Winter's Maiden 2

Winter's Magic Part 2

L. STARLA

Disclaimer: This is a work of fiction. Names, characters, businesses, places, events, locales, and incidents are either the products of the author's imagination or used in a fictitious manner. Any resemblance to actual persons, living or dead, or actual events is purely coincidental.

WINTER'S MAIDEN 2

To request permission, contact the author:
laelia@starlaarts.com

Cover illustration © Jana Hoffmann
Graphics & book design by L. Starla
Editing by Felix Staica

First edition 2021.

ISBN-13 (Paperback) 978-0-6488424-5-3
ISBN-13 (eBook) 978-0-6488424-4-6

Self-published.

Author's Note

This book contains coarse language and explicit scenes, including depictions of sexual violence and minor BDSM that may upset or offend some readers. There is also a partial cliff-hanger for one of the characters, which is somewhat resolved in *Winter's Thrall.*

Dedication

—In loving memory of Joan Elizabeth. Your legacy is the love you inspired in the lives you touched.

Epigraph

"Equality is not a concept. It's not something we should be striving for. It's a necessity. Equality is like gravity. We need it to stand on this earth as men and women, and the misogyny that is in every culture is not a true part of the human condition. It is life out of balance, and that imbalance is sucking something out of the soul of every man and woman who's confronted with it. We need equality. Kinda now."

—Joss Whedon

Playlist

"Stronger" by The Score
"The Dark Side" by Muse
"Spit It Out" by IAMX
"Mischief Maker" by All Systems Know
"Now or Never" by Metric
"Danger to Myself" by The Unlikely Candidates
"Pure Morning" by Placebo
"Play with Fire" by Sam Tinnesz & Yacht Money
"I'm So Sorry" by Imagine Dragons
"Oh My Dear Lord" by The Unlikely Candidates
"Hellfire" by Barns Courtney
"High" by Anavae
"Evil Night Together" by Jill Tracey
"No Harm" by Editors
"Stay Around" by American Authors
"Mad About You" by Hooverphonic
"Bloodsport" by Sneaker Pimps
"Legendary" by Welshy Arms
"Yellow Sea" by Landroid
"Touched" by Vast

Playlist available on Spotify.

The Cast of Characters

The Council of Mages, Fleurieu District

High Magus:
Kieran Lane, Monique's father (Mayor)

Seat of Aether Mana:
Alannah Winters (Conjurer, Dress Maker)

Seat of Elemental Mana:
Liam Winters (Warlock, Police Officer)

Seat of Organic Mana:
Ross Winters (Abjurer, Doctor), Liam & Brendan's father

Seat of Emotional Mana:
Nora Winters, née Maher (Shaman, Vet), Liam & Brendan's mother

Seat of Energy Mana:
Steve Maher (Alchemist, Pharmacist), Liam's cousin

Seat of Names Mana:
Monique Lane (Alchemist, Council's Secretary)

Seat of Cosmic Mana:
Lucas Ó Máille (Clairvoyant, Lawyer), Liam's friend

Seat of Physical Forces Mana:
Clayton Rowan (Warlock, Police Officer)

Seat of Matter Mana:
Mr. Duncan Sheridan (Alchemist, Pharmacist)

Seat of Senses Mana:
Mr. James Maher (Illusionist), Steve's Father & Nora's brother

Pure Blood Mages

Brendan Winters, (Pure-mage Enchanter, School Counsellor), Liam's brother

Jessica Ó Máille (Clairvoyant), Lucas' younger sister & Monique's friend

Claudia Rowan (Shaman, Dancer), Clayton's twin sister

Chester Rowan (Conjurer), Clayton's younger brother

Danielle Sheridan (Abjurer), Monique's friend

Reginald (Abjurer), Eyre Peninsula district

Wendy (Shaman), Eyre Peninsula district

Richard Lane (The Inquisitor), Kieran's brother

Other Magicals

Cara Hughes (Half-mage Shaman, Conservationist), Alannah's best friend

Jacob Bennett (Boggart, Gangster), Brendan's best mate

Nick Patterson (Orc, Orchardist)

Ben Sanders (Weredingo, Vet Assistant)

Caleb Hawthorn (Fae- Endarkened, Unemployed)

Bridey Hawthorn (Fae- Endarkened), Caleb's older sister

Connor Foley (Half-mage Abjurer, Marine Biologist)

Bailey Dougherty (Half-mage Warlock, Bartender)

Bianca Oakley (Fae- Wood Nymph, Cabaret Singer)

Amy Smith (Dwarf, Metallurgist & Council Blacksmith)

Prologue

Three Years and One Month Since Alannah's Eighteenth Birthday

Returning to her office, the woman settled in behind the solid oak desk and turned on the Waterford crystal lamp. She withdrew a pad and fountain pen from the drawer to her right and commenced:

Alannah,

While I understand it is not customary for a mage conceived at Beltane to concern themselves with the identity of their biological father, it has come to my attention you are pursuing such knowledge. If this is indeed the case, I have some insights of great value to offer.

Rising from her desk, she deliberated over the wording of her next paragraph while peering out through the tempered glass of her window. The street below buzzed with the city nightlife one would expect from Sydney on a Saturday night. She looked forward to joining them, but she needed to finish the letter. *Time to stop procrastinating.* Returning to her seat, she resumed writing:

Sharing this information puts me at risk, so it will not come free. If you are willing to meet at a secure location, I am sure we can strike a suitable deal. Rest assured I mean you no harm and I guarantee a safe rendezvous. It is of no consequence to me should you choose to disregard this letter and decline my offer. However, accepting my invitation would be of much benefit to you.

If you decide to seek me out, please contact Patrick, my agent, to arrange a time and place. I have enclosed his business card.

Regards,
Scarlett.

She allowed the ink to dry, detached the top sheet from the pad and neatly folded the page. Her deft hands slipped it into the envelope addressed to Alannah Winters of Gaeilge Shores, South Australia. She tucked the letter into her handbag and grabbed her coat. After riding the elevator down ten floors, she left the office building and stepped out into the cool, early September air. She stopped at the red post box a few metres down the street and dropped the letter inside before ducking into her favourite cocktail bar.

Chapter One

Five Days later

High Magus Kieran was the epitome of pompous ass. 'Thank you, Councillor Rowan. Councillor Alannah Winters, do you have anything to report?' He stared at her with a stern eye. Her appointment to the Fleurieu District Council of Mages still displeased him, and it continued to show in his open hostility at every meeting.

'There has not been much activity involving the use of Aether, Your Honour, and none of it has caused any negative energy.' As the representative for all mages attuned to Aether in her district, one of Alannah's responsibilities was to remain open to this mana source to detect any misuse and investigate the issue. Given how few mages were even capable of channelling the divine element, she had an easy time of it.

Being one of a handful of mages in the state with this attunement had its benefits. There was no competition when she applied to fill the seat vacated by the late Shaun Ó Máille in August of the previous year, a few days after her twentieth birthday. But even with the community endorsements she received following her epic showdown with Tara all those years ago, the High Magus was not happy about having a Winters woman on the Council.

'Are you certain of this?' Kieran did not second guess the other Council members.

He is such a chauvinistic bastard. Clenching her fists in her lap beneath the table, she bit back the sarcastic retort on the tip of her tongue. 'Yes, Your Honour.'

'Very well. On to our next matter of business…'

Most mages regarded the seat of Aether with reverence because the mage in that role has a direct link to the Gods. Alannah recently learned the High Magus treated her predecessor with far more respect. Kieran had always insisted Shaun Ó Máille present his report first rather than last. Still seething, she tuned out while Kieran harped on about some bureaucratic nonsense, catching the odd buzzword here and there like commendation, sanctioning, and authority. Using mindfulness meditation, she calmed herself.

This is so damn boring. Alannah had expected more focus on hunting magic criminals when she signed up for the Mages Council. It made her mourn the days of fighting her grandmother's threats. Gaeilge Shores may have been a dangerous place with Tara Winters around, but it was a hell of a lot more exciting.

A sudden nudge in her side brought Alannah's attention back to the room. She looked at Liam, the owner of the offending elbow, and met his frown as he gestured in Kieran's direction.

'Huh?'

The High Magus gave her a death glare. 'I asked, if you had an opinion on the matter, Councillor.'

'Oh. Sorry Your Honour. No, I have nothing to add.'

'I look forward to the day when you have anything at all to contribute to these meetings, Miss *Winters*.' His cronies sniggered.

Aunt Nora, representative for emotions, smiled at her with pursed lips. As one of three women on the Council, along with Monique Lane, she understood the difficulties Alannah faced in such a patriarchal system.

Kieran glanced at his watch, and turned to face his daughter, Monique, who took the minutes.

'I would like to call the meeting closed at seven fifty.' He stood up and the room filled with the sound of chairs scraping against wooden floorboards as everyone else rose. Standing whenever the High Magus was on his feet in the Council Chambers was important etiquette.

They all waited for him to exit the room before collecting their belongings and leaving.

After saying goodbye to Ross and Nora, Liam spoke in a hushed tone as he followed Alannah outside. 'You shouldn't take your place for granted Lana. Kieran could easily step down into your seat if you keep pissing him off.'

She huffed. 'I doubt he'd be willing to give up his position of power. That said, it's not like I'm actively trying for top spot on his shit list. He's never liked me and my being on the Council is enough to make him hate me. Besides, it's not my fault bugger-all mages practice necromancy in this area.'

Pausing when they reached the car, Liam sighed. 'I know. But you could at least try to pay attention to the rest of the business.' He unlocked the car but waited for her.

'Why? It's pointless paper pushing. Where's the real action?' She slumped into the passenger seat.

He dropped into the driver's side and shook his head. 'I warned you it wouldn't be all fun and games. I get as much admin work as a police officer, if not more sometimes.'

'The whole bloody system needs reforming. When I become High Magus, my first order of business will be to liven up those damn meetings.'

'I hate to burst your bubble, yet again, but you know that'll never happen. They would never allow a woman to head up the Council.'

'Never say never, sweetheart. I will get there or die trying. Once I get my fourth and fifth attunements, it's game on.'

They rode the remaining two blocks from the Town Hall to their seaside terrace house in silence. Council meetings were long and draining, and neither of them felt up to walking on such nights. Getting home to eat and sleep was the priority.

Shortly after earning his badge on the force, Liam had asked Alannah if she wanted to buy a house in town with him. They had been in a solid relationship for years by that point, so it made sense and she had been keen to move into her own place. While Alannah had drawn up an extensive list of requirements, Liam only voiced two criteria: a place in town close to work and easy access to the ocean. Even with all his responsibilities to the Council and the police force, her boyfriend lived and breathed the surf. It took them a while to find somewhere suitable, so it was like a dream come true when this place became available almost a year ago.

Liam groaned at the sight of his brother's Jag as they pulled into the driveway. She could not blame him. Alannah understood Liam's moods and anyone's company, other than her own, was the last thing he wanted to deal with when exhausted. But she did not mind. Spending time with her best friend and cousin, Brendan, was exactly what she needed to lift her spirits.

'Dagnammit!' Brendan jumped at the sound of the front door slamming, cursing as he dropped a serving spoon on his foot. He had almost finished laying everything out on the dining table for dinner. *At least I wasn't holding a plate!*

Liam stormed into the open-plan living area and threw his keys at the kitchen bench. 'Don't you have a home of your own?'

'Well hello to you too, bro.' Brendan still lived with his parents on their country estate, and while the privacy of the guest house was great for taking chicks home, on school nights he much preferred the convenience of a place to crash in town, especially one Alannah lived in. Pushing past the grumpy sack, he placed the rogue piece of cutlery in the dishwasher and grabbed a replacement from the drawer. 'And is that any way to talk to your chef?'

After casting a cursory glance at the plastic containers on the table, Liam turned his scowling face back to Brendan. 'Unless you're now moonlighting as a Chinese chef at the local take-away, I doubt you can claim any credit.'

He smacked Liam hard on the shoulder blade. 'Well, you're welcome.' Turning aside from his ungrateful brother, he grinned at Alannah and drew her into a hug. 'Hey, gorgeous, how's life?'

When they stepped out of the embrace, she gave him one of her award-winning smiles. 'Mostly good. Although I came close to dying of boredom and frustration in that meeting. I need a drink. You guys want one?' She approached the bar fridge.

'I can't. I have an early start tomorrow,' Liam complained.

Brendan returned to the table and took a seat. 'I'll have a pale ale, thanks, Lana.' He also had work the next day, but a couple of beers wouldn't be a problem for his job as school counsellor.

Alannah handed Brendan the drink in a stubby holder and sat across from him. Reaching forward, she clinked the tip of her own bottle with his. 'Cheers.' Tilting her chin and lifting her gaze skyward, she took a huge swig of her drink.

Damn, that woman makes drinking beer look sexy.

Returning her attention to him, she smiled again. 'So, how's work and stuff treating you?'

'Same old, same old. Work's not bad, but the ol' social life could use some more excitement.' He took the opportunity to check her out while she filled her plate. He liked Alannah's new habit of wearing her long black hair in a half ponytail. It reminded him of Katie McGrath as Morgana.

Sitting back, she gave him an impish grin. 'Social life, or sex life?'

'Both, but you're right, I do need to get laid soon. How's tomorrow night looking for you?'

She snorted before turning on the smoulder. 'I'll check my calendar.'

Liam growled as he pointed his chopsticks at Brendan. 'I know the flirting is part of your stupid game, but please spare me. I'm not in the mood to put up with your bullshit.'

Brendan had gone to serious lengths to assure his brother there was nothing going on with him and Alannah, after messing up and almost kissing her four years ago. He even managed to convince Alannah he was not interested in a relationship with her. As much as it pained him, especially when Alannah first expressed interest, it was for the best. He reasoned he would end up hurting her. Not to mention getting a major arse whooping from Liam—almost one-hundred kilos of pure muscle with perfect aim when rapid firing lightning bolts—not someone whose bad books you wanted to be in.

He narrowed his eyes at Liam. 'Right, 'cause your mood is the only one that matters. I was trying to cheer up Lana.' As an enchanter attuned to emotions, Brendan could tell Alannah felt miserable. He could sense it through his empathic link.

Rising from his chair, Liam pressed a kiss to the crown of Alannah's head before grabbing his plate. 'I'm sorry, gorgeous, but I'm exhausted. I'll take this to bed and see you there later.'

'Okay, night.' She stood to peck him on the lips, and he deepened the kiss in a possessive display obviously intended for Brendan's benefit.

The tension in the room lifted and Alannah heaved a huge sigh as though breathing freely for the first time in hours.

'What got up his arse and died?' Brendan asked.

'Well aside from his mundane work being relentless, High Magus Kieran got snarky with me tonight. I know these things get to him. And I didn't help matters when I zoned out again.'

He laughed. 'I don't envy you, Lana. Those meetings sound like a big waste of time.'

She went quiet for a few minutes and toyed with her food. Biting her lip, she gazed up at him. 'Maybe you should look at renting a place in town. As much as I love having you here, the frequency of your visits is wearing at Liam's patience. He can't relax when you're here this often.'

'That man can't relax properly full stop.' He sucked a noodle into his mouth and sighed. 'But you're right. I'll start searching this weekend.'

Stretching her arm across the table, she placed a hand over his. The warmth of her touch sent a jolt of pleasure through his nerves. 'Hey, you are still welcome here and I'll drop in to see you. If you have your own place, we could both escape Liam's moods.'

'I know. I guess it's time I grew up and cut the apron strings.'

Humour returned to Alannah's visage. 'Just don't grow up too much. I love your carefree attitude.'

A hearty laugh escaped his throat. 'Trust me, that'll never happen. I'm a playboy for life, remember?'

'Right.' Her fingers were still resting on the back of his hand, and he perceived their rough pads brushing against his skin. Hours of sewing every week for years had produced callouses on the tips of her otherwise soft hands. The sensation was strangely erotic.

Flipping his wrist, he grabbed her hand as he stared into her eyes and probed her mind. Brendan knew he should not invade her private thoughts, not only for the immorality of it, but because knowing the truth would be futile either way. But he could not help himself.

She grinned, but there were no thoughts suggesting she wanted him. Only the usual *'I'm not gonna let him win.'* Over the past few years Alannah had become a lot better at Sleazy Chicken, a flirtatious game they started playing at the age of six, although he still won most times.

Rising to his feet, Brendan pulled her up against his chest and planted soft kisses along her arm, running from her hand towards her neck. He watched her face for signs of blushing. There was no hint of colour in her cheeks as she gave him bedroom eyes that made his blood rush. It was just as well he was able to magically control his erections; else he might give away his true feelings.

Closing in on her shoulder, he could no longer see her face when she drew an audible breath. 'Stop. You win.'

A wicked grin formed on his face when he stepped back to look at her. 'The reigning champion keeps his crown.'

'You will have to give it up to me one day.'

'Oh, I promise I'll give it to you one day, Lana. I'll give it to you real hard.' He winked at her, seized his beer, and chugged down the rest of the bottle.

After tiptoeing across the bedroom floor, avoiding the squeaky floorboards, Alannah slipped into bed alongside Liam's sleeping form. He looked handsome beyond compare when asleep, the stress and fatigue gone from around his eyes.

Liam must have sensed her presence, despite her best efforts to avoid disturbing his sleep, because he snuggled in closer to her. He groaned the moment their bodies connected, and his eyes flittered open. The bright moon peeking through a slit in the curtains was the only light illuminating the room, but it was enough to reveal the features of his face. He smiled. 'Hey gorgeous.'

'Sorry for waking you.' Although Alannah was secretly glad she had, still feeling horny after the game of Sleazy Chicken.

'You're the one person who doesn't ever need to apologise for that.' His deep voice was raspy from sleep, and it heightened her arousal. 'I love you, Lana. You are the most incredible woman to walk this earth and I feel blessed to call you mine.'

Her heart melted at his words. Rendered speechless, she inhaled sharply and claimed his mouth with a heated kiss. Before long she straddled Liam's naked body, grinding against his pelvis. Her hands skated along his muscular arms as she immersed herself in the addictive sweet and salty taste of his mouth.

After making out for ten minutes, Liam rolled them sideways and fell back asleep. Alannah sighed - another typical weeknight, with Liam exhausted after work and mage commitments. She would be calling on her rabbit again soon

Brendan beelined through the front bar of Doyle Dougherty's, the only pub in Gaeilge Shores, and found his mates in a booth. It was Friday, the night following his dinner at Alannah's. Ben and Nick were arm wrestling, giving the girls around them a

show of bulging tatted muscles. Connor had an arm wrapped around Amy, whispering sweet nothings in her ear. Bailey and Caleb were showing each other memes and sharing metalcore music on their smartphones. And Cara sat in Jacob's lap, sucking his face off. *Yup, business as usual. Except someone was missing.*

Bailey looked up as Brendan approached. 'Hey, Brendo. How ya doin', man?' He extended his hand out for a fist bump.

'Okay, I guess. What's up with you all? And where's Bianca?' He slid down next to Caleb, an endarkened fae and the only member of their group to have more piercings than Brendan. Caleb gave him a silent nod before vaping some sweet-smelling herbal stuff.

Jacob came up for air a moment later, giving Brendan an impish grin. 'Didn't you hear? Bianca has a dark cabaret band now. They're rehearsing tonight.' The red-headed boggart had become his best mate in the years following the death of Lachlan Munroe. The goofy goblin had been Jacob's closest friend at school and losing him in their battle with Tara Winters had been heartbreaking for all his crew. The passing of Austin Pearce, Brendan's previous bestie, also contributed to their growing bond. Although Austin was dead to Brendan when he date-raped Alannah.

'Yeah, they are gearing up for a regular spot at some cabaret lounge in Adelaide,' added Bailey.

'Oh? This is all news to me.' *How am I the last to hear about all this?*

Nick, the punkish orc, tittered. 'I guess you guys are always too busy boning to talk about her side hustle.'

While true to some extent, it was not like they *never* talked. But it had been a few months since he had invited Bianca to his bed. He did not want to give her the wrong impression, even if she was the best lay he could get in town. Commitment was a dirty word to Brendan in most cases. Leaning back into the seat, he sighed. 'I guess I'll have to hook up with a human tonight.' Brendan did not mind human girls, but they did lack the magical talents of a nymph like Bianca.

'Well Chelsea's had her eye on you since you arrived.' Ben directed his head of long, caramel coloured hair towards the table of girls a few metres away. The weredingo's attention shifting to that group of girls did not surprise Brendan. Ben's reputation as a man-whore was almost as notorious as Brendan's.

Brendan shook his head. 'Been there, done that too many times. I need a challenge. I want more excitement in my life.'

'What about her?' Ben's gaze travelled to the door where a stunning woman with long black hair entered. Legs reaching the sky were on display beneath a short black skirt. She completed her outfit with a purple brocade corset and silver necklace. Her curvaceous figure alone took Brendan's breath away. The moment he looked up at her face, he found himself drawn into her eyes. As dark as night and outlined with purple makeup, they scanned the room. Peering through the veil of her glamour, he glimpsed pointy ears lined with silver studs from lobe to tip. *Most likely fae and her dark colouring suggests unseelie.*

'Son of a gun!' Caleb's eyes widened, as though he had seen a ghost.

As if hearing Caleb's muttered curse, the woman turned her attention to their group and grinned, eyes darting to each of them before settling on Caleb. She advanced and Brendan felt Caleb trembling beside him. Reaching the booth, she scrutinised Caleb as she spoke in a deep, rich voice, 'Hello, Brother dearest.'

Chapter Two

'And done.' Having sewn on some black lace as the finishing touch to her latest dress, Alannah sat back to admire her work. *It is damn sexy, if I do say so myself—and I can't wait to wear it out.* Modelling her designs was an important marketing strategy for her business. She cracked her knuckles and stood for a few stretches.

A cursory glance at the old grandfather clock on the wall told her the afternoon was ending. *Liam will get home soon. I ought to think about cooking dinner.* Needing some fresh air first, she strolled out to the letter box to collect the mail.

After sifting through the advertising, which went straight in the recycling bin, and the bills she threw on the buffet in the hall, Alannah found one item of interest: A letter addressed to her in a neat cursive script without any sender details, but the postmark was from Sydney. She walked into the loungeroom to get comfortable and opened it. The business card of a Mr. Patrick Douglas dropped into her lap as she unfolded the letter.

> *Alannah,*
> *While I understand it is not customary for a mage conceived at Beltane to concern themselves with the identity of their biological father, it has come to my attention you are pursuing such knowledge…*

She inhaled deeply and took a moment to process the contents of the letter. *My bio dad?* Alannah's mind buzzed. *Could he be alive?* Her heart thrummed, playing a rhythm of hope on her ribs like a xylophone, but she put a stop to it by calming her breathing. Nothing about Scarlett's words suggested anything of the sort. Only a fool would entertain such fantasies. Yet she could not deny wanting to know who her real father was.

The sound of keys jingling at the front door broke her reverie. Alannah jumped to her feet and tucked the letter and Patrick's card into her handbag. She needed to talk to someone about this letter, but Liam would not understand, so it would have to wait.

Liam met her in the kitchen, where they embraced. He beamed, blue eyes bright and full of life. 'Hi, gorgeous. I hope you haven't started cooking yet. I want to take you out for dinner.'

Alannah's whole face lit up and she kissed his full lips, running her fingers through his mid-length brown hair before replying. 'As it happens, I haven't yet. I'm keen to eat out.' Pausing, she gazed upon him. 'So, what has you in a marvellous mood?'

'It's Friday night and I have a full weekend off work. I want to make the most of my time with you.'

'Gods, I love you. Give me a few minutes to get ready.' She was still wearing her usual work attire: trackpants and an old, tattered t-shirt.

He followed her into the bedroom. 'I want to change too. And I need a shower. Care to join me?'

When she turned to look at him, the unbuttoned shirt displayed his eight-pack. Heat coursed through her blood at the sight. 'How can I refuse an invitation like that?' *There is no urgency to get to dinner. It's not like I'm hungry… for food anyway.*

The strong fragrance of violets assaulted Brendan's nose.

'Bridey? W...what are you doing here?' Caleb frowned at his sister.

So, this is Bridey Hawthorn, Brendan thought. He had never met the girl, but Caleb had told him a lot about her. Like the fact she grew up with their dark mage (read: rogue) father in the city while their elven mother raised Caleb in the country. They originally lived in the Adelaide Hills where their parents' marriage declined when their dad's eye turned from his wife to his teenage daughter. Unfortunately, Bridey had no qualms pandering to daddy's desires. She was every bit as perverted as he was and even put the moves on an unwilling Caleb when he first hit puberty. This was the final straw for their mother, who packed up and fled with Caleb to Gaeilge Shores to hide. It was smart. Few dark mages would chance a run-in with the High Magus and the Council.

No wonder poor Caleb trembled. Brendan placed a supportive hand on the guy's shoulder as he spoke up. 'Well, well, well. The wayward sister returns.' He pierced Bridey with a glare.

Bridey shrugged off Brendan's hostile vibes. 'And you are?'

As he read her aura, he saw curiosity at first. As her gaze intensified, the tell-tale bright red flicker of lust pulsed around her. She licked her lips seductively and his cock instantly hardened. *Gods! Have I met my match? Get a grip, dude.* He took a deep breath and refocussed his mind. 'Brendan Winters. Perhaps you've heard of me?'

A wicked grin lit up her features. 'Oh, indeed. The infamous enchanter of Gaeilge Shores. I didn't realise my brother had such interesting friends. Mother did such a stellar job of hiding him from me.' She looked at Caleb and smiled. 'Relax, darling. I'm not going to hurt you. I'm here on business and I'd like your help connecting with the magic community in town.'

'Just business?' Caleb narrowed his eyes.

'Yes sweetheart, *just* business; unless you want more.' She gave him a lewd grin and he shivered. Bridey's head fell back as she cackled. 'Oh, Caleb, you are precious. And far too much like our sweet Mother. But your friends?' Her eyes travelled around the group before settling on Brendan. 'I think your friends will be a blast. And I'm all for mixing business with pleasure.'

It took all of Brendan's willpower to hold back the groan threatening to escape his lips as his dick stirred. She arched her right brow at him. *Hell! Is she an enchanter too?*

'May I sit?' She directed her question at Brendan.

He shrugged. 'It's a free country.'

There was no room for her on his side of the booth, so she perched herself in Brendan's lap, leaving him to splutter as she ground into his erection.

Caleb stared aghast at their display.

Scowling, Bailey rose. 'I'm getting another round of drinks. Who's in?'

Everyone pushed their glasses forward. Brendan doubted lowering inhibitions around Bridey was wise, but he needed some alcohol to take the edge off.

'I'll have a Purple Haze, thank you darling,' Bridey demanded.

Bailey frowned at her. 'A what?'

'*Pur-ple Haze*. It's a cocktail. Don't tell me this backwater doesn't know about cocktails!'

'Sure, we know about cocktails,' Bailey retorted. 'We're just not pretentious enough to care.'

'Oh dear. I see I'm going to have my work cut out for me with you. What's your name, handsome?'

After a moment of hesitation, he replied. 'Bailey. Bailey Dougherty.'

She gasped with delight. 'As in *the* Doughertys? Owners of this fine establishment?'

'Exactly. So, I suggest you show this *backwater* more respect if you don't want piss in your fancy-schmancy drink.' Bailey turned on his heels and strode off to the bar.

'Wow. What a gem.' Bridey's tone oozed sarcasm. 'So, Caleb, who else do we have here?'

Caleb reluctantly introduced everyone. Ben and Nick were both drooling when Bridey cast her eyes over them. She even distracted Jacob, who was oblivious to the stink eye his girlfriend, Cara, sent Bridey's way.

At least I'm not alone. This woman is trouble with a capital Oh Hell!

Bursting into Brendan's room in the Cailleach Estate guesthouse on a Saturday morning always came with risks, Alannah knew that. But she figured she had seen it all, multiple times in fact. And the girls? She had seen them all too. Most of them had grown accustomed to Alannah, but a few still freaked out or got irritable when she intruded.

Yet nothing could have prepared her for the scene greeting her that morning. They were *still* at it. All four of them. Grunting and groaning filled the room and Alannah wondered if she had accidently stumbled onto the set of a porno film.

She had no idea who the fae girl was, but she recognised the inked skin of Ben and Nick.

While Alannah thought three men taking one woman at the same time was outrageous, none of it compared to seeing Brendan in action. The thing she knew he was most reputed for was the one thing she had never see him do. Pressing her back to the wall, she covered the gasp slipping from her mouth. Ben may have been the weredingo and Nick was the orc with staghorns, but Brendan was the one who fucked like an animal: biting, clawing, and slapping as he thrust into the fae chick. *So damn hot!* Brendan's transformation into a ruggedly handsome man only enhanced the hotness factor. His face had filled out more over the years, transforming his gaunt appearance into a strong, well-defined jawline covered in designer stubble. He had also cut his fringe back, so it no longer slipped down over his right eye, but the choppy strands were still long enough to cover most of his forehead.

She should have left, but she could not tear her eyes away. She should have announced her presence, but she could not bring herself to stop them. She wanted to touch herself as she watched them but did not dare. Explaining *that* to Brendan would be difficult. So, instead she stood there, frozen.

Several minutes later, Brendan turned his head and glimpsed her. He did not stop. His full lips curled into a lascivious grin and his green eyes pinned her in place as he continued pounding into the back of the fae chick. *Oh Gods!* She squirmed and felt her cheeks flush but did not break the eye contact.

Alannah had worked hard to shut down any feelings of lust around Brendan in the last four years. She did not want to risk him reading such feelings in her. But in the heat of the moment, she let her guard down and she was so busted. *Right—time to deflect.* She shifted her attention to the other guys, hoping Brendan would think it was the sight of them turning her on. She even contrived to bite her lip.

Brendan spoke in her mind, *'I guess I should tell Liam to get some tats on his buff bod.'*

There was no need to feign the blushing.

'Don't worry, I won't tell Liam, or these guys. But to save yourself anymore discomfort, I suggest stepping out before they see you. We'll finish soon.'

She took his advice, waiting beyond the door. About ten minutes later, the porno party emerged.

'Oh, hi, Alannah,' Nick greeted her on his way past.

Ben followed with his arm around the fae woman. 'Hey, girl.' He winked at her as he passed.

Catching a proper glimpse of the woman, Alannah startled at her striking looks.

'Who was that?' Alannah heard the woman's deep voice ask as they left the guest house.

The sound of Brendan clearing his throat drew her attention back to his bedroom doorway. He stood there in nothing but a pair of red satin boxers. The scent of sex mingled with his musky cologne—*or is it his natural odour?* 'I had no idea you were into voyeurism, Lana.'

Forcing her eyes to focus on his face, she exhaled sharply. 'Neither did I. First time for everything, right?'

His eyes narrowed on her. 'Right. So, to what do I owe the pleasure? With you, that is. My previous pleasure was obvious enough.'

Alannah snorted. 'Who was that girl anyway? I've never seen her around before.'

'Caleb's sister.'

'Caleb has a sister?'

Brendan frowned. 'Yup. They grew up apart, with separated parents. He doesn't like her much, so please don't tell him about what happened.'

'I guess we both have some new secrets to keep.'

Humour returned to Brendan's visage. 'I still can't believe…'

'Can we drop it, please? I need to talk to you about something.'

'Okay. Give me a sec to clean up.' Brendan moved to the bathroom. When he came back, he joined Alannah on the couch in the living area, smelling cleaner. 'What's up?'

'I received this strange letter yesterday. I want your opinion.' She handed him the offer from Scarlett.

Brendan read in silence, folded the letter and returned it. The right side of his face lifted for a moment. 'Have you shown this to Liam?'

'No, only you. Liam won't understand my need. He's an old-fashioned sort, big on tradition and whatnot.'

He nodded. 'True. How did the letter come to you?'

'Through the post. It came from Sydney, but there was no return address.'

Brendan put his feet up on the coffee table and reclined into the couch. 'I don't like it. The letter reeks of suspicion and evil agendas. It's a pity we aren't friends with a non-Council affiliated clairvoyant.'

'I know, right. I really want this info, but I don't trust this Scarlett. What should I do?'

'I dunno. The letter doesn't stipulate meeting alone, but her agent might insist on it. If you contact him, ask about taking a bodyguard. Don't agree to going alone.'

'Fair point. But who would be a suitable bodyguard? Most warlocks we know are loyal to the Council. Even Bailey.'

'So, don't take a mage. What about Nick?' Brendan winked. She began to object when he stopped her, pressing a finger to her lips. 'Think about it. The guy can kick some serious butt. And he can channel the elements almost as well as a warlock.'

She sighed. 'I suppose.' Alannah considered her options. 'Okay, I'm gonna do this. I'll start by asking Nick, then see what I can arrange with this Patrick dude. Thanks for your help.'

'Anytime, Lana. Just be careful, okay?' Brendan's forehead creased.

'Yeah, of course.'

'Can you keep me updated, too?'

With a plan in place, Alannah smiled. 'Sure thing. Well, we better head into the house. Your mum is cooking brunch and Liam will come drag our arses out there soon.'

Brendan collapsed into one of the hammocks on the front porch and sighed as he watched Liam's SUV carry Alannah away.

'Quite the minx, isn't she? If I didn't know better, I'd think she was a succubus.'

Startled by the unfamiliar man's voice appearing out of nowhere, Brendan jumped to his feet. When his eyes fell upon the red glowing eyes of a demon, his skin prickled. Noticing the blue courier uniform, he exhaled. Demons copped a bad rap thanks to humans and mages alike. While the Gods did curse the evil doers and banish them to the Underworld, most of these poor souls inherited their fate. When summoners beckoned them to the mortal plane, they entered a pact requiring full obedience. Their bosses were the ones to worry about.

'Lovely day, isn't it?' The demon courier smiled, withdrawing some paperwork from his satchel. 'One package for a Brendan Winters of Cailleach Estate, Gaeilge Shores. Are you the Brendan in question?'

'Yup, that's me.'

'I'm so glad. Now you need to sign for it. In blood, please.' The courier's skeletal hand extended, offering him a clipboard.

Brendan took it and inspected the delivery documents. *No mention of the sender's name. Makes sense, given the use of forbidden blood magic*. He pricked his finger using the quill pen tied to the binder and signed the parchment. As soon as he returned the clipboard, a large book-shaped parcel wrapped in brown paper materialised in his hands.

'Right then. Have a great day.' The demon vanished.

No way I'm showing my parents an item delivered by a demon courier using blood magic. He walked around the side and headed into the guesthouse.

Sitting on the couch, he tore away the brown paper to reveal a black leather-bound book. The cover was blank, devoid of any symbols suggesting the content. Not sensing any nefarious magic at work, he opened the tome.

'Ho-ly shit!' He drew a deep breath before flicking through the rest of it. After scanning the bulk of the pages, he leaned back to process the significance of what he was holding. The more he thought about it, the more he realised he possessed the proverbial goldmine of potion craft: the most extensive collection of magic tinctures, elixirs, tonics, and poisons known to the magic world. There were potions for every attunement, with multiple recipes for every spell effect. The best part? It was all in English, so he would not need to spend time translating anything. This volume would even put the recipe section of Alannah's Book of Shadows to shame.

Who sent this book and why? What do they expect me to do with it?

A tapping noise on the guesthouse door broke his train of thought, so he shoved the compendium inside the ottoman.

His best mate, Jacob, waited at the door, a wide grin revealing his sharp boggart teeth. They fist bumped as Brendan let him in. 'Hey, man.'

'Hey. You wanna drink?' Brendan made his way to the bar.

'I'll have a coldie. Thanks.' Jacob took a seat on the couch.

Once they were both settled with their beers, Brendan withdrew the leather volume from its hiding spot. 'Check this out. A demon courier dropped it off.'

Taking the large book, Jacob's brows drew together. He whistled through his chompers as he perused the content. 'Who was your benefactor?'

'No idea.'

Jacob read out some of the potion titles in the Emotions section. 'Love potions, narcotics, and stimulants. Curious. There's a recipe for a tincture that's pretty much the magical equivalent of ecstasy. You could make a fortune by making and selling this stuff.'

'It could be interesting to try some of these potions. You wanna help me?'

Jacob's eyes lit up. 'Hell yeah.'

'But this stays between us, alright. I don't want too many people knowing about this book, or what we are cooking up.'

Chapter Three

'Ugh. This place is way too modern for my liking. It lacks warmth and old-world charm.' Alannah followed Brendan into the apartment's master bedroom. His invitation to attend an open inspection on Monday afternoon had excited her until she discovered all his taste was in his mouth.

After glancing around the space, he gazed at her in the floor to ceiling mirror on the built-in wardrobe. 'Modern is exactly what I'm after. Old places are often in disrepair.' He grinned. 'And they don't usually have as many mirrors in the bedroom.'

The eyeroll was instinctive. 'I bet we could find an old place in shipshape condition.' After a pause she added, 'And you can always add your own mirrors.'

'I like modern places, okay. They are more efficient with energy use and space.'

Alannah shook her head. 'Gawd, it feels like we're on an episode of *House Hunters*.'

Brendan blinked as he cocked his head.

'It's a show where couples with different tastes look for their dream home.'

He leaned in close to her with a mischievous glint in his eye. 'Are you implying we are like a couple, Lana?'

She snorted. 'In your dreams, buddy.'

An eyebrow shot up. 'How did you know about those dreams? Have you been training as a clairvoyant?'

Without thinking, she smacked his arm, hitting a hard bicep. 'Even if I had, I wouldn't want to know about your filthy dreams.'

Grabbing her arm by the wrist, he drew her close, bringing their chests together. 'I bet you would though, given your recent propensity for voyeurism.'

Damn. I can't deny I would love front row seats to a viewing of his wet dreams. They remained locked in a stare down until the real estate agent cleared her voice from the doorway.

'Would you like to complete a rental application, Mr. Winters?' Sylvia Green eyed them askance. The tall, blonde woman of mixed-mage-blood was a few years older than Alannah. She was also a notorious bigmouth.

Brendan gave her a big smile. 'Yes, this place is great.'

Sylvia beamed, gesturing with a manicured hand for them to follow her down the hall.

Alannah pulled herself free of Brendan's grip and whispered in his ear. 'Just as well we aren't a couple. You don't need to take my preferences into account.'

He looked at her and all humour faded from his visage.

When they reached the living area, Sylvia directed her attention to Brendan. 'Is Miss Winters signing the lease as well?'

'No—' Alannah began.

But Brendan threw his arm over her shoulder and cut in. 'What my dear cousin was about to say is she won't be living here. But I'm sure we will have plenty of sleepovers, so let's put her on the lease. Just in case, you know?'

Alannah stiffened in his hold under the sidelong gaze of the agent. *Gods! What must Sylvia think?* Gossip travelled fast in a small town like Gaeilge Shores, especially if the news involved the founding families.

'Well, here's the form. You can either email or fax it through to me.' The agent handed Brendan the paperwork. 'And here's my card. Don't hesitate to call if you have any questions.'

Brendan took the business card, giving her the smile that inspired half the female population to drop their panties. 'Thank you, Ms. Green.'

'Please, call me Sylvia.' She reached out for a handshake.

When he took the offered hand, he drew it up to his lips and kissed it. 'Then you can call me Brendan.'

The woman's eyes darkened, and Alannah knew they would end up calling each other all sorts of inappropriate names.

Outside, Alannah stopped Brendan on the curb beside his Jag with a firm hand on his shoulder. 'If I get word of any nasty rumours after the stunt you pulled, I will strangle you.'

He spun around to face her with a lascivious expression. 'Kinky. I love a bit of breath play.'

She shook her head. 'Is there any form of kink you don't like?'

Narrowing his eyes, Brendan licked his lips. 'Do you really want to go there?'

Hell yes, she thought. 'No. It was a rhetorical question.'

Brendan hitched his eyebrows.

Oh crap! Am I projecting my aura? Alannah had spent years suppressing all inappropriate thoughts and feelings for Brendan after he rejected her. Not to mention her love for Liam and the guilt she felt over harbouring desires for his brother. 'Can we go now?'

'Yeah. I gotta get to one more inspection.'

Alannah felt like a fish out of water in the sailing club. When she told Liam about forming a women's group, he suggested using the clubrooms for meetings. The idea was rational at the time, but the splendour of the place gave her doubts, as did the glances she got from some of the elite as they peered down their toffee-stuffed noses. *Perhaps I should dress up more next time.* On this occasion, she wore jeans and her favourite t-shirt: the black one with an Irish whiskey logo.

As the last of the ladies entered, she closed the door and stood at the head of the boardroom table. 'Thank you all for taking time out of your Tuesday evening to attend.' She glanced at Cara, beyond grateful her best friend had magiported in from work for this meeting. Cara offered her an encouraging smile, giving her the strength she needed to continue. 'I have a confession to make. I haven't invited you all here for the sole purpose of chatting over Devonshire tea. I have some important issues to discuss with you all.'

A few murmurs and the general sound of discontentment filled the air.

She projected her voice. 'That said, I have still provided tea and scones for you to enjoy at the end of my speech. Please hear me out first. If you decide you are not interested in my cause, you are still welcome to enjoy the refreshments before you take your leave.'

The din settled and all eyes were on her.

'It is time the women of the magic world push for change on the political front. Our society is behind the times when it comes to women's rights in the Western world. The country we live in has already had a female prime minister. Other countries have had women in leadership roles, yet we have still never seen a female High Magus, let alone adequate representation on most district Councils.

Stunned silence.

'But this isn't only about seats of power. How many of you would like the opportunity to register as warlocks?' Alannah directed her gaze at Claudia, a woman she knew to have the attunements of a warlock, forced to become a shaman simply because she lacked a Y-chromosome.

Claudia nodded for her to continue.

'Or to choose your own field rather than having the men in your family dictate what you can register as?' This time she glanced at Monique, who would have made an excellent conjurer, but her father insisted she be an alchemist because he did not want to risk her going to war if the summons came.

'I am proposing we form a lobby group to campaign for change in the Mages Council, to push for equal rights. If enough of us get our voices out there, the momentum will grow across the country, then across the world. Together, we can fight for what we deserve. Who's with me?'

Every single woman in the room rose and applauded her.

Monique approached Alannah when the group had broken for tea. 'Compelling speech. I can see you making a great High Magus one day.'

'Thanks, but doesn't it bother you I might oust your dad from his position?'

'Dad's resilient. He will probably use the opportunity to advance in the mage ranks. Or to gain a sideways promotion. So, what do you plan to focus on first?'

Looking around the room at the assortment of female mages—both pure and of mixed-blood—she considered her next course of action. 'We should push for a gender quota on the Council in every district. Once we achieve that, we can form a women's faction, making it easier to pass the rest of the bills.'

Monique smiled. 'For someone who falls asleep at most Council meetings, you have a lot more political nous than I gave you credit for.'

'Those meetings are rarely about real politics or even magic. There's also something to be said for growing up in the human world.'

'So how are we gonna do this?' Jacob sat in an armchair, turning his gaze upon the potion book on the coffee table.

Brendan handed Jacob one of the beers he carried and slumped onto the couch. After chugging down a large mouthful, he put the bottle aside and picked up the book. Casting his eyes over the recipe, he made a mental note of the ingredients they needed. *Essence of joy, essence of excitement, essence of lust, 30% ethanol.* He flicked to the section of essences. 'Hmm. Some of these recipes are quite vague in their instructions. I guess that's why they call potion craft more of an art than a science.

'Yeah, I guess. How can I help?' Jacob sat on the edge of his seat; anticipation painted all over his face.

The professional counsellor part of Brendan reared its concerned head at Jacob's enthusiasm for making what was essentially a recreational drug. But the more dominant hedonistic side of him was keen. 'I'll have to make the essences because they involve emotion-based mana channelling. How about you get us the ethanol? We could either source it pre-diluted or prepare it ourselves with the concentrated stuff and some purified water. We also need an imbuement funnel.'

'A what?'

'It's an enchanted funnel that allows the magical properties of the essences to transfer into the end product.' Brendan paused to consider their options. 'I'd ask Alannah to make one for me, but I don't want her getting mixed up in this. It might put her seat on the Council at risk. Can you ask Amy?' Most dwarves were skilled conjurers, and it was likely their dwarven friend could craft what they required.

'Yeah, sure. Is there anything else we need?'

'Just some standard laboratory glassware, although we need to consecrate it. Is that something you can manage, or should I do that?'

'How about I get the glassware and you consecrate it? I'm not into all that ritual mumbo jumbo. Never needed to be since I started life with my one and only attunement.'

'Sounds like a plan. Please don't tell me how you acquire the stuff.' Brendan knew boggarts were notorious for theft (an easy feat when they were skilled illusionists) and Jacob was no exception.

'Okay fine. Just don't tell me how you go about preparing them essences.'

Brendan chuckled as he reached for his beer. 'By the way, I plan to move into town soon. I accepted an offer for a small rental house near the school.'

'Sweet. That'll make mornings easier for you.'

'And my brother less crabby with me.'

Jacob's brows rose. 'You've been overstaying your welcome there, haven't you?'

He sighed. 'You might say. Getting my own flat was Alannah's suggestion. That girl has been giving me all sorts of mixed messages lately.'

'Oh?'

'After she shut me out of her thoughts and feelings for years, I caught glimpses of her mind again recently.' Brendan thought back to their previous night of house hunting. 'Her head is a mess, let me tell you.'

Jacob gave him an impish grin. 'Read any interesting thoughts?'

Letting his own devil horns show, Brendan smirked. 'Yup.'

The moment Liam left for work on Wednesday morning, Alannah jumped in her blue hatchback. She had contacted Nick on Sunday to arrange a meeting, and this was the earliest suitable time. With what she was about to ask him, she did not want to use an unsecure phoneline.

When she reached the end of her street, she took the road leading to the southern exit out of Gaeilge Shores. Passing through the outskirts of town, she braked as something caught her attention: the tell-tale shimmering of a glamour spell. And it came from the old ruins which had once been the heart of a large farmstead before they crumbled into disrepair.

Alannah killed the engine and concentrated on peering through the veil. It was the most powerful illusion she had ever encountered, clearly meant for hiding something from mages as well as humans. Luckily, Alannah was gifted with exceptional magic sight.

A few minutes later, the veil faded, and her eyes widened at the sight of a warehouse within the ruins. *Odd.* Questions of who, what, when, and why flooded her mind, but she pushed them aside and made a mental note to investigate this place later. She had somewhere to be.

Driving straight to Nick's house took fifteen minutes, crawling along the bumpy dirt track forming his driveway for five of those. Alannah did not mind though, because the Pattersons' orchard was a stunning place, the entrance lined with blossoming almond trees.

Nick waited on the front porch for her, leaning against the stone veneer wall with his arms crossed. His orcish muscles bulged from beneath a tight black t-shirt, showing heavily inked arms that reminded her of his naked body merging with a fae chick in Brendan's bed. He shaved most of his head, leaving medium length strands of pink and black streaked hair to cover the right side. That was the colour he broadcast with his glamour. She knew his hair was in fact dark brown, his olive-coloured skin leathery, and he had stag horns and pointed ears. Alannah considered herself a tad shallow, because when it came to her magical friends who were not mages, she preferred to look at their projected image.

Once she parked, Nick pushed off from the wall and reached her in a few long strides. The moment she emerged from the car; he squeezed her tight in an embrace. 'Hey, little lady.' He was the only guy she did not reprimand for calling her little. Like most orcs, Nick's stature was mammoth, both in height and width, dwarfing almost everyone. Yet despite his build and punk image, Nick was a big softie.

'Hey Nick,' Alannah replied as soon as he released her, returning air to her lungs.

He gave her a playful grin. 'So, what's with the secret rendezvous? Have you come to your senses and decided to ditch those cousins? If we leave now, we might hit the state border by nightfall.'

'Ha! Why drive when I can use ley lines?' She made a show of wiping away the imaginary drool from Nick's chin. 'Seriously though, you know Liam's the only cousin I'm involved with, right?'

'Yeah, but we all see the sexual chemistry between you and Brendo. It's out of this world. Just a matter of time, sweet.' He put his arm across her shoulders to lead her inside. 'Come on then.'

Alannah rolled her eyes. 'You know the flirting is fake, right? It's part of the game we play.'

'If you say so. Here, take a seat.' He gestured to the Victorian settee that matched the rest of the antique furniture but did not fit with the rugged appearance of the farmhouse's occupants. 'Can I get you a drink? Tea, coffee… something cold?'

'A coffee, thanks.' *It is still morning after all.*

When Nick returned, he set the drinks down on a coffee table and sat in one of the sturdier armchairs. 'So, what's up?'

'I need a bodyguard.'

Nick's eyes narrowed, but he remained silent, allowing her to explain.

'This is something I don't want Liam to know about.' She gave Nick the letter from Scarlett.

'I can see why,' he agreed as he returned it. 'I'm in. What's the plan, sweet?'

Alannah smiled. 'Thanks, Nick. The next step is to call this Patrick dude and make the arrangements. Mind if I use your phone?'

He pushed his iPhone across the table.

'Thanks.' Taking a deep breath, she dialled the number.

The call connected after three rings. 'Patrick Douglas speaking.'

'Uh, hi Mr. Douglas. My name is Alannah and I'd like to arrange a meeting with Scarlett.'

'Certainly. What is your location, please?' He sounded formal and proper.

'Gaeilge Shores.'

'That's in South Australia, yes?'

'Yeah.'

'Just a moment, please.' Putting her on hold, he subjected her to some horrendous easy-listening music. She was thankful when Patrick returned a couple of minutes later. 'Scarlett can meet you in Adelaide on Friday night. Will this time suit you?'

'Yeah, that's fine.' Pausing, she glanced at Nick, who gave her an encouraging smile. 'Is it okay if I bring my bodyguard?'

'Scarlett will permit one escort, but she would like to know their name before granting approval.'

Being able to take someone surprised her. 'His name is Nick Patterson.'

'Very well. I will contact her and send you a message to confirm the details. Can I text you on this number?'

'Yes, please.'

'Great. Thank you for your call, Alannah.'

Well, that was odd.

Nick's brows rose. 'So, how'd it go?'

'Fine, I think. Patrick needs to check if Scarlett will allow you to accompany me, but apparently, I can take one person with me. He will text your phone with the details. We are meeting on Friday night; I hope that's alright?'

'All good. I'm sure the lads won't mind if I skip pub night to help you.'

'Excellent.' Alannah sculled her tepid coffee.

'So, uh, how much did you hear going on in Brendan's room on Saturday morning?'

Her heart fluttered as memories of four sweaty bodies colliding together flashed before her. She bit her lip.

His eyes narrowed. 'That much, huh? You know, I'm not usually like that. I don't know what came over me on Friday night. I…'

Alannah raised a hand to stop him going on. 'It's okay, Nick. You don't need to explain. What you guys do behind closed doors is none of my business and I don't think any less of you for it.'

'You're such a sweetheart. I sure hope I can find a woman like you one day. Liam's such a lucky bugger and I bet he doesn't fully appreciate what he's got with you.'

Does Nick have a thing for me? 'Uh, thanks.'

A text came through on Nick's phone. 'It's Patrick. He says Scarlett will permit me to attend as your bodyguard and we should meet at some place called The Magic Martini at ten. You know the place at all?'

'Yeah. It's a fae cocktail lounge in the East End. Bianca took a few of us there once.'

Nick frowned. 'Hmm. Sounds swanky. I s'pose I'll have to buy a suit.'

'Not a bad idea.' She reached into her purse and retrieved a wad of cash. 'This should cover most of it.'

He pushed her hand away. 'Don't be silly. I can buy it myself. I'm doing this to help out a friend and I don't expect any money.'

'Ah, okay. Thanks, Nick.' She smiled. 'You're a legend.'

'No biggie.'

Alannah rose. 'Well, I should get going. I've got work to get back to. Let's meet here at half-past eight on Friday night.'

'Righto.' Nick followed her outside, giving her another bear hug before letting her leave.

Alannah stopped outside the old ruins on her way back into town and rang Liam.

'Hey, gorgeous. How are you?'

She grinned into the phone, feeling all warm and fuzzy from his greeting. 'I'm fine. Listen, I spotted something strange as I was driving past the old ruins. Can you meet me there?'

'Yeah, of course. Give me ten.'

'Okay, great. See ya soon.'

'Will do. Love you.'

Alannah never tired of hearing him say it. 'Love you too.' After hanging up, she got out of the car and took a short stroll down the road to South Seas Café, figuring there was enough time for a coffee. Assuming Liam was in town, she would be able to see his patrol car passing by.

Brigette, the human barista—who was around a year younger than Alannah—greeted her with a warm smile. 'Hi hun. Will it be the usual today?'

'Yes please. Oh, and an extra muffin to go, thanks.' Alannah was addicted to their white choc and raspberry muffins. She took her usual seat by the window, where she watched the world go by. It humbled her to think much of humanity went about their business oblivious to mages and magic.

Once Brigette had delivered her order, Alannah's eyes swept the room. Catching the gaze of one of the older ladies sitting up the back, she offered a polite smile. But the woman frowned and shook her head, whispering something to her fellow cronies. The rest of them sneered at Alannah.

'What the?' she whispered to herself. Those ladies had never been rude to her before, despite the way she dressed. Turning back to face the street, Alannah tried to ignore the hostile vibes emanating from the rear of the coffee shop and focussed on her morning tea. As she downed the last of her latte, she spotted Liam driving past.

He walked towards the café when she stepped out. 'Figured you'd be waiting in there.' Pulling her into a warm embrace, Liam kissed her passionately. 'This is a pleasant surprise.' His grin ran from ear to ear.

'As tempting as it is to pull you into the back of your car and waste the morning, I need to show you something.'

Liam laughed. 'I wouldn't complain, but what did you want to show me?'

Alannah tugged on his hand, leading him back to the old ruins. She pointed toward the warehouse. 'Can you see through the glamour spell?'

Narrowing his eyes, Liam focussed on the spot in question. 'Hmm… not unaided.' He pulled out a potion vial from a small pouch on his belt and swallowed it. A moment later his eyes widened with alarm. 'Doesn't bode well. Whoever uses that warehouse must be up to foul play if they are hiding from mages.'

'That's what I figured.'

He glanced around the street, then at Alannah. 'Let's take a closer look. I wanna scout the place out. Do you have any invisibility potions?'

She shook her head. 'I wasn't expecting to need any when I left home this morning.'

'Here, take mine.' He retrieved another vial from his pouch and gave it to her.

'But what about you?' she protested.

'Your safety comes first. Please, Lana,' he pleaded. 'Besides, I can defend myself more readily.'

She sighed. 'Fine.' After drinking the bitter tincture, Alannah grabbed both of Liam's hands, allowing him to see her, and put her phone on silent. They had worked enough stealth missions—both real and in training drills—to be able to fall into an effective routine. Trailing Liam with silent footfalls, she kept her eyes and ears peeled.

They both needed to moderate their pace when they reached a section of ground covered in rubble from a busted stone wall: one wrong step would not only risk a fall, but it would give them away. Reaching clear, level ground, Alannah let out a breath she did not know she held.

When they reached the warehouse, Liam tried every door to no avail. Not even his lock picks worked. 'They must be magically warded'. After a full perimeter sweep, they returned to the roadside. 'What are your thoughts, Lana?'

'I'm worried about the lack of windows. Could it be a nest of fugitive vamps or ghouls?'

'Unlikely. They wouldn't have access to such strong wards and glamour magic, not without a lich. And as you saw with our grandmother, liches prefer more luxurious quarters. Whoever is using the facility wants to keep prying eyes out of their business. It could be a dark mage or unseelie operation. Possibly even dark elves, but we haven't seen them around this state for decades.'

'Hmm. Should we report this to the Council?'

'Yes. I'll ask Kieran if we can assemble a special taskforce to get inside. For now, I need to get back to work. Will you be all right to get home, or did you want a lift?'

'I'll be fine. My car's over there.' Alannah pointed to where she parked across the road. 'See you tonight.'

They kissed with a fervour to rival their greeting until Liam took his leave.

Alannah gave the mysterious warehouse one last glance before making her way home.

Chapter Four

Having finished in the Sailing Club's showers, Liam made his way over to the bar to join his cousin, Steve Maher, for a quick drink. While the rascal had always run with Liam's crew, the death of Blake, Liam's best mate and Steve's big brother, had solidified their friendship. Liam felt he owed it to Blake to watch out for Steve, especially when Blake had sacrificed his life to save Alannah.

Steve leaned on the bar with his left arm while his right hand raked a few tangles out of his wavy blond hair. 'Hey man, awesome swell you conjured for us out there.'

When it came to surfing, Liam's talent for elemental magic was often sought-after. He grinned. 'I'm glad you could handle it. Lucas was such a Barney out there. Did you see him wiping out?'

'Hey, I heard that. Not cool bro!' Lucas chided from down the bar, but there was humour in his tone.

As he glanced in his mate's direction, Liam noticed a group of middle-aged men at a nearby table staring at him as they whispered and laughed. *What the hell?* The moment he considered confronting them, the sound of Aqua's 'Barbie Girl' chiming from his pocket interrupted his thoughts. 'That little shit!' He knew who was ringing even before seeing Brendan's name on the caller I.D. His brother had developed a nasty habit of hacking Liam's phone over the last few years and pulling stunts like changing the personalised ringtones for certain contacts. He always set the most irritating tunes for his own entry so Liam would get annoyed and even embarrassed when the twerp rang him. 'What is it, Barbie?'

Brendan laughed. 'Did you only just discover that one? Or did you keep it because you secretly love the song?'

'Is there a point to your call, other than tormenting me?'

More laughter. 'Mum wants to know what time to serve dinner. Oh, and Lana is already here. I gave her a lift on my way out of town.'

He glanced at his Omega watch. *I must have lost track of time.* 'I'll be there in fifteen minutes.'

'Super. We're all famished here, so don't keep us waiting any longer. You know how lethal

Lana gets when she's hangry.' Alannah giggled in the background and Brendan groaned. 'Ouch! Hell, woman. You're just proving my point.'

Liam tensed his jaw at the sound of them flirting. 'I'll see you soon.' He hung up, not waiting for Brendan's response. Looking up from his call, he noticed everyone in the club fixed their eyes on him. He leaned in close to Steve, adopting a hushed tone. 'Do you know why everyone is gawking at me and whispering?'

Steve's eyebrows rose. 'You haven't heard the rumours yet? You're normally one of the first to catch wind of gossip.'

He frowned. 'What rumours and why am I only hearing about them now?'

Gulping, Steve's Adam's apple bobbed as he combed his fingers through his hair. 'Um, I'm sure they're bollocks, that's why I didn't bring it up with you.'

Liam's clenched his fists. 'What. Damn. Rumours?'

'About Alannah and Brendan hooking up.'

Liam's heart skipped a beat, his blood froze, and he saw red. Without further hesitation, he stormed out of the Sailing Club and dived into his SUV, paying no heed to Steve calling after him. He did not care about speed limits as he gunned it all the way to Cailleach Estate. A single thought occupied his mind on the torturous drive: *If Brendan has touched Lana, I will spill his blood.*

Upon arrival, he burst through the door, ignoring his mother's greeting as he stalked down the hall. He found the two of them laughing in the living room, sitting much too close. Rage coursed through his blood and the moment Brendan looked up, he paled at the sight of Liam's advance. To avoid a show in front of their mother, he grabbed his brother up from the sofa and dragged him out the back where Liam shoved Brendan up against the double-brick wall of the house.

Alannah rushed outside after them, shouting, *'What the hell, Liam?'*

Liam focussed his seething eyes on the rogue before him. 'Did you touch her?'

Brendan smirked. 'Who? You mean Lana? Of course I touched her. I touch her all the time.'

His fist collided with Brendan's jaw.

'Liam! Stop it!' Alannah's screams barely registered.

'Did you screw her?' He hissed the question.

'What? No!' Alannah cried in protest. 'What's gotten into you?'

Turning his head to the side, Brendan spat blood on the ground before casting his insolent scowl back on Liam. 'Why don't you ask Lana? Or is your relationship so insubstantial you don't trust her?'

Ross emerged from the house. 'Liam? What's going on here?'

Maintaining his grip on Brendan's shoulders, Liam turned to his father. 'That's what I'd like to know, Dad. Would anyone here like to tell me why all of Gaeilge Shores are under the assumption my brother is sleeping with my girl?'

'I'm sure it's only a vicious rumour, Son.'

Snapping his attention back to Brendan, Liam glowered. 'Is this because of your stupid flirting game?'

'Maybe.' Brendan smirked, tempting Liam to wipe the expression away with his fist.

'I warned you about pulling shit in public. As Council members, Lana and I both have reputations to uphold. This doesn't only hurt me.'

All trace of impudence left Brendan's visage as he hung his head. 'I'm sorry, Lana.'

When Liam released his hold of Brendan, he turned to Alannah and his heart sank at her red-faced, wide-eyed visage.

'Ross and Liam, can you please go back inside. I'd like a word with Brendan.' Alannah's mouth set in a hard line.

Liam hesitated as he watched his dad walk inside.

She pierced him with a glare. 'Liam, please.'

Alannah watched Liam stride through the door with deflated shoulders, back into the house where the mouth-watering smell of Nora's cooking called to her. First, she needed to confront Brendan about the stunt he had pulled. Shaking her head, she turned back to him. 'Why did you do it, Brendan? You haven't started a game out in public since I got back with Liam. Why now? Was it to get a rise out of him?'

'Pretty much,' he deadpanned.

'And what of the backlash I'm gonna have to deal with?'

Brendan lowered his gaze. 'I didn't think things through.' He sought her eyes again. 'I'm sorry, Lana. I didn't want to hurt you.' Stepping closer, he drew her into his arms. 'Hurting you is the last thing I've ever wanted.'

'Yet you keep doing it,' she mumbled under her breath.

His body stiffened. 'What?'

As she pulled back out of his grasp, Alannah noticed how wide his eyes had grown. 'Nothing. Don't worry about it.'

'How do I keep hurting you, Lana?'

She feigned a smile. 'Damn your magic hearing.'

Brendan's gaze narrowed on her. 'Stop deflecting. How do I keep hurting you?'

A vice gripped her heart. 'Can we forget I said anything?'

He shook his head and grabbed her shoulders. 'There's no way I'm letting this slide. Tell me, Lana.'

And there's no way I'm telling you about the wound inflicted by your rejection and how every time we play Sleazy Chicken, I'm reminded of that pain. Tears threatened to escape her eyes as she attempted to suppress her thoughts and feelings. Breaking free of his hold, she moved toward the house. 'Come on, dinner's going cold.'

The air of tension at the dining table was thick enough to plunge a fork into. The Winters family's dysfunctional dynamics had always added some discomfort to their fortnightly dinner. Brendan's resentment over Ross favouring Liam was a big part of it, along with several other sibling rivalries between the boys. *And now I'm one such dispute.*

Liam alternated between puppy dog eyes directed at Alannah and death stares pointed at his brother. Brendan, with his attention focussed on Alannah, failed to notice Liam's glare. Meanwhile, Alannah welcomed the distraction of tasty roast pork and veggies.

Nora broke the excruciating silence: 'So Alannah, have you got any new dresses to show me tonight?' The woman's beaming smile and loving blue eyes warmed Alannah's heart.

'Yes, actually. I'm planning to show it off in the City on Friday when I go out for a girls' night.'

Liam cleared his throat. 'You never mentioned anything about this girls' night.'

'I just did. Consider yourself notified,' she clipped at him, still pissed he did not come to her about his concerns first. *Does he not trust me?*

A snicker slipped from Brendan's mouth. 'Damn that was hot.'

Along with the rest of the group, Alannah turned her own evil eye on Brendan.

His heated gaze remained fixed on her as he crunched through a piece of crackling.

'*Get out!*' Ross roared at him.

'To hell with you, old man.' Brendan spoke with a mouthful of food.

'Brendan, please leave the table,' Nora begged.

After an exaggerated sigh, he rose, pushing his chair back with enough force it clattered as it struck the floor. Grabbing his meal, he stormed off toward the guesthouse.

'I wanna throttle the jerk,' Liam mumbled.

'Liam, please,' Nora pleaded. 'Enough is enough.' She placed a comforting hand on Alannah's arm. 'I'm sorry, sweetheart. I don't know what's up with my boys at the moment.'

Liam made a guttural noise akin to a growl. 'Don't feign ignorance, Mother; it's not very becoming. You know exactly what's going on.'

After shooting Liam another scowl, Alannah turned her attention back to Nora.

Nora sighed. 'You know I can't share the insights I gain from my attunement to emotions. It's not my business.'

After finishing their meal in silence, Alannah and Liam made a quick escape. As soon as they got home, Liam beelined for their home gym and slammed the door.

Alannah sank onto the couch and let it all out with a gut-wrenching cry. Once her sobbing had subsided, she found Liam punishing a punching bag with the angry screams of the Dropkick Murphys blaring through the stereo. She lowered the volume, prompting him to look at her. Crossing her arms, she tried to remain calm when she addressed him. 'Why didn't you ask me? Why did you go straight to Brendan?'

He dropped his boxing gloves and took a reluctant step toward her. 'I was furious when I heard the rumours.'

'But how could you even believe a word of that gossip? Don't you trust me?'

'The thought of him touching you flicked a switch in my brain. I wasn't thinking rationally. I'm sorry, Lana.'

'There must be some aspect of mistrust for that switch to even exist. How many times do we have to reassure you neither of us harbour any of those feelings?'

'Don't be so damn naïve, Lana. Brendan's always had designs on you. And don't take me for a fool. The fact he hasn't tried anything further until recently also tells me you must have done something to encourage him.' He drew closer, a fierce expression in his eyes. 'I'd like to know what you did.'

After gaping at him, she frowned. 'I haven't *done* anything. I can't believe how little faith you have in me or in us.' The wound in Alannah's heart wept and her eyes were not far from joining it. Liam was not ready to resolve matters, so she left him to his own devices and collapsed on the bed in the guestroom.

Brendan stood upon Jacob's threshold and listened to footfalls scurrying toward him.

Jacob threw open the door. 'You got the stuff?'

'Yup. Here's the secret sauce.' He handed over the vial containing the combined essences.

After glancing at the white contents, Jacob raised a brow. 'Do I want to know what's in here?'

Brendan grinned. 'Probably not.' Gaining a precious glimpse at Alannah's thoughts the previous night had renewed his hope. It provided him with all the inspiration he needed to feel joy, excitement, and lust. He simply had to bottle those feelings while channelling their power.

Jacob screwed up his nose. 'Well, it's comforting to know we are working with a homeopathic potency and you're a pure mage.'

'Oh, why's that?'

'Because you guys don't get any of those nasty human infections.'

Laughing, he slapped Jacob on the back. 'Come on, let's get on with it.'

'Right. The equipment is all in the kitchen.'

Brendan followed him down the hall of his cottage. The kitchen blinded him, with its lemon yellow Laminex bench tops, powder blue cupboards, and black and white checkerboard linoleum floor. The most hideous feature was the wallpaper depicting ice-creams and doughnuts in pastel shades of pink, yellow, and blue.

After throwing up in his mouth, Brendan focussed on the dining table, covered in potion vials, glass beakers, volumetric flasks, measuring cylinders, and pipettes. The first step was consecrating the glassware, so he got to work with setting up a ritual circle. Jacob helped him move the table to the middle of the room. Brendan checked the cardinal points with his compass and drew a pentagram on the floor around the table in thick white chalk. He placed a candle at each point; red to the North, yellow to the East; green to the South, blue to the West, and silver at the apex. Symbols for each of the elements joined the candles.

Jacob watched casually from one of the dining chairs at the edge of the room. With everything in place, Brendan glanced at him. 'Once I start this, you can't enter the pentagram under any circumstances. Doing so will break the circle and screw up the whole ritual. Do you understand?'

'Yeah, got it.'

'Good.' Brendan cast the circle, calling upon each of the elements as he lit the candles. He picked up a beaker in each hand and took them to the red candle and passed them a safe distance above the flame. 'I call upon the Guardians of the North to consecrate these beakers and charge them with emotional energies. I purify them this night and make them sacred.'

Brendan moved through each point, finishing at the apex. 'I call upon Cailleach, mother of mages, to consecrate these beakers and charge them with your energies. I purify them this night and make them sacred.'

He repeated this process for all the potion making equipment. By the time Brendan drew his athame across the chalk line to break the circle, Jacob was snoring in his chair. Laughing, he poked his friend in the ribs.

Jacob startled as he awoke. 'Gods! I'm glad I don't have to share a bed with you. So not cool, man.'

Brendan grinned. 'Don't worry. I treat any lady lucky enough to share a bed with me to a more pleasurable wakeup call. I finished consecrating everything. It's time to mix the potion.'

'About time. That ritual rubbish took hours.'

'What do you expect with so much equipment? Now pass me the box containing the imbuement funnel, and whatever you do, don't directly touch it.'

'O-kay. Why can't I touch it? Is it dangerous?' Jacob stared at it with wide eyes.

'Relax bro, it's not dangerous.'

'Yeah but Amy enchanted it with some magic voodoo stuff. I don't know these things.'

A roaring laugh escaped Brendan's belly. 'You crack me up man. I've known humans less ignorant of magic than you.'

Jacob frowned. 'I'm glad you find me amusing. Here's your damn funnel.' He thrust a white cardboard box at Brendan's chest.

'The reason you can't touch the funnel is I've consecrated it for personal use. If you touch it, we will lose some of the power within it. The same goes for the rest of this glassware.'

'Well bugger. What can I do to help now, seeing as I can't touch anything?'

'You can pass me the ingredients as I ask for them. You should be able to touch the potion vials too since they will hold the finished product. They have been specially made to protect the magical energies within.'

Jacob nodded his understanding. 'Right. Let's do this.'

Brendan grabbed a one-hundred millilitre volumetric flask, a measuring cylinder, and a couple of different beakers. 'I need the water and the ethanol first.'

'Here.' Jacob handed him two glass flagons each holding about two litres. One contained '95% ETHANOL', while purified water filled the other.

After decanting an approximate amount of both liquids in separate beakers, Brendan poured the ethanol into the measuring cylinder until he obtained the desired volume. Given he had failed high school chemistry, it was fortunate Brendan got roped into helping his father prepare healing potions during his teenage years. He tipped it into the flask and topped it up with water to the graduated mark. With the stopper in place, he gave the mixture a gentle shake. 'That's our alcohol made. Now I need the mother tincture.'

Jacob blinked. 'The what?'

'The secret sauce. Its technical name is mother tincture.'

'Oh right. Here.' Again, he grimaced as he held the mixture out for Brendan.

Brendan used a pipette to measure the essence mixture into a second flask, making up the volume with diluted ethanol. He repeated the process until they had used all the mother tincture, at which point he decanted the potions into vials. 'Now my man, we are done.'

Jacob beamed. 'Sweet! It's time to party!'

Nick sighed. 'As much as it kills me to say this, I'm with Liam on this one.'

'What?' Alannah glanced at Nick, her bodyguard for the night. His massive bulk barely fit within the confines of her hatchback. She had confided in him about the family drama, hoping for a sympathetic ear. Normally, Cara would have been her go-to on matters like this, but her fiery haired shaman friend worked a fly-in fly-out job which involved revegetation around the state, and she was only home on weekends.

Brendan still had not spoken to Alannah since that dinner and the few words she had had with Liam in the last two days were bitter and distant. Before leaving in the morning, he had demanded she stop playing the Sleazy Chicken game with Brendan.

Returning her attention to the road in time for the expressway entrance, she huffed. 'I thought you had my back?'

'In most things, I do. But if you were my girl, there's no way I'd tolerate your flirting game with Brendo. It wouldn't matter if there were feels on either side, or neither. It would make me uncomfortable, and it obviously gives some people the wrong idea about you two.'

'Does it give *you* the wrong idea?'

'Depends on how you and Brendo honestly feel. The impression I get is you are both hot as hell for each other. If not, I guess I have the wrong idea. I'm not attuned to emotions, so I don't have an accurate read on things by any means. But the only valid opinion here is Liam's since he's your actual boyfriend. How would you feel if Liam continually flirted with one of his female friends? If you're still in love with him, you need to shut that shit down.'

Alannah took a deep breath. 'You're right. Brendan and I have been playing this game for so long, I stopped thinking about how others perceive it. It all started out as innocent fun, you know?'

'That's where an outside perspective can help.'

'Yeah, I guess.' Her voice trailed off as she let her thoughts enter dangerous territory.

'Are you okay, sweet?'

'What?' She glanced at him.

'You were lost in your thoughts. I'm wondering if you're okay?'

Alannah bobbed her head. 'Ah, yeah. I was contemplating something you said about getting an accurate read on things. Do you know much about Sylvia Green?'

'The real estate chick?'

'Yeah, her.'

'Not much, why?'

'She probably started the rumour after I went to an open inspection with Brendan. What if she is attuned to emotions?'

'Why would that matter? It was only a rumour, right?'

'Because I want to know if she got an accurate read on either of us.'

'Holy cow!' Nick bellowed. 'You *are* lusting after Brendo!'

Alannah sucked on her lip. 'Promise me you won't tell a soul. Especially not Brendan.'

'You have my word, but you know there's no hiding your feels from that man.'

'Well, I've made him promise he won't intentionally read me. I've also worked hard to shut off my emotions around him, so I don't project my aura.'

'This may be a stupid question, but if you've got the hots for Brendan, why are you wasting time with that asshat boyfriend of yours?'

Alannah stifled a laugh. 'I happen to be in love with that asshat of mine. Besides, Brendan turned me down four years ago when I was good and ready for it. To put it simply, Liam's a sure thing, while Brendan is not.'

When stopped at a red light, she observed the gobsmacked expression on his face. After a minute of silence, Nick spoke up. 'I had no idea. I'm sorry, sweet.'

She shrugged. 'It is what it is.'

After finding a street park a few blocks away, they walked among the Friday party crowd hopping in and out of bars, cafes, and night-clubs. While not as busy as Melbourne, it was one of Adelaide's more vibrant evenings.

Their destination, The Magic Martini, was in the basement of a human bar, disguised as a private function space. At first glance, the doorman resembled the typical burly bouncer, but after piercing the glamour, Alannah saw a lizard-like humanoid known as a kobold. They were a species of fae resulting from elves mating with dragons or wyverns who act as knights and vassals for the Seelie Court.

This kobold had golden scales instead of skin and when he cast his eyes on Alannah, he looked her up and down, offering an appreciative grin before opening the door for them.

She muttered 'pervert' under her breath as they entered.

'Well you do look sexy as sin in that dress,' Nick pointed out.

Alannah shook her head as she continued down the stairs. 'Why do so many of my friends have magic hearing?'

'I'm gonna assume that's a rhetorical question.'

'Good call.' She scanned the room upon entry, taking in the sensual ambience, complete with café jazz playing in the background. The colour scheme was deep reds, dark browns, and warm metallics. Antique-style filament globes hung at various heights throughout the room and the interesting patterns on the floor and ceiling, combining straight lines and curves, reminded Alannah of Art Deco.

Nick ordered their drinks, a mocktail for her and a Coke for himself, and followed Alannah to a table near the back of the room. 'What's the plan?'

'Now we wait. I presume she will recognise me and approach us. I have no idea what she looks like.' Alannah checked the time on her phone. 'We're a few minutes early.'

'Hmm. You nervous?

'Hell yeah. You?'

'A bit, but only because I don't know who we're dealing with. I figure the whole bio dad thing is adding to your anxiety.'

She sighed. 'It's weird you—'

'Hello, dear child.' The familiar voice inside her head was like a knife twisting in her heart.

'Are you okay sweet?' Nick's brow puckered. 'You look like you've seen a ghost.' He glanced around the room searching for the hidden face in the crowd.

'Before I reveal myself, I want to assure you I mean you no harm.'

Alannah jumped to her feet. 'Let's get out of here.'

He stood with her. 'Why, what's wrong?'

She started walking toward the door.

'Wait child! Please, give me a chance. I can tell you all about your father.'

Something deep in her subconscious stopped Alannah in her tracks. Strangely, she felt she could trust those words.

'Alannah? What's going on?' Nick's tone was urgent.

Returning to her seat, Alannah beckoned Nick to sit next to her. 'Fine. I will listen if you show yourself.'

Nick's eyes squinted as he sank beside her.

A second later, a woman in a scarlet-red cocktail dress appeared on the seat across from them. She had dyed her once white hair black and styled it a French knot. Coloured contacts gave her white eyes their brown tint. The name change and disguise would have fooled most people, but there was no hiding her identity from her granddaughter.

'I thought I killed you. How are you alive?' Alannah hissed in a hushed tone.

Nick glanced at her, then in the direction she faced. 'Who are you talking to, Alannah?'

Alannah narrowed her eyes on Scarlett. 'Show yourself to my friend here, or I will leave and report you to the Council.'

Scarlett sighed. 'Very well. But you have to ensure he will not scream bloody murder.'

She turned to Nick. 'Scarlett is here, but she is currently hiding from you. I need you to promise you won't do anything to give her away unless she threatens me.'

'I promise.' Nick nodded. When he turned back to face Scarlett, he gasped. 'You!'

'Please, Nick. You promised.'

His Adam's apple bobbed as he gulped. 'I know. Give me a sec.' He took a moment to calm his breathing. 'Okay.'

Scarlett smiled. 'Splendid. Now, to answer your question Alannah, I am a lich. You cannot kill me by the same means as other cursed. I am truly immortal.'

Alannah's eyes widened. *How is this not known to other mages?* 'Do you still want to curse and control me?'

Her grandmother's head shook daintily. 'No dear. I am no longer the Queen of the Cursed; I do not hold such power. I simply seek your forgiveness and an opportunity to get to know you better.'

She eyed the woman suspiciously. 'Why?'

'Because you are my granddaughter, and you have a great aptitude for magic. It would be my honour to help you realise your potential.'

'How can I trust you not to kill me, or those whom I love?'

Scarlett grinned. 'Because if I wanted to kill you or your loved ones, you would already be dead.'

Alannah rolled her eyes. 'Still as arrogant as ever, I see. So, what's the deal? What do you want in return for info on my dad?'

'I would like the opportunity to teach you. I know you are seeking to further your position on the Council, and I want to help. Train with me and you will have your five attunements in no time. Once you have those attunements, I will tell you all you want to know about your father.'

'Is that it? I don't see what you get out of the deal. What's the catch?'

'Tsk, tsk. Such a cynic. As I said before, I want to spend time with you and help you achieve your goals. Call it vicarious living if you like.'

Alannah considered the terms for a few minutes. The deal was too remarkable to be real, warranting a cautious approach. Scarlett likely wanted to manipulate her and use her as a puppet if she became High Magus, but her natural scepticism ought to guard her. 'Fine, but how are we going to meet? We can't train at my house—Liam would go ape if he found out.'

'An astute observation. I will prepare a space and contact you when it is ready. May I have your direct contact details?'

The fact her grandmother knew Alannah had given someone else's number did not surprise her. She withdrew a pen and scrap of paper from her clutch. After scribbling down her number she pushed the slip of paper forward. 'Here.'

'Thank you. Expect to hear from me within a week.' Scarlett disappeared.

The sound of Nick's throat clearing brought Alannah's thoughts back to the room. 'Well, that was… uh… interesting.'

'Indeed.' She looked at him and smiled. 'Thanks for backing me up. I'm sure it goes without saying you won't breathe a word of this to anyone.'

Nick arched a brow. 'Not even Brendan, who knew you were meeting Scarlett tonight?'

'Especially not Brendan. He would freak. That woman took a lot from him. Besides, I'm consorting with a fugitive, so the Council could name anyone who knows an accessory to my crime.'

He frowned. 'I don't like it, but I get it. Although, if anything happens to you, I won't be keeping my lips sealed any longer.'

'Fair call. Now, the night is still young. Wanna party?' She batted her lashes.

Exhaling, he smiled. 'Okay. But first I need to shoot Brendan a text to let him know the meeting is over and you are safe and well.'

She retrieved her own phone to message Cara: **Meeting finished. I'm thinking of seeing some bands. Wanna come into the city?**

Cara replied straightaway: Already in the city. At a nightclub. Come join us.

Alannah winced. **A nightclub? Really?**

{Cara} **Really. It's not half bad. Lots of eye candy.**

Even though Cara could not see it, Alannah rolled her eyes. She knew Cara and Jacob had an open relationship, but the whole thing was strange to her.

Did you just roll your eyes? Cara's text made her laugh. The girl knew Alannah too well. **Get your sexy little arse over here.**

Glancing up, Alannah planted a stupid grin on her face. 'The other guys are in the city tonight. Cara invited us to join them. You wanna?'

He nodded. 'Let's go.'

Chapter Five

When Jacob first proposed a nightclub, Brendan hesitated because the music usually sucked balls. But after stepping through the doors of The Vault, Brendan admitted the club impressed him. A smoky haze filled the air, intensifying the coloured light beams radiating from the stage and ceiling, and scantily clad chicks danced in cages dotted around the perimeter. The official dancers were not the only ones showing a lot of skin. One glimpse of the writhing bodies on the dancefloor and Brendan understood why Jacob had suggested the place.

Ben stepped up close beside him. 'Gods, man. Look at all that tail.'

An arm fell across Brendan's shoulders, and Jacob's head jutted in between his and Ben's. 'Gentlemen, this is the ultimate candy store. Now let's go treat ourselves.'

Brendan handed them both a potion vial and popped the lid from his own. 'Here's to a wild night.' After tapping their vials as though they were drinks, he threw the tincture down his throat.

'How long before this takes effect?' Ben asked. He was the only other friend Brendan felt comfortable sharing their test batch with. Not only was the weredingo a bigger party animal than either of them, but he also possessed an insanely strong constitution.

Brendan shrugged his shoulders. 'I dunno. This is the first time any of us are trying it. Come on, I'm buying the first round.' He made his way to the bar, his mates following close behind.

With beers in hand, the group clustered around a table overlooking the dancefloor. Brendan was taking it all in when Cara placed a hand on his shoulder, speaking in his ear: 'What was that potion I saw you guys taking?'

Brendan laughed. 'You don't miss a thing, do you? It was a magical pick-me-up.'

'Figures. Where's mine?'

'I only had three. Sorry.'

She slapped his arm. 'Sharing's caring, jerkwad. Why didn't you get one for me?'

When he turned to face her, his heart almost melted for the pleading puppy dog eyes. 'We don't know if this stuff is safe. Jacob didn't want you taking the risk.' His lip curled into a lewd grin. 'But hey, I'm sure you'll reap the benefits from him later.'

Cara huffed as their phones beeped.

He had a message from Nick: **Meeting with Scarlett finished. It went well and Alannah is safe.**

Brendan let out a sigh, releasing the knots of stress Alannah had planted in his shoulders. **Thanks man. You're a champ.** With that business over, he was truly free to let loose. Seeing Cara still busy texting, he made his escape. He downed the rest of his drink and pushed his way through the crowds and onto the dancefloor.

Ben was already putting the moves on a group of bleach-blonde girls who appeared close to their age. Catching sight of Brendan, he smiled. 'Hey man, come meet my new friends!' he shouted over the thumping bass. 'Ladies, this is my mate, Brendan. Let's see if I have this: Tina, Simone, Chloe, and Madison. Am I right?'

The girls all nodded and giggled. 'Are you single too?' inquired the one closest to Brendan. She wore a short red dress with a plunging neckline showcasing her ample assets.

He gave her his most charming smile. 'Madison, was it?'

She nodded with vigour.

Brendan moved closer, leaning toward her. 'Tonight, I can be whatever you want me to be.' He heard her suck in a breath before he drew back to peer into her sparkling eyes.

'So, in essence, you're available right?'

He gave her his seductive laugh. 'Yup. That's what I meant.'

Madison's huge smile was more radiant than the sun. Before he knew it, she was bumping and grinding up against him. He was clueless when it came to dancing to this electronic noise, so he scanned his surrounds to see how other guys were moving. A few were getting right into it, but most swayed on the spot, letting the chicks do most of the work. He chose the latter approach.

A few minutes later, his heartbeat quickened as a rush of endorphins coursed through his system. *This must be the potion kicking in.* He groaned as light beams brimmed beneath the surface of his skin and bokeh bubbles flashed in his field of vision. Without thinking, he slid his arms around Madison's waist, prompting her to giggle. Within seconds, his body was magically in tune with hers and the rhythm she danced. It occurred to him he was passively channelling emotional mana. *Is this a side-effect?* It felt sensational to have magical power flowing through him without the need to concentrate. Closing his eyes, he lost himself in the experience.

Minutes passed—or it might have been hours. Time ceased to mean anything to Brendan until a sudden awareness yanked his attention back into the room. Something or someone was amplifying the emotional wave he was riding. His eyes flickered open, and he looked at Madison, wondering: *is she doing something new?* But she was only dancing. He glanced around to see how his mates were doing.

Ben was beaming with two of the girls flanking him, while Jacob was making out with the fourth blonde. He scanned the room further to check Cara and Bianca were safe. The moment he spotted them; he saw the reason for his surging hormones. *By the Gods! She is so damn sexy.* His dick jumped to attention and Brendan wanted nothing more than to ravish her.

Alannah's eyes pierced him from where she stood on the edge of the mezzanine level balcony. She sipped her drink casually as her heated gaze locked onto him with her lust-filled aura on display for the whole magic world to see.

Oh hell!

While the music the DJ pumped out was not to Alannah's usual taste, it was alright. Heavy and full of energy, there was a level of complexity to it unlike what she had come to expect from most dance music.

Heading for the bar, it did not take long to find the girls. Cara dived at her, pulling her into a bear hug. 'Gods, I missed you!'

'I missed you too. Sorry about last weekend. Liam had time off so—'

'So, he monopolised all of your time. I get it. Liam doesn't like to share you. At least not with us.'

As she pulled back from their embrace, Alannah gave Cara an exaggerated eyeroll. 'Well, we're fighting at the moment, so you will get me for most of this weekend. I might even need to crash at your house.'

Cara's eyebrows rose sky high. 'Sounds serious. Wanna talk about it?'

Alannah nodded. 'Line up at the bar with me and I'll fill you in.'

They left Nick and Bianca immersed in a conversation of their own.

'I love that dress, by the way. Is it your latest work?'

'Yeah'. Alannah wore a skater style dress of layered black lace, incredibly short with a V-neckline of scandalous dimensions.

'Nice. I might have to order one of those. So, what was this fight about?'

'Brendan.'

'Ah, what now?'

Alannah sighed. 'A rumour has circulated through town about me hooking up with Brendan. It started because he initiated a round of Sleazy Chicken when we were house hunting. Long story short, Liam lost it, punched Brendan, accused the two of us of cheating on him, and got pissy with me for provoking Brendan. Liam wants me to stop playing the game now.'

Cara's jaw dropped. 'I'm away for a week and I miss all that. I'm gonna have to find a new job closer to home. Did anything happen between you and Brendan?'

'Of course not. I would have rung you during the week otherwise. But there was an incident last weekend and things have changed between us.'

'Oh my Gods, what?'

A bartender approached Alannah, putting their conversation on hold. She ordered a beer, moving to the edge of the balcony to resume their chat. 'I walked in on him having sex. Let's just say I enjoyed the show a bit too much.'

A hearty laugh broke free from Cara's lungs. 'Holy shizza, woman! Did he see you watching?'

'Uh huh.'

'Damn. So, what are you going to do about Liam?'

'I dunno…' her voice trailed off the moment her eyes landed on Brendan, ambushed by a surge of desire. He danced with a blonde who made Barbie dolls look real. His movements were incredibly erotic, and she imagined herself replacing the bimbo. She was vaguely aware of Cara laughing and moving away. But Alannah focussed on the man stirring emotions which, until a week ago, she had kept dormant for years.

When Brendan's gaze locked with hers, her instincts initially told her to look away, but a devilish idea occurred to her. *Perhaps this is my opportunity to test Liam's theory.* Letting all those pent-up feelings out, she narrowed her eyes in a lust-filled stare and broadcast her aura to ensure there was no mistaking what she wanted.

His gaze raked her up and down before returning to her eyes. He filled her mind with his voice, *'You're playing with fire, Lana.'*

If she had been able to reply telepathically, her retort would have been, *'Who says I'm playing?'* But instead, she settled for a lascivious grin.

Plastic girl drew his attention away. A moment later, they were kissing and feeling each other up.

Alannah sighed. *So much for that theory.*

'I know I'm a simple guy, but if you want him, you should tell him,' Nick whispered in her ear.

She snorted. 'Were you watching?'

'We all were. You weren't exactly subtle.'

Glancing at her friends, Alannah caught Cara and Bianca looking at her with raised brows. *Crap!* She forgot Bianca—a wood nymph attuned to emotions—was standing nearby. If the nymph did not know how Alannah felt about Brendan before, she sure as hell knew then. It was time for some damage control. She stepped closer to the girls, addressing them both. 'Promise me you won't tell a soul about what you saw.'

'You know I'd never talk shit about you behind your back,' Cara reassured her.

Alannah turned her attention to Bianca. 'I know you saw my aura.'

Bianca grinned. 'Yeah, I did. And I'm beginning to wonder if the rumours are true.'

Alannah crossed her arms and glared. 'I haven't cheated on Liam if that's what you're insinuating.'

'Not yet, but I can see you want to.'

She shook her head. 'I don't want to cheat. I—'

'It matters naught to me which of those brothers you bone, nor whether you make a clean break from one before bedding the other. You know I'm not a gossiper, Alannah.'

Her shoulders relaxed as she breathed easier. 'I know. I'm sorry for doubting you.'

Bianca smiled. 'All good. Now let's go dance.' She dragged Alannah and Cara down onto the dancefloor. The three of them had a blast dirty dancing together through several songs.

Leaving her alone with Bianca, Cara exposed Alannah's back, providing the perfect opening for male attention. A solid chest pressed up against her back and a hand slid around her waist, prompting Bianca's eyes to widen. Alannah almost broke out of the hold, but a familiar musky scent filled her nose. Instead, she spun around to face him. 'What happened to your Barbie doll?'

Brendan's eyes glazed over, and she wondered if he was high. 'She had to leave with her friends.' Their bodies swayed together of their own accord.

'Oh. I'm sorry.' Alannah laced her tone with sarcasm. 'She would have been an easy lay.'

With his best attempt at bedroom eyes, he reeled her in closer. 'I'm not worried. There's still plenty of time to get lucky tonight.'

'Why are you dancing with me? You should be making your next move.'

A wicked glint lit up his eyes. 'What if I want to get lucky with you?'

Her breath hitched. 'This game has to stop, Brendan.'

'Who says I'm playing, Lana?' he replied, throwing back the retort she had thought of earlier.

Gods damn, is he a mind reader now? 'I'm serious, Brendan. No more Sleazy Chicken. It makes Liam too uncomfortable.'

Brendan scowled. 'I don't give a rat's arse about Liam's comfort. Besides, he's not here right now.' His hand found its way to her thigh and his fingers travelled beneath her hemline.

Alannah almost jumped out of her skin from the contact. 'Brendan, please.'

Leaning in, he brushed his lips against her ear as he spoke in a gruff voice. 'Mm. I love hearing a woman beg.' His fingers had reached the edge of her panties. Any closer and he would feel how wet she was.

'Brendan, please stop.' She knew her plea lacked conviction.

'Stop what? Do you mean these?' His fingers tickled her bikini line. 'If you wanted them gone, I'm sure you would have swatted my hand away by now.'

The emotional tornado spinning around inside her came to head as Alannah burst free of his grip. '*Stop all of it!*' she screamed; 'the flirting, the touching… all of it. I can't deal with the games anymore.' She turned and fled toward the door, only stopping once she was outside and able to breathe in the fresh air.

The sight of Jacob's bare arse greeted Brendan when he stumbled out of his guesthouse bedroom on Saturday morning and threw a blanket over him. 'Bloody hell, man! You could at least wear some undies when sleeping on my sofa bed.'

Rolling onto his back, Jacob groaned, rubbing his eyes. 'Old habits, sorry. What time is it?'

'Nine something.'

'How and why are you awake so damn early?'

'I didn't sleep well after what happened with Lana.'

Jacob's brow creased. 'Ugh. Sorry bro.'

He strode across the loungeroom, toward the door. 'I'm grabbing some coffee from the main house. You want one?'

'I thought you'd never ask. And how about some of you dad's hangover cure?'

'Sure.' When he found the main house empty, Brendan breathed easy, glad he would not have to face his parents. It felt like someone had spent the better part of the night going at his head with a jackhammer while pouring caustic soda down his throat. He grabbed the magic green elixir and poured two shots, downing one himself. After giving it a few minutes to kick in, he ran the other out to Jacob before making the coffees.

Jacob had dressed, and the sofa bed folded up when Brendan returned to the guesthouse. Slumping onto the couch, he heaved a heavy sigh.

After sipping on his brew in silence for a minute, Jacob smiled. 'So, that potion was the best juice I've ever taken, I gotta say.'

'Same here. Pity my own high was short lived. I was hoping to see what it did for me in the bedroom. Maybe I should give Madison a call and see what she's up to tonight.'

'You mean the blonde with the boob job? She looked lively.'

Brendan snorted. 'That's one way of putting it.'

'Didn't strike me as your usual type though.'

He arched an eyebrow. 'I didn't realise I had a type.'

Jacob laughed. 'Of course you do. Except for Monique and now this Madison bird, I've never seen you hook up with blondes. You usually go for the dark-haired beauties. Can't think why.'

He glared at Jacob. 'You're treading on thin ice, man.' The wound of Alannah's rejection had re-opened and it still felt raw. Trying to shake it off, he stretched his neck. 'Maybe I just need to shake things up.'

Jacob slapped a hand on Brendan's shoulder. 'Be sure to include me and some of her friends in your plans. I need some action too after the stunt you pulled with Alannah got me exiled from my own bed.'

Brendan rubbed his palm against his forehead. 'Even with all my experience, I still don't get women. Why the hell did Cara kick you out for my stupidity?'

'Because Alannah is staying at our place and Cara didn't want to put her up on the couch. I could have used it, but I figured you'd need the company.' Jacob grinned. 'Besides, your sofa bed is much more comfortable than my crappy couch.'

His ears pricked up at the news of Alannah. 'Why is she staying at your house?'

Jacob shrugged. 'I dunno, something about relationship problems with Liam. Cara wouldn't give me any details.'

'Hell! I had no idea their relationship got so rocky. No wonder she freaked out last night.'

'Does this have anything to do with the latest news on the rumour mill?'

'Yeah, but you know that's all bull. It all started when I flirted with Lana in front of Sylvia Green. I guess she read something in my aura and jumped to conclusions.' Recalling the previous night, Brendan's mind drifted away for a while.

When Brendan's attention returned to his friend, Jacob drained the last of his coffee, and frowned at the empty cup. 'Is there more?'

Brendan laughed. 'There's still plenty in the pot. Help yourself.'

'Cheers man. Back in sec.'

As Jacob returned, Brendan decided to air his thoughts. 'You know, after last night, I'm wondering if my aura wasn't the only one Sylvia saw something in.'

One of Jacob's brows shot up. 'Oh?'

'Before Alannah stepped onto the dancefloor last night, she was watching me from the balcony. Her eyes were dark with lust, and she was broadcasting her aura as clear as day. I thought she wanted me. That's why I came on strong with her later.' Brendan sighed. 'I dunno what she wants. I'm so damn confused.'

'Hmm.'

Narrowing his eyes, he pinned Jacob with a serious stare. 'What?'

'Has it occurred to you that Alannah's struggling with feelings for you because she's in a serious relationship with your brother?'

'Damn. When did you get all wise and whatnot?'

Grinning, Jacob took a leisurely, reflective sip from his cup. 'From now on you will address me as Sensei, *young Grasshopper*.' His Mr. Miyagi impersonation cracked Brendan up.

'Too funny, man.' Brendan let out a belly laugh.

'What has you amused, *young Grasshopper*?'

After laughing until he struggled to breathe, Brendan punched Jacob playfully in the arm. 'Killer. Just killer.'

'So, getting back to this potion. I'm convinced we could make a fortune selling this on the Unseelie Market.' He referred to the magic world's black market, controlled by various criminal syndicates of unseelie origin.

Brendan's expression turned grave. 'I dunno, man. Sounds a bit too hardcore. Some of those thugs are lethal.'

Jacob narrowed his eyes on Brendan. 'You know I'm one of those thugs, right?'

'Sorry bro, I didn't mean any offence. But unlike you, I wasn't born into that world and the stories I've heard about unseelie gangs are terrifying. I can't reconcile that stuff with the Jacob I know.'

Leaning back, Jacob sighed. 'It's not all bad you know. There is such a thing as honour among thieves. If you handle the production side, you could let me take care of the business transactions. And we split the profits down the middle. What do ya say?'

Brendan reclined his head and closed his eyes to mull over Jacob's proposal. On the one hand, he knew there were risks dealing with Jacob's associates; and if The Council of Mages caught him dealing unsanctioned potions on the Unseelie Market, he would be up shit creek. On the other hand, this opportunity might provide the excitement he had been seeking. He turned to Jacob with a wicked grin. 'Okay, but we need a suitable street name for this stuff.'

Tapping his chin, Jacob stared into space. 'What do you think of Rapture?'

Arching a brow, Brendan laughed. 'Isn't that the drug in *Spider Man*?'

'Good point. What are some other ecstasy synonyms? Bliss, elation, euphoria, delight…'

Brendan roared with laughter. '*Delight?* Do you honestly want to market a drug with the name Delight? Sounds more like a brand of herbal tea for grannies. We may as well go with Glee.'

Jacob frowned. 'That's a TV show, dude. Besides, I'm just throwing words out there until something sticks.'

A lightbulb turned on inside his brain. 'How about Rhapsody?'

Chapter Six

Four days had passed since Alannah's outburst in the nightclub, and life was returning to normal.

Brendan rang on Saturday afternoon to apologise for 'acting like a dick,' as he put it. Turns out he *was* high on Friday night, explaining how he had not been thinking straight when he came on to her. He even smoothed things over with Liam, reassuring him there would be no more Sleazy Chicken. It certainly made interactions more civil for them all when they helped Brendan move into his apartment on Sunday.

But life could never be truly normal for Alannah Winters: living the life of a pure blood mage had seen to that. And even though her mother had tried her darndest to protect Alannah from the magic world, to hide her from the most powerful woman in the world, there was no keeping Alannah from her calling. The magic in her blood would never allow her to continue her old mundane existence.

By all appearances, Alannah was enjoying a cup of the best coffee in Gaeilge Shores, sitting in her favourite seat by the window where she could watch the normal world go by. But in a world where magic was real, appearances were always deceptive. This was especially true on that fine spring day because no one else could see or hear the woman in a red dress sitting across from Alannah.

Her grandmother had called in the morning, instructing Alannah to meet her at the South Seas Café at one o'clock.

'Surely you have a less conspicuous location arranged for my training?' Alannah did not voice the question, she merely thought it.

'There have been some complications with the location I had procured. The local unseelie had promised a strongly glamoured warehouse down the road, but their magic was not strong enough to hide it from the Council. Warlocks ransacked the place on the weekend. I will need to set up new training grounds. I will choose a place further out of town this time.'

Alannah's eyes widened. *'The place in the old ruins was yours?'*

Tara—who had been going by the pseudonym of Scarlett—huffed out a laugh. 'I am guessing I have you to thank for the Council discovering the place? Figures. At least that restores my faith in unseelie magic.'

Alannah smiled, happy to resolve the mystery of the warehouse, at least for herself. '*So, what's the plan for today. I guess my training will have to wait.*'

Her grandmother sighed. 'You look like your mother when you smile.'

The comment wiped the smile right off her dial. '*The same mother who died at your hands.*'

'My son has clearly filled your mind with half-truths about our history.' Scarlett's eyes glistened with the faint threat of tears. 'I loved Aileen and I never wanted her to die. I did not even raise my own hand against her. The Council poisoned her against me and my sister. So, when she confronted us, she took us by surprise. Had she known the secret to killing a lich, she would have succeeded but she wasted her energies trying in vain.'

If Alannah's jaw could have dropped any further, it would have struck the table. She regained her composure, not wanting to arouse suspicion. '*Why would the Council send Mum against you?*'

'Aileen was their best hope of taking me down. My power threatens them—power I obtained by forbidden means according to their laws. They were not content to label me an outcast for my supposed sins. If you are to survive in their world, dear child, you will need to learn about the true nature of your precious Council. This is the premise of your first lesson, which starts right now. Theory should always come before practice, after all.'

Brigette approached the table. As she picked up Alannah's empty cup, she smiled sweetly. 'Is business slow this week?'

'Yeah, it is quiet, but I need the break.'

'I hear ya. Can I get you another coffee?

'Yes please.' Alannah retrieved the coin for her drink and dropped it in the girl's free hand.

'Thanks, hun. I'll bring it right over.'

She looked back at Scarlett. '*Go on*.'

'We are all taught there is only one way to find our attunements, but that is the Council's way of controlling us. By focusing on specific mana sources, we close ourselves off to the ultimate source.'

Alannah gasped and inclined her head to her phone to give the impression of reading something interesting. '*You're talking about the primordial?*'

'Yes, dear. That is exactly what I am referring to. It is the power of the universe. Not only does it open us to all mana sources, but it is also the key to instinctive spell casting.'

'Why would they not share the power with all registered mages? It would make our job of policing the magic world a lot easier.'

'I like the way you think, Alannah. Now you are beginning to see the tip of the corrupt iceberg we call the Mages Council. They argue such power should not be going around unchecked. But who is watching the watchers?'

Brigette returned with Alannah's cappuccino. 'Here you go, hun. Let me know if you would like anything else.'

'Thank you so much.' After taking a sip of the cocoa-coated foam, she cast her gaze back to Scarlett.

The woman shifted in her seat, crossing her left leg over her right. 'Have you ever heard of the Secret of the Beltane Blessing?'

She nodded. *'I've heard rumours of such, but I have no idea what it is about.'*

'What the big wigs of the Council do not want to tell the general population is blessed children, such as you and me, possess innate gifts.'

'Makes sense. It explains why I could perform magic before my initiation.'

'Here is the real kicker. The reason we have these natural abilities stems from our inherent attunement to the primordial. We just need to learn how to channel it effectively.'

Alannah was gobsmacked and utterly lost for words.

'If we are to continue training, you need to decide if this is something you want to learn.'

A golf-ball sized lump formed in her throat when she considered the consequences for dabbling with such magic. *'Will my use of the primordial be traceable, like the other major sources are?'*

'No, dear. The Council can only detect spell effects related to a specific source. If you cast an illusion spell while channelling the primordial, it will show up as use of senses mana. I will ask you again: do you want to channel the primordial?'

'Yes, I absolutely want to channel the ultimate source.'

Standing in a dark alleyway reeking of piss, Brendan's stomach felt like knotted Shibari ropes. It was a Monday night, so the west end of the city was dead, with only the occasional thumping bass of a car stereo or police siren to break the silence. He tried to shut off his emotions as he looked at Jacob. 'Remind me why I'm needed at this meeting. You were meant to handle all the business dealings.'

Jacob, clearly in his element, was the very image of composure. 'Apparently the new Underboss wants to meet the mastermind behind our operations. And when such a figure of authority requests a meeting, you don't decline.'

Brendan shook his head. 'Have you met this new Underboss?'

'Not yet. But Violet's reputation precedes her, so I feel like I already know her.'

He narrowed his eyes on Jacob. 'What sort of reputation?'

'Well… apparently she's sexy as fuck.'

'And?'

'And… uh… ruthless. Quite the femme fatale and all that.'

Brendan snorted. 'Great. I hope we can at least raise enough to cover our funeral expenses.'

Jacob waved his hand dismissively. 'Oh, ye of little faith.'

Movement at the northern end of the lane drew their attention to where three figures approached. Shadows masked their faces, but their body-shapes suggested a tall, curvaceous woman and two bulky men. Brendan gulped, wishing he had brought Nick and Ben as backup.

'Relax man,' Jacob hissed.

As soon as the party of three stepped beneath the soft, pink neon light of an adult emporium sign, Brendan sucked in a breath as recognition hit. 'You.'

The woman gave him a wicked grin. 'Oh, this is too good. I should have known those potions were the work of the infamous enchanter of Gaeilge Shores. I *have* experienced your work firsthand, after all.'

Jacob spun to face Brendan. 'Wait. You slept with her? Thornsy's gonna be pissed if he finds out.'

'Shut it, Associate. You will not speak until I address you directly,' Bridey snapped.

'Sorry, Madam.'

The endarkened woman returned her gaze to Brendan and licked her lips. 'Another member of the Winters clan turns dark. This will please the Boss.' She drew closer, bringing her hands up to Brendan's chest. 'Mm, your heart is beating fast for me again.' Bridey wore another purple corset emphasising the cleavage of her D cups.

Sweat poured from every follicle on Brendan's body despite the cool night air. 'What do you want, Br—'

'Uh, uh. When it comes to Syndicate business matters such as these, you will address me as Madam or Lady Violet.' Leaning in close to his ear, she whispered, 'But you can call me whatever you like in bed.'

Brendan felt his dick twitch. *Oh hell! Not again.* 'Sorry, *Madam*. Why is it you wanted to meet me tonight?'

She slid a finger along his cheek. 'You mean aside from putting this delectable face to the potion known as Rhapsody, a tincture so potent it took the magic underbelly by storm in one weekend?'

A sharp breath escaped through Brendan's teeth. He knew they had been successful in selling the first full batch of vials over the course of the previous weekend, but he had no idea how much popularity the magic drug had gained. Memories of all the wild sex he'd had during his own high brought a smile to his face.

'Quite the ego boost, isn't it Mr. Winters? But getting to the point, I have a proposition for you.'

'Go on.'

'The Boss wants to spread Rhapsody throughout the country. And I have an offer you can't refuse.' Leering at him, she winked. 'You do your bit with making that secret sauce and sell us the method for turning it into happy juice. When this stuff hits the streets, I promise your cut will make you a rich man.'

Brendan's lips curved into a slight grin. 'How much mother tincture will you need to start with, and when?'

'As much as you can manage. At least ten vials to start us off would be great.'

He was in the middle of setting up his new apartment, but ten lots of the stuff should still be achievable in a week. 'Okay, fine. I'll let Jacob haggle the price.'

Bridey grinned as she traced a fingernail along the throbbing artery in his neck. 'Terrific. It has been an *absolute pleasure* doing business with you, Mr. Winters.'

When Alannah walked out to the parking lot of the sailing club, Monique approached her. 'Alannah, you got a minute?'

'Sure. What's up?'

'Another great meeting tonight. I'm excited to get some more of the girls onto the Council. I was thinking about approaching some of the guys who might be willing to support our campaign. What do you reckon?'

'Did you have anyone in mind?'

'Well, I assume Liam's on board, right?'

Alannah grinned. 'Yeah, of course he is. He knows better than to oppose me on this stuff.'

'Right. We can use some other family and friends ties to garner support. Like getting Claudia to win Clayton over, and it wouldn't take much for Jessica to talk Lucas around. Could Liam talk Steve into voting our way?'

She gave it some thought. 'Possibly. Getting the majority vote in our own district won't be hard. Thing is, we need to get the other districts following suit if we are going to bring about constitutional change, which is why reaching out to women everywhere else in the state is an important first step. But I like your idea. When we do make contact, we can ask the other women to take a similar approach. Can you get into your dad's files to dig up some info on who's who in the other districts? This might allow us to go with a more targeted approach.'

Monique beamed. 'Totally on it. I'll email you the deets.'

'Thanks.'

'No probs. See ya round.'

'See ya.' Alannah waved as Monique got into her silver SUV, watching as the vehicle disappeared around the corner.

'I never thought I would see the day when you and Miss Lane got along well.' Scarlett's voice came from close behind her.

Alannah jumped. 'Gods, woman! You scared the hell out of me. Don't sneak up on me.' She paused to catch her breath before retorting in a bitter tone, 'You know, we have you to thank for our friendship. Nothing like bonding in a dungeon cell.'

Her grandmother smiled. 'Come, we must hurry if we are going to achieve anything.'

One eyeroll and a huff later, Alannah stepped into the back of the red Mercedes, alongside Scarlett. She glanced at the driver, doing a double take at the demon behind the wheel. But she remembered her grandmother no longer had power over the living cursed. 'You employ demons now?'

'Of course. They are useful and do not demand a salary.'

'But they are evil. Not to mention the risks of channelling nether.'

Scarlett laughed. 'You have much to learn, dear child.'

Alannah feared asking, so she continued the rest of the journey in silence. They reached their destination twenty minutes later, pulling up to an old wooden shack in the middle of dense scrubland. The hut resembled the sort campers used, but it had fallen into disrepair. KEEP OUT signs warned visitors of danger and as they walked past, and Alannah noticed half the roof was missing, breathing easier when she realised the dilapidated structure was not going to be her training room.

Rounding the corner, a large, galvanised steel shed came into view. It looked a lot like the warehouse she had shown Liam at the old ruins. The Federation green building sparkled and shone, at odds with the natural environment. When they stepped inside, Alannah welcomed the cool air. She had expected the metal to act as a heat trap, but there was a split system air conditioner moderating the temperature. Aside from modern office furniture, Scarlett had arranged the space much like the cellar at Cailleach Estate, complete with a large pentagram painted in the middle.

'This place is yours, Alannah. Your own personal training grounds. The property title and deeds are in those drawers, along with forged identification documents pertaining to your own pseudonym.' She pointed toward a large filing cabinet beside a bookshelf. 'And these are yours.'

Speechless, Alannah stared down at the set of keys in Scarlett's outstretched hand. It took her a whole minute to come to her senses and accept the offer. 'Uh, thanks.'

'From now on, when we communicate, you are Ebony, and you will address me as Lady Scarlett or Madam. Is that clear?'

Looking at Scarlett, she nodded.

'Now let us commence. I want to see you cast the ritual circle.'

Calling upon the guardians of the elements had become second nature to her over the years. As a matriarch in training, it was one of many duties expected of her. With the candles lit and the circle drawn, both women knelt on the floor.

Scarlett gave her a silver ring with a pearlescent blue stone. Upon closer inspection, the gem also had a black streaky pattern. 'This is labradorite, a volcanic rock as old as the world. I want you to meditate on this ring and open yourself to the mana surrounding us.'

Alannah placed the ring on her finger, closed her eyes and breathed deeply. *In, one-two-three, hold one-two-three, out one-two-three.*

Her grandmother's voice was soft and soothing as she continued her instructions: 'As you reach out to a mana source, do not try to focus on one. Free your mind of all limitations and seek out the underlying power in all things.'

The soft white glow of celestial clouds had been her usual visual since opening a permanent connection to the Celestial element. But she reached beyond and saw various molecular structures woven together, transferring from one state to another. She felt the power of matter drawing her in but resisted the pull and tried to find the link between it and Aether. But she could not see it. 'I can't.'

'Do not worry. It is rare for a mage to succeed on their first attempt,' Scarlett reassured her. 'Even when we are blessed.'

Feeling deflated, Alannah opened her eyes and looked at her grandmother. 'Did you?'

'No, I did not. But I know what might help. Sunstone crystals provide a stronger connection to the primordial. The one I used to use is in your uncle's cellar. If you bring it to our next session, along with some other quartz crystals, you might get some results sooner rather than later.'

Alannah sighed. 'I dunno.' She hated the idea of stealing from her uncle.

'It is not theft, dear. Remember, you are now the matriarch of the Winters family. Everything in that ritual room belongs to you.'

She eyed Scarlett, searching for signs of deceit in her features. After a moment, Alannah forced a smile. 'Okay. I'll get the crystals.'

The moment Brendan stepped into the family home; his father called him into the study.

'What's up, Dad?'

'Take a seat.' He pointed to one of the two leather armchairs situated in front of the fireplace. The old country house was often chilly at night, even on a warm spring day such as they had, so he welcomed the heat of the gas fire.

He slumped down into the seat. Dad only ever summoned him for private chats when there was bad news or to lecture him—neither had occurred since he left high school.

Ross sat down, placing one leg across the other knee. 'It's time you stopped messing around with all the riff-raff. You are twenty-one now and it is time to start thinking about the future, which means finding a suitable woman.'

Taken aback by his father's sudden interest in his life, Brendan's blood boiled. 'Are you for real?'

'I couldn't be more serious, which is why I took the liberty to invite someone to dinner.'

'What the actual fuck?'

'You would also do well to tone down your language and start acting like a gentleman. I honestly thought you'd grow out of your infantile behaviour by now. I was married and a proud father by your age.'

'Well times have changed, pops.'

'Not in our world, they haven't. As pure mages, we have obligations—you've always known that. Why is it a constant struggle with you? Your brother accepted his fate long ago.'

Brendan let out a derisive laugh. 'Your golden boy can do no wrong, but he's always had it easy.'

Dad scowled at him. 'Liam has worked extremely hard to get where he is. He also gave up on the love he once harboured for Cara because he knew it could never go anywhere.'

'Yeah, and now he has the only decent pure blood woman out there.'

'Is that what this is about? For everyone's sake, Son, you need to get over your pointless obsession with Alannah and move on. Starting right now. Get out there and be nice to our guest.'

He rose. 'Whatever.' Brendan made his way down the hall.

The smiling face of Jessica Ó Máille greeted him when he entered the living room. 'Hi Brendan.' The girl was pretty enough, with long, wavy, auburn hair and bright green eyes; but she was still a townie, one of Liam's crew, all of whom he had made a point of avoiding. Well, except for that one time with Monique.

'Uh, hi, Jessica.'

His mother entered, holding a couple of glasses and a bottle of chardonnay. 'Oh, hi sweetheart.' She smiled as she put the wine down, crossing the room to embrace him.

'Hi Mum.' Stepping back, he decided he needed something stronger to get through the evening. 'I'm gonna grab a drink. Be right back.'

When he returned with his whiskey on ice, he found Jessica laughing with his mum. 'Thanks for the wine, Mrs. Winters.'

'Oh sweetie, please call me Nora.'

Jessica beamed.

His mum signalled for Brendan to join them. 'Come and sit with us, Brendan.'

As he moved toward an armchair, Jessica giggled. 'I won't bite, Brendan. Please sit next to me.'

Hell! I should have grabbed the whole bottle. After hesitating a moment, he eased himself carefully onto the couch.

'How are you, Brendan? Gosh, how long has it been since I saw you last?'

'I've been fine. The last time would have been high school.'

'Wow. I guess so. Why don't I ever see you at the Spring Equinox?' She lowered her voice, attempting to sound seductive. 'Or at Beltane?'

'I prefer to celebrate with the wider magic community.'

'But…' she began, stopping herself and settling for a meek 'Oh.'

Distant voices sounded from the direction of the front door, followed by footsteps.

'Sounds like the rest of the family are here.' Mum smiled, standing to leave the room.

A hand clamped onto Brendan's thigh, and Jessica whispered in his ear, 'Tonight doesn't have to be awkward for us, Brendan. Let's enjoy each other's company. From what I hear, you're the fun-loving type.'

When he looked at her, he glimpsed a red flash of lust in her aura.

Movement in the doorway caught his attention. Alannah walked into the room, the neck of a beer bottle halfway down her throat. She gazed at the pair of them. 'Uh, hi Jessica. What are you doing here?'

Lowering the glass of wine she had been daintily sipping, Jessica smiled warmly. 'I'm Brendan's date this evening.'

Alannah's eyes bugged out as beer sprayed from her mouth. '*What the?* Can I have a word with you, Brendan?' She glanced at Jessica. 'Excuse us a moment.'

He sighed and rose from the couch.

After exiting through the back door and walking as far as the guesthouse, Alannah spun around to face him. 'Since when have you been dating her?'

Brendan could not read Alannah, yet her petulant tone aroused his suspicions. 'For the most awkwardly contrived half-hour of my life. Why? Are you jealous, Lana?'

Her face turned an intoxicating shade of pink.

Gods I love making her blush.

'What? No.'

Drawing closer, he let his breath tickle her neck. 'Prove it. Let me read your aura.'

She stepped back and narrowed her eyes. 'Brendan, please don't.'

'Don't what? See your true feelings for once? You call me your best friend, yet you constantly shut me out. Why is that Lana?'

'Please don't do this, Brendan.'

'I'm serious. I want to see those pretty emotions of yours. You do still have those, right? Or has your heart turned to stone?'

Alannah gaped, and her expression darkened like storm clouds. 'Why do you even care?'

Groaning, he threw his hands in the air. 'Oh, I dunno. How about the fact you're my cousin and used to be my best friend? We were close once, Lana. What happened? Is it because of Liam?'

She sighed. 'I guess so. You know how he can be. He gets paranoid about the nature of our relationship.'

'But he doesn't have anything to worry about, does he?' Then it dawned on him. Grabbing her shoulders, he reeled her in close enough to hear his hushed words. 'Or is that why you close yourself off from me, Lana? Do you worry I'll read feelings you shouldn't have?'

Pushing him back, she rolled her eyes. 'Get over yourself, Brendan. Not every woman in town is in love with you.'

She's deflecting. She is so *deflecting!* 'I don't give a damn about most women, but I do care how you feel.' He smirked. 'And if you don't start showing me your colours, I'm gonna assume you're in love with me.'

'Ugh, you're so full of it.'

The sound of snapping twigs ended their conversation. Looking up, Brendan saw Liam approaching with a glare. 'Dinner's ready.' He reached for Alannah's hand.

As the three of them walked together, Alannah jabbed Brendan in the arm. 'So, what are you going to do about *your date*?'

He shrugged. 'No point wasting an opportunity to get lucky.'

Liam growled in that alpha wolf way of his. 'You better not mess with Jessica if you know what's good for you. Her brother will kick your arse so hard you won't be sitting for days.'

Raising his hands in supplication, he grinned. 'Not my fault if she can't keep her hands off me.'

Richard smiled warmly as he stepped out of his rental car and cast his eyes upon the beaming face of his niece. He had not seen her for a few years and her elegance and maturity impressed him. With his line of work, he had never managed to settle down and have kids of his own, so Monique had always been a daughter to his heart.

She flew into his arms and squeezed him tight. 'Hey, Uncle Ricki.'

'Hey, Pumpkin. Have you missed me?'

'Damn straight, I've missed you. We all have.'

He laughed. 'Your dad stopped missing me when I became the better mage.'

'That's still debatable.' Kieran's voice drew Richard's attention to where the man stood on the porch with a rare glint of humour in his eyes. 'Hello, little brother.'

Richard released Monique and took a few long strides toward his brother. 'Hello, Kieran.' They exchanged a firm handshake. 'Good to see you again.' Aside from some minor sibling rivalry when it came to magic, the Lane brothers respected each other and got along well enough.

His sister-in-law drew him into her arms. 'Welcome home, Ricki.'

'Thank you, Janice.' They shared a polite, formal hug befitting the founding families.

Kieran followed him when Richard returned to the car to grab his luggage. 'Why didn't you magiport?'

After shutting the boot and locking the vehicle, he handed one suitcase to his brother. 'I like to fly under the radar when on official business. Channelling risks alerting the rest of the Council, and word travels fast around here. I can't afford to lose the element of surprise.'

'Hmm. Smart move. Come and get yourself settled, then I'll brief you on the issue.'

They always kept his old room for him and as such, the décor represented his minimalist taste. The only personal touches were the trophies and ribbons from his youth, when archery and guns had been his biggest passions. He might have joined the army if The Council of Mages allowed it, but they forbade pure mages from engaging in human warfare. So, he did the next best thing, and became a federal agent. The job was perfect for granting him access to high-level government intel and the networking opportunities were invaluable. But it was all a cover for his real role in the magic world. After tossing his jacket on a chair, he removed his tie, put his clothes away and made his way back downstairs.

Kieran was in his office. 'Please, come in and shut the door.'

Richard complied with the request, taking a seat across from his brother. 'So, why do you have need of the Inquisitor?'

'It has come to my attention we have a rogue mage problem I need you to investigate.'

Chapter Seven

The doorbell announced the first of Brendan's party guests. He fastened the last of his shirt buttons and gave himself a quick spritz of his favourite musky cologne before answering.

Alannah stood upon the threshold, beaming. 'Happy housewarming!' She leapt into his arms for a bear hug.

Liam—who stood back in awkward silence holding a potted plant—glanced at Brendan's hands on the small of her back, giving him the old stink eye.

Brendan averted his eyes to focus on Alannah. 'Thanks, gorgeous.'

Liam's predictable growl followed. The dickwad hated it when Brendan used that term of endearment for Alannah. To be fair, Brendan had been calling her gorgeous long before she started dating the tosser.

As Brendan ushered them into the hallway, Liam handed him the plant. 'This is for you.'

After glancing at the herb, he squinted at Liam.

'It's lemon balm,' Liam replied flatly.

'I know what it is. I did learn some things during our herbology lessons. I'm wondering why you are giving it to me.'

Liam shrugged. 'It was Lana's idea.'

The sound of a hairdryer starting up in the ensuite bathroom reminded Brendan of his other houseguest.

Alannah cast an inquisitive eye in the direction of the noise before returning her attention to him. 'Plants are a traditional housewarming gift. I figured you'd find this one useful.'

He studied her and smirked. 'I appreciate the gift, but you know I don't need to use herbal aphrodisiacs with my mad skills.'

A hint of pink flushed her delicate cheeks. 'I read this stuff is useful in several different enchanter's potions. I'm sure you'll find a use for it.'

Brendan led them down the hall and put the lemon balm by the large window filling his modern kitchen with lots of natural light.

A moment later, his latest hook-up appeared in the open plan living area. 'Oh, hi.' She smiled at Liam and Alannah, who sat on one of the couches before turning to Brendan. 'I didn't realise you had guests.'

'We are early for the party, but being family means we have certain privileges, right Brendan?' Alannah's teased. 'I hope we weren't interrupting anything.'

'Not at all, Madison was just leaving.'

The blonde ignored him, making her way further into the lounge area. 'Did you say party? What's the occasion?'

A wicked gleam shone in Alannah's eyes. 'Brendan's housewarming.'

She spun to face him. 'Oh wow, that essentially means you just moved into this place, right?'

'Right,' he replied with an exasperated breath.

'So, Madison, was it? I'm Alannah, Brendan's cousin.' She rose to shake the girl's hand. 'And this is my boyfriend, Liam.'

'Hi.' Liam remained seated and inclined his head in her direction.

Madison's eyes bounced back and forth from Alannah to Brendan. 'I can see the resemblance. You essentially look like twins, right?'

Alannah laughed as she dropped back to her seat. 'Ironic, when Liam and Brendan are the only siblings here.'

Brendan nodded. 'It's true. Liam's my older brother.'

Madison's brow furrowed as she processed the information in her tiny little brain. Several seconds later she gasped. 'Wait, that *essentially* means Alannah and Liam are related right?'

Crossing his arms, Brendan casually leaned against the breakfast bar. 'Yup.'

'That's *essentially* incest, right?'

Alannah squirmed as Liam stiffened. The magic community did not have a problem with their relationship because it was common for first cousins to marry for the sake of maintaining bloodlines. But the human world viewed these things differently, and they had copped a bit of flack for it over the years. 'No, Madison,' Alannah explained, 'the term incest only relates to closer relatives, like siblings or a parent and child. It is legal and safe for cousins to become intimately involved.'

'Oh, okay.' Madison accepted Alannah's explanation without question.

As the tense atmosphere dissipated, Alannah smiled. 'What are you up to tonight, Madison?'

The question made Brendan stand up straight. He glowered at Alannah as he projected his thoughts into her mind: *'Don't you dare!'*

She winked before turning back to Madison. 'Oh, not much. I'm essentially free.'

'Why don't you stay for the party? Madison's *essentially* welcome, *right*?' Alannah directed the last question at Brendan with a big grin.

Oh hell! 'Yeah, whatever.' Brendan shrugged with resignation. 'The more the merrier, *right*?' He glared at Alannah for a second. She knew who else was coming to his party. *'I will get you back for this, Lana.'*

Alannah snorted. 'Right.'

With the music cranked and the arrival of more friends, Brendan was able to avoid Madison's grating voice and unwind. He even snickered to himself when 'Mischief Maker' by All Systems Know played through his stereo.

Arms wrapped around Brendan's torso and a warm body moulded to his back when he retrieved a beer from the fridge. 'There you are. Happy housewarming, darling.'

He turned within Jessica's grip. 'Uh, hi.' Before he could do or say much more, she devoured him. Brendan took his fill of her, loving the pressure of her full lips and the way her tongue probed his mouth. 'Quite the greeting.'

'What can I say? I missed you last night.' She was glowing, thanks in part to the bright orange dress giving the sun a run for its money.

'We spent both Wednesday and Friday night together and you're still not sick of me huh?' He tried to keep his tone light-hearted even though he felt tense, silently cursing himself for taking things as far as he had. Not that he knew how clingy she would be when Dad set them up earlier in the week.

After trailing her tongue along the pulse point in his neck, she giggled. 'I'd never grow sick of you, Brendan. The things you can do to my body… let's just say I've never known such pleasure before.'

He should have put a stop to her antics then and there, but he was a sucker for flattery coming from a hottie like Jessica. That and the way she was touching him was… *Mm*. Turning on the bedroom eyes, he gazed at her. 'Well, you know what they say.'

'Maybe, but tell me, what do they say?'

'Enchanters do it better.'

She giggled. 'So true. Well, at least with you. You're the only enchanter I've been with.'

A flash of movement near the French doors caught Brendan's attention and spying Madison made his pulse erratic. He leaned in close to Jessica's ear. 'Hey, why don't we go have our own private party?'

More God damn giggling. 'I like your thinking, but I want to catch up with a few people first.'

Oh hell! Madison walked directly toward them. *Six steps… five steps…*

'How about a quickie first?' He pouted.

Four… three.

'I appreciate your enthusiasm, sweetheart, but I know you could never be quick.'

Two… one.

'Oh, hey Brendan. Your friends are essentially hilarious, right? Thanks for letting me stay.'

And boom!

Jessica glanced down her nose at the blonde. 'Who are you?'

'Hi, I'm Madison. And you?' She reached out her hand.

But Jessica ignored the invitation to be civil. 'I'm Jessica, Brendan's girlfriend.'

Madison paled. 'Oh.' She shot a dagger at Brendan. 'You told me you were single.'

Jessica spun to confront him. 'Wait, don't tell me you cheated on me with this slut?' Her hand thrust out toward Madison and waved furiously.

'*Excuse me, you bitch*! I am *not* a slut.' Madison moved up close to them and poked Brendan in the chest with her index finger. 'Don't call me again. I will not be a part of your cheating, not even for sex that awesome.' She stormed out in a huff.

'If I knew it'd be so easy to get rid of her, I'd…' *Slap!* Brendan's face stung from the impact of Jessica's hand.

'You bastard! How could you?'

His friends were gathering around to watch the drama unfold. Recovering his composure, Brendan grabbed Jessica's arm and pulled her down the hall and into the spare room. 'We've seen each other what, twice this week? Just 'cause we slept together both times; doesn't mean we are a couple. Did you ever hear me define our relationship as anything other than casual sex?'

Her lip trembled. 'But I thought…'

Clenching his fists, Brendan's tone turned bitter. 'Well you thought wrong. You know my reputation, so you have no excuse for misreading things.'

Jessica scowled. 'I'm telling your father and my brother about this.' She marched out of the room, out of his house, and with any luck, out of his life.

Alannah found Brendan hiding out in his room. 'Well, that was *essentially* an entertaining shitshow, *right?*'

Brendan sat up on his bed, cradling a glass of stiff amber liquid. He snorted. 'You love to watch the trouble my dick gets me in, don't you?' A lewd grin took over his face. 'Among other—'

She marched up to him and placed a silencing finger over his mouth. The contact sent tingles dancing across her skin, almost forgetting herself as she gazed upon his lips. Brendan's whole body stiffened at her touch and his eyes blazed. The air between them was more electric than a thunderstorm. Breathing in sharply, Alannah took a much-needed step back. 'So, uh, your dad's gonna shit bricks when he hears about Jessica.'

He laughed. 'Screw him. Besides, he'll just invite the daughter of another founding family to our next dinner.'

'You could at least try to be monogamous for a bit.'

'Nah. I'm good.'

Rolling her eyes, she sat beside him. 'Why do you live like this?'

'Just because my life isn't perfect like yours, doesn't mean I can't have my pleasures. It's not like I can love any of those women, so I may as well enjoy sowing my wild oats.'

'Why can't you love any of them? I've gotten to know most of those girls, and they aren't too bad.'

He polished off his drink, reclining against the headboard. 'I can't love anyone else because a girl took my heart years ago and never gave it back.'

This is news. 'Who?' she whispered.

'Na uh, I'm not going into it now.' He squeezed his eyes closed for a few long minutes.

Alannah felt a lump in her throat. *Is that why he didn't take a chance with me all those years ago? He still loved this other girl, whoever she was.* 'My life isn't perfect, you know.'

Brendan's eyes shot open and narrowed on her. 'Oh really? You've got your dream job, a seat on the Council, and the requited love of a suitable partner who will probably marry you one day and give you lots of pure mage babies to carry on your legacy. You've had it pretty easy compared to me, Lana. You haven't lived in your sibling's shadow, struggling to gain the approval of your father and the rest of the mage community. And… you won't be forced to marry someone you don't love.'

'It's not all rainbows and unicorns for me, Brendan. For one thing, my parents are dead; it's not like I've got any expectations to live up to. As for my seat on the Council, it's a constant struggle for me to get anywhere because I'm a woman. Then there's this whole business of trying to find out who my bio dad is. You don't even know the extent of my predicament.' She felt a single tear slide down her cheek.

'Oh, Lana. I'm sorry. I didn't mean to upset you. Come 'ere.' He reached out and drew her into his arms. 'You know I'm here for you, always. Talk to me. Tell me what's going on with your father.'

Alannah clung to his familiar warmth. 'I still don't know anything. Scarlett struck a deal with me, and it could be months, or even years before I can uphold my end of the bargain.'

Brendan's body tensed, but he kept her tucked against his chest. His heart beat rapidly. 'What sort of deal?'

'She wants to train me to channel my next two attunements.'

'So, Scarlett's a mage?'

She braced herself for the lie she needed to tell. 'Of sorts.'

He shifted their position so he could peer into her eyes. 'Hold up. What do you mean "of sorts?" She's not a dark mage, is she?'

Biting her lip, she hoped averting her eyes would deflect from the truth.

'Ah hell, Lana! What have you gotten yourself into?'

'It's not as bad as it sounds. I'm not doing anything wrong.'

He shook his head. 'You mean other than consorting with an outlaw?'

Alannah cringed. 'It's not like I'm helping her with anything illegal.'

Brendan pulled her back against his chest and stroked her back. 'I get that, gorgeous, but do you realise you're risking your seat on the Council by working with her?'

'I know. That's why she set up a secret training site and forged a fake ID for me.' She scoffed. 'I even have a codename. She calls me Ebony now. Apparently, people in her organisation have some sort of colour themed name.'

She heard Brendan's breath hitch.

'What?'

'This woman sounds dangerous, Lana. I'm worried about you.'

'I know she's dangerous, Brendan. I'm not naïve, nor defenceless. I can handle her. I'm just not sure if I've got what it takes to achieve what she's trying to teach me.'

He tugged on her chin, forcing eye contact. 'Hey, you're Alannah Fucking Winters. If there's anything I've learnt about you in the last five years, it's you are a kickass mage. I know you'll get those attunements in no time.'

Alannah felt herself getting pulled into his enchanting green eyes. Brendan's hand remained on her chin, and the awareness of their skin contact sent a surge of desire down to her core. Drawing her bottom lip between her teeth, Alannah's eyes fell to his mouth for a split second. When she released her lip, she looked up again to see Brendan's attention focussed on her mouth. His thumb glided along her bottom lip. 'Brendan?' she whispered.

'Hmm?' He continued to stare at her mouth.

Her heart skipped a beat. She would have given anything to know what he was thinking. *Does he want to kiss me? Please, Gods, let the answer be yes.* Some of the walls she had carefully constructed around her heart over the last few years began to crumble away. 'I told you, no more games.' She spoke in a hushed, but firm tone.

His eyes flicked up to hers, but his hand remained on her chin. 'I'm not playing any games, Lana.'

In an instant the rest of her walls crashed down as their eyes locked together. Brendan smirked and Alannah knew she was in trouble.

A loud knock at the door broke whatever was going on between them. Brendan released his hold of her as Liam entered. 'Ah, there you are.' He cast them a sidelong glance when he observed Alannah's proximity to Brendan. 'What's going on?'

Alannah jolted upright, spurting her explanation in rapid fire, 'We were just discussing Brendan's Jessica predicament.'

Liam sniggered. 'You are boned. She already posted the news online. You might want to see the comment from Lucas. I feel pretty justified with an *I told you so*.'

'Meh. I'm not scared of that clairvoyant pussy. What's he gonna do? Hit me with predictions of my future?'

'How about his raw strength?'

Brendan cocked a brow. 'Have you seen me fight recently?'

Liam grinned. 'Actually, no. We haven't had a decent sparring session in months. Perhaps we should remedy that.'

'You're on, bro. But not tonight. I'm too plastered already.'

Alannah's thighs quivered at the thought of Liam and Brendan brawling, both shirtless of course.

Brendan leered at her as his voice entered her mind. *'Looking forward to the show, are you gorgeous?'*

Yep, so much trouble.

Thanks to Liam having the public holiday off, the rest of Alannah's October long weekend passed with plenty of reasons to stay away from Brendan. After their *moment* at his housewarming party, she did not trust herself alone with him. But avoidance would be more difficult with school holidays spelling the start of Brendan's leave. When he rang Tuesday morning to ask if they could meet, she told him she had an urgent order for a set of ritual robes. It was not a complete lie: she only fibbed about the urgency.

As she embroidered the last of the details, she put the velvet garment aside and checked the time. Six o'clock. *Phew, one day filled*. Liam was working late, as he did most Tuesdays, so she fixed herself a quick dinner with some left-over pasta.

The doorbell broke the trance she had entered when her she finished her meal. Clearing her mind of all thoughts pertaining to Brendan, she snatched the bag she had filled with various crystals and made her way to the door.

Scarlett greeted her with a passive expression. 'Are you ready?'

'Yes, Madam.' Alannah locked up and followed her. It was a different car this time. When they reached the black Tesla, Alannah drooled over her dream car: sexy and ecofriendly.

'I want you to drive us there this time. It will help you remember the way.'

Alannah gazed upon her grandmother with the grateful eyes of a child who had received her most desired Christmas present until reality sank in. 'How am I going to explain this to Liam and my friends?'

'I am sure you will think of something.'

Sighing, she let the gears spin wildly in her mind as she tried to come up with a valid lie. 'I'll need the keys.'

'You already have them on the keyring I gave you. This car is yours too and the registration papers are in the glovebox.'

She was gobsmacked. 'Um, thanks.' Alannah noticed the custom numberplate: EBONY02. 'Why the two on the end? Am I the second Ebony?'

'No. It relates to your birth year.'

Once they were in the vehicle, Scarlett gave directions. The Tesla was a smooth ride and Alannah was in love with it by the time they arrived at the hidden training sanctuary.

'Now, set up the crystals on the altar, and cast the circle.'

Alannah placed the sunstone front and centre, surrounding it with a variety of quartz crystals—amethyst, rose, smoky, citrine, and clear—along with one she could not identify, resembling a clear quartz with a strange red glow.

Scarlett stepped forward and showed her how to construct a crystal grid using a mandala template on parchment paper. With the geometric pattern complete and the circle cast, Alannah began meditating. But as much as she tried to focus, her mind kept returning to her moment with Brendan. *Crap!* She felt defective. She had never had trouble concentrating on magic because of guys before, not even when she was a teenager. Denying that Brendan was getting under her skin was getting harder. He was seeping into the empty cracks in her heart and soul.

She could almost feel Brendan's thumb on her lip as well as the heat of his gaze. The memory sent scorching waves coursing through her blood. *Oh Gods! Such intense arousal!* The feeling became amplified, and she almost climaxed right there on the floor with Scarlett in the room. 'What the hell?' she muttered.

'You are channelling emotions.' Scarlett's voice sounded distant. 'Or rather, you are channelling one specific emotion. A rare gift. Most mages attuned to emotions are unable to filter out all the different emotions surrounding them when channelling. I want you to create your visualisation for this mana source. Make it your new attunement.'

An easy request. Alannah already possessed the perfect inspiration for her visualisation. She pictured Brendan again, but this time he was naked, and she could see his warm yellow aura surrounded by shades of bright pink and red. The intensity of the emotional power source flowed through her.

'Now I want you to find the underlying cause of this feeling. Use a visual focus if you have to.'

Isn't Brendan the underlying cause?

'No, he is the inspiration.'

Oops of course Scarlett is reading everything going on in my filthy mind.

'The cause is fundamental to all life.'

Focussing on the mana doing all sorts of naughty things to her body, she realised it would be an effective form of masturbation. *Did Brendan jerk off when channelling like this? Gods! Did I just think that? Focus, woman!* After a few deep breaths, she pictured people having sex around the Beltane fertility fires. It hit her: babies are born from these feelings—we have these feelings because we are born—the cycle of life is tied to our emotions.

'Now dig deeper and think back to a time before people; before animals.'

Tracing the origin of species backwards in time, she could see each precursor in the human evolutionary line. She pictured the formation of the Earth at the hands of the creator Gods. *Were the Gods the cause?*

'No. The primordial came before the Gods.'

Of course! The Earth was relatively young compared to the age of the Universe. Supposedly, it all started with the big bang. She visualised the creation of the Universe and the formation of stars which produce hydrogen. *Matter and energy.* But before they even existed, there was something: *Primordial power.* She could see a red-hot glow from which everything originated. She felt it! *Holy hell!* The surge of power was unreal. It felt like she caught fire. Her body pulsed between euphoria and agony; unlike anything she had ever experienced.

'Excellent. Now solidify your visualisation. Become attuned to the almighty power source.'

Imagining what the birth of the Universe was like became her visual focus. When she opened her eyes, she grinned, feeling high from the power flowing through her.

'You have done well. Next week I will show you how to use the primordial to tap into other mana.'

Chapter Eight

Alannah sat alone at the boardroom table of the Council chambers when she really wanted to just curl up in Liam's arms and sleep. Thoughts of Brendan kept haunting her, distracting, exhausting, and plaguing her with guilt. Every time she woke from one of those wet dreams, she glanced at the man sleeping beside her—the man who loved her—and dread settled into the pit of her stomach. It became impossible to get back to sleep.

So, as she waited for the rest of the Council to arrive, she rested her head on her arms and tried to get some shut eye.

'Oh look, Alannah's already nodding off and Kieran's droning hasn't even commenced.' The voice of Liam's cousin, Steve, cut through her slumber.

A warm hand rested on her shoulder blades. 'Are you okay, Lana?'

She gazed into Liam's bright, cobalt eyes. 'Yeah, I just haven't been sleeping well.'

His brows furrowed as he sat down beside her. 'That's normally my problem, not yours. Has something been bothering you?'

'Yeah, but I don't want to talk about it here.' *Or at all with you.*

'Okay. Maybe you should ask to present your report first so you can take your leave and get some rest.' Liam's caring warmth made her smile.

'Not a bad idea. You won't mind?'

'Of course not, gorgeous. Your wellbeing will always come first.'

She kissed his lips chastely. 'I love you so much.'

'I love you too, babe.'

'Naw, you guys are adorable.' The booming voice of Lucas announced his arrival. The man's larger-than-life presence and muscular bulk even made the likes of Nick and his Orc clan appear scrawny. What Lucas lacked in magical power, he made up for in physical strength *and* intellect. 'Yo Liam, just a heads up—I plan to pummel your brother into the dirt.'

Liam laughed. 'I did warn him.'

'Maybe someone should cut his dick off,' Steve suggested.

Oh Gods, what a horrifying thought. Alannah's stomach turn. Brendan might be a cad, but that dick of his had been a source of immense pleasure for a lot of women. Along with those hands, and those lips…

'Whose dick are we cutting off?' Clayton asked as he entered the room.

Lucas glared at him with his fists clenched. 'Whose do you reckon?'

Clayton laughed. 'Oh right. I'm guessing you mean our resident enchanter. I say power to him. If I had half his magical talents, I know I'd be wanting to share them with the lady folk.'

Alannah snorted. She had always liked Clayton. He was less uptight than most pure-bloods and she would never forget the first time she saw him and his twin sister, Claudia: their fire dancing at the Spring Equinox gala had been spectacular.

Lucas' left eye twitched. 'I doubt you would feel that way if he'd done the dirty on *your* sister.'

Clayton shrugged. 'Wouldn't bother me. Claudia's a big girl—she can take care of herself.'

'Evening all.' Ross walked in, putting an end to all talk of Brendan.

'Hello boys and Alannah.' When Nora saw Alannah's eyes, her smile disappeared. 'Oh sweetheart, are you okay? You look terrible.'

She forced her lips to curve into a smile as Nora sat next to her. 'Just sleep-deprived.'

'So, I gotta know,' interrupted Clayton. 'Who owns that shiny black Tesla in the carpark? That thing's a real beauty.'

Alannah beamed. 'That'd be mine.'

Liam whipped his head around to gape at her, while the other guys stared. 'Since when?'

'Since I bought it today,' she lied. She had hidden the car at her hideout for as long as it took to sell her old rust bucket.

'Why didn't you consult me first? Are you sure we can afford the finance?'

'I bought it outright, with my own money, so I don't see why I needed your permission first.' She spoke with more defensive bitterness in her tone than intended and hoped it did not give away her secret.

Liam narrowed his eyes. 'How the hell did you afford it? Those things cost a fortune.'

'I've been saving.' It was an absolute crock of shit and Liam probably figured as much, but they had kept their finances separate so he had no idea what her bank account looked like.

He shook his head as a couple of the older Council members took their seats quietly and turned to his mates to talk about surfing.

Nora continued to study Alannah. 'You're not hiding your aura anymore.' She spoke in a whisper: 'I can see something's eating at your conscience. If you need to talk about it, you can always come to me. You know that, right?'

This time, Alannah's smile was genuine. 'Thanks, Nora.'

Monique rushed in and stood behind her chair. 'All rise for the Honourable Richard Lane and High Magus Kieran Lane.'

What is the Inquisitor doing here? Alannah stood with the rest of the Council as the two powerful men strode into the room with smug confidence. They both wore charcoal business suits, pressed to perfection. The only difference in their attire was their choice of tie: Kieran's was blue and gold, while Richard's was black.

'Thank you, Lady Monique.' Richard scanned the mages assembled around the table. 'Please be seated.' When everyone settled, Richard prompted Kieran to speak.

'I am opening the meeting at four minutes past seven. We have an important matter taking precedence over all other Council business this evening. I know many of you are wondering why the Inquisitor is with us tonight.'

Alannah nodded along with several other members at the table.

'I have evidence to suggest we have a rogue mage in our midst, so I have called upon the services of the Honourable Richard Lane to help flush them out.'

Oh crap! Does he mean…

The piercing stare of Richard's frosty, dark eyes of steel cut Alannah's thought short. He cocked his head as his brows arched.

Not good!

Kieran continued speaking. 'After Lady Nora's last report on the spike in emotional mana channelling, I did some digging of my own and came across this.' He placed a potion vial on the table.

Breath returned to Alannah's lungs. Richard was not here for her.

'This is an unsanctioned potion that found its way onto the Unseelie Market and into the hands of magical people who frequent urban clubs.'

Alannah inspected the potion. It was almost clear, with a milky white tint. It was a tincture of some kind.

'According to my sources, it goes by the street name Rhapsody, and it elicits a high much like the human drug ecstasy. However, the side effects are quite different. Being mystical in nature, this potion does not harm the physical body of a magic person. This stuff is dangerous because it opens a user to emotional mana, causing them to passively channel the power source and giving them access to magic abilities beyond the understanding of those untrained in the area.'

Oh wow, that's some potent magic.

'It is also highly addictive. The demand has been high enough to prompt mass production around the country.'

Ross raised his hand.

'Yes Councillor?'

'If this potion is all over the country, why is the Inquisitor *here*?'

'An excellent question, Lord Ross,' Richard replied. 'I have been in contact with all of the districts in this state as well as across the Nation. The spikes in emotion channelling reported elsewhere have only recently begun. They originated from the Adelaide area prior to the spread.'

Ross nodded. 'Thank you, Your Honour.'

Richard continued to address the room. 'My investigation will begin with the routine questioning of all Council members, followed by the registered mage community. This is standard protocol and nothing for upstanding citizens to fear.' His attention focussed on Alannah, sending a chill down her spine. 'Please make yourselves available upon my request.'

'It's a good thing I love you so damn much, Lana. Seeing your smile makes sacrifices like this worthwhile.' Liam gave Alannah an impish grin as he linked his arm with hers and escorted her into Doyle Dougherty's. The bar was nothing special: a typical country pub with nondescript wooden furniture and a floor covered in beer-stained carpet that might have been red once. But this place was always buzzing on a Friday night.

'Oh come on! My friends aren't *that* bad.'

'I guess most of them are okay. But I still don't like seeing you hang out with unseelies.'

Alannah shook her head. 'Jacob and Caleb are harmless. You should know. In all your time as a cop, have you ever had cause to arrest them?'

He sighed, conceding she had a point. 'No. But I still don't trust them.'

An arm fell across his shoulder, and a second later Brendan's head poked in between Liam and Alannah. 'Hey there fam. Who don't you trust, bro?'

'You and your sleazy arse for one,' he retorted, tensing at the sight of Brendan's other hand on Alannah's shoulder.

Brendan recoiled and clutched his heart in an exaggerated manner. 'I feel so wounded, Brother. My arse is the least sleazy part of my body.' The twerp winked at Alannah, grabbing her hand and pulling her over to their booth.

Liam watched Alannah greet the rest of her friends with hugs as he ambled his way over. By the time he got there, she was deep in conversation with Cara, so he slipped into the seat next to her. Her hand naturally gravitated toward his thigh, where he clasped it in his own. He smiled, thinking he would never grow tired of the small gestures of love in their relationship.

After a few minutes, Alannah straightened and smacked the table to get everyone's attention. 'So, did you guys hear the Inquisitor is in town?'

Cara waved a hand dismissively. 'Bah. He's probably visiting his family.'

It was no secret the Inquisitor was High Magus Kieran Lane's brother.

Liam shook his head. 'This time he's on official business. We arrested a couple of unseelie folk for dealing unsanctioned potions in the city last weekend, so Richard's here to shut down the whole operation.' He directed an accusing eye at Jacob. 'You wouldn't happen to know anything about this drug ring?'

Alannah punched his bicep in the adorable way that hurt her fist more than his arm. 'Liam! Don't be rude to my friends.' She shot Jacob a smile. 'I'm sorry.'

Jacob shrugged. 'It's okay. And to answer Liam's question: no, I don't know a damn thing. My ties to the family business are "tenuous" at best.' He even used air quotes.

'Any idea where these potions might be coming from?' Brendan directed his question at Liam.

'If I were to guess, I'd say a dark mage is the source. Most unseelie fae aren't known for their potion making skills and we don't have many endarkened in this district. Richard explained he is going to systematically question every registered mage in town to rule us all out before he moves on to flushing out any outlaws living in our midst.'

A snicker came from across the table and all eyes landed on Caleb.

Liam glared at him. 'What's amusing, freak?'

Caleb scowled. 'You guys have no idea what you're in for. I've seen that man at work and it ain't pretty. His methods are barbaric. Think full-fledged effin witch-hunt. Your so-called pure blood won't help any of you because he don't discriminate. Every little secret you mages are keepin' will be brought to light and if you try to keep him out of your heads, he'll torture you until you let him in.'

Connor, Bailey, and Brendan all stared at him with wide eyes. When Liam glanced at Alannah, he saw the same expression on her face, so he squeezed her hand. 'It's okay, babe. We don't have anything to hide. We'll be fine.' When her eyes connected with his, she bit her bottom lip, sending a heavy lump down his throat and into the pit of his stomach. *What is she hiding?*

Brendan could hardly breathe. Having the Inquisitor in town would have been bad enough but knowing the most powerful Council member in Australia was investigating his racket sent him into palpitations. He exchanged a look with Jacob and spoke to him telepathically. *'We need to shut down our operations. I can't have Richard Lane finding all the gear in my shed.'*

Without reacting, Jacob mentally replied, *'Keep your calm, bro. Acting this suspicious will give the game away.'*

'How can you expect me to be calm? You heard what Caleb said.'

'If you pull out of this deal, Violet will skin you alive. We'll move the lab and I'll get you a mind shield so Richard can't read your thoughts.'

Brendan drained the last of his beer, already feeling the need for something stronger. *'Thanks for the reassurance, I feel so much better knowing I have to worry about that psycho bitch as well as the sociopathic Inquisitor. Oh and—'* A glance at Alannah broke his concentration.

She was in a silent stare-down with Liam, her eyes wide while Liam's gaze narrowed upon her.

'You're not hiding anything, are you Lana?' he queried.

Oh hell! Brendan remembered what she told him about Scarlett.

She hesitated. 'No.' Her eyes shifted to Brendan, pleading with him.

Liam glanced at each of them and paled.

Brendan maintained a neutral expression.

'Is this why you haven't been sleeping, Lana?' Liam sneered. 'Have you been sneaking off to meet Brendan in the middle of the night?'

'What? No!'

'Or is it when I'm at work?'

'There's nothing going on between Brendan and me.' She kept eye contact with Liam.

'Then what's going on? I know something is bothering you and it's been keeping you awake at night.'

Deciding it was time to step in and help, Brendan spoke into both their minds. *'Lana has been receiving magic training from someone of dubious repute. She's concerned the Inquisitor will find out.'*

'Dubious how?' Liam's eyes narrowed on Brendan.

'Unregistered, but not dark. Right, Lana?'

'Right.'

'Damnit! Do you realise the trouble this could bring down on us?' Liam snapped.

'I know. I'm sorry.' Alannah was on the verge of tears. 'I'll fix it, I promise.'

Brendan looked at Jacob. *'Can you get us some* selective *mind shields?'*

He gave a single nod. *'Given enough time and money, I'm sure I could.'*

'Brilliant. Get one for Lana too.'

'Okay, but who's paying?'

He could see Liam and Alannah were still arguing. *'I'll front the bill for all of them. And make sure they are quality.'*

When Liam rose and stormed off in a huff, Brendan moved around to take the vacated seat. 'Don't worry, Lana. I've got a plan to help protect you from the Inquisitor.'

She smiled at him. 'Thank you. And thanks for defusing the situation with Liam.'

'No probs.' Brendan knew he had Alannah trapped in the booth, with Cara and Jacob flanking her. Grinning, he grasped the golden opportunity. 'Now, Lana, how about telling me why you've been avoiding me all week. Does it have anything to do with those sleeping difficulties Liam mentioned?'

Her face lit up like a brothel light. 'No, of course not.'

'You're a terrible liar, Lana. Something you will have to work on.'

She frowned. 'Why do you assume I'm lying?'

'For one thing, you avoid eye contact. Also, the pitch of your voice rises.' He lowered his voice and gave her a suggestive grin. 'Why don't you come back to my place tonight and I'll give you a lesson in effective bluffing?'

'That's unwise. Liam's already in a pissy mood. I should get home and sort things out with him.'

'You know as well as I do Liam will need a few hours to calm down before he sees reason. Stop making excuses, Lana. What's the real reason you don't want to spend time alone with me?'

Creasing her forehead, she stared at him. 'You seem to know, so why don't you tell me?'

He arched a brow. 'Are you giving me permission to read you?'

'You may as well. I'm sure you've caught enough glimpses lately anyway.'

She had let her guard down again last weekend, allowing Brendan to see the extent of her arousal. He leaned in to whisper in her ear: 'I think you're afraid of your feelings for me, Lana. Some inappropriate feelings, given your situation. Am I right?'

Alannah bit her lip. 'I'm in love with Liam and I'm not going to cheat on him.'

Bloody Liam! What did she see in the asshat? Brendan leaned back and crossed his arms. 'You needn't worry though. It's not like I'd try anything.'

She clenched her eyes.

Dagnammit! Lana must have mistaken my meaning.

But before he could explain, Jacob tugged on his sleeve. 'Hey bro, we gotta clear outta here *now.*'

'*What*?' he clipped, annoyed by the interruption.

'Richard's here. We should go lay low for now.'

Brendan glimpsed the entrance and observed both Richard and Kieran making their way to the bar. *Oh hell! What were they doing here?* That sort usually went to the sailing club to socialise.

As if sensing their apprehension, Bailey piped up. 'I'll show you out through the staff exit.'

He grabbed Alannah's arm as he rose. 'Come on, you better get out of here too.'

She nodded and followed them.

Once outside, Brendan turned to Alannah, but before he could say anything, she magiported away. 'Gods damnit woman!'

Alannah lay in bed hours after Liam got up for work on Saturday morning, curled in a ball and staring blankly at the closed window. She knew pining over Brendan's constant rejection was illogical. *It's not like I can act on my feelings anyway.* Her love for Liam was real and requited, affirming her determination to remain faithful. But she could not help indulging in a pity party, especially since Liam was still in a foul mood when he left.

The first two times the doorbell rang, she ignored it. But the sound of someone bashing at her door roused her. Throwing on a plush dressing gown and matching pink slippers, she shuffled down the hall. Glancing through the peephole, she froze.

'Open up, Councillor Winters. I know you are home,' the Inquisitor's deep voice demanded.

She took a deep breath and opened the door. 'Sorry, Your Honour. I was still in bed.'

Richard took in her dishevelled state and simpered. 'Rough night?'

'Something like that. What can I do for you?'

'I have a few routine questions to ask you. May I come in?'

'Certainly.' She opened the security screen and stepped aside. They moved into the front sitting room. 'Please give me a minute to get dressed.'

'Of course.'

She returned to her room to change, before shooting Brendan a text: **Inquisitor at my house now! What was that plan of yours?**

His reply came promptly: **Damn! ... I was going to get you a selective mind shield ... Try to focus on anything other than Scarlett ... Even if you have to imagine me naked :P**

Alannah rolled her eyes as she deleted their message history. She took another deep breath and walked back to the front room. 'Sorry for the wait, Your Honour. Can I get you a drink?'

He gave her a warm smile. 'Just a glass of water, thank you.'

She got them both a glass and brought a jug of chilled water out from the fridge. Having poured their drinks, she sat on the edge of her seat. 'What would you like to know?'

'To start with, can you please tell me your full name and date of birth?' He withdrew a notepad and pen.

'Alannah Kayleigh Winters, born thirty first of July, two-thousand and two.'

After jotting something down, he regarded her a moment.

Is this a scare tactic? Alannah tried to redirect her surface thoughts. Images of Brendan's naked body were the first things to enter her mind. *Damn him!*

Richard sipped from his glass and smiled. 'Tell me what you know about the potion called Rhapsody.'

'I only know what you and High Magus Kieran told us at the Council meeting.'

'And when was the first time you learnt of this potion?'

'At said Council meeting.'

Richard dabbed his pen against the notepad as he studied her. 'Have you heard of the Dark Syndicate, Lady Alannah?'

'No, Your Honour.'

He stopped tapping his pen and crossed his legs. 'What about the Unseelie Market?'

'I have heard of it. Its existence is common knowledge to the Mages Council.'

'Of course it is. Do you know anyone within the Unseelie Market?'

'Not directly, no.'

Richard leaned forward in his seat. 'Please explain your use of the word *directly*.'

'I have a couple of unseelie friends. While they are not part of any criminal organisations, I assume they have relatives who are. But I don't know their families, nor have I heard of anything to support my assumptions.'

'Indeed. Who are these unseelie friends?'

'Jacob Bennett and Caleb Hawthorn. I went to school with them, Your Honour.'

'You have some interesting friends, Councillor. Most mages of your status would not associate with the magic underclass.'

What an insufferable snob! 'I was friends with them before I knew what they were, or what I was for that matter.'

The hint of a frown touched his features before his poker face returned. 'What do you mean, before you knew what you were?'

'My parents raised me ignorant of my heritage to protect me from my grandmother. I did not know anything about the magic world until I returned to Gaeilge Shores at the age of sixteen. Even then, it was some time before my cousins told me anything.'

'Ah yes. The infamous Tara Winters. She tried to curse you, did she not?'

'Yes, Your Honour.'

'Strange how she disappeared after you killed her. Do you know what happened to her body?'

Her thoughts wandered to the memory of Brendan's thumb on her lip and the desire to kiss him. 'Uh, sorry Your Honour… what was your question?'

Richard smirked. 'Something is distracting you, Lady Alannah. I wonder, how would Lord Liam react if he knew of the feelings you're harbouring for his brother?'

Alannah gasped and her chest constricted.

'Don't worry, I won't tell him.' He winked at her. 'That concludes my questioning for now. Thank you for your time.' He rose from the chair.

'No worries.' After standing, Alannah walked him to the door.

Stepping outside, he turned to her. 'Oh, did you know Tara's sister, Dana, now sits on the Cursed Throne?'

What? This is news! 'No, Your Honour, I had no idea.'

'It is a little-known fact. Have a great day, Councillor.' He turned and left.

Chapter Nine

Pacing the living area, Brendan mulled over Alannah's message about her visitor. 'Dagnammit!' When she did not reply to his last text after a few minutes, he scrolled through his contacts. Finding Jacob, he hit the call button.

'Hey bro, what's up?'

'I need those mind shields *now*!'

'Gods, Brendo! I told you these things take time.'

'We don't have time. The Inquisitor is at Alannah's house right now.'

Silence.

'Jacob? You still there?'

'Yeah, I'm here. I thought we agreed not to tell her about the potion making.'

'I haven't told her jack. This isn't about that. But she has her own secrets and I promised to protect her from the Inquisitor.'

Jacob's exhaled breath almost deafened Brendan. 'Heck, bro. You had me pissing myself for a minute there. I'll see what I can do. But if the Inquisitor is there now, it might be too late for her.'

Brendan slumped into an armchair and tossed his head back against the backrest. 'Just see what you can do, okay?' He hung up, sending Alannah another message: **Call me when Richard leaves. Better yet, get your sexy arse over here.**

As soon as he sent the message, his doorbell chimed. 'Thank the Gods!' He ran to the door and flung it open, expecting to see Alannah; but she was not the Winters woman standing on his doorstep. His already pale complexion must have turned as white as the ghost before him.

'Hello Brendan, dear. Miss me?' Tara Winters was there in the flesh, wearing a red dress and appearing different to the last time he saw her corpse lying cold on the ground.

'Not on your life, or unlife. How are you here, and what do you want?'

'You have lots of questions, I am sure, but time is of the essence. I want to help you and Alannah with your Inquisitor predicament.'

'How do you know about that?'

'Did I not say we do not have time for all of your questions? Word on the Syndicate grapevine is you need these.' She held up three silver amulets, each engraved with the shield Celtic knot.

'You're in the Dark Syndicate?'

'Oh, sweetheart, I *am* the Dark Syndicate. Now, are you going to take these or what?' She thrust her hand toward the security door.

'How much do I owe you?'

'Nothing.'

He eyed her askance. 'What's the catch?'

'No catch. I am protecting my investments. I am glad you found my book useful, by the way.'

'That came from you?'

Tara smiled. 'Oh yes. Alannah cannot be the only one with a Winters family heirloom, after all.' She swung the amulets like pendulums. 'Take them or leave them. I will not stand here all day.'

'Okay, fine.' He opened the screen door and snatched them from her bony fingers. 'Now get the hell out of my face.'

'As you wish. Oh, and send my regards to Alannah.' She turned and strode toward a red Mercedes.

Brendan watched Tara leave. When she climbed into the car parked in his driveway, he glanced at the number plate. As SCARLETT64 took off down the street, he collapsed to his knees and screamed, '*Fuuuuck!*'

Well, that could have gone much worse, Alannah thought as she watched Richard leave. After having her morning coffee, she returned to her room to collect her phone and noticed the text from Brendan. Smiling at his reference to her arse, she grabbed her purse and keys and made her way outside. Feeling the need for fresh air, Alannah travelled the short distance to Brendan's house on foot.

When Brendan opened his door, he yanked her inside and threw his arms around her. 'Thank the Gods you're okay.'

Alannah clung to him as if he were a life raft on a stormy sea. In some ways, his hugs had always comforted her regardless of whatever was going on between them. He was still her best friend. 'Brendan—'

'Shoosh. Let me hold you.'

She had no idea how long they remained locked in each other's arms, but it was easily the longest embrace of her life; yet when he pulled back from her, it was too soon.

'Come on.' He led her down the hall. 'Jacob will arrive in a minute, then we need to talk.'

'Maybe we should talk before he gets here.'

There was an expressionless mask on his face as he shook his head.

'I need to tell you about my chat with Richard.'

'Wait for Jacob.'

'But Brendan—'

'No, Lana. Things are more complicated than you realise.'

She wanted to protest more, but the doorbell cut her off, so she made herself comfortable in an armchair.

Jacob entered the room a moment later. 'Oh, hey Alannah.' He shot Brendan a look. 'What's she doing here? I thought we—'

'Sit down,' Brendan snapped.

Jacob threw his hands up in supplication. 'Whoa man. What crawled—'

'Sit. The. Hell. Down.'

Gods! Alannah could not remember the last time she had seen Brendan in such a state, if ever.

After picking his jaw up from the floor, Jacob sat on the couch.

Brendan paced the room, stopping in front of her. 'We have a serious problem. Lana, remember the letter you received from Scarlett?'

She nodded.

'You weren't the only one to get some mysterious mail.' He retrieved a book from inside the ottoman and dropped it on the coffee table. It landed with a loud thump, startling Alannah. 'Inspect it thoroughly.'

It was a large volume, requiring two hands to pick up. She noticed the cover was black leather, much like her Book of Shadows. But there were no markings on the front of this one.

'Turn to page two-hundred and fifty-three.'

Opening the book, she found a recipe for an enchanter's tincture. As she read about its effects, the penny dropped. 'Oh crap! This is Rhapsody. Does this mean you're the source?'

'Yu*p*.' He popped the P. 'And Jacob here. He's my partner in crime.'

'What the hell, Brendan?'

'Oh, it gets better. You see, I learnt who sent me the book. None other than your friend Scarlett.'

Dread took root in the pit of her stomach.

'Alannah knows Lady Scarlett?' Jacob blinked, eyes bouncing from Brendan to Alannah and back again.

'Oh yeah, they go way back. Don't you Lana?'

Crap! Does he know?

'What I'd like to know, Jacob, is how well you know the Boss lady?'

'Never met her, why?'

Brendan studied Jacob for a few seconds. 'Scarlett paid me a visit today. She wanted to deliver these in person.' He pulled three amulets from his pocket and thrust them on the table.

Jacob grabbed one. 'Heck yeah! You got the mind shields.'

But Brendan paid him no heed. He stared at Alannah. 'And she sends her regards to you, Lana.'

'Oh crap!' she mumbled.

His gaze became challenging. 'When were you going to tell me? I'm at least hoping for before she stabs us all in the back. Or are you Team Scarlett now?'

'I'm sorry, Brendan. I was trying to keep her away from you and Liam.'

'Don't you mean keep us from her? Because after what she did to us all, I feel pretty justified in ripping her heart out and feeding it to her.'

'Wait, what am I missing here?' Jacob wrinkled his forehead.

They both ignored him as Brendan's hands came to rest on the arms of her chair, caging her in as he towered over her. His eyes glowered. 'How much do you know about the Dark Syndicate, Lana?'

Second time today someone asked me about the nefarious gang. 'Nothing.'

'That's interesting, considering you're a high-ranking member.' He snorted. 'I can't believe it didn't occur to me before.'

'Wait, Alannah's in the Syndicate?' Jacob took a deep breath and eased it out.

'Oh right, I believe introductions are in order.' He stood upright. 'Jacob, meet Lady Ebony; Lady Ebony, meet Associate Jacob.'

When she looked at Jacob, his eyes widened. 'That's where you got the new car from?'

Alannah squinted. 'What are you talking about, Brendan?'

'The Dark Syndicate is a powerful criminal organisation comprising of dark mages and unseelie. They like to give their top-ranking members colour themed codenames to protect their identities. What's your rank, Lana? Captain? Underboss?'

The blood simmering away beneath Alannah's skin overboiled. 'I told you, I don't have a damn clue! Today is the first time I heard mention of this Syndicate. Besides, it's not like you can talk. You're selling them unsanctioned potions.'

Brendan took a deep breath. 'I guess she's playing all of us and we're goners if we don't work out her endgame soon.'

'Hold up. Who's playing us?' Jacob inquired.

'Lady Scarlett.' Brendan turned to face Jacob. 'Or should I say, Tara Winters?'

'Bloody hell! Scarlett is Tara? As in *the* Tara?' Jacob was pale, panting, and trembling.

Brendan might have felt sorry for him if the rascal had not gotten them into this mess in the first place. Tara must have known Jacob's family were Syndicate members and manipulated the situation to bring Brendan into the fold. He turned back to Alannah. 'What has she been teaching you?'

'We've only had a couple of training sessions thus far and she's focussed on getting me to channel the primordial.'

He shook his head. 'That takes an Arch Mage apprentice years to master. How the hell can she expect you to do it? Or is that her plan: to drag the training out and not give you the information you want?'

Alannah sighed. 'I had my first breakthrough on Tuesday night. It won't take me long to become fully attuned.'

His eyes were bugging out. 'Are you for real?'

She nodded. 'Apparently, I was born attuned. Something about the secret of the Beltane Blessing.'

'By the Gods!' he whispered.

'Did I hear right? Is Lady Scarlett—I mean Tara—training Alannah?'

'Yes, Jacob,' they replied in unison.

'I told you she had her secrets,' Brendan added with a sly grin directed at Alannah.

'Her endgame is pretty obvious.'

Brendan turned to face Jacob. 'Oh?'

Jacob nodded. 'She's going Palpatine on your arses.'

They both wrinkled their brows.

'You know, Emperor Palpatine from *Star Wars*?'

He glared at Jacob. 'I know who he is, asshat. But what do you mean?'

'Tara wants to bring you both over to the dark side.'

Brendan contemplated Jacob's theory. 'But what does she stand to gain from turning us dark?'

'She wants us to be allies, not enemies,' Alannah replied. 'It's been my theory all along. She is preparing me for a seat of power in the Council. I figure she's trying to manipulate me so I can be her puppet when I gain said position.'

Brendan dropped into an armchair and grinned at Alannah. 'See, I always knew you were much more than just a pretty face.'

Her eyes smouldered, and Brendan caught another glimpse of her lusty aura. She crossed her legs, bringing attention to her thighs as her short black skirt rose.

When Brendan lifted his gaze, her gleaming eyes narrowed on him, and her lips puckered.

Jacob cleared his throat, breaking the hold of Alannah's emerald eyes on Brendan. 'So, what's the plan?'

'I say we continue business as usual and use our positions to search for Tara's weakness.' Alannah suggested.

Brendan arched a brow at her. 'What weakness?'

'A way to bring about her true death. We can't kill liches by conventional means. That's why she didn't stay down when I killed her the first time.'

Damn, she is sexy when strategising. 'Okay, but we will have to be extra cautious. We should use these around the Syndicate, as well as Richard.' He held up one of the mind shields. 'Speaking of Richard, how did things go with him this morning?'

After picking up her own amulet, Alannah smiled. 'Better than expected. Your deflection technique worked. Although…'

'Although what?'

'Your visualisation suggestion worked too well.'

Brendan's eyes widened. 'You didn't?'

Those sweet cheeks turned pink as she bit her bottom lip.

Hot damn! His mind ran through all the dirty things he wanted to do to her right then and there. Thankfully, Jacob was present, else Brendan's resolution to keep his hands off her might have crumbled.

Alannah blinked, humour vanishing from her visage. 'Richard also told me something potentially useful. Apparently, Tara's sister, Dana, is now Queen of the Cursed. I don't know what their relationship is like, but we should investigate it.'

'Stupendous idea,' Jacob agreed.

'On that note: I'm gonna head over to Cailleach Estate and do some research.'

As soon as Alannah was on her feet, Brendan drew her into his arms. 'Please be careful, Lana. I can't bear the thought of losing you.'

'Likewise, Brendan.' Her head dropped into the crook of his neck, and he felt her inhale deeply. Pulling free, she glanced at Jacob. 'See ya.'

Jacob saluted her. 'Laters.'

Sighing, Brendan slumped back into his chair.

'Bro, it's as clear as my mum's obsessively cleaned windows how much Alannah wants you.'

'You don't need to tell me, or are you forgetting who's the enchanter here?'

Jacob shook his head. 'Sometimes I wonder if you're blind when it comes to her. But if you know how she feels, what's holding you back?'

'She's still with Liam.'

'So? What has he ever done to earn your loyalty?' Jacob retorted. 'Alannah is ripe for the picking and if you don't act soon, you might lose your only chance to get the girl.'

Brendan sat up in his chair, his heart thrashing erratically. 'You're right.'

Jacob grinned. 'Of course I'm right, *young Grasshopper*. Now let's get the lab moved. I got us a glamoured warehouse in Lonsdale.'

Most of the women had assembled in the Sailing Club meeting room. Alannah listened to Jessica Ó Máille and Danielle Sheridan gossiping about the girls their brothers were dating. On occasions like this, she missed Cara immensely. Even though the girls had warmed up to Alannah, she still felt like an outsider.

Unable to concentrate, she turned her attention to the window to watch the springtime drizzle trickling down the glass. Mesmerised by the view, she slipped into a meditative state. The familiar tingle of mana flowed through her, although she did not recognise the source.

A flurry of movement at the door drew everyone's attention and Alannah lost the connection. Monique strode into the room, flanked by Claudia and Charlotte Rowan. Alannah began to rise, but Monique pinned her in place with a deadly glare. 'Sit down.'

'Um, o…kay.' Alannah's heart thumped wildly. *What is going on?*

Monique moved to the head of the table. 'Ladies, it has come to my attention Alannah here is no longer a suitable leader for our group.'

'What? Why?' several voices queried.

'As you would all know by now, my uncle, the Inquisitor is in town.'

Oh Gods!

'And he has officially declared Alannah a *person of interest*. He won't say why, but it doesn't matter. His suspicions are enough to taint her reputation.'

A chorus of gasps shot through the room, including Alannah's. *Why am I hearing this from*

Monique rather than Richard or Kieran? All eyes fell on her. 'I swear to the Gods I have no idea why he suspects me of anything. I haven't done anything wrong.'

'Monique's right, it doesn't matter. Your reputation will hurt our campaign,' Jessica retorted. Several others concurred with nods and muttered words.

Charlotte stepped forward. 'I nominate Monique to head up this lobby.'

'I second that,' Jessica agreed.

'No!' Alannah whispered, her heart racing as she felt her life spiralling out of control.

Danielle stood. 'All in favour of Monique Lane taking Alannah's Winters' place as our campaign leader?'

All but Alannah thrust a hand in the air. They may as well have plunged knives into her heart. At least she would not live to feel the sting of betrayal for long. Her stomach swam as she drifted toward the door.

Monique grabbed Alannah's arm as she passed and glowered. 'I told you I don't tolerate rogues.'

Yanking her arm free, Alannah returned the evil eye, and stormed out of the room.

When she got home, Alannah let the tears flow and her first thoughts turned to Brendan and his comforting hugs. Without thinking, she rang him.

'Hey, Lana.'

'Can you come over?'

'Hell! It sounds like you're crying. What's wrong?'

She choked back the lump forming in her throat. 'I need you here, Brendan. Please.'

'I'll be right there.'

A few minutes later Brendan burst through her front door without knocking. Panting heavily and imitating a drowned rat, he approached her in the front sitting room.

Alannah spoke through her sobs. 'Did you… run here?'

'Of course I did.' He tugged his wet t-shirt over his head and threw it over the bar heater. The sight of his bare chest sent a sudden jolt of heat to her core. Brendan had bulked out since high school, sporting an eight pack to rival Liam's. A twinkling of light caught her attention, highlighting the silver sleeper piercing his left nipple.

He dropped beside her on the antique divan, grabbed the soft fleece blanket she huddled under and wrapped it around them both as he pulled her into his arms. 'What happened, Lana?'

'You know the women's group I started?'

'Yeah.'

'Monique stole my position and ousted me from it tonight.'

'*What?* That bitch!' Brendan's tone was seething. 'Why did she betray you?'

'Apparently I am a *person of interest* in Richard's investigation.'

'Oh hell!' He squeezed her tighter. 'I'm sorry, Lana. This all my fault.'

'Brendan, don't. Please just hold me, okay?'

He sucked in a deep breath. 'Okay.'

The sound of rain pelting against the roof lulled Alannah to sleep in Brendan's warm embrace.

Chapter Ten

Brendan did not whistle often. It usually took an incredibly wild night in the sack to elevate his mood enough, but all he needed this time was the memory of Alannah's warm body sleeping in his arms. Even visions of the murderous blaze in Liam's eyes—when he had come home from work—to find them curled up together could not kill Brendan's current buzz.

Placebo's song 'Pure Morning' played as he drove to his parents' place for the fortnightly family dinner. The lyrics resonated with him all day, and he whistled the tune as he stepped out of the car and walked toward the house.

'You sound cheerful this evening.' Nora, glancing up from salad preparation, smiled at him as he entered the kitchen.

He leaned over and planted a big wet one on her cheek. 'That's 'cause I am.'

Laughing, she wiped her cheek dry with the back of her hand. She stood upright and studied him a moment. 'Hmm. You're swooning. Just don't tell your dad. He's already angry with you after the stunt you pulled with Jessica. There's another girl here tonight. Her name's Wendy and she's from the Eyre Peninsula.'

Brendan grabbed a beer from the fridge, leaning against the pantry. 'Well, this Wendy form the Eyre Peninsula should go home because I'm not interested.'

Mum rolled her eyes. 'You haven't even met her yet. She is very pretty.'

'I don't care if she is Australia's next top model. Dad has to learn he can't dictate my love life.'

'You know he will keep trying until you settle on a pure mage.'

'Then he can stop trying because I've already settled on a bloodline babe.'

Her eyes widened, and she smacked his arm. 'Why didn't you say so before? Now don't keep me in suspense. Who is she?'

Raised voices sounded at the front door. 'Ah, that'd be her now. But shoosh; don't tell Dad.' He winked.

As soon as Nora recognised Alannah's voice, she frowned. 'Your joke is in poor taste.'

Hell! Are Liam and Lana arguing out there? 'It's not a joke. You'll see.'

Liam entered first. 'Hi Mum.' He embraced her briefly, glimpsed Brendan and gave him a death glare. 'What are you looking so smug about?'

'I don't know what you're talking about.' Brendan gave Alannah his best panty-dropping smile as she walked in. 'Hi gorgeous. How'd you sleep last night?'

Slamming the fridge after grabbing his drink, Liam growled and left the room.

'Brendan, must you…' Mum began, but she looked at Alannah and froze. Because of her Council position, Nora Winters was always open to emotions mana. There was no doubt she saw it too.

'Hey,' Alannah replied to Brendan as though he were the only person in the room. Crossing the floor, she squeezed him in a bear hug. All the while, her aura was broadcasting not only bright red, but bright pink too: the tell-tale mix of lust and love.

He glanced over Alannah's shoulder at his mother and gave her a satisfied grin.

Shaking her head, Nora mouthed '*Be Careful.*' She did not need to tell him. He knew he was playing with fire—quite literally in Liam's case—but Brendan had gained new determination to win Alannah fair and square.

When Brendan entered the living room, he did a double take at the sight of their two guests. *Woah! Aboriginal mages*. You did not see many of them around anymore. White settlement wiped most of them out, resulting in the migration of European mages to Australia during the Eighteen-Hundreds. His mum was right: the girl was attractive, but she was not his Lana.

Dad stepped forward. 'Brendan, I'd like to introduce you to Reginald and his daughter Wendy. They are from the Eyre Peninsula district.'

'Hi.' He shook their hands.

Following the remaining introductions, they all sat in the lounge area for their aperitif.

'So, Alannah… I heard you are leading a women's lobby group,' prompted Wendy.

Alannah's shoulders slumped. 'I was, but they kicked me out.'

'What?' Liam and Nora formed a chorus.

She focussed her attention on Liam. 'That's what upset me last night. According to Monique, Richard has declared me a *person of interest* and the rest of the group voted me out because of it.'

'Oh Gods, that sounds awful.' Wendy was trying to retreat into the depths of her chair. She was such a contrast to fire-cracker Jessica, the first of Dad's failed matchmaking attempts.

'Wait, why would Richard have reason to suspect you of anything?' Liam gave her a sidelong glance.

Alannah sighed. 'He interviewed me on Saturday. I didn't think he read anything to arouse suspicion, but I guess I was wrong.'

'And you failed to mention the Inquisitor came to visit? I'm sick of all the secrets, Lana.' Liam folded his arms and flared his nostrils.

'I wouldn't need to keep them from you if you were more tolerant and understanding.'

'Is that why you go crying on Brendan's shoulder instead of mine?'

'I've had enough of this.' She vaulted from her seat and escaped out the back door.

Brendan rose to follow her.

But Liam jumped in front of him. 'Where the hell do you think you're going?'

He glanced into the blue storm clouds staring back at him and smirked. 'To give her a shoulder to cry on.'

'Stay. The. Hell. Away. From. Her.' Drawing up to his full height, Liam towered over Brendan.

'Screw you, bro.' Brendan shoulder checked Liam as he strode toward the door, pausing to smile at Wendy. 'I'm sorry you had to see our family drama.' Without further ado, he took off.

After trudging along the side of the house, Alannah settled into one of the wicker hammocks on the front porch. She was taking stock of the epic clusterfuck she called her life when she heard footsteps approaching. Tensing at first, she released her breath as Brendan rounded the corner.

'Come on, Lana, let's get outta here.'

'I can't just leave.'

He smiled. 'Sure you can.'

'But Liam—'

'Is a douche canoe who needs to get over himself.' He reached out a hand to help her up. 'Now come on. It's time to pay our friend Jameson a visit.'

The hint of a smile crept onto her face. 'How do you always know what I need?'

His left brow, the one with the piercing, arched in the sexy way it does. 'Is that a rhetorical question, 'cause you know what my attunements are, right?'

She grabbed his hand and pushed herself out of the hammock. 'Yeah, but I reckon it's more than that.'

'Oh, you do, do you?'

'Yeah, I do.'

When they reached his Jag, Brendan opened the passenger door for her. After getting into the driver's seat, he looked at her. 'What do you think it is?'

'Hmm... I'm not telling.'

'I bet I can get you to tell me after a few drinks.'

Alannah sank into the comfortable upholstery and closed her eyes. The scent of leather blended with Brendan's cologne: an intoxicating mix. 'We'll see.' She loved his playlist too.

They stopped at the bottle shop in town before driving down to the beach front where Brendan found a secluded spot to park. He killed the engine, but kept the music going. 'Mind passing the two shot cups from the glovebox?'

She gave him a sidelong glance. 'Is drinking in your car a frequent occurrence?'

'Frequent enough. Are you gonna pass them over, or make me come and get them?'

Hmm, now there's an idea. She grabbed the two small plastic cups and examined them. 'Do you drink with all those girls you bone? I'm not gonna catch anything from using these am I?'

He chuckled. 'Firstly, you're a pure mage so you can't get human STIs. Secondly, I don't have the second cup for my hook-ups.'

'Then who do you drink with?'

'Jacob mostly. Sometimes one of the other guys.'

Relieved she was not about to share a shot glass with half the town's female population, she held them out for Brendan to pour their drinks. Alannah welcomed the burn of the whiskey going down. 'Gods, that feels awesome.' A moment later, she was reaching her hand out for more.

Brendan was smiling at her with amusement in his eyes.

'What?'

'You've always been my favourite drinking buddy.'

Alannah felt her heart swelling. 'Why?'

There was an impish grin on his face as he poured another round. 'That information will cost you.'

She laughed. 'Name your price.'

'An exchange of intel.'

'Nice try, but you won't get it out of me so easily.'

Brendan's pout was adorable. And too damn sexy. 'Shame. I guess I'll keep my secrets too, then.'

Sam Tinnesz and Yacht Money were singing 'Play with Fire', so Alannah closed her eyes and immersed herself in the strong, sensual beat. 'I love this song. You have much better taste in music than Liam.' Wondering why he did not make a smartass retort, she peeked at Brendan and sucked in a sharp breath.

His eyes were blazing. 'You're pretty pissed with him right now, aren't you?'

She nodded.

'I have an idea.' Brendan continued. 'How about you tell me all the ways I'm better than Liam and I'll tell you all the reasons you're my favourite drinking buddy.'

Alannah snorted. 'Can your over-inflated ego handle it?'

'When it comes to how I compare to Liam, I will take all the ego boosting I can get.' Given their history, Brendan was telling the painful truth.

'Okay, it's a deal. We'll go piece for piece. Since I began, you need to tell me something now.'

Grinning, Brendan poured more drinks, and settled back into his seat. 'For one, you hold your liquor better than most, Jacob included.'

'Wow, okay. Well, you are more tolerant and understanding than Liam.'

'I'll drink to that.' He downed his shot. 'You laugh a lot when drunk and I love your laugh.'

'You're a better fighter than Liam, both armed and unarmed.'

He gasped. 'Damn it's gratifying to hear it. You're more attractive than the others.'

'Hmph, the others are blokes and you're straight, so that's not hard.'

'Hey. I'm including Cara, Amy, and Bianca here.'

Her heartbeat sped up. 'You think I'm prettier than Bianca?'

Brendan smiled. 'Much.'

Considering Bianca was the girl he slept with the most, Alannah felt flattered. 'You have a better sense of humour than Liam. His jokes always make me cringe.'

'Ooh, damn, that's quite the burn. Which brings me to my next point. You throw shade better than anyone I know.'

'I don't need alcohol for that,' she scoffed.

'True, but it doesn't hurt. Speaking of which.' He held the bottle out and poured her another.

After throwing it back, she looked at Brendan and whispered. 'You give the best hugs.'

'Oh, Gods! You melted my heart, Lana.' He leaned back and closed his eyes a moment. Brendan's lids remained closed as he spoke. 'We click more than I do with the others. It feels like we have this deep understanding of each other. Being with you is more exciting and more… meaningful.'

Woah! Talk about heart-melting. 'That's why...' she whispered.

His eyes flicked open. 'What did you say?'

Alannah found herself leaning toward him to keep her voice hushed. 'That's why you always know what I need. You know me better than anyone else.'

'Better than Liam?'

She nodded. 'Yeah, even better than Liam.'

Brendan bit his lip and winced. 'Damn that bastard. There's still one way he knows you better.' When his penetrating gaze turned on her, Alannah's cheeks flushed. His eyes flashed and he brought his fingers up to her face, brushing his knuckles along her burning skin.

Power surged through Alannah and an acute headache struck, forcing her eyes closed. In her mind she saw Brendan bending her over a bed and fucking and spanking her hard while her screams of pain induced ecstasy rang through the air. Suddenly, Liam barged in and shot Brendan with a lightning bolt. She opened her eyes again as the vision ended.

'Are you okay, Lana?' Brendan's voice trembled.

While short, the vision packed one hell of a punch. And she knew it was a cosmic warning.

'Lana?' His hand cupped her chin.

As the pain eased, she looked at him. 'I'm okay. It was just a headache. I think I've had enough to drink.'

Brendan screwed up his face but held his tongue. Something on her nose drew his attention. 'Okay.' He tapped her diamond stud. 'I have an idea.'

'Oh-oh. Sounds dangerous.'

'You know I live for danger.' He winked and started the car. Five minutes later he parked the car. 'How about we get some new body bling?' Brendan gestured toward a shop with a small white neon sign: *Brocade Spider, Body Art and Piercings*. 'My treat.'

When they stepped back out of the salon, Alannah no longer felt tension in her shoulders. Meredith, the lady who pierced her belly button, was a hoot.

Brendan linked her arm with his. 'Where to now, my lady?'

Not wanting to tempt fate, she sighed. 'I should go home.'

His brows furrowed. 'Are you sure?'

'Yeah.'

'Okay.' They walked to the car in silence. Music filled the short drive, lessening the tension in the air.

Liam's car was absent from the driveway when they arrived, alleviating the knots in Alannah's shoulders. She hated dealing with his moods. Brendan followed her inside and down the hall. When they reached the kitchen, she glanced at him. 'Coffee?'

'Sure. Thanks.'

While Brendan sipped his drink, she studied him.

He glanced up from his cup and cocked his left brow. 'What?'

'I'm wondering what you had pierced tonight.'

Brendan smouldered. 'I'll show you mine if you show me yours.'

'Fine.' Alannah put her coffee down and unbuttoned her jeans. She gasped when he did the same. She was expecting him to lift his t-shirt to show her a second nipple piercing since she could not see anything new on his face or ears.

His eyes widened. 'Now I'm intrigued.'

'So am I.' *Where exactly did Brendan get his bling?* All sorts of images filled her mind, none of them wholesome.

'How intrigued?' He nudged his waistband down while his mouth twisted into a lewd grin.

'Did you seriously get a cock piercing?'

'Yup. Now tell me if you *want* to see it.'

'This feels like a game of Sleazy Chicken.'

'Once more, for old time's sake?' His eyes pleaded with her.

'Okay, I'll bite. Besides, it's not like I haven't seen you naked before. But I doubt you'll show me. Willingly baring yourself to me is different to incidental exposure.'

'This isn't a question of how far *I'll* go; it rarely is. The issue here is whether you truly want to see it. Do you want to feast your eyes upon my dick, Lana?'

Alannah's cheeks flamed as lust pooled at her core.

Brendan rushed her, pinning her against the wall. 'Do you know why I usually win Sleazy Chicken?'

Swallowing hard against the tension mounting in her throat, Alannah held his gaze. 'Because you're a bigger sleaze than me.'

He inched closer. 'Wrong answer.'

'Okay, then why?'

'Because I'm never bluffing.' Brendan pushed his weight against her and hissed telepathically in her mind. *'I. Want. You. Lana. I've wanted you for as long as I can remember. When I said I wasn't in love with you; I lied. And right now, all I want to do is kiss you senseless, throw you down, and bang your brains out.'*

Another of her instinctive powers manifested, showing her Brendan's aura. The bright red flickering of lust within the bright pink colour of love confirmed the truth. Not to mention the bulge in his pants. *'Fuck!'* she whispered through clenched teeth.

'Exactly.' His expression turned wild and wicked.

The sound of keys unlocking the front door, followed by approaching footsteps resounding off the wooden floorboards of the hall sent Brendan darting across the room. He fastened his jeans with expert deftness, as though he had been in similar situations countless times. *Then again, he probably had.*

Her own jittery fingers fumbled with her button fly, scarcely getting the last one as Liam entered the room. Bracing herself for his rage, she bit her bottom lip to stop it trembling.

But when he slumped against the kitchen bench there was no spark left in him. 'I didn't think you would come home tonight.'

Alannah's heart broke. Stepping up to Liam, she wrapped her arms around him. 'I'm sorry,' she whispered.

Bringing his own arms up to encircle her, Liam peered into her eyes with barely constrained tears. 'It feels like I'm losing you, Lana.'

'I'll see myself out.' Brendan's bitter tone cut through the air and into Alannah's already aching heart.

She wanted to go after him, but Liam needed her too. *When did it all become so complicated?* Pressing her forehead to Liam's, she felt a tear slide down her cheek. 'You haven't lost me. I'm right here.'

He claimed her mouth in a hungry kiss. She could not remember the last time they had kissed with such raw passion. The taste of choc-mint on his breath mingled with her own coffee and whiskey aftertaste, fuelling the fire of desire in her core. Alannah wrapped her legs around Liam's waist, clinging to his body like a monkey. They continued kissing as he walked them through the hallway and into the bedroom.

After he took his sweet time making love to her, Liam enfolded her in his arms. 'I'm sorry, Lana. I haven't been here enough for you. I'm taking some time off work to spend with you.' He tucked a strand of hair behind her ear. 'If you still want me?'

Tears were streaming from her eyes as she nodded.

'Hey, we've just had a hiccup, but we'll get past it. And I promise to support you more. I love you so much, Lana.'

'I love you, too,' she sobbed. *And my heart tears in two.*

Chapter Eleven

The next morning, Liam needed to head into the police station to finish some paperwork and tie up a few loose ends before taking leave. So, Alannah took the opportunity to confront Brendan. After ringing his bell twice, she beat down his door.

He eventually answered, yawning as he opened the door. 'What the hell, Lana? Do you know how early it is?' Brendan's jet-black hair was more dishevelled than usual, and his only clothing was a pair of low-hanging baggy grey track pants. Under different circumstances the sight might have been a serious distraction for Alannah.

'Stop your whingeing. You'd be at work by now if you weren't on holidays. Can I come in?'

Crossing his arms, he narrowed his eyes. 'Depends.'

'On what?' She could feel her patience slipping away.

'Are you here because you dumped my lunkhead brother and want to spend the day trying every position of the *Kama Sutra* with me?'

'What? No! Brendan—'

'Then my answer is no.' He slammed the door in her face.

Crap! What a disaster. Grabbing her keys, Alannah let herself in. '*Brendan!*'

He was halfway down the hall. 'Why did you bother asking if you were gonna barge your way in?'

'I was trying to be polite. Now stop being a dick and listen to me.'

When they reached his living room, he sprawled out on the couch and scowled at her. 'I'm all ears.'

Letting out a sigh, Alannah pushed his feet off the sofa and sat next to him. 'Are you seriously sulking because I won't screw you?'

'You also woke me up. And you know I'm not a morning person at the best of times, let alone when hungover.'

She shook her head. 'You only had four shots last night. I drank more than you.'

He pulled an empty whiskey bottle from under the couch. 'Finished it when I got home. I'll give you three guesses why.'

Alannah blinked at him.

'What? Not even one guess? Fine, I'll tell you why. Only minutes after I bared my heart to you, Lana, you went running back into Liam's arms. I honestly thought I was getting somewhere with you last night, but once again the golden boy comes in and sweeps you up.'

Speechless. She was utterly speechless for several long minutes while staring at him. Averting her eyes, she inhaled deeply. 'Why did you have to wait until now to make your move? Now things are serious for Liam and me? You had plenty of opportunities in the past.'

'You truly want to know?'

She turned back to face him. 'Yes, Brendan. It's about time you were open and honest with me.'

He sniggered. 'Like you're one to talk.'

'What's that supposed to mean?'

'You're the one who's been shutting me out these last four years.'

'I've had my reasons.'

Tucking his thighs up to his chest, Brendan dropped his chin to his knees. 'Just as I had reasons for keeping my feelings under wraps. There has never been a right time with you, Lana. When we were kids, you were always like "Liam this, Liam that." I'll never forget the night following your mum's funeral. That day was doubly painful for me: not only did I lose Aunt Aileen, but I felt like I lost you too.'

Alannah's brow creased. 'What are you talking about?'

'Liam and I came to check on you that night. When we stopped outside your door, we overheard you talking to your Melbourne friend, Emma.'

She gaped at him, recalling the personal chat.

He continued, 'You remember it, don't you? Sometimes the conversation replays in my mind:

Emma started it. 'So, those cousins of yours are way hot.'

You giggled before responding, 'Yeah, they are.'

Liam and I exchanged glances and he almost went to leave, clearly feeling guilt over eavesdropping. But I grabbed his arm and gestured for him to stay quiet and remain listening with me.

'So, you're down with kissing cousins?' Emma queried.

'Hell yeah. I would totally let one of the guys comfort me in bed tonight.'

I got painfully hard hearing your admission. Then I saw the surprise in Liam's eyes and almost laughed out loud. He was so innocent for a fourteen-year-old guy; something that was an endless source of amusement for me.

Emma asked the question Liam and I were both dying to hear you answer: 'Who would you choose?'

The time you took to consider your answer was a nerve-racking moment for the two of us. We stood there staring at each other, waiting with bated breath.

You cleaved my heart in two when you replied, 'Well, I've had the biggest crush on Liam for as long as I can remember, so it would feel divine to have him kiss my tears away.'

The biggest grin I've ever seen formed on the mofo's face, and he stared at me with smug satisfaction. Not wanting to cause a scene on such a sombre occasion, I flipped him off and hightailed it out of there.

Heaving a huge sigh, Brendan leaned back and pressed his head against the back of the couch.

He shut his eyes for a second. Still reclined, he turned his face to her. 'When you returned to us, I kept trying to read you, to see if your feelings had changed; but aside from the odd flash of lust, you didn't give me hope of mutual affections.'

'So, what's changed? Why now? I'm more in love with Liam than ever.'

'I know, and it scares me, Lana. I figured I had to act before I lost my chance entirely.' Moving closer to her, Brendan grabbed the nape of her neck and gazed down upon her. 'The morning you walked in on me with Thornsy's sister, you let your guard down, just as you have a few times since. Not to mention the nightclub.'

She closed her eyes to suppress the threatening tears brought on by the painful memory of that night.

'Open your damn eyes, Lana.'

'I can't.'

'Why do you keep shutting me out?'

It was no use. The tears broke free as she pushed out of Brendan's grip and jumped to her feet. She glared at him as she screamed, '*Because it hurts to let you in*. Every time I opened myself to you, and to the possibility of intimacy with you, you rejected me. I don't know what twisted game you are playing with my emotions, but if your goal is to inflict maximum pain, you won. Congratulations for breaking my heart.' Unable to take anymore, Alannah fled from Brendan's apartment.

'Oh hell.' Brendan raced after Alannah but stopped at the door, remembering he was half-naked.

After a quick shower, he threw on the first clothes he could find in the washing basket, jumped in the Jag and gunned it until he reached Alannah's house. But when he saw Liam getting out of his SUV, Brendan refrained from leaving his own car. *What the hell is he doing home already?*

The arsehole turned toward Brendan with a smug grin.

'*Damnit!*' He smacked the steering wheel and took off.

One roadhouse coffee and steak sandwich later, he found himself driving aimlessly around the countryside. *How did I botch things so much with Lana? I am meant to be the expert when it comes to reading people*. He floored it as soon as he hit the highway. Brendan needed a rush—any rush to numb the pain! And he did not even care when a speed camera flashed behind him. But even the thrill of riding his second-favourite girl was not enough to get his mind off the first.

His subconscious drove him to Bianca's estate, not surprising him at all. The nymph waited for him on the porch as usual because she could always sense him coming. 'Well hey there, stranger. It's been a while.' She styled her long black hair in the usual pigtails and wore a short black mesh dress that left nothing to the imagination.

He grabbed her arms in a vice grip. 'Quit with the pleasantries and screw me already.'

Bianca giggled and the green vine pattern all over her tanned skin glowed as she channelled mana. 'Your rotten mood tells me this is gonna be some angry sex. I can't wait!'

'Then why are you still talking?' Brendan growled as he pulled her into his arms and devoured her mouth.

Clothes flew to her bedroom floor in a frenzy and only his satin boxers remained as they crashed onto her bed. Their lips and tongues duelled for several minutes until Brendan drew back to grab a foil packet from his wallet.

With the distance between them, Bianca gasped; her eyes wide as she stared at him.

He flinched. 'What? Do I have a nasty bruise or something?'

She shook her head gradually as she whispered, 'Your aura.'

'Tell me sweetheart, what do your nymph eyes see? Aside from the healthy red glow telling you I'm about to rock your world.'

Her eyes sought his, killing the mood when he saw tears swelling in them. Dropping back on the bed, Brendan reached out to place a comforting hand on her shoulder, but she backed away. 'You're freaking me out now, B. What's wrong?'

'What have you done, Brendan?'

His brow creased as he approached her, prompting her to retreat further. 'What do you mean, what have I done?'

'Your inner aura. It's tainted with shades of grey. You've been practising dark magic.'

He recoiled. 'Damn! I didn't realise how nasty things were. Promise me you won't tell anyone?'

The tears slid down Bianca's cheeks. 'I'm not gonna tell anyone, but whatever you've been doing is wrong Brendan, and it's damaging your soul. You need to stop as soon as possible. If you don't, you're gonna do permanent damage. Once your inner aura goes completely dark, there's no coming back.'

He rubbed the side of his face. Brendan did not know the potion making was dark enough to corrupt his soul. He understood Bianca's warning though. The fall of the dark warrior was among the parables Dad had read to him as a bedtime story. It was a lesson taught to all young mages meant to keep them in line:

'Stick to the right-hand path, Son, and your soul will never darken. Mages who defile their souls by performing unsanctioned magic become dark mages.'

'What is a dark mage, Dad?'

'Outlaw mages who lose their way—like Donovan, the dark warrior. He became so obsessed with power for its own sake his soul darkened over time until it turned black. Once that happened, he could no longer seek redemption. Upon his death, Donovan's soul joined the cursed in the Underworld. And he fathered children with tainted souls too.'

Tara's plan is working. 'Thanks for the warning, B. I'll try to stop, but it won't be easy to get out of the mess I'm in.'

'Does this have anything to do with the Inquisitor investigating Alannah?'

Hearing Alannah's name was like having the knife in his heart twisted. 'You know about that?'

Bianca nodded. 'Yeah. Cara told me.'

Leaning back against the headboard, Brendan sighed heavily. 'Everything's complicated right now. It's best if I don't tell you anything, for your own sake.'

'Oh, sweetheart, I'm sorry. I can see how much you're hurting. Come here.'

And so, Brendan lost himself in Bianca's arms, forgetting his grief for a few sweet hours.

Alannah had survived the start of pub night by confining herself to the corner of their booth with Cara for quality girl chat. But when her bestie headed for the bathrooms, Jacob stalked after her, giving Brendan an opening.

He slid across the seat and leaned in. 'Are you still avoiding me, Lana?'

She eyed his beer. 'Depends.'

'On what?'

'If you're buying the next two rounds.'

Brendan slapped some money down in front of Bailey. 'Be a pal and get us two more jugs, will you?'

Bailey frowned at him. 'I'm not your damn beer wench, bro.'

'Please, pretty please?' Brendan gave him a pouty face complete with batting lashes.

'Fine, but I'm keeping the change.'

With Bailey gone, Caleb was the only person left at their table and he was busy scrolling through memes on his phone. Ben and Nick were playing pool, and Connor and Amy had taken off early for some couple-time.

Moving in close enough for their thighs and shoulders to touch, Brendan whispered in her ear, 'I've been trying to catch you at home since yesterday morning, but Liam's been hanging around you like a bad smell.'

'He took leave from work to spend time with me.' Alannah stole Brendan's drink and chugged it down in one go.

'Bloody hell, woman, you're killing me.' He grinned. 'So, where is that bad smell tonight?'

'The Council summoned him for business. The Inquisitor has his pet warlocks on the prowl trying to sniff out anyone using or dealing Rhapsody.'

A wicked gleam appeared in his eyes. 'Did you call Liam a dog?'

'What? No!'

'You totally did. You said, and I quote, "A pet on the prowl trying to sniff people out." Sounds like a dog to me.'

'Hmph! Liam's more like an alpha wolf.'

'Touché.' He waggled his brows. 'Don't tell me you have a thing for weres now, Lana?'

Alannah snorted. 'No way!'

'*Sure…* Tell me, did this furry fetish come on before or after you saw Ben in action?'

She punched his arm. 'Will you ever let me live that down?'

'Hell no!' He laughed.

Bailey delivered their jugs of ale and resumed his conversation with Caleb.

After taking a decent mouthful of her drink, Alannah giggled as the alcohol buzz kicked in. She pressed her mouth to Brendan's ear. 'You know the only reason I looked at Ben and Nick that time was so you wouldn't see who initially drew my attention.'

'Hmm, is that so?'

She nodded.

'So, you weren't getting aroused by the sight of so much inky muscle?'

Alannah let out a hearty laugh. 'Nope. Tats don't do it for me as much as piercings.'

Brendan shot the other guys a cursory glance before whispering, 'Hell! I better not let you see Thornsy naked.'

'You are treb… turb… terrible.'

He grinned at her. 'And you're drunk.'

'No shit, Sherblock.'

Brendan burst out laughing and Alannah joined him. When he was able to catch a breath, he gazed at her and nodded. 'Yup, still my favourite drinking buddy.' But then his expression turned serious. 'I'm sorry, Lana.'

Her brow furrowed. 'For what?'

'For messing everything up between us.' Reclining against the backrest, he closed his eyes. 'I thought I was doing the right thing when I gave Liam a second chance with you.'

She inhaled sharply. 'What do you mean?'

Brendan looked at her with glistening eyes. 'Remember the time he left you and hooked up with Monique because he misread the situation with Austin?'

Wincing at the memory, she sobered. 'Yeah.'

'Our drinking session that night was the first time I sensed you wanted me. It took every ounce of willpower in my depraved brain to keep my hands off you.'

Alannah's eyes widened. 'Why *did* you… (swallow)… keep your hands off me?'

'Because we needed Liam on our side in the war against Tara.' He took a deep breath. 'And if I'm honest with myself, it's 'cause I'm a damn coward for heeding Liam's threats.'

Biting her lip, Alannah found her mind churning through a bunch of what-ifs.

'What are you thinking about, Lana?'

'I wonder how different things might have been if you'd stuck around to hear the rest of that conversation with Emma.'

'Why?'

'Because if you had stayed, you would have heard me tell Emma I wanted you.'

Brendan stared at her in silence.

'After I told her about my crush on Liam, she retorted:

'But Brendan looks so fuckable.'

'Ah huh. Which is why he'd be my choice for the night. That guy is like a wet dream walking, and I'm sure he'll feature in mine for years to come.'

Emma snorted, 'Ha! Come! I get it.'

I gave her one of my eyerolls before continuing. 'There's nothing I wouldn't let him do to me. With the bad boy look he's got going, he's like all my wildest fantasies come to life.'

'Wait, does that mean you want them both?'

'Yeah, I suppose it does.' I shrugged with a devilish grin.

'Gods damn, woman, I am so hard for you right now.' Brendan paused for a deep breath. 'Explains why Liam didn't comfort you in bed that night. He must've been fuming.'

'Crap! Was he still listening after you left?'

Brendan nodded. 'Probably wanted to hear you go on about him some more.'

'No wonder he always worries about the two of us.'

Pinning her with a scorching gaze, Brendan rested his hand on Alannah's thigh as he addressed the elephant in the room with a deep, toe curling voice, 'Question is, should we give him a real reason to worry?'

Chapter Twelve

After sealing the last of the mother tincture vials, Brendan glanced up from his work to see Jacob entering their industrial hideout. 'Hey, man.'

Jacob stepped up for a fist bump, casting his eyes over the stainless-steel bench. 'Woah, bro, is that a double batch?'

Flopping down on a couch in their make-shift lounge area, Brendan stretched his arms victoriously, and placed them behind his neck. 'Yup. Let's just say inspiration struck.'

'Good work. This should keep Violet off our backs for a while.' Jacob joined him on the sofa. 'Does this inspiration have anything to do with a certain goth beauty?'

'Maybe.'

'Ah, come on, man. I saw how cosy the two of you were last night. Did anything happen after I left?'

Brendan drew a deep breath, easing into the backrest. 'Nothing physical, but I made a breakthrough with her. Lana admitted she wants me.'

Jacob's face lit up. 'That's great, Brendo.' Contorting his face, he leaned forward. 'So, why aren't you spending your weekend making sweet, sweet love to her?'

'Because she won't cheat on Liam. She also needs time to think before making her decision because of some misguided affection for the wanker.' Brendan had had a lot of wicked thoughts since parting ways with Alannah at the pub and a new one was forming. 'I have to keep proving to Lana I'm her best option. Liam's bound to slip up eventually.'

'That's the spirit.' After rising to his feet, Jacob returned to the bench and grabbed half the vials of potion concentrate. 'I better get one of these batches in Syndicate hands before they send the collectors after me.'

'Collectors?'

'They're the brutes who get sent to collect on late shipments; with interest, mind you.'

The idea made Brendan's skin crawl. 'Would I be right in guessing the interest isn't anything with monetary value?'

'All depends how generous their boss is feeling on any given day. Besides, most things carry monetary value on the Unseelie Market.'

A shiver travelled down Brendan's spine. 'That's dark, bro.'

Jacob shrugged. 'Welcome to my world.'

'I'd rather stay as far away from your world as possible, thanks. Once we work out a way to deal with Tara, I want out of this potion business.'

'For real?' Jacob's lips pressed tight together as his forehead creased.

'I'm sorry, man, but this venture is destroying my soul, literally. It's been fun and all, but I won't turn dark for it.'

Jacob sighed. 'Fine. Speaking of fun, have we got any spare Rhapsody of our own? I'm planning on hitting the clubs with Cara tonight.

'There's plenty in the fridge.'

'Sweet.' After grabbing a few vials, he held one up in Brendan's direction. 'You wanna come with?'

He shook his head. 'Liam's busy tonight, so I'm gonna work my magic on Lana some more.'

Jacob arched his brow. 'You sly devil. Good luck.' As he approached the exit, he turned around with an impish grin. 'Just don't do anything I wouldn't do.'

Brendan laughed. 'Sounds like free reign to me.'

He snorted as he reached for the doorhandle.

'Oh, and Jacob?' Brendan called after him.

Jacob glanced over his shoulder. 'Hmm?'

'Be careful out there. The Inquisitor has every warlock in the state on the hunt tonight.'

'Thanks for the heads up,' Jacob nodded before leaving.

With Liam on annual leave, Alannah did not know when she would get another opportunity to see Scarlett for a while. She decided to kill two birds with one stone and emphasise the platonic condition of meeting Brendan.

As soon as Brendan answered his door, Alannah hugged him, savouring the feel of his body pressed against hers. Reluctantly releasing him, she strode toward her Tesla. 'Come on, we'll take my car.'

'Wait up a minute. Shouldn't *I* be taking *you* out?' He waggled his brow.

After suppressing her traitorous hormones with a deep breath, Alannah simpered. 'Not a date, remember?'

He let out an exaggerated sigh. 'So you keep reminding me.' Sitting in the car, Brendan connected his phone to the stereo. 'But I still get to choose the music.'

Alannah shrugged as she started the engine. 'Fine by me. We like all the same tunes anyway.' When he did not reply, she glanced at him and caught the biggest grin she had ever seen on his face. 'What?'

'I was remembering all the ways *you* think I'm better than Liam.'

She giggled. 'You're relentless.'

Brendan leaned in close to speak in her ear. 'And you're gorgeous.'

Exhaling sharply, Alannah tried to ignore the flutters in her stomach and focussed on the road. His first song choice— 'Play with Fire'—had not escaped her attention. *Figures Brendan is playing dirty now the cards are all on the table.* Liam's ignorance of the situation gave Brendan an unfair advantage and she needed to keep reminding herself of that at times like this.

As soon as they left town, Brendan shifted in his seat, turning to gaze upon her. 'So, where are we going?'

'You'll see.'

'Hmm, colour me intrigued.' His voice was deep and sexy. 'What are we going to do when we get to this *mystery* location?'

'You'll see.'

'If you don't give me any clues, I'm gonna start imagining all manner of erotic things.'

Alannah snorted. 'You can imagine what you like; it won't change the reality.'

'True, but it will get my cock hard, and when you see the effect you have on me, your thoughts will go there too.'

Her mind was already there thanks to his filthy mouth.

'And there he goes,' Brendan remarked.

Unable to help herself, Alannah glimpsed the tent in his jeans. As her eyes rose, Brendan's gaze caught her. The distraction was enough to make her swerve onto the other side of the road. 'Crap!' *Thank the Gods there was no oncoming traffic.*

'Eyes on the road while driving, Lana. But if you want a better view, you could always pull over.'

She rolled her eyes. 'Nice try.'

'I'm just getting started, gorgeous.'

Something occurred to Alannah. 'If you did not bluff when playing Sleazy Chicken, how is this only the second time I've seen your arousal?'

'I'm sure there have been more times when you didn't notice, but as a rule I used magic to control my own emotions.'

'I suspected as much.' Glancing at Brendan, she gestured to his erection with a flick of her eyes. 'You might want to do something about *that* before we arrive because we will have company when we get there.'

'Would you like to help me?' Again, with the voice.

'I'm not touching your dick tonight, Brendan.'

He sighed. 'Shame.' The sound of a zipper opening hit Alannah's ears.

She willed herself not to peek. 'What are you doing?'

'Do you want a detailed description? Firstly, I've lowered my fly, so now my hand…'

Alannah felt her cheeks flush. '*Brendan*! Don't you dare jerk off in my car!'

'Hey, you told me to take care of it.'

'I meant by using your emotion controlling powers.'

'Then you should've specified.'

She shook her head. 'You're incorrigible.'

'Only when it comes to you.'

Alannah felt sceptical. Brendan's history with girls and his self-professed need for variety were the main factors weighing against him and they were biggies. But she did not know how to approach the issue with him.

Brendan fell silent, focussing on his breathing, until they reached the old wooden hut. 'Mm.' His tone was suggestive.

'Mm, what?'

'A secret rendezvous in the woods. This seems less like a date and more like skipping straight to the part where we rip each other's clothes off and…'

When they rounded the corner, Scarlett's Mercedes came into view, shutting him up. Alannah parked alongside the red car and turned to face a gaping Brendan. 'You were saying?'

'Hell, woman! You could have warned me!'

'I thought you might not agree to come with me,' Alannah admitted as she grabbed her mind shield and put it around her neck. Holding the silver charm, she focussed on blocking all thoughts about Scarlett and the Syndicate. She activated the illusion spell by pressing the blue lace agate in the centre, rendering it invisible against her chest.

Brendan did the same, narrowing his eyes on her. 'For the record, I'd rather walk into the pits of the Underworld with you than enter the Celestial realm without you. I just want to be with you Lana, regardless where.'

Her breath hitched at his words.

After a pregnant pause, Brendan broke the silence by clearing his throat. 'So, what's the plan here?'

'Tell her you're here to make sure I'm safe because you still don't trust her. Then watch the training session and suss out the situation. We will debrief afterwards.'

His brow rose. 'Is that it? Won't Tara alter her approach with me present?'

'It's possible, but I suspect she trusts you because of your ties to the Syndicate.'

Brendan sighed. 'Okay, let's get on with it.'

Scarlett smiled as they entered the sanctuary. 'Hello Brendan. What a pleasant surprise.'

He scowled at her. 'I'm here to make sure Lana's safe.'

Their grandmother nodded. 'Of course. I would not expect any less from you, given the depth of your love for her.'

Hearing Scarlett confirm Brendan's feelings knocked the air out of Alannah's lungs. When she glanced at him, his eyes fixed on her.

He spoke in her mind. '*It's true, Lana.*'

Scarlett stepped closer. 'Well Brendan, do you want to enter the circle, or watch from the lounge?'

'I'll take my chances *in* the circle, thanks,' he replied.

'Very well. You know what to do, Ebony.'

Alannah commenced casting the circle. When they sat, she placed her athame between herself and Brendan. This would allow either of them to cut their connection to the circle.

Scarlett looked at her. 'I want you to attempt the channelling exercise I talked you through last week, only without my guidance this time.'

She sank into a meditative state. Before long, the familiar rush of primordial power flowed through her.

'Excellent, dear child. Have you been practising?'

'Yes,' Alannah admitted.

'Keep it up. Once it becomes second nature, you should be able to keep the channel open in much the same way as you do with Aether. This will allow you to access any other mana source you want.' Scarlett leaned forward and retrieved a large white crystal cluster from the altar. 'Do you know what this?'

'No.'

'This is apophyllite, often used in healing magic—but it has a hidden property few mages know.' She looked from Alannah to Brendan, and back again. 'It provides a safe way to channel the stygian element.'

'*What?*' Brendan interjected. 'There's no way you're teaching Lana that shit.'

'Brendan, please.' Alannah's eyes pleaded with him, and his jaw stiffened as he stopped himself from talking. She returned her attention to Scarlett. 'I don't like the idea of messing with nether.'

'Just hear me out, please. I will not force you to do anything you do not want. In fact, I only planned to give you a demonstration tonight. It is true working with nether has its dangers, the least of which being the use of the highly toxic cinnabar crystal. Apophyllite does not only negate the need for a mercury compound, but it also protects the mind, body, and soul from the necrotic effects of nether.'

'What about the moral and legal repercussions of channelling such an evil power source?' Brendan glared at her.

Scarlett laughed. 'Your concern surprises me, considering your recent activities. But to answer your question, there is nothing innately evil with channelling nether; how you choose to use the power matters. But because the Council is stubborn with rules, it is illegal to even access it, which is why there is no representative for it. The flipside is the Council cannot detect use of the stygian element.'

Alannah leaned in. 'Aside from summoning demons, what use is there in channelling nether?'

'It can also be used to negate the effects of other spells, which is what makes it useful, but also dangerous in the Council's opinion. They reserve such knowledge for Arch Mages.'

'Yet more secrets,' Alannah mused.

Scarlett grinned. 'Exactly. Now, can I show you how?'

Alannah nodded. 'Yeah, okay. Just don't summon any demons.'

The drive back to Brendan's place was silent and tense, with Alannah losing herself in thought. Gods knew what was going through his mind. Intending to drop him off and go straight home, she pulled up along the curb.

Brendan sucked in a breath and stared at her. 'You coming in?'

'I don't think I should.'

'We still need to debrief. And Liam doesn't get home for hours yet.'

Alannah sighed. 'Fine.' She followed him through the small cottage garden leading to his apartment.

When they reached his open plan living area, Brendan grabbed a bottle of expensive whiskey and two glasses. 'I don't know about you, but I need something to take the edge off.'

'Thanks.' Settling on the lounge, Alannah turned her whole body to face Brendan. 'So, what do you make of everything?'

After draining his glass in one mouthful, he gazed at her. 'Your theory about her grooming you to be a puppet is pretty accurate. The woman's manipulations are subtle and effective. And the worst part? She let me read her the whole time, so I know she wasn't lying.'

'What if she's a convincing liar?'

He shook his head. 'With the way I read her, there's no way she could have been. That's not to say she wasn't lying by omission, but the words she spoke were true. Every single one of them.'

'Damn. So, why is she manipulating me?'

'Am I right in guessing she's been drip feeding you high level Council secrets each time you meet?'

Alannah took a moment to think back over their previous meetings, finishing her drink as she did. 'Pretty much, yeah.'

Brendan nodded. 'She wants to turn you against the Council so you'll challenge their authority and push her agenda. And it's already working. I could see how pissed you were about all the secrets they keep from us.'

Rage flared through her blood. 'Aren't you? They have no right to keep this crap from us.'

A lascivious grin formed on his face. 'You are so damn hot when you get fired up like this. I'd love to translate your anger into passionate sex.'

Her jaw dropped to the floor, and she punched his bicep.

Brendan grabbed her wrist upon impact. 'Do you have any idea how much your small outbursts of violence turn me on?'

Speechless, Alannah shook her head.

His eyes lit up with wicked intent a second before he pulled her onto his lap such that she straddled him. Her skirt rode up, exposing her most intimate parts to the sensation of Brendan's arousal grinding against her through his jeans.

Alannah's core flooded with desire.

His eyes darkened with pure lust. 'Oh hell! You are so damn wet, Lana.'

A small moan escaped her mouth when his deep voice uttered her name, and again as both his hands tightened their grip on her wrists.

'You are so horny I bet I could take you over the edge with friction alone.' He bucked his pelvis a couple more times.

Alannah let her head fall back as her throat released a guttural sound. Brendan was right; her climax was imminent.

'If you don't stop me now, Lana, I will do it. I will make you come all over me.' His tone was low and threatening in the sexiest way possible.

A distant part of her brain screamed at her to stop, but she could not hear it over her groans. She was putty in Brendan's hands and resistance was useless. His movements became harder and faster, tipping her over the edge. '*Aaah!*' He ripped the scream from her, along with her orgasm.

'Wowsers!' Brendan mumbled as she collapsed against him. He encircled her with his arms, and whispered in her ear, 'Was that possible because I turn you on like no one else can, or because Liam hasn't been taking care of your needs?'

'Could you shut up for a minute?' she mumbled against his hard chest. Guilt and shame mixed with the sweet pleasure of her afterglow.

When Brendan caressed her head, Alannah trembled. It was too much to process. She clambered free of his hold and curled up on the opposite side of the sofa.

He regarded her with darting eyes, as though she was a wild animal.

After a few deep breaths, she relaxed her muscles. A glimpse of the wet patch on Brendan's jeans set her cheeks on fire. 'You… uh… might want to change those.'

'Nah, I'm good. In fact, I doubt I'll ever wash them again.'

She screwed up her nose. 'That's disgusting.'

'There's nothing gross about your sexual juices, Lana. I didn't have you pegged for the type to be self-conscious about them either.'

'I'm not, but those jeans will turn rank after a while.'

He grinned. 'I'll cross that bridge when I come to it.'

Alannah sighed. 'I still haven't made my decision, Brendan.'

After jumping to his feet, Brendan spun to face her. 'What else is there to think about? You've already listed about six ways in which I'm better than Liam, some of which are a pretty big deal in my opinion. And the chemistry between us is *so* off the charts you just sprayed the evidence all over me. What more do you need?'

Rising, she faced him head on. 'I need commitment—something I can't trust a playboy like you to give me.' She escaped down his hallway as tears burst forth, cascading down her enflamed cheeks like the rains of a summer storm breaking a heat wave.

When she reached her car, Alannah pressed her forehead against the cool metal roof and tried to catch her breath. But she did not get to draw in the much-needed air because her head filled with immense pain, turning everything black as her legs gave way.

'Hot damn, Lana! They look like real handcuffs.'

Alannah smirked at Brendan as she cuffed his naked body to the bed. 'I stole them from Liam. Now I have you, there's no way I'm letting you escape.'

He felt his already hard cock twitch in response. 'I've already promised to never leave you, but if this is what it takes to convince you, I won't complain.'

Squeezing his dick in her dainty hands, she smirked. 'I don't see any complaints here either.' She ran her calloused fingers along his shaft, drawing a loud groan from his diaphragm. A moment later, she eased herself onto him, wrapping him in her tight, wet folds.

'Gods, you feel incredible, Lana.' The sight of her long black hair falling across her bare breasts as she mounted him was the most erotic thing Brendan had ever seen. She rode him. Hard. So hard, the sound of the bed banging against the wall deafened him.

'Oh Gods! Slow down, gorgeous, or I'm not gonna last.'

But she did not listen to him. Her own climax came within seconds, curtailing Brendan's guilt when his own release poured into her seconds later.

Oddly, the sound of the bed banging against the wall continued even as she collapsed in his arms. *And why is the strawberry scent in her hair fading?*

Brendan jack-knifed into a sitting position on his bed. The vivid dream left his face dripping with sweat and his legs sticky from his own release. And the damn knocking on his front door persisted. He was tempted to ignore it, *but what if it's Lana*? After cleaning himself with a tissue, he slipped into his track pants and dragged his sluggish body to the door.

Instead of bright green eyes, glacial blue ones burning like dry ice greeted him. 'Where is she?' Liam demanded.

'What?' he blinked his bleary eyes, wiping away some sleep.

'I swear to the Gods you're as good as dead if she slept with you.'

'Hold up bro, what the hell's your problem?' Not wanting to air their dirty laundry outside any longer, Brendan opened the screen door to let Liam inside. He stalked down the hall in search of much needed coffee.

'Alannah! Get your arse out here,' Liam screamed as he barged into Brendan's room.

Wow! He never uses her full first name. Did she tell him what happened last night? Brendan opened a jar of instant coffee. It was inferior to the real stuff, but it did the trick when he was desperate for a quick fix. 'Lana's not here.'

'I call bullshit! Why is her car still parked out the front after she didn't come home last night?'

The jar slipped from his fingers and smashed on the floor as Brendan's jaw dropped. 'What?'

Liam grabbed Brendan by his throat. 'You heard me. Now where is she hiding?'

A snarl escaped Brendan's lips. 'I told you, she's not here. Lana didn't stay here last night. If she didn't go home, something happened to her.'

'Shit!' Liam dropped Brendan and moved into the lounge area where he paced across the floor.

Brendan swept the broken glass to the edge of the room, too frantic to bother picking it up. 'You should have more faith in her, *Brother*. You never deserved Lana.'

'And what makes you think a perverted player like you has any right to her either?'

'Fuck you.' He was not in the mood to argue. Alannah was missing. 'We have bigger things to worry about right now.'

'Do you have any idea where she might be?' Liam begged.

'No, but I could use my emotional connection with Lana to track her magically.'

Liam scowled at him and sighed. 'Fine. I'll put a call in at the station to see if I can get a unit deployed to help.' He approached the front door and paused. 'Call me as soon as you get a read on her.'

'Trust me, Brother, if I get a read on her, I'm not gonna wait for you before tearing into the arsehole who is doing Gods know what to her.'

Liam winced. 'Just call me, okay!' He stormed out of the house.

As soon as Brendan finished dressing, he rang Nick.

'Hey man, what's up?'

'I need your help. We have a serious problem.'

Pain was the first thing Alannah noticed when she awoke. Agony. Her head throbbed with the intensity of a hundred hangovers, and the skin of her wrists and ankles was raw from chaffing against the metal cuffs shackling her against the bumpy metal wall. But despite the aching and stinging, she found the strength to meditate.

A deep laugh cut through the dark room. 'Good luck escaping those restraints, Miss Winters. They are pure, cold iron: the only material known to block the flow of magic.'

Why is his voice familiar? Alannah's skin prickled as she took stock of her physical state. Her clothes remained, except for the boots, and she sensed the amulet against her chest. *Thank the Gods!*

'The feel of your fear flowing through me is quite intoxicating, Alannah. More so than the naughty orgasm you shared with your lover's brother.' Her captor's voice drew closer.

'W…what do you w…want?' Her lips trembled. A match came to life in her face and she squinted at the sudden brightness.

When his face came into focus, he leered at her. 'The truth. It's all I've ever wanted. But I should know better than to expect it from a woman. You're all filthy, lying whores, the lot of you.' He extinguished the match against Alannah's inner arm, bringing forth her gut-wrenching scream. 'Do you know what they did to whores like you in the witch-hunts of old?' The Inquisitor lit another match.

Alannah glared at Richard with tears welling in her eyes.

'They burned them alive.'

He doused the flame on the exact same patch of skin and she screamed louder still.

'Tell me, Alannah, what do you know about channelling nether?'

She gasped, failing to draw in enough oxygen. 'It's dangerous and against the law. Use of the stygian element is the only known way to summon demons.'

'How very textbook of you.' He lit another match. 'Now tell me who has channelled it recently.'

'I don't know anyone who messes with nether.'

'I think you do.' He blew the match out in her face, the smoke stinging her eyes as it filled her nostrils.

When he stepped away, she breathed again. The flicker of another flame brought the room into view and Alannah realised he was lighting a few candles on a small table a metre away. But her eyes fell on the torture instruments beside the candles and her heart sank into the pits of the Underworld.

'Here's what we're going to do, Alannah. You're going to tell me everything you know about the practice of dark magic in this state. I want names and locations. Including anything involving the production of Rhapsody. And in turn, I won't satisfy this strong desire I have to break your mind, body, and soul.'

'I don't know anything.'

A rictus grin formed on his face. 'I'd hoped you'd resist for a bit because I am going to enjoy this.' Richard stepped up to her with a scalpel in his hand. He cut her shirt down the middle and ran the blade across her bare stomach.

It stung like nobody's business and a small line of blood trickled down her front.

'Do you have anything to tell me now?' he demanded.

'I honestly don't know anything or anyone.'

Another cut, this time along her chest. 'How about now?'

'No,' she spat out.

The Inquisitor continued to inflict small cuts upon her body until the torment became unbearable and she passed out, praying the Gods would take her soul.

Chapter Thirteen

'Is this Scarlett's doing?'

Brendan shook his head. 'No. I got a pretty clear read on her last night. She doesn't want to hurt Lana.'

Nick sighed. 'So, I guess you know who Scarlett is?'

'Yeah. And thanks for the heads up, bro.'

'Hey, Alannah swore me to secrecy. I can't go breaking her trust.'

'I know. I'm sorry.' Brendan closed his eyes to focus on the link. 'Turn left at the end of this street.'

'How do you know her captor wants to hurt her?'

After taking a deep breath, Brendan opened his eyes. 'Because I can feel her pain.' *And it hurts beyond the Celestial Realm*. After their intimate moment the previous night, Brendan was more in tune with Alannah than ever. She was almost a complete mana source on her own.

'Oh. Sorry man.' Nick fell silent.

Brendan did not complain. The quiet helped him concentrate on the connection. As much as it pained him, it also drew him closer to finding her; to freeing her. Holding on to that scrap of hope kept him going. He refused to entertain the possibility of being too late.

Ten minutes later they drove along an unfamiliar dirt track and Brendan was thankful for the four-wheel drive feature in Nick's car. 'Stop here.'

'But there ain't nothin' here.' Nick was half right: they had reached a desolate paddock without so much as a single cow in sight.

'I can feel her close. There has to be something hidden here.'

'Okay, I'm trusting you on this.' He parked along the embankment and jumped out.

Brendan followed him, closing his eyes after a moment to tune into Alannah again. 'This way.' He took off at a run.

'Wait up, man!' Nick's feet came pounding after him.

They were sprinting at break-neck speed when Brendan slipped and fell down a set of concrete steps recessed in the ground. '*Ah, bugger!*'

Nick squatted beside him. 'You okay?'

'I twisted my ankle. Who leaves a damn hole in the ground like this unguarded?'

'Whoever it was didn't expect company. Look,' Nick pointed.

Peering further into the depths of the pothole, Brendan's eyes landed on a door. Alannah's signal was weak, but he was sure she was beyond the door.

'Here, let me help you up.'

He accepted Nick's hand, leaning on him as he limped down the steps. The corrugated iron structure buried in the ground put Brendan in mind of the old Anderson-style bomb shelters from World War II. The dishevelled nature of the materials suggested that very purpose.

The lock on the bunker did not deter Nick. The orc made quick work of the door with the old hip and shoulders.

As soon as they entered, Brendan gagged at the smell of burnt flesh. The room was gloomy, with only a hint of light coming in through the door. It took a moment for his eyes to adjust, but when they did, his heart sank. 'Oh hell.'

Alannah slumped, unconscious in her chains. He limped up to her and checked her for signs of life. His own breathing resumed when he felt the faint tickle of air escaping her parted lips. As soon as he noticed the tattered scraps of fabric failing to cover her, Brendan swallowed the bile pushing its way up. 'What kind of sick bastard did this to her?!'

Nick, who had remained near the door, sauntered over. 'By the Gods. Are they burn marks?'

'Looks like it, along with a million shallow cuts.' Brendan was hard pressed to find an unharmed patch of skin on the front of her body. It took all his strength to fight back the threat of tears. It was not time to let them out; Alannah needed him. 'Give me a hand with these manacles.'

With another display of raw strength, Nick ripped the chains from the wall, releasing Alannah's limp form into Brendan's hold. He stumbled under her miniscule weight, forgetting his injury.

'Why don't you let me carry her? You shouldn't put too much pressure on your ankle.'

'Don't. I need to do this.' There was no way in hell he was letting her go until she woke up, even then he might not. Reminding himself the discomfort he felt was nothing compared to what Alannah had gone through, he ignored the pain.

'The arsehole who did this is pretty lucky we didn't catch him.' Nick mused as they walked up the steps. 'I wouldn't be able to stop myself from killing the prick if he were here right now.'

'I know how you feel.' Brendan conceded to Nick's supporting him as they crossed the paddock. Once he had settled into the back seat with Alannah resting against him, he got on the phone.

'Yes, Brendan?' Ross answered with the sounds of a social gathering in the background.

'Drop whatever you're doing and meet me at your place.'

'Brendan I won't—'

'Lana is unconscious and injured. I pulled her out of some nightmarish torture dungeon, so don't give me your damn excuses.'

'Okay, calm down son. I'll be there. Maybe open with that next time.'

'Whatever, just be there.' He hung up and considered ringing Liam. But when he gazed down at Alannah, the tears threatened again. Liam could wait. It did not even matter if Nick was witness to his breakdown. It was happening. One loud sob after another resounded through the vehicle's cabin. Brendan did not cry often, but when he did it was always because of Alannah: she was the only woman who got under his skin and tugged on his heart strings.

Even Ross paled at the sight of Alannah when he greeted them. 'Bring her into the first guestroom.'

Brendan hobbled in through the front door with Nick's help. 'Thanks man, I'll take it from here. I'll call you when she's awake.'

'No worries.' Nick slapped him on the back and left.

'Looks like you're injured too,' Ross observed.

'I'll be fine. Focus on Lana.'

'Oh Gods!' Mum gasped as soon as she approached. 'The poor, sweet girl.'

With Alannah settled on the bed, Brendan sat beside her and removed what was left of her clothes. He rested a hand on her arm.

'I need room to work, son.'

'You'll have to work around me, 'cause I'm not moving from her side until she's better.'

Ross started to argue but sighed and got to work. He set up her drip, before cleaning and dressing her wounds with healing ointments. When he reached her pubic region, he looked at Brendan. 'Do you know if…'

Fresh tears sprang to Brendan's eyes. 'No idea.'

After a deep breath, Ross Winters adopted a professional mask to perform the internal examination. 'There is no sign of tearing or discharge in either opening.'

Brendan let out the breath he had been holding. 'Thank the Gods.'

Once her visible injuries were tended to, Ross used his attunements to assess the extent of her head injuries. 'She has a severe concussion. I'll give her a magical boost; the healing tincture in her drip should do the rest.' Laying his hands upon her forehead, Dad closed his eyes and performed his magic. Rising, he handed a potion to Brendan. 'She'll be okay. Take that for your injury.'

Brendan nodded and skulled the tonic. 'Thanks.'

'Does Liam know?'

'Not yet. I'll contact him in a minute.'

'Okay. Call me if either of you need anything.' His father left the room, closing the door behind him.

Being careful not to dislodge the drip, Brendan turned Alannah onto her side to snuggle up behind her. Not wanting to risk touching any of the wounds on her front, he kept his free hand on her shoulder blade. He drew the blanket up to cover them both, letting the rest of his tears flow free.

About an hour later, Alannah stirred and moaned. 'Urghm.'

'Are you okay, Lana?'

'Brendan?'

'Yes, Lana?'

'Did you save me?'

'With Nick's help, yeah I got you out of there.'

'Thank you.' She sucked in a deep breath. 'Everything hurts and I'm tired.'

'I know. I'm sorry, gorgeous.' He kissed her shoulder. 'Go back to sleep. We can talk later.'

'Please hold me.' She spoke with a faint whisper.

'I am holding you.'

'I mean properly.' She reached back for his hand and pulled it forward.

'Are you sure? I don't want to hurt you.'

'This is fine.' She let his hand rest on her bare stomach.

Brendan felt the new piercing in her belly button and half a smile tugged at his lips. It was a bittersweet feeling to have Alannah sleeping in his arms given the circumstances.

Liam was on the verge of conniptions when he got off the phone to his dad. *That little punk didn't call!*

He had spent the better part of the day driving around in a daze searching for Alannah when Brendan had rescued her over two hours ago.

As soon as he got to his parent's place, he flew through the door and into the first guestroom. The sight of Brendan spooning Alannah brought his blood bubbling to the surface. 'What the hell do you think you're doing?'

Brendan glanced up at him and Liam was taken aback by the red, puffy appearance of his eyes. 'Shoosh. She's sleeping.'

It had been years since he had seen evidence of Brendan crying. Liam sat on the edge of the bed and peered down at her. She appeared peaceful. 'What happened?' he whispered.

'I don't know. She was out cold when I found her.' Brendan sucked in an audible breath. When he continued speaking, his voice shook with emotion. 'Her condition was nasty, Liam. Covered in millions of cuts and burns.'

'Gods!' Liam ran his fingers along the side of Alannah's face.

Her eyes flickered open. 'Liam?'

'I'm here, gorgeous.' He leaned down to press a kiss on her lips.

'Please hold me.'

Liam smiled. 'Of course, baby.' He glared at Brendan. 'You can go now.'

'No, please. I need both of you.' She batted her lashes atop her brilliant green orbs.

When he glanced at Brendan, Liam half expected a smirk, but there was no trace of levity in his brother's expression.

Liam sighed as he removed his boots. 'Okay, gorgeous.'

She was asleep again when he returned. Lifting the blanket, Liam was greeted by another infuriating sight and he glared at Brendan. 'The hell? She's naked. Get your filthy hands off her, you pervert.'

'Calm your crazy, bro. Lana's injured. There's nothing suss going on.' Brendan slid his hand across her stomach, along her hip, and up to her shoulder.

'Looks pretty damn suss to me.' Liam slipped under the blanket and nestled up to Alannah's front.

'Get over yourself, Snowflake, and be a good boyfriend for once,' Brendan deadpanned.

Liam felt a growl slip from his throat, but he bit his lip to hold back from arguing.

Alannah felt safe, warm, and loved as she lay there cocooned in the arms of her two favourite men. It was a shame her blissful bubble would have to burst once she recovered. *Can I pretend for a while? It sucks that I needed to be injured to get both Liam and Brendan in bed with me at once.* Visions of a threesome consumed her, sending a rush of blood through her veins.

Brendan chuckled in her mind. *'Are you having sexy thoughts, Lana? Are they about me or Liam?'*

Alannah blushed. With payback in mind, she nudged her backside against Brendan.

But he reciprocated by pressing his hardon against her, sending more signals through her bloodstream and straight to her core.

She should have known better, after all their years of playing Sleazy Chicken. *He was never bluffing.* Nonetheless, Alannah loved pushing Brendan's boundaries, or lack thereof.

After another small thrust from Alannah, Brendan's hand moved from her shoulder down to her arse and swatted it. *'Careful, Lana, or I'll bang you right here, in front of Liam.'*

A small moan slipped out as arousal pooled between her legs.

'Or is that what you want?' Brendan's hand slid down her arse until his fingertips brushed against her clit. *'Mm. I love how wet you get for me, gorgeous.'*

Clenching her teeth did not stop the hissed curse escaping: *'Jesus!'*

Liam's eyes shot open with concern. 'Shit! Are you okay, Lana? I didn't hurt you, did I?'

When Brendan's hand moved back to her shoulder, she sucked in a deep breath. 'No. I'm okay.'

His countenance relaxed. 'How are you feeling?'

'Much better.'

'That's reassuring.' Liam touched the cannula on her hand. 'You probably don't need this anymore. Are you awake, Brendan?'

'Yeah.' Brendan's breath tickled Alannah's neck as he spoke.

'Why don't you go get Dad?'

'Okay.' But Brendan did not budge.

Liam growled. 'Now would be good.'

'Relax, bro, I'm sending him a telepathic message.'

Tension formed in the set of Liam's jaw, but he let the issue slide and focussed on Alannah. 'Do you know who did this to you?'

Alannah had tried to recall the source of her injuries a few times as she drifted in and out of sleep but kept drawing a blank. 'I don't remember.'

Liam's hand, which had been resting on her waist, came up to her face. 'Fair enough. It must have been too traumatic.'

'What happened to me? What were my injuries?'

Glancing over her shoulder, Liam looked to Brendan. 'Should I tell her?'

Brendan took a deep breath as he rubbed her arm. 'Yeah. Lana's ready.'

When Liam peered into her eyes, tears welled in his own. 'You must have been abducted when leaving Brendan's place last night. Your car was still out front this morning. I'm sorry, Lana, but I assumed the worst of you when you didn't come home. I knew you were at Brendan's because I saw your Tesla there on my way home. I spent the night waiting up for you and… But if I'd gone to confront you earlier…' A tear slipped from his eye.

She brushed it away with her thumb. 'It's okay. Go on.'

'Brendan found you in an old bomb shelter. You were chained to the wall with cold iron and…' His Adam's apple bobbed. 'Your clothes were ripped to shreds and you were covered in cuts and burns.'

They burned them alive. Alannah remembered the smell of burning flesh, her flesh. And the pain. 'Oh Gods, I'm gonna spew.' She sat up.

Liam seized a bucket from the floor. 'Here.'

As she leaned forward to empty her stomach, Brendan pulled her hair back—a simple yet touching gesture. He topped it off by stroking her back with his other hand.

Ross entered as she finished retching. 'Hmm. It might be too early to remove your drip.' He pressed his hand to her forehead and frowned. 'You're still concussed, Alannah. Can I see the rest of your wounds?'

Alannah bobbed her head as she handed her sick bowl to Liam. It felt awkward having her Uncle see her naked, even if he was a doctor. She lowered the blanket.

'Look away now, Brother,' Liam demanded.

'Are you forgetting how I found her?'

'Don't make me poke your eyes out.'

Alannah sighed. 'And the truce ends.' She had removed the blanket by this stage and looked down at herself. Aside from a lot of ointment residue, there were no signs of the cuts and burns that had covered her skin.

'They have healed well,' Ross observed. 'You can put a night gown on now.'

Liam let out a sigh of relief as he grabbed a white cotton slip from the bedside table. He disconnected the tubing from Alannah's hand and helped her into the nightie.

She watched as Ross replaced the empty IV bag with another pouch of clear fluid. He refitted the tube to her cannula and studied her with knitted brows. 'How's your stomach feeling? Are you ready for food?'

Her stomach growled as if on cue. 'I think that's a yes.'

Ross smiled. 'I'll see if Nora can fix you a sandwich.'

'Thanks.' When he left, Alannah sat back against the headboard and closed her eyes. The rest of her memories hit her, and she winced. *The Inquisitor*.

Brendan stiffened beside her as if he had read her mind.

'Liam, could you please get me a clean change of clothes from home?'

'I'm sure Mum has something you can wear when the time comes,' Liam suggested.

She sighed. 'I need to talk to Brendan. Alone.'

Liam's eyes flashed through a symphony of emotions. But rather than voice his thoughts, he leaned forward and kissed her lips before leaving the room.

'Caleb wasn't wrong about Richard's love of torture.'

'Oh hell! What was he trying to extract from you?'

'Everything I know about dark magic in the state, including the production of Rhapsody.'

Tears shimmered in Brendan's eyes, which were red and puffy. 'I'm so damn sorry, Lana.'

'Hey, don't you dare blame yourself. Besides, the potion business wasn't his main reason for capturing me. Richard's primary concern was the recent channelling of nether.'

Brendan's eyes burst wide open. 'But Scarlett said it couldn't be detected.'

'I guess there are some Council secrets she doesn't know. I'm going to arrange to meet her tomorrow and put a hold on the training sessions for now. We all need to lay low while the Inquisitor is in town.'

Brendan gnawed at his lip a moment. 'Did he, uh, get anything from you?'

'No. The shield was still active until I passed out the first time. By the time he found and removed it, I was too weak to think about much at all. He mentioned something about bringing in an abjurer to heal me and start the process all over again. I guess you found me while he was out.'

'Yeah, not a minute too soon either. You were barely holding on when I got there.' A few tears slid down Brendan's cheek. 'I thought I was going to lose you, Lana.'

She pulled him in for a hug. 'Hey, it's okay. I'm fine, thanks to you.' Alannah let him sob in her arms for a few minutes.

A knock sounded at the door before Nora entered with two plates of sandwiches. 'I thought you might be hungry too, Brendan.'

Still clinging to Alannah, Brendan turned to face Nora. 'Thanks Mum.'

'I'll leave them here.' She put the plates on the dressing table and dashed out the door.

'I reckon Nora knows something's going on between us.'

Brendan wiped his face with his sleeve and smiled. 'She's always known how we feel about each other.' He rose and grabbed their food.

Alannah nibbled at her sandwich, not wanting to risk a relapse of the upchucks. Brendan, on the other hand, scoffed his. As she watched him eat, a question formed in Alannah's mind that she could not hold back any longer. 'How did you find me?'

He looked up from his meal and swallowed his last bite. 'I could feel you.'

She gasped. 'What do you mean?'

After placing the empty plate on his bedside table, Brendan shuffled closer to her and placed his hand on her bare thigh. 'I have a strong empathic link to you, Lana. Since you returned five years ago, I've been able to feel what you feel, even with a bit of distance between us. It's not always active and I can switch it on at will if I need or want to.'

She stared at him. 'Do you have the link with anyone else?'

'No. I need to be actively channelling to feel other people's emotions; and even then, I can't pinpoint who is who unless I can see their auras.'

The air around her felt like a sauna. 'What does it, uh, feel like?'

'I imagine I feel whatever you do. The same emotions, identical sensations.' He trailed a finger up her leg. 'Just like I can feel this on my own leg as well as the pleasure response it evokes. The main difference—' his hand reached her apex—'is when you feel something on or in your *feminine* parts.'

Alannah whimpered as he flicked her swollen bud, almost dropping her sandwich.

'In that case,' Brendan continued toying with her as he spoke in his deep bedroom voice, 'my body translates the feeling into something more *masculine*.'

She flung the rest of her food aside and arched her back as the intensity of her arousal increased. *Holy heck! He isn't even inside me, but Gods do I want him to be!*

'Do you want more, Lana?'

Biting her lip, she nodded.

Grinning with wicked delight, Brendan plunged two fingers deep inside, pulling an orgasm straight out of her. 'I'd love to do much more to you, gorgeous, but you are still recovering from head trauma. Best if we go easy on you, yeah?'

'Thanks,' she rasped.

'For the orgasm or the reprieve?'

Alannah smiled. 'Both.'

'My pleasure, *as you know*.'

Chapter Fourteen

The woman in red used powerful illusionary magic, which most mages would not detect, to hide herself. But Richard's secret attunement allowed him to pierce the veil. Sitting in a dark corner of the café, he watched as she took her usual seat by the window. *Strange how she chooses to sit facing in rather than make the most of what her seaside vista has to offer. Perhaps it is to avoid an unsuspecting human sitting in her lap.*

Grabbing his tablet, he opened the file he had been compiling with what he knew about her thus far. After rereading his last entry: *Powerful magic user, but not a registered mage. Possible dark mage or cursed?* He glanced at her again, adding: *Also appears familiar, but from where?*

Richard almost called for another coffee refill when a new arrival caught his attention.

'Hi hun. Will it be the usual today?'

'Yeah, thanks Brigette.' Alannah Winters stood at the counter looking as healthy as ever. She had been laying low since her escape from his custody a few days ago, only stepping out in public with one of her devoted cousins. But this time she had an orc with her. *Curious.*

His interest piqued further when she sat at the red woman's table. Richard used a far-sighted spell to get a better view of the two women together. *Holy realms! No wonder Red is familiar!* The family resemblance was striking.

Red smiled at Alannah. 'Hello, dear child.' She glanced at the orc. 'Hello, Nick.'

'Hello, Madam,' Alannah's replied telepathically.

The orc remained silent.

Thinking quick, Richard grabbed an amethyst chip from his satchel and inserted it into the SD slot of his smartphone. The magic tech would allow him to record telepathic communication. He took a quick photograph of them together and opened a voice recording app.

'Do you wish to schedule another training session?'

'No, Lady Scarlett. We need to put those on hold for a while. At least until the Inquisitor leaves town.'

Scarlett, huh? Fitting name. Why didn't I think of it? It is better than Red.

'Oh?' Scarlett inquired.

'Don't ask me how, but he detected your channelling the other day.'

Bingo! Richard's intuition never led him astray.

Scarlett laughed. 'The shady fellow must have some unsanctioned tricks of his own. He sounds like a worthy opponent.'

'Please be careful of him. He's cruel and sadistic; something I barely lived to tell you about. If Brendan hadn't...'

Scarlett's eyes widened. 'He caught you? What did you tell him?'

'Nothing. And I'm fine now, Grandmother, thanks for asking.'

Wait? Did she address Scarlett as her grandmother? Richard grinned. *Oh, this is too good.*

'I told you to address me formally, you silly girl.'

'It's not like anyone is listening right now.'

'That we know of.'

Alannah paled, scanning the café.

Richard pretended to read the paper as he sipped from his empty cup. He was confident his own glamour spell would hold up, so mages would only see an old human man sitting there.

'There are no magic auras here,' Alannah observed.

Having enough evidence, Richard folded the paper, ceased the recording and snuck out of the café, not sparing either of the women or the orc another glance.

With Liam and Brendan both back at work, Alannah had spent the days following her abduction hanging out at Nick's orchard. She refused to go out in public without one of the guys with her, and Liam agreed she needed the protection. Liam still did not know who had kidnapped her, but he knew Alannah was keeping secrets again and he did not hide his displeasure from her. She might have felt guilty if he had not been such an aloof ass about it.

Brendan, on the other hand, had been vigilant, checking in on her every chance he got. He also toned down the flirting and intimate contact after telling Alannah the ball was in her court. It was odd. He was almost the perfect gentleman. Almost. Brendan would always be mischievous and cheeky to some extent, but she would not have him any other way.

Following the afternoon meeting with Scarlett, Nick dropped Alannah off at Brendan's apartment.

The door flew open, and Brendan pulled her inside for a massive bear hug. 'Hey, gorgeous. Miss me?'

Alannah tried to laugh with the small amount of air left in her lungs, but it came out as a wheeze.

'You're squashing her,' Nick remarked.

Brendan released her and bumped Nick's fist. 'Hey, bro, thanks for looking after my girl.'

She gave Brendan an exaggerated eye-roll before turning to Nick. 'Thanks again. Same time tomorrow?'

'No worries, sweet.'

As soon as Nick left, Alannah walked down the hall. 'Got any movies in mind for tonight?'

'No. I was gonna let you pick.' Brendan followed close behind her.

'Do I still get to pick the pizza toppings?'

'Of course.' When they reached the living area, he grabbed her arm, spinning her around to face him. 'Hey, how'd the meeting go?'

'Fine. Scarlett agreed to postpone further training.'

'That's a relief.' He pulled out his phone, loaded the food delivery app and handed it to her. 'Here, go wild.'

She arched her brow. 'You should be careful about giving me such open invitations.'

He laughed, pushing himself up to sit on the kitchen bench. 'Why? There isn't anything I wouldn't let you do to me.'

Alannah sucked in an audible breath. 'Anything?'

Brendan nodded. 'Yup.'

A wicked grin tugged at her lips. 'Even spinach pizza?'

'Oh hell. Are you trying to kill me, woman?'

She huffed. 'Fine. We'll go with the usual unhealthy crap.'

'I'm glad we have an understanding, gorgeous.'

After submitting the pizza order, Alannah slumped on the plush suede couch and slipped her shoes off. She started flicking through movie options on a streaming app when the doorbell startled her. 'That was quick.'

Brendan rose. 'I'll get it. You keep searching.'

Alannah heard voices at the door, followed by two sets of footsteps approaching. Her eyes grew wide when Liam appeared. 'Oh, hey. I thought you had a Council Meeting tonight.'

'I do. And so do you.'

She frowned. 'Liam, we talked about this. I don't feel comfortable about going after what Monique did.'

He sighed. 'I know, but High Magus Kieran specifically requested your presence tonight.'

Alarm bells rang in her head. 'Why?'

'I don't know. He just asked me to make sure you show up.'

'And if I don't?'

'I'm not going to force you, Lana. But I can't imagine you'll still have your seat if you refuse an official summons.'

'Fine.' She put her shoes back on and dragged herself up. 'Sorry, Brendan; looks like you'll have to eat my share of the pizza tonight.'

Brendan shrugged. 'I can take one for the team.' During their farewell embrace, he whispered to her, 'Good luck, gorgeous.'

Liam clutched her hand and led her out to the car.

Bat sized butterflies held a party in Alannah's chest as she sat in the Council meeting room. The other councillors' glares did not help either. At least Liam kept a supportive hold of her hand.

Monique entered to announce both Kieran and Richard's arrival and Alannah's heart did backflips as she rose with everyone else.

'Please be seated,' Kieran ordered. 'Now, before we commence our usual business, Inquisitor Lane has an important matter to bring to the table.'

'Thank you, High Magus.' Richard grinned at Alannah.

Crapola!

He pulled a phone out of his pocket. 'While I know the main purpose of my visit has been to find the source of that accursed potion, Rhapsody, another dark magic problem has come to my attention—one I can't ignore. I present my first piece of evidence.'

After hitting a button on the touch screen, a voice recording commenced: '*Do you wish to schedule another training session?*'

Dread settled in the pit of Alannah's stomach when she heard Scarlett's voice. *Surely Richard didn't get the other side of the conversation?*

Her own voice came through clear as day.

'*No, Lady Scarlett. We need to put those on hold for a while. At least until the Inquisitor leaves town.*'

Every eye in the room was on her. With a trembling lip, she turned to Liam for help. His mouth drew a hard line as he leaned in and whispered, 'Is this about the unsanctioned training?'

She nodded.

Liam's eyes widened. '*Damnit!*' He squeezed Alannah's hand and held her gaze in a show of support. At the mention of Richard's torture, compassionate tears hovered in his eyes. But they vanished as he dropped her hand and gaped the moment the recording revealed Scarlett's identity.

When the recording ended, Richard stood, and his malicious voice boomed across the table. 'Warlocks, seize Councillor Alannah.'

Clayton jumped to obey, but Liam moved in slow motion.

Tears streamed down her face as they pulled her from the chair.

'Alannah Winters, by the authority of The Council of Mages, I am placing you under arrest.'

Cold iron cuffs clamped her wrists behind her back.

'You are charged of treason and under suspicion of practising dark magic.'

Liam stood gobsmacked and frozen in front of her while Clayton frisked her for weapons and magic tools. She winced when he groped her between the legs.

'You are not obliged to say anything, however anything you do say can be used in evidence against you.'

Clayton led Alannah out of the room, with Liam close beside her. The holding cells were in the Council chamber's basement, sparing her the humiliation of walking outside in public view.

They stopped in a stuffy storage room where Clayton shoved her into Liam's arms. 'Out of respect for you, Liam, I'll let you do the strip search, but I will have to watch to make sure you don't miss anything.' He grabbed two empty plastic tubs from the shelves and placed them on a nearby bench. The yellow one for *Personal Effects*, while the red one was for *Evidence*.

Liam turned her around and looked down at her with arctic eyes as Clayton removed her cuffs. 'Remove all of your clothes slowly and hand each item to me.' None of the usual tenderness or excitement laced his request. As she removed her panties, Alannah heard Liam growl. 'Stop enjoying yourself, Clay.'

'I'm sorry, man, but it's not every day we get to apprehend such a fine piece of arse.'

Her cheeks burned.

Liam glared at Clayton, his eyes turning from arctic ice to molten lava. 'Shut your trap before I do it for you.'

Clayton raised his hands in supplication. 'Okay, chill out, bro. Please, continue.'

Liam grimaced when his attention returned to Alannah's naked body. 'You have to squat and cough now.'

She blanched, slipping into stunned silence. *I can't believe the Council uses such an intrusive procedure.*

'Alannah, please don't make this any harder than it needs to be.' His eyes pleaded with her.

She gulped, sinking to the floor in a squatting position. After coughing, she opened her mouth for Liam to peer inside with a small torch. *It is absurd. What the hell am I going to hide in my throat or mouth?*

'It's a routine precaution, Alannah,' Liam explained. 'If I don't go through the motions they could accuse me of nepotism, or worse.'

Alannah gave a silent nod, closing her eyes as Liam's hands continued searching the rest of her cavities. *At least it is Liam's hands,* she reminded herself.

'You can stand up now.'

Releasing the breath she had been holding, Alannah rose.

Liam handed her a set of teal pants and t-shirt reminiscent of surgical scrubs, along with clean white cotton underpants. 'Put these on.'

Once she finished dressing, the men logged her belongings and put them away before taking her into the bowels of the building. When the cage-like door of her cell closed her in, Clayton left. Liam remained with a sneer on his face. 'I have to return to the meeting, but I will return to talk to you as soon as it finishes.'

Probably for the best. Alannah felt too choked up to talk to him. Nodding, she took stock of her dimly lit surroundings. The first thing she noticed was the single bed, followed by a drinking fountain to her right, along with a toilet and wash basin sat in the left corner. The walls were some type of granite judging by the grey and white colouring. They were all lined with metal bars extending across the ceiling and floor. Collapsing on the bed, she discovered a lumpy mattress full of broken springs, and groaned. Evidently, her comfort was not a concern for the Council. She sighed and breathed deeply, to calm the storm of emotions brewing within.

A few hours later, Alannah sprang to her feet when she heard people approaching. Clayton and Liam both wore sombre expressions when they stepped up to her prison.

'Stand back from the door,' Clayton ordered. As she did so, he unlocked the cell, letting Liam in before locking it again. 'I'll give you fifteen minutes. Buzz me if you want out earlier.'

'Thanks, man,' Liam replied.

When Clayton left, Alannah ran toward Liam, but he put a hand up to stop her. She gasped. 'Liam?'

'Don't touch me, Alannah. I'm here to clear a few things up because my head is spinning right now.' He crossed his arms and leaned against the stone wall.

Her heart sank. 'Is this an official interrogation?'

Liam sighed. 'No. They wouldn't put me in charge of your case even if I wanted them to. You and I are going to have a personal chat.'

She nodded, and sat on the bed, avoiding the worst of the springs that were hell bent on giving her a proctocolectomy.

'I don't even know where to start.' He paced the floor. A minute later, he stopped in front of her. 'Was Tara training you?'

'Yes.'

'Why *the hell* were you training with her?'

'It was a condition of obtaining the information I wanted. She promised to tell me who my bio dad was if she could help me obtain two attunements.'

Liam shook his head. 'Which attunement have you gained so far?'

'I'm not sure if it counts, but she reconnected me to an innate source I have because of the Beltane Blessing.'

'What—was it—Alannah?'

She shivered at the impersonal way he used her full first name. 'The primordial.'

His eyes bugged out. 'What the…?'

'I know, that's what I thought at first. But it's true, Liam. I can now channel any mana source I want because of it.'

'Does the Inquisitor know this? Is this why he kidnapped you?'

'No. He was more concerned about the channelling of nether.'

'*What?*' Liam's voice rose several decibels.

'She only showed me how to do it safely. I haven't attempted it myself. I swear to the Gods I have not practised any dark magic.'

He collapsed on the bed next to her and slumped into his raised knees. 'And here I thought your big secret was an affair with Brendan.'

'Liam—'

'But this is much worse.' He glared at her. 'How could you do something so dark and dangerous, with our arch nemesis, no less?'

'I—'

'And don't give me the bio dad bollocks. I'm not buying that excuse as enough to warrant the risks you took.'

'It was about my father at first. But I became invested in what Tara taught me about the primordial. For the record, I didn't know Scarlett was Tara's pseudonym when she first wrote me.'

'When did she make initial contact?'

'Early September.'

He went silent for a few minutes. 'Is Brendan part of this?'

'Not directly. He didn't even know about Tara at first, but when the Inquisitor showed up, I went to him for help.'

'Why do you always run to him, Alannah? Why didn't you come to me for help?'

She searched her heart for the truth. 'Because Brendan has always been there for me. And I was afraid you would react like this. What would you have done if I'd told you about Tara back then?'

'I would have put a stop to it and gone after the bitch.'

'It wouldn't have helped me, Liam. I needed protection from the Inquisitor, not Tara. Even when she had me locked in a dungeon cell; Tara never tortured me like Richard did. Sure, she did some messed up things, but at the end of the day, Tara didn't *want* to hurt me or my mum.'

Liam looked at the ceiling as if it could provide some insight. 'I can't believe I'm hearing this. Tara is poisoning your mind.'

'No, Liam. The Council is poisoning our minds… like hiding the truth of the Beltane Blessing.'

'I've heard enough of this rubbish.' Jumping up, he grabbed the bars of the door, pressing his forehead against them. He turned to glare at her. 'Now tell me the damn truth. Have you been screwing Brendan?'

'No, Liam. How many times do I have to tell you?' *Those two unexpected orgasms didn't count, right?*

'But you've wanted to, haven't you?'

She bit her lip, unable to deny it, especially knowing Liam heard the conversation with Emma all those years ago. 'That doesn't make me a cheater, Liam.'

'No, but it might be emotional infidelity. Are you in love with him?'

'Liam—'

'It's a simple question, Alannah. Are. You. In love with Brendan?'

She exhaled sharply. 'Yes, but—'

'Then you can call him to bail you out. We are done.' Liam pressed the intercom button, standing in silence as he stared out into the hallway.

'Liam, please listen to me.'

'No.' He continued facing away from her.

'I'm still in love with you too, Liam.'

'Doesn't matter anymore.'

'Why?'

Liam spun around to face her. 'Because you're a traitorous whore.' Pure hatred dripped from every pore. His words stabbed Alannah in the chest like a hot poker, knocking the wind from her.

Clayton appeared a moment later.

After leaving her cell, Liam paused to glance at her one last time. 'Dad was right about the women in our bloodline: you're all a damned disgrace.' He turned and left, leaving Alannah to grieve more than the loss of her freedom.

Hours passed. Alannah could not surmise more without a clock or window to the outside world. Having cried herself dry, she clambered up to the drinking fountain, savouring the feel of the cool water on her parched lips. Alannah's hands were no longer cuffed, but all attempts to connect with her attunements proved useless. She figured the bars must be cold iron, acting like a Faraday cage to block magic. She returned to the bed and attempted to rest. Sleep was futile, so she did the next best thing and slipped into a meditative trance.

The sound of a door slamming broke her reverie and she jumped to attention. Clayton appeared at her door wearing different clothes, and he was alone. 'Morning, Alannah.'

'Gee, is it morning already? How time flies.'

'That's a hilarious mouth you got there. If you weren't expected upstairs right now, I'd be tempted to learn its other talents.'

'You're a creep, Clayton,' Alannah spat in a seething tone.

He grinned wickedly. 'Don't taunt the alligator, *sweetheart*.' His pearly whites flashed at her as he leered and snapped them. He pulled a set of keys from his pocket and dangled them in front of his face. 'Now turn around and bend over the bed like a good whore.'

She stood there defiantly.

Sparks formed on his fingertips. 'Do you want me to hurt you?'

Swallowing bile, she turned and placed her hands on the bed.

The sound of the door opening and clicking shut reverberated through the room. She felt Clayton's body ram against her backside. 'Liam's not gonna defend you now, *sweetheart*.' He thrust his pelvis against her and pinched her arse. 'Mm. I bet he was too much of a prude to take you back here.' His hand slipped inside her pants and rubbed against her bare cheeks. 'Question is, have you let anyone else in this tight little hole? Like your vampire ex, perhaps?'

Alannah's eyes brimmed with tears as she shook her head.

'No? What about Brendan? I doubt he would hesitate to claim your arse, given the chance.'

She continued shaking her head.

'Hmm, this is a virgin arse? Lucky me.' His finger pressed against her puckered opening. 'You know, I've been dreaming about this ever since your striptease last night.' He removed the offending limb with a sigh. 'But my gratification will have to wait.' Tugging her arms back, he cuffed her wrists and pulled her upright. 'Come on. The High Magus wants to see you.'

Alannah squinted when they entered the ground floor corridor. Too much sunlight poured in through the windows after she had become accustomed to the gloom of her prison. She blinked with relief when they entered the lift taking her up to Kieran's office.

The High Magus did not even look at Alannah's face when she arrived. 'Please remove her restraints and leave us, Warlock Clayton.'

'Yes, Your Honour.' Clayton released her hands, slapping her on the arse before making his exit.

Kieran did not bat an eyelid at the obvious sexual harassment. 'This is your official notice of dismissal from the Council.' He handed her an envelope. 'Seraphina will finish the booking process with you, after which you will have the opportunity to post for bail.' Already appearing bored, he returned to his desk and resumed working on his computer.

His brunette half-mage secretary escorted her into an adjacent office. 'Please be seated, Miss Winters.'

Alannah sat in one of the gas-lift chairs, welcoming the relative comfort of a soft seat.

'I need you to complete this paperwork confirming your registration details.'

She reviewed the form. As a registered mage, the Council had all her vital information, including mug shot, fingerprints, blood group, and DNA samples. After Alannah signed a declaration, Seraphina handed her the *Application for Bail* form.

'Please read the conditions of bail carefully, especially the part about remaining within this Council district and making yourself available for a court appearance.'

When Alannah returned the completed papers, Seraphina signed as a witness and looked at her. 'Is there someone willing to act as your guarantor?'

Alannah's first thoughts went to Liam's hurtful dismissal, and she had to choke back the lump forming in her throat. 'I'd like to ask Brendan Winters.'

A faint smile broke the woman's otherwise neutral expression.

Oh hell, had Brendan slept with her too?

Seraphina handed her a desk phone and directory. 'Very well. Call him.'

Alannah grabbed the phone and dialled without need for the listing. Brendan's number was one of three she had memorised.

Three rings. 'Hello, Brendan Winters speaking.'

'Hey, it's me.'

'Oh, Gods, Lana, are you okay? When Mum told me what happened, I was frantic. I couldn't even sleep.'

She inhaled deeply as his deep voice flowed through her, calming every nerve. 'Yeah, I'm okay. They are letting me out on bail, but I need a guarantor. I was kinda hoping—'

'Of course, I'll do it. I'll be right over.'

Alannah smiled. 'Thanks, Brendan.'

'Anything for you, gorgeous.'

Chapter Fifteen

The memory of Alannah's ordeal kept Brendan grounded like sandbags on a hot air balloon. Without those weights, he would have floated away. *She rang me, not Liam!* He knew he should not have jumped past the conclusion and straight into epilogue territory, but neither his heart nor cock were listening to that part of his brain when he hit the pedal to the metal.

After flying across town, he parked right in front of the Council chambers, ignoring the *NO STANDING* sign, and burst through the glass doors.

'Oh, hey handsome,' the receptionist greeted him. The redhead was familiar, but he could not remember her name. She fluttered her lashes at him. 'Can I help you?'

'I have business in Kieran Lane's office.'

Her face drooped before she put her emotions in check. 'No worries, hun. I'll buzz you up. Do you know where to go?'

'Yup.' Brendan had never been in this building, but he didn't need a map. He beelined for the lift, hating every second it took to climb the five floors separating him from Alannah. He could feel her racing heart and wanted to squeeze every ounce of that worry and fear out of her, filling her with nothing but positive emotions.

The door opened on the top floor. He strode up to an office with the name plaque, *SERAPHINA BLACK*. *Oh joy, another one-night stand*. He knocked on the door.

The moment he caught sight of Alannah; their gazes locked. He pushed past the other woman and scooped Alannah up in his arms. 'Everything will be okay, gorgeous.'

Seraphina cleared her throat. 'Excuse me, Mr. Winters, but I need you to sign for Alannah's bail.'

He reluctantly let Alannah go. 'Right, of course.'

After pushing through the tedium of bureaucracy, he turned to Alannah and noticed her attire: the awful prison uniform. *Poor Lana*. 'I should have thought to bring you a change of clothes.'

'You can have these back now, Miss Winters.' Seraphina placed a yellow tray on the desk that including last night's dress. 'There's a bathroom down the hall you can change in.'

When Alannah was ready, she marched straight up to Brendan, grabbed his hand, and kept walking. 'Please get me out of this Gods forsaken place.'

Trying to keep things light, he saluted her. 'Yes, ma'am.' Truth be told, he could not wait to get out of the stuffy place either. There was a stench in the air that was far worse than defecation: it reeked of affectation.

Once seated in the Jag, Brendan smiled at Alannah. 'Let's get you home.'

Alannah took a deep breath, stopping Brendan from releasing the park brake with her hand on his. 'No. Please take me to your house.'

He tried to ignore all the cells in his body as they high-fived one another. 'Not that I'm complaining, but why my house? Have you—'

'Liam dumped me.' She spoke with a voice void of all emotion, looking at him with hollow eyes. But Brendan knew it was a mask. He could feel the pain she suppressed.

'Oh, hell! I'm sorry, Lana.'

'Why? It's what you've wanted isn't it?'

Brendan had indeed dreamt of the day that Alannah broke up with Liam, but he never wished for it to be at her expense. He had imagined her being the one to kick Liam's sorry arse out on the street. And in his fantasy, it was because she had chosen him. 'Not like this, Lana. Not with you hurting.'

She flinched.

Squeezing her hand, he gave her a reassuring smile. 'My place it is.'

The fridge was Alannah's first port of call when they got home. Brendan's new place had become a second home for her after all. She glanced over the door and grinned. 'Is that my pizza?'

'Yup. I worried about you too much to eat last night.'

It did not take her long to devour the food and wash it down with a beer, all while standing in the kitchen.

Brendan watched, his dick at half-mast while he half-frowned. 'Are you okay?'

She grabbed a couple more beers and bumped the fridge door closed with her arse. 'I feel a hell of a lot better now I've eaten. I give the hospitality in that place minus five stars.'

'Wow, okay.'

Alannah handed him one of the beers and moved to the couch.

He sat beside Alannah, pulling her into his arms. 'You don't have to hide your emotions from me anymore, Lana.'

She sighed. 'I'm not hiding them, I'm processing. And… trying not to fall apart. I feel like I've already cried enough for two lifetimes lately. I don't know if there are any tears left.' She took a few deep breaths. 'I feel so damn angry.'

'Angry with who?'

'The lot of 'em.' Alannah closed her eyes. 'But mostly Richard. And Clayton—that creep needs to burn.'

The hairs on the back of Brendan's neck prickled and violence churned deep in his gut. He sat up and gazed deep into her eyes. 'Did that bastard touch you?'

Alannah bit her lip.

'Oh hell!'

Before he could say anything more, she shook her head. 'Not like that. He couldn't keep his hands to himself; but no, he didn't take it far. Although I wouldn't put it past him, given the opportunity. I'm glad I didn't have to spend another night locked up there.'

'So am I. And I swear to the Gods next time I see the wanker I'm gonna teach him a lesson in respect.'

'Don't, Brendan. Please don't go caveman on his arse.'

'Are you kidding me? He needs to pay.'

'I agree, but Clayton's a powerful warlock and he's protected by the Council. We need to fight smarter, not stronger. The same goes for taking Richard down.'

'Why does it sound like you're cooking up a plan?'

Something mischievous gleamed in her eyes as she gave him a lopsided grin. 'Because I am.'

After picking up a few things from home, Alannah collapsed on Brendan's couch with another beer.

He cocked a brow at the sight of her sprawled out. 'You wanna skip the pub and stay in tonight?'

She gave him two thumbs up. 'Once again with the knowing what I need.'

Brendan smiled. 'I bet I know what else you need.' He chuckled at her side-eye. 'You assume I'm going to say something dirty, don't you?'

'Well you usually do.'

'Touché. But not this time. Despite popular belief, I don't always think with my dick.' He moved her legs to sit on the sofa, but instead of letting her feet drop to the floor, he pulled them into his lap, and massaged one.

Alannah threw her head back as the pleasure of his touch shot through her. 'Oh, Gods, that feels unreal. Are you sure this has nothing to do with sex?'

'Only if you want it to.'

Pulling her other foot back, she aimed a kick at his chest, but Brendan caught the offending foot.

'Careful now, Lana. A degenerate like me might mistake your actions for foreplay.'

She glared at him. 'You expect me to believe your intentions are honourable when you say stuff like that?'

He gasped. 'Hell, Lana. You think I'd pressure you? Your side of Liam's bed hasn't even grown cold yet and I know your heart still aches for him. Please, give me more credit. I was only trying to lighten the mood with some flirting.' Sighing, he pushed her feet from his lap and grabbed his own beer.

'I'm sorry, Brendan. I didn't mean to imply you would.'

Humour returned to his eyes as he gave her a big grin. 'I bet the sex with Liam was lousy.'

Alannah did not say anything, she simply rolled her eyes.

'What? Too soon? Isn't it a best friend's job to throw shade on your ex when they break your heart?'

'Yeah, but that's more Cara's domain. Things are more… complicated between us.'

'But you gotta satisfy my curiosity because you know how competitive I get with my brother. Was he any good in the bedroom?'

She sighed. On the one hand, it felt wrong to divulge this stuff with the one person that would never let Liam live it down, but on the other hand…*screw him*. 'You're right. The bedroom chemistry was way off. He wasn't into anything kinky, and he left me unsatisfied most nights of the week because he was too tired.'

'Hell! I'd never leave a woman wanting, no matter how tiring my day was. I figured he was dull, but that's unforgivable.'

Shaking her head, she tittered. 'Not everyone has your insatiable appetite for sex, Brendan. People are entitled to a rest. Besides, priorities change over time in long-term relationships.'

'Not that a playboy like myself would know much about that, though huh?' A hint of acrimony laced his tone.

Alannah snorted. 'Will you settle down if you find the right woman?'

His right eyebrow almost lifted off his face. 'That's a loaded question.'

'How so?'

His left brow joined its friend, and his eyes bored into her. 'The question assumes I haven't already found the right woman.'

She forgot to breathe for a split second. 'Have you?'

'I don't know, Lana. You tell me.'

She struggled to breath in that moment. 'So much for giving me time.'

'You asked. I'll give you all the time you need. But know this, gorgeous: none of those other girls were you. That's why I didn't commit to any of them.' Brendan leaned in close, his breath tickling the sensitive spot on her neck as he spoke into her ear. 'And as soon as you give me the green light, I will bang you six ways from Sunday.' He sat back with a twinkle in his eyes. 'I haven't forgotten your comment about kink either. I bet you like it rough.'

Alannah's lips curved into a half-smile. 'Maybe.'

'Do you like to dish out the pain, or receive it?'

She paused a moment to consider her answer, but also to read Brendan's aura. There it was: his emotions pulsed bright pink and red, confirming how much he loved and desired her. 'Receive it, mostly.' She observed the lust intensify and felt her skin tingle all over.

Puffing his breath through pursed lips, he shifted in his seat. 'That sweet mix of pleasure and pain makes for some of the steamiest sex. Just thinking about doing that stuff with you is turning me on.' His eyes narrowed: 'As you can see in my aura.'

A gasp escaped her mouth. 'I'm sorry.' She attempted a coy smile. 'But how did you know?'

'It's okay. I don't mind having you read me like a book. As for the *how*…' Brendan smirked. 'You're not the only one with a secret power or two.'

'Tell me, Brendan. How did you know?'

'I read your thoughts.'

Alannah's jaw dropped. 'When did you start reading minds?'

'When we were sixteen.'

Her skin was heating, and it began to prickle.

Brendan swept in close and seized her hands. 'Now before you get mad, hear me out. I don't always read your mind, and even then, I only get the surface thoughts.'

'But you still read me. Why?'

'Come on, Lana. Stop pretending you don't get me. When you asked me to stop reading your aura, I wanted to respect your request, but I needed a way to gauge your feelings for me.'

Glaring, Alannah shook her head. 'My thoughts are a lot more personal than my aura.'

'I know, which is why I only caught the occasional glimpse when I needed to know if things were still unrequited. And you did an effective job of shutting me out of your mind over the last few years anyway.'

Sighing, Alannah reclined into the couch. 'Before tonight, what was the last of my thoughts that you heard?'

'You were asking me about my empathic link as my finger trailed up your leg.'

She bit her lip as the memory of their sensual moment stirred the same heat and moisture between her thighs.

'You remember what was on your mind then, hmm? I wasn't planning to take things further, but it was hard to resist your mental plea to plunge that finger deep inside you.'

Withdrawing her hands from his grip, Alannah closed her eyes and focussed on a quick breathing exercise. She needed to get her hormones in check. Tempting as it was to jump Brendan's bones then and there, she needed a full night of rest after her tribulations.

'I won't read your mind again if you don't want me to.'

She opened her eyes and smiled at him. 'It's okay, Brendan. I kinda like having you in tune with me. I wish I could read *your* mind.'

He laughed. 'You sure you want in there? It's a pretty filthy place.'

Alannah grinned. 'It could be fascinating. And I am capable now with my primordial attunement.'

Brendan smirked. 'Be my guest, gorgeous. Just don't expect me to pay for your therapy bills.'

As Alannah drained the last of her beer, a huge yawn escaped. She dropped the empty bottle on the coffee table and snuggled into Brendan's side. 'Don't worry Brendan, you're the only therapist I need.' She closed her eyes.

'Gods, I love you, Lana.' Brendan's arms tightened around her as she drifted off to sleep.

Alannah inspected the crystal grid she had made with apophyllite at the centre. The gems took up all the space on the small wooden altar in Brendan's cramped training room. She stood up and faced him. 'It's ready.'

'Are you sure about this, Lana?' Brendan surveyed the altar before eyeing her.

'Yeah, I am. Smarter not stronger, remember? This is the best option.'

He sighed. 'I understand your plan, I do, but I still hate it. There must be another way. I don't like risking you. What if I do it?'

She shook her head. 'You will get in a lot more trouble if they catch you. Besides, there is still the Clayton issue to deal with.'

Grimacing, he stepped closer and pulled Alannah into his arms. 'I dislike that part of your plan the most.'

After swallowing against the lump in her throat, she squeezed both his biceps. 'I appreciate you willing to make the sacrifice, but time is not on our side. It could take you months to gain access to the stygian element. My trial date is just over two weeks away. I have a better chance of learning how to harness the power in time.'

'What if we run away and hide?'

'No. I have to do this.'

Brendan dropped his forehead to hers and sucked in a deep breath. A couple of tears fell from his eyes, dripping onto her lips. 'You are the bravest person I know.'

Her tongue darted out to taste the salty residue of Brendan's pain. The motion drew his eyes to her mouth, transfixing his gaze. She did not need to read his mind to know what he was thinking. Alannah thought it too. Her resolve teetered on the edge but giving in to the primal need would distract her too much from the bigger picture. She pushed back from him. 'I'll be okay Brendan, I promise.'

'How can you promise when dealing with such unpredictable, sadistic arseholes?'

'Because I have something they don't.'

'What?'

She smiled at him. 'Someone worth fighting for.'

He exhaled through pursed lips. 'You're pushing the limits of my restraint here.'

Yours and mine both.

Brendan's eyes flashed as he took a step toward her.

'Crap, did you hear that?'

Nodding, he took another step. One more would bring them toe to toe.

'I need to focus on the task at hand, Brendan. But if I succeed with the channelling today, we can celebrate tonight.'

The left side of his lip curled into a lopsided grin. 'Celebrate how, Lana?'

'Like a date.'

His brows launched into outer space. 'For real?'

'Yes, for real.'

'Fuck!' He beamed from ear to ear.

'Later,' she offered with a mischievous grin.

Brendan's eyes were ablaze as he leapt at her. Alannah squealed as she ducked out of the way, but he still managed to grab her by the arm and whirl her around, pinning her against the closed door. 'That better be a promise, Lana, because it's some vicious teasing if not.'

'Damn it, Brendan, you're making things hard.'

'No, Lana. *You're* making things hard.' He thrust his pelvis into her to prove his point. Do you have any idea how close I am to bending you over the altar and defiling both you and this sacred space?'

'Okay, point taken.'

Brendan gave her a lewd grin. 'Not yet, it's not. You know, I'm wondering if it might be better to screw all this sexual tension between us away before attempting to practise the dark arts.'

The fires of the Underworld would have been cooler than Alannah's skin. Biting her lip, she considered telling him.

'Tell me what, Lana?'

'Crap. That mind reading is getting frustrating.'

His right hand moved to her left breast and pinched her hard, aching nipple. 'Do you need me to redefine frustration? *Tell me.*'

Squirming from his continued torture, she let out an exasperated sigh. 'I need the sexual tension for my channelling exercise.'

Brendan's mouth fell agape, and his right hand dropped to his side. But he kept her trapped against the door with his left arm and body weight. 'Since when? Tara never mentioned anything of the sort.'

'I read about it in my book of shadows. When channelling nether, pent up sexual energy helps a newbie achieve results quicker.'

After staring at her in stunned silence for nigh on a minute, his gaze turned fierce. 'Did you just play me, Lana?'

'What? No, of course not. You should be able to feel how much I want you with your empathic link. We just need to hold out a tad longer.'

Still caging her in, he drew his bottom lip between his teeth and sucked on it. Her skin dripped with perspiration and if he did not move soon, Alannah knew she would cave.

'Please,' she pleaded in a whisper.

He drew a deep breath, stepping back. 'Fine.'

Alannah dashed across the room and snatched up the gas lighter to start the ritual before it was too late.

Brendan let out a low, sexy laugh. 'I love your enthusiasm, gorgeous.'

She would have chastised him, but he dropped to his knees on the edge of the pentagram and fell quiet. After casting the circle, Alannah channelled the primordial. Only this time, she hardwired the images in her mind to keep the channel open. 'Phew. Step one complete.' She looked at Brendan. 'Now the tricky bit. You know what to do if things get hairy?'

He nodded. 'Cut the circle and drag your sexy arse out of here.'

'Right.' Closing her eyes, she slipped back into a mindful state and visualised the Underworld, starting with the upper layer—a large, barren desert—and working her way down through the freezing tundras and glaciers, putrid swamps, and finally the Volcanic Pits that were the source of nether.

She made use of her carnal desires in those pits, picturing herself chained up as a demonic form of Brendan ravished her. The heat was sweltering, and she could feel the power start to flow through her. *By the Gods!* She thought it was pleasurable channelling lust and the primordial, but this was something else. It was like comparing the light rush of blood following a minute of hanging upside down with the adrenaline high of abseiling.

Alannah had a decision to make. She could either stop the exercise and sever her link to the most erotic power source of all, or she could keep the gateway open. Her body cried out for a release; so, she moved her hand between her legs to bring on the climax she yearned for. As the release came, Alannah made her connection to the forbidden mana permanent, thus sealing her fate.

Opening her eyes, she glanced at Brendan's gobsmacked expression and grinned. 'It's date time.'

Brendan licked his lips. 'Can I bang you first?'

She laughed. 'That's not how dates work, Brendan. The sex usually comes at the end of the night *if* you're lucky.'

He scoffed. '*If I'm lucky*? I was right there in in your head during those visions. I know what you want, and I intend to make every one of your wild fantasies come true.'

She arched a brow. 'Is that a threat or a promise?'

'To satisfy *your* kinks, Lana, it will have to be both.'

Alannah rose. 'Well then, time's-a-wastin'.'

'The city, huh?' Alannah queried as the Jag turned onto the highway.

Brendan glanced at her; an infectious grin plastered on his face. 'I'm hardly gonna take you to the local pub on our first official date, gorgeous. I've dreamt of this night for at least a decade. It's gonna be special.'

Alannah's heart performed acrobatics again. It had become such a habit of late, that she was thinking of giving the organ a stage name. 'Wow. And here I thought your idea of a dream date would be tying me to the bed and drinking shots from my navel between rounds of coital bliss. Who knew you could be romantic too?'

He laughed. 'There you go spoiling my surprise for the second date.' After parking in a secure garage, Brendan turned to her. 'Wait there a second.'

She could only manage a nod while calming her breath.

Brendan got out of the car and circled around to open her door. 'My Lady?'

Gods! This was almost too much. But Alannah loved every second of it. She gave Brendan her hand, letting him help her up as she smoothed down her short, red cocktail dress. Not a colour she had worn before, but she felt like a change.

Her date wore a black suit. From what she understood, Brendan hated formalwear, but he had gone all out for her.

Once out of the car, Alannah took a moment to admire the vision in front of her. 'Damn you look hot in a suit, Brendan. You should wear them more often.'

Linking his arm in hers, he leaned in and pressed his lips against her ear. 'Anything for you, gorgeous.' His voice was deep and erotic, eliciting a rush of hormones through her bloodstream.

They walked in comfortable silence for a block until they reached a dimly lit, non-descript door. It led them down a dingy staircase into a narrow corridor toward a red glow. Alannah gave him the side eye. 'If we weren't dressed to the nines, I'd be thinking sex dungeon right about now.'

Brendan replied with a deep, throaty laugh. He pulled her to a stop in front of a kobold bouncer who stood in front of a black door beneath a red lightbulb.

The draconic man gave them a polite nod. 'Good evening, sir, Madam.' He stepped aside to let them pass.

As soon as they stepped beyond the black door, Alannah froze, stunned by the beauty before her. 'Wow, what is this place?' Warm, sparkling light glittered from crystal chandeliers and bounced from the reflective walls which contained specks of quartz. A stage at one end of the room drew her attention. She watched a seelie ensemble performing sensual, jazzy music. A nymph in a long, sleek, black dress covered in sequins fronted the band. Upon closer inspection, Alannah recognised Bianca.

'The Crystal Cabaret. It's a popular hangout for magicals and a refuge from pure mages. They only let me in because I'm friends with a bunch of fae and they know I won't cause trouble.'

'And me?'

'Well, they know you're not exactly in the Council's good books right now.'

Alannah snorted. 'Putting it mildly.'

'*Wowsers!*' Brendan muttered as he gazed at her.

'What?'

'Your eyes. They burned red for a split second. Must be a side effect. Do you feel okay?'

She grinned. 'Better than okay. I should have mentioned I kept the channel open. I guess there's a little demon in me.'

Brendan exhaled sharply, leaning in close to speak in her ear. 'I wish I was that demon right now.' Grabbing her hand, he led her through the club.

Alannah turned to him as they reached the bar. 'You wanna be a demon, huh?'

'I told you, Lana, if you go to hell, I'm following you there.' He focussed his attention on her, sending her heart down the road in a series of cartwheels.

Hmm, how about The Magnificent Flipping Felicity?

'What can I get you to drink?' a soft voice asked.

Alannah faced the bartender, but the gem encrusted counter bedazzled her, sparkling in every colour imaginable. The bartender himself was a clurichaun. Serving drinks was a fitting job for fae born of alcohol-induced debauchery.

She returned the man's smile. 'I'll have a single malt whiskey, thanks. Whatever you recommend.'

'Make that two.' Brendan handed over a wad of cash.

With drinks in hand, they settled into a booth where Brendan's left arm rested across Alannah's shoulders. She took a moment to study their surrounds. 'No one's using glamour in here.'

'This club is off limits to humans. It is one of the few public places where magicals can be themselves. Most find it liberating.'

She nodded. 'I guess it would be exhausting to keep up those illusions all the time. We are lucky we appear human.'

'I guess. But it's not why I'm feeling lucky tonight.' Brendan's eyes fixed on her as he spoke in that bedroom voice of his.

Blushing, she bit her lip and turned her attention to the stage. 'Bianca's got some pipes.'

'I suppose she has.'

Alannah sipped her drink, enthralled by the music when Brendan grabbed her and pulled her onto the dancefloor.

His arms held her close, and they swayed to Bianca's deep, sensual voice singing about spending an 'Evil Night Together.'

'You know, I don't normally dance to jazz music.'

'This isn't jazz, it's dark cabaret. Also, shoosh.' He wrapped his arms around her, dancing with their bodies pressed close.

Alannah's blood still hummed with the effects of nether flowing through her, although the intensity had waned since first connecting with the power source. But another sensation slid across her skin and seeped into her pores and Brendan's hands—clamped on her backside—were the source. Resting her head against his chest, she inhaled his rich, musky fragrance. 'Are you trying to enchant me, Brendan Winters?'

'Not intentionally. Holding you like this feels incredible and I'm instinctively channelling your touch.'

Looking up at him, she found Brendan staring at her, his eyes blazing with passion. Alannah glanced at his lips, full and kissable, drawing her in.

Brendan licked those luscious lips, tilting his head down. His mouth was a hair's breadth from hers when his head jolted upright, glimpsing something over her shoulder. '*Damnit!*' He swung Alannah around and stood in front of her like a shield.

When she peeked out from behind his broad frame, Alannah felt the blood drain from her face as two warlocks approached.

'I see you waste no time, *Brother*,' Liam hissed.

Brendan tried to block their access to her, but Clayton dodged around him and grabbed her.

'Keep your damn hands off her!' Brendan seethed.

As the cuffs clamped around her wrists, Liam grimaced. 'Alannah Winters, you are under arrest for the crime of channelling the stygian element.'

Damnit! She did not think they would come for her this soon.

'You will be held in custody until your trial without the option of bail,' Liam continued.

'*No!*' Brendan cried as he moved toward them, but Liam pinned him against the wall with a forceful gust of wind. Brendan's eyes filled with tears that streamed across his cheeks like a waterfall. His voice entered Alannah's mind. '*I love you, Lana. Stay strong for me, gorgeous.*'

She caught a final glimpse of Brendan as Clayton ripped her away from the warmth and safety of his presence. She hoped he heard her parting thought. *I love you too, Brendan.*

Chapter Sixteen

There were some days when Liam detested being a warlock and this was one of them. Even after everything that happened, and all the pain Alannah had caused him, it killed him to arrest her. Seeing how she had rushed into Brendan's arms, and most likely his bed, did not help Liam's mood either.

It was late when he got home. He threw his keys at the buffet, kicked his boots off in the hall, and beelined for his bedroom. As he flicked on the light, he jumped out of his skin. '*Holy shit!*' When he recognised Brendan slumped over the edge of his bed, Liam's pale face turned red. 'I knew I should have changed the locks. Why the hell are you lurking in the dark like a creeper?'

When Brendan looked up, the raw emotion on display floored Liam. 'Oh good, you're home. I need your help, bro.'

'I might be your brother, but I'm not your damn bro. That ship sailed long ago when you started putting the moves on my girl.'

Brendan sighed. 'Be honest, Liam: that ship didn't even dock in the first place. Lana was never your girl; you just hated seeing how close she was to me and drove yourself between us like a wedge over and over. But I'm not here to debate the finer points of our age-old rivalry. I need your help; or rather, Lana needs your help.'

He tensed. 'There's nothing I can do to help her now; she dug her own grave.'

Brendan shook his head. 'I can't believe you dumped Lana over this business with Tara. Did you even get her side of the story, or was your head stuffed too far up Richard's arse to hear it? You should know her heart and soul are too pure to turn to dark magic without decent reasons.'

Liam heaved the air from his lungs and collapsed on the edge of the bed beside Brendan. 'I was angry about the Tara stuff, but it's not why I broke things off with her.'

'Then why?'

'Are you dense, Brendan? Why do you think she went running to you?'

'Because you left her in a time of need, yet again.'

'But why *you*, Brendan? Why not Cara, or Mum? She always went to you, even when I *was* there for her.'

Brendan gulped as he stared at Liam. Seconds later, a smug grin developed.

'Congratulations Brendan, you got the girl. Pity she's in prison. Now get out of my house before I throw you out.'

His expression sobered. 'Wait! Do you still care about Lana at all?'

'Of course, but—'

'Then I'm guessing you don't want her to get hurt by sadistic arseholes while in prison.'

Holding his breath for a second, Liam processed Brendan's meaning before exhaling. 'It's okay, Richard doesn't have access to her in there and no one can bribe the elven guards.'

'Richard might not be able to get to her, but his buddy Clayton can, and that man's torture methods are lot more sexual in nature.'

White hot rage boiled his blood. '*The hell?* What. Did. He do?'

'So far? Only a bit of handsy harassment, but I worry he will make good on his threats over the next two weeks.'

Liam rocketed off the bed. 'I'm gonna kill him.'

'*Liam*! Wait!'

He paused at the door.

'Lana has a plan. A super sucky plan, but I promised her I'd stick to it. Sit down and hear me out.'

Turning, he returned to the bed. 'Fine.'

Over a week had passed. Eleven days by Alannah's count, but she based her assumption on the regularity of her twice-daily meals. The guards never spoke to her when they delivered the food, even when she asked them questions. At least they were feeding her this time.

The only regular visitor who talked to her was Liam, but she did not want to talk to him. His previous hurtful words and abandonment still stung. When he had come the morning after her arrest, he had apologised:

'I'm sorry, Lana. Brendan told me everything.'

She looked up from her seat on the bed. 'Will you help with my plan?'

Liam winced as he nodded. 'Yes. I get what you're doing with regards to Richard, but I hate the risk you are taking with Clayton.' He slipped a phone beneath her mattress. 'I've set the voice recording app to start, and I'll swap it out daily with a freshly charged burner.'

'Good.' She turned around to face the wall.

'I really am sorry. I said all those things because I was hurting, but I didn't mean any of it. Please, you have to forgive me.'

'I don't have to do anything for you, Liam. Please leave me alone.'

She heard him sigh, but he did not press the issue.

Memories of Brendan kept her going through the agonising loneliness and stifling silence. The feel of his strong arms wrapped around her; the sound of his deep, erotic voice saying dirty things; those inviting lips almost kissing her and the desire in his eyes promising much more. Their almost-kiss drove her wild at night when she tried to sleep. *When I get my freedom back, kissing the hell out of those lips is the first thing I will do.* She prayed her chance would be sooner rather than later.

On the verge of sleep, Alannah woke with sudden awareness chilling her to the bone. Her eyes flicked open, and she tried to scream.

But his strong, rough hand clamped over her mouth. 'Did you think I would forget about that fine arse of yours, *sweetheart*? I've been waiting for the right opportunity to come and claim it,' the horribly familiar voice growled.

She tried to fight him off, even biting his hand, but nothing deterred him. The bastard was naked, and the more she struggled, the more obvious his arousal became.

'Guess what, *sweetheart?* These walls are soundproof, so you can scream all you like. It will only make me harder.' He pulled his hand from her mouth and flipped her over.

'You'll burn in hell for this, arsehole!' she cried out.

He sniggered as he cuffed her hands to the bars at the head of the bed. 'And you'll burn right alongside me, you filthy dark mage whore. Mm, I guess I'll get an eternity of fucking this arse in the afterlife. Lucky me.'

Alannah's legs flailed as he tore her pants from them. She hoped to kick him in the nuts but being on her front made it impossible to aim. When his solid body pushed her down against the bed, she swallowed hard. She knew resistance was futile at this point, but her fighting spirit would not let go. '*No!* Get off me you creep!'

Clayton's putrid breath oozed across her neck as he spoke in her ear. 'Not gonna happen, *sweetheart*.' Pulling her hips up, he forced her to kneel. He ran the tip of his cock along her back passage. 'Can you feel how big I am, Alannah? I won't lie: this is going to hurt.' He drove himself inside her with lethal force.

She screamed bloody murder. While she had never tried anal with a partner before, she had read about it and knew it took a lot of foreplay and lubrication to prepare for an enjoyable experience. Clayton tearing her open was the least pleasurable experience of her life. Her eyes watered as she cried out.

When it became unbearable, her breathing slowed, and she prayed. *Oh Gods, please make the pain stop*. Then it did. She could not feel the physical ache, or the grief. In fact, she could not feel anything except a wonderful sense of peace.

Opening her eyes, Alannah gasped at her surrounds. No longer kneeling on the wretched bed of broken springs, she stood in an open field full of purple wildflowers as far as the eye could see. *Stunning*.

An oddly familiar stranger in blue velvet robes approached her. White wispy clouds surrounded him, and his aura was strong and pure. 'Hello, dear child.'

'W-where am I?' she stammered, not quite sure how to address the powerful man.

'The Celestial Realm.'

She blinked a few times. *Yep, still here.* Peeking down at herself, Alannah observed her own white and wispy form. 'A-am I… dead?'

He gave her a sympathetic smile. 'No, Lana, your soul just needed a holiday from your body.'

'How did I get here?'

'Through your Aether connection.'

'I thought the cage prevented my access to mana.'

This time his smile broadened. 'Some magic is more powerful than anything earthly… like love, or the bonds of family.'

A few of the words the man had spoken dropped into place for her. Child. Love. Family. Unable to suppress her hope, Alannah wagered her heart on a hunch. 'Dad? You're my real dad?'

'Yes, I am. It is lovely to finally meet you, Lana. I've been keeping an eye on you over the years and you have done much to make me proud.'

A sobering thought occurred. 'Wait, if you're up here, that means you are dead.'

'Please don't mourn for me, dear child. While I do not live in your realm, I am happy living here. And one day, when your time does come, you will join me.'

If she could cry, she would have. 'But with all I have done, I might not get the chance to return.'

'You will, I promise. All the Gods know your intentions are honourable. You are a strong and brave woman, Lana. The strongest of Cailleach's daughters yet. I hope you can take heart in my words and the knowledge that you are on the right path.'

The feeling of peace returned, and she felt herself smile. 'Thanks.'

'I must go now, and it is time for you to return home. Remember what I have told you, okay?'

'Okay.'

'Goodbye for now, dear child.' He turned and walked away.

'Wait! I didn't get your name.'

But her dad had already vanished, and she felt her body tugging at her soul.

When consciousness returned, Clayton had gone, but the burning sensation remained.

Whimpering, she turned to face the wall, away from the security camera, and reached under the bed for the phone Liam had smuggled in. After sending a quick SOS text, she curled up in a ball under the blanket and sobbed with the last of her energy reserves.

Alannah must have fallen asleep because the next thing she knew, Liam shook her. 'Hey Lana, I'm here. Everything will be okay now.'

But she was too tired and weak to move.

He pulled the blanket away, sending bitter chills dancing across her bare skin. '*Oh Gods!* You're bleeding, Lana. Dad! There's so much blood! You've gotta help her.'

'Give me space, Son,' Ross commanded in a calm tone.

Liam stepped back, and Alannah felt her uncle's hands on her head. His hand shifted to inspect the damage.

'Why is she bleeding?' Liam gulped.

'She has a large anal fissure.'

'*Shit!* That bastard is going to pay for this.'

'Alannah, honey.' Ross' voice was warm and soothing. 'I don't know if you can hear me, but I need to take some samples now. I will try to be gentle, but some of this might hurt.' The first few swabs were external, brushing her thighs and buttocks with a tickle, but she did not flinch. The first of the internal swabs was vaginal—uncomfortable, but not painful. But the anal swab was a different story. Her eyes shot open wide as her leg jolted, but Liam caught it before she could move far.

'It's okay, Lana, everything will be okay,' Liam's voice trembled. 'The bastard won't ever touch you again, I promise.'

Ross moved into her field of view. 'I have all the samples I need, Lana.' He handed her a potion vial. 'Here, drink this. It will help with the pain.'

Alannah gaped at him.

'*Oh Gods!* She's in catatonic shock, Dad.'

'I know.' Ross sat on the edge of the bed and pulled her into his arms, wrapping the blanket around her. After opening the vial, he tilted her head back and encouraged her to drink the potion.

Liam growled. 'She needs a therapist and to get out of this hell-hole.'

Ross sighed. 'I agree, but you and I both know Richard won't allow it. The best we can do for her now is process the evidence so we can put Clayton away.' He stroked the side of her face. 'I'm sorry this happened to you, sweetheart.'

Boom!

Alannah turned manic, pushing away at the hands holding her. '*No! Get off me you creep!*' she screamed.

'Get back Dad!' Liam knelt in front of her. 'Lana, it's okay. No one here wants to hurt you. You are safe now.'

This time she blinked through the tears. 'Liam?'

'Yes, princess, I'm here. You're safe now. Dad has the samples, and we are going to destroy the man who did this to you.'

Alannah nodded. 'Good.' She reached for the phone. 'Here. There's an audio file on it to prove my lack of consent.'

Liam took the phone, reaching out to touch her face but she recoiled from him. 'Lana?'

'I'm still pissed with you.'

Shoulders sagging, tears swelled in his eyes. 'I'm so sorry, Lana.'

'Please leave me be. Both of you. I'm tired.'

'Yes, of course. You've need to rest and heal,' Ross agreed. 'If you still have pain tomorrow, get one of the guards to call me, okay?'

She nodded, curling up under the blanket again.

Liam hesitated.

'Come on, Son. Give her time.'

Alannah drifted off to sleep as the cage door locked.

Alannah glanced around the courtroom: smaller than she had expected from watching television and movies. Scanning the room confirmed Clayton's absence, which eased the tension in her shoulders. Liam was the warlock to escort her into court, under Monique's supervision. He sat beside her, while Monique stared daggers at her from the Clerk's desk.

Her eyes lit up the moment Brendan entered the room, walking straight up to her. His voice entered her mind on approach. *'Hi gorgeous, miss me?'*

She scoffed. *'Understatement of the year.'*

As Brendan reached her, she moved in for a hug, but he shook his head and whispered, 'Not here. We have to show decorum and whatnot.'

Alannah nodded. 'How did you score front row seats?'

He grinned. 'I convinced the Council to let me represent you.'

'For real? You're not even a lawyer.'

'Doesn't matter. A lot of the best magic lawyers are enchanters. And I did a crash course in legal studies during your confinement. I'm considering a career change now.'

She gaped at him.

'Plus, it beats doing this by yourself. You've been through enough lately.' He frowned.

'All rise for the honourable Kieran Lane.'

The High Magus entered and took his place at the judge's bench. Once everyone returned to their seats, he addressed the room. 'Good morning, ladies and gentlemen. Calling the case of Alannah Winters versus the magic State of South Australia. Are both sides ready?'

Lucas Ó Máille stood up and Alannah heard Brendan curse under his breath. 'Ready for the State, Your Honour.'

Brendan rose. 'Ready for the defence, Your Honour.'

Kieran instructed Monique to swear in the jury, a diverse cross section of the magical community. Alannah did not recognise any of them from town. Kieran turned his attention to Lucas. 'I call the prosecution forward for an opening statement.'

Lucas stepped up. 'Thank you, Your Honour.' He turned to face the jury, reading from his notes. 'Ladies and gentlemen, the defendant has been charged with the crimes of treason and for practising dark magic. A witness will testify the defendant met with Tara Winters on the nineteenth of October to discuss unsanctioned training. This will be supported by audio and visual evidence. Following bail, the same witness discovered the defendant channelling the stygian element on the twenty-first of October. The evidence I present to you will prove without doubt the defendant is guilty as charged.' The room fell quiet as he returned to his table.

'I call the defence forward for an opening statement.'

Brendan winked at Alannah and rose to face the jury. 'Greetings, Your Honour and ladies and gentlemen of the jury. Please recall that according to law, my client is innocent until proven guilty. I will show you there is no case against my client. Firstly, Alannah Winters worked to undermine Tara Winters and secondly, there is no evidence to suggest she ever used her channelling for nefarious purposes. Therefore, my client is not guilty.'

When he returned to the seat beside Alannah, she smiled at him, thinking: *You seriously rocked that speech.*

He grinned. *'Thanks, gorgeous. When this is all over, I will rock the rest of your world.'*

She clamped her legs together. *Damn.*

'The prosecution may call its first witness.'

Their heads snapped forward as Lucas called Richard to the witness stand. After running through all the evidence of Alannah's meeting with Tara, Lucas moved onto the more pertinent question. 'Please describe the dark magic you witnessed the defendant practising on the twenty-first of October.'

'Certainly. I monitored her following her bail. On the day in question, I saw her use a ritual circle to open a connection to the nether. As you know, magic law strictly forbids this mana source because of its connection to demonic forces.'

Lucas nodded, pausing for dramatic effect. 'How did you know she channelled nether?'

Alannah and Brendan both edged forward on their seats.

Richard stared straight at her, his lips curling into a smirk. 'Because I could read her mind when she performed the visualisation exercise.'

She paled at the thought of Richard being party to such an intimate experience.

'Can you describe the visualisation?'

'I will spare you all the explicit details, but the gist of it is Alannah performed sexual acts in the volcanic pits of the Underworld.'

There were a few gasps from the jury and a couple of sniggers.

Brendan placed a reassuring hand over hers as he spoke telepathically. *'Don't let him get to you, Lana.'*

Lucas shook his head. '*Tsk, tsk.* Thank you, Inquisitor. No further questions.'

Kieran looked at Brendan. 'Does the defence have any questions?'

He stood. 'Yes, Your Honour.'

'You may approach the stand.'

'Your Honour, I seek permission to use the Cuffs of Truth.'

Kieran's eyes narrowed on him. 'The witness has already sworn an oath, Mr. Winters. What grounds do you have to require such an archaic method?'

'I have evidence to support a possible mistrial, Your Honour.'

The High Magus arched a brow. 'What type of evidence?'

'Testimony by means of cross-examination to prove the prosecution's witness is guilty of misconduct and obtaining evidence by wrongful means, Your Honour.'

Kieran frowned. 'Very well. Warlock Winters, please deploy the Cuffs of Truth.'

Brendan and Liam exchanged nods and glances before Liam stepped up to the bar to present an old wooden box. He withdrew an old set of cold iron manacles from the chest.

Monique inspected them before announcing, 'I confirm the deployment of authentic Cuffs of Truth, Your Honour.'

Liam took the cuffs up to a disgruntled Richard and fastened them to the Inquisitor's wrists before returning to Alannah's side. Aside from humiliation, the cuffs themselves were not designed to hurt. They did, however, prevent Richard from using his own magic to hide the truth. Their worth came from what an enchanter could do to their wearer.

Alannah's pulse became manic. This was the moment she had been eagerly anticipating. She had planned to have Brendan present, working his magic in the background; but having him right there to challenge Richard was even better.

Brendan stepped up to the witness stand. 'Tell me, Inquisitor, are you certain Alannah Winters channelled nether? Perhaps her vision was part of some wild sexual fantasy.' He glanced over his shoulder and winked at Alannah.

More titters from the jury.

'Yes, I am certain.'

'What makes you certain?'

Richard glowered at Brendan with a twitch in his eye. 'I detected the channelling.'

'Hmm, interesting. How, pray tell, was that possible?' The two men became locked in a contest of wills as Brendan attempted to pull the truth out of him.

'B-because I have an open nether channel.'

The intake of breath drawn by every single jury member was more predictable than a Skrillex bass drop.

'Are you admitting to the same magic practice for which Alannah has been charged?'

'Objection, Your Honour,' Lucas cried out. 'The witness is not on trial.'

Kieran shot Brendan an annoyed glance. 'Sustained. Keep to the facts, Mr. Winters.'

'Fine. What do you use the stygian element for?'

'Detecting other users, obviously.'

'Obviously. Anything else? Such as the summoning of demonic sex slaves perhaps?'

Richard gasped. 'What? No! I've never summoned demons. That is true dark magic. I also use it to block the effects of other people's spells.'

The jury murmured.

'Silence!' Kieran demanded.

'Interesting. So, you don't think channelling nether is true dark magic?'

'I know it isn't. Dark magic taints the soul, but the simple act of channelling nether doesn't.'

Brendan turned and grinned at Alannah for a second before turning back to Richard. 'Had you suspected my client of channelling nether on a previous occasion, Inquisitor?'

'Yes.'

'Was this because of your own nether channel?'

'Yes. But also because I sensed she was hiding something when I conducted my first interview.'

'Indeed. How did you go about questioning her the second time?'

Richard's brow furrowed. 'Please clarify the question.'

Brendan drew closer to the stand. 'Fine. I'll spell it out for you then, shall I? Did you abduct and torture Alannah Winters in an abandoned bomb shelter?'

The eye twitch returned. 'N-yes.'

'And did your torture involve chaining her to a corrugated iron wall with cold iron manacles so you could cut into her with a scalpel and burn her flesh with a cigarette lighter?' Brendan's voice rose with each accusatory word.

'Yes.'

He glanced at the jury's wide eyes and slack jaws before returning his attention to Richard. 'Did you know such methods of extracting information from a suspect have been illegal in the magic world for over a century now?'

Richard sighed. 'Yes.'

'Why did you do it?'

This time a wicked grin formed on Richard's face. 'Because I enjoyed it.'

Alannah's stomach churned.

Brendan oozed disapproval. 'Did you enjoy watching the surveillance footage of your friend Clayton raping Alannah in prison?'

Lucas jumped up. 'Objection Your Honour, that is not relevant to this case.'

Kieran sighed. 'Are you going somewhere with this line of questioning, Mr. Winters?'

'Of course, Your Honour,' Brendan replied.

'Then carry on.'

Brendan nodded. 'Thank you, Your Honour. Please answer my question, Inquisitor.'

'Yes. I enjoyed the show.'

The bile climbed up her throat.

'Did you know Clayton was going to do it? *Did you let the arsehole brutalise her?*'

'*Mr. Winters!*' Kieran cried out. 'Watch your language and temper in my courtroom or I will have you removed.'

'Sorry, Your Honour.' Brendan took a deep breath and paced. 'Inquisitor Lane, were you complicit in Clayton's plan?'

'No. I didn't know he would violate her.'

'But you didn't stop him or reprimand him when you saw the live video feed?'

'I didn't stop him, no, but I chastised him for potentially compromising this case.'

Brendan stopped pacing and scowled. 'Rather than arresting him for such a violent crime, you gave him a smack for putting your own work in jeopardy. Was that before or after shaking his hand and thanking him for the unsolicited porn?' Lucas rose to object, but Brendan put his hands up in supplication. 'Rhetorical question. So, to summarise, Inquisitor, have you practised magic deemed illegal unnecessarily because it is not dark, and mistreated my client to gain the evidence for this trial?'

Richard growled. 'Yes.'

'No further questions, Your Honour.' Brendan returned to his seat with a victorious smile Alannah felt compelled to return.

'Warlock Winters, please take Inquisitor Richard Lane into custody.' Kieran's words were sweet, sweet music to her ears.

'With pleasure, Your Honour,' Liam replied as he moved toward the witness stand.

Alannah fixed her gaze on Brendan, who spoke in her mind. '*Telepathic high five, gorgeous.*'

Heck yeah!

'I'd like to call a short recess. Monique, will you escort Miss Winters into the defendant's waiting room?'

'Yes, Your Honour.'

Chapter Seventeen

The stuffy air was full of tension, owing in part to the cold iron lining the walls, but mostly to Monique's glowering presence.

'What?' Alannah snapped.

'You will pay for what you did to Uncle Ricki.'

'Oh, I'm sorry, Monique. Did you have a close relationship with the sadistic arsehole? Remind me to be more mindful of your feelings next time I consider retribution for torture.'

Monique went to open her mouth, but there was a knock at the door, so she rose to answer. 'Get lost, Brendan. The defendant is not permitted visitors during recess.'

'She has a right to speak with her legal representative though.'

Huffing, Monique stepped aside to let him in, and slammed the door.

'*Gods!* Someone's turned into a serious grumplestiltskin.'

If looks could kill, Brendan would have been travelling express to meet his maker.

Brendan turned his attention to Alannah and pulled her into a bear hug. 'Gods, I've missed you. How are you holding up?'

'Better now after your kick-arse performance. But I'm still pissing kittens about the verdict.'

Still holding her close, he sighed. 'I know what you mean. I had hoped Kieran would throw the case out of court after all the crap Richard pulled, but I guess nepotism and corruption run deep in the Council.'

'Shut up, Brendan,' Monique hissed.

'Hey, Lana? Can you hear an annoying buzzing sound?'

She snorted. 'See, this is why you're the only therapist I need. Between the hugs and laughs, you've got it covered.'

'We haven't even gotten to the sex bit yet, gorgeous,' he whispered.

Every nerve in her body tingled. 'I can't wait.'

'Fuck, I'm gonna need a cool shower before returning to the courtroom. My usual magic tricks aren't working.'

Alannah chuckled. 'That's because we're in a cold iron room, jackass.'

She could feel his chest rumble against hers as he stroked her head. 'I totally knew that.'

'Are you guys gonna stand there grinding against each other the whole time? It's making me nauseous.'

'Hmm, there's that buzz again,' Brendan retorted.

'Don't mind Monique, she's just jealous. You should hear what she told me about your mad skills.'

'*Alannah!* You are such a bitch!'

A loud knock sounded at the door, followed by one of the court officials popping their head in. 'Recess is over.'

Brendan released her. 'Go on. I'll join you in a moment.'

Alannah studied him with uncertainty until his eye movements gestured to the tent situation in his pants. She bit her lip to suppress the grin threatening a global invasion of her face. 'Okay.'

When everyone settled back in their places, Kieran addressed the room with is his eyes focussed on Alannah. 'After some deliberation I have decided to exclude all existing evidence pertaining to the charges of dark magic. In the absence of permissible evidence, I am dropping these charges.'

Alannah beamed.

'However, there is still the matter of treason, for which the existing evidence remains legitimate. The remainder of this case will focus on such charges.'

Her heart sank again.

'Does the prosecution wish to call any further witnesses?'

Lucas rose. 'No, Your Honour.'

'The defence may call its first witness.'

After a quick squeeze of her hand, Brendan stood. 'I wish to skip straight to the defendant's own testimony, You Honour.'

'Very well.'

Liam led her up to the witness stand. After swearing a sacred oath to the Gods and stating her name for the record, Brendan approached.

'Is the audio recording in question an accurate record of a conversation had by you on the nineteenth of October?'

'Yes.'

'In this conversation, you referred to the other woman as Scarlett, except at one stage, when you addressed her as Grandmother. Is this woman really your grandmother?' Brendan turned toward the jury for a moment.

'Yes. Scarlett is her nickname, but her real name is Tara Winters.'

He spun on his heels. 'But didn't you kill Tara Winters four years ago?'

Amused by his antics, she tried hard to suppress a smile. 'I thought I did, but being a lich, she was able to come back to life. She told me this the first time we met following the incident. Apparently, there is only one way to bring true death to a lich.'

'And how does one bring about this true death?'

Alannah sighed. 'I don't know. I was hoping to learn this by meeting with her.'

Brendan shot her a grin. 'Can you please explain the true purpose of your meetings with Tara Winters?'

'Certainly. As far as she knew, they were training sessions in which she tried to turn me against the Council. But I saw them as an opportunity to gain her confidence and learn her secrets so I could put a stop to her once and for all.'

'So, does that mean you were working against Tara, not with her?'

'Yes, that's right.'

Brendan gave the jury one of his charming smiles before continuing. 'Why didn't you bring this matter to the Council?'

'Because I knew it would compromise my situation and potentially endanger the people I care about.'

'Thank you, Alannah. I have no further questions, Your Honour.' He returned to his seat and winked at her.

'Does the prosecution have any questions?' Kieran asked.

'Yes, Your Honour.' Lucas approached her. 'Miss Winters, what was the nature of the training Tara facilitated?'

'She was teaching me to reconnect to an innate power source I have because of my Beltane Blessing.'

Lucas raised his brows as if intrigued. 'What mana source?'

'The primordial. She explained all blessed children have this gift and we can access all other mana via this power source.'

The entire courtroom erupted in chatter.

'*Silence!*' Kieran cried. But no one paid attention and he needed to use the gavel to bring order back.

'Did you succeed in channelling the primordial, Alannah?'

'Yes. And I now have a permanent connection.'

The room fired up again but fell silent as soon as Kieran shot a lightning bolt at the roof.

'Why didn't you register your new attunement, Miss Winters?'

'Firstly, it isn't new—I was born with it. Secondly, I was arrested shortly after confirming the connection.'

'I have no further questions, Your Honour.' Lucas slumped into his seat.

Kieran looked at her. 'The witness is excused.' When she sat down, he focussed on Brendan. 'Does the defence rest?'

Brendan bobbed up to reply, 'Yes, Your Honour.'

After issuing instructions to the jury, Kieran asked if the final arguments were ready.

Both representatives rose. 'Yes, Your Honour.' Lucas stepped up to the jury as Brendan returned to his seat. 'Ladies and gentlemen of the jury, the High Magus has asked for proof of three criteria. Two of these are simple. Firstly, as a registered mage of South Australia, the defendant has sworn allegiance to the State. Secondly, the defendant has admitted to engagement with Tara Winters, a known enemy of the State. Therefore, all we must prove is the intent to assist the enemy. The defendant admitted Tara was using their training sessions to gain influence. Knowing this, the defendant still complied with the enemy's wishes by going along with the training. Training, which, I might add, opened an incredibly powerful mana channel she could use against the State. This shows the defendant *intended* to assist the enemy. The evidence proves the defendant is guilty of treason.'

Brendan approached the jury as Lucas retired. 'Ladies and gentlemen of the jury: remember my client is innocent until *proven* guilty. Alannah Winters has explained she had no intent to assist Tara Winters in any plots against the State. She said, and I quote, the training sessions were "an opportunity to gain (Tara's) confidence and learn her secrets in order to put a stop to her once and for all." Does this sound like intent to assist the enemy? It is the prosecution's job to prove beyond reasonable doubt they satisfy all three criteria. Has the prosecution *proven* Alanna Winters assisted Tara by agreeing to training sessions? It sounds more like Tara assisted Alannah. Perhaps Tara should be the one on trial for treason.' That earned him a few laughs. 'Seriously though folks, there is reasonable doubt here. Alannah Winters is clearly not guilty. I rest my case.' He took a melodramatic bow and returned to his seat.

Alannah was struggling to contain her own laughter as the jury stepped out to deliberate.

'True calling, just saying,' Brendan whispered.

She snorted. 'Gods! Kieran would have a coronary if he had to deal with you on the regular.'

A few minutes later, the jury returned.

'Has the jury reached a unanimous verdict?' Kieran queried.

The jury's foreperson stood. 'Yes.'

Alannah took a deep breath and held it.

Monique collected a sheet of paper from the foreperson and took it to Kieran.

The High Magus glanced at the page, looking up to announce, 'The jury finds the defendant not guilty. Alannah Winters may continue meeting Tara Winters to gather intel, but must report back to me with everything she learns.' He concluded the hearing by striking his gavel against the sound block.

She heaved out that breath with the force of a tornado.

'*Yes!*' Brendan cheered, high fiving her for real.

'Now get the hell out of my courtroom.' Kieran smirked at them.

As soon as Liam unlocked Alannah's handcuffs, Brendan grabbed her hand and dragged her outside at breakneck speed. He scooped her up in a whirlwind embrace and she hooked her legs around his waist, laughing and crying with joy. The moment Alannah caught her breath, she crashed her lips against his in an all-consuming kiss.

Kissing Brendan was everything Alannah had imagined and more. His intoxicating musky scent filled her senses as her skin tingled from the contact. Hungry lips devoured her as though she was their first and last meal. His stubble grazed her chin, a foreign yet exhilarating sensation.

'Mm. I've been dreaming of this moment.' His husky voice spoke against her lips.

Alannah pressed her forehead to his. 'I've been craving this since the Council stole the moment from our first date.' She smacked her lips to his again. Cheers and wolf-whistles summoned her awareness of the crowd gathering around them. Alannah tittered, feeling the heat rise in her cheeks.

'There I go making you blush again. Gods, I love seeing these turn pink.' He brushed his nose against her right cheekbone. 'Knowing only *I* have this effect on you has always given me such a thrill.'

She drew her bottom lip between her teeth, savouring the residual salty taste of Brendan's kiss.

'Hey, Brendo, stop monopolising all the Alannah hugs,' Nick's voice boomed as he approached from the courthouse.

When she glanced over Brendan's shoulder, still with her arms and legs gripping him tight, she saw Jacob elbow Nick in the ribs. 'Shut the hell up, bro,' Jacob chastised. 'They just had their first kiss.'

'Ah bugger! I take a whizz and miss all the action.' He grinned and turned to Ben with an outstretched hand. 'Pay up, man.'

Scanning the crowd around the courthouse doors, Alannah realised most of her friends were there watching them. Liam was sulking in the shadows, arms crossed as he leaned against one of the pillars. She averted her gaze.

Jacob's eyes widened. 'Wait! You guys bet money on them hooking up?'

Nick shrugged. 'What? It always seemed inevitable to me. Ben's the one who lacked faith.'

Squirming, she hid her face in the crook of Brendan's neck.

Brendan's laugh vibrated against her and he pressed his mouth to her ear. 'You wanna get out of here?'

'Yeah.'

He started walking her away.

'Oi, dipshit!' Cara cried out. 'Don't even think about stealing her from me yet. We've got some serious celebrating to do!'

'O.M.G. Cara!' Alannah squealed as she slipped out of Brendan's hold and ran into Cara's arms. 'You came to see my trial?'

'Of course, hun. There's no way I'd miss something so important. Not that the Council allowed us inside the courtroom. Are you okay, sweetheart?'

Boom!

'No! Get off me you creep!' Alannah pushed away from the hands holding her.

Brendan pulled her into his arms, calming her with his magic touch. 'Hey, gorgeous, it's okay. I've got you.'

Alannah noticed Jacob helping a startled Cara up from the ground and turned in Brendan's arms to get a better view. 'What happened? Cara, are you okay?'

Cara brushed off her knees. 'Yeah, I'm fine, but what the hell was that? You decked me.'

Glancing at Brendan, Alannah's brow knitted together. 'I did?'

His eyes were wide as he nodded. 'I don't know what happened, but you freaked out and pushed Cara away.'

'It was a PTSD episode,' Liam explained as he drew closer. 'The same thing happened when Dad held her in gaol. Cara must have said or done something to trigger her.'

Cara's mouth dropped open. 'What did I do?'

Sighing, Liam shook his head. 'I don't know, I wasn't close enough to tell.' He pulled a memory card from his pocket and handed it to Brendan. 'I know you didn't want to see this before, but you should watch it to better understand her potential triggers. I synced the video and audio.'

Alannah gasped. 'Is that what I think it is?'

Liam gave her a solemn nod. 'I also have news that might help your recovery. Kieran announced the declaration of two divine verdicts.'

Brendan took the SD card and pulled her in closer to his side.

'Two?' Alannah queried.

'Yes. The Gods have sentenced Richard to exile from the mage community, officially stripping him of all his titles and property. He won't be allowed to set foot in the State again and if he does, we have been ordered to execute him.'

Alannah exhaled.

'And the other arsehole?' Brendan demanded.

'Life in maximum security magic prison,' Liam replied.

She huffed. 'Is *that* all? Austin got the death sentence and he only *date* raped me. At least that was pleasurable as far as I can remember.'

Liam cringed as Brendan tensed beside her. 'You know his attempts to curse you played a role in his punishment. The main thing is the bastard can't hurt you ever again.'

'Hopefully some ogre will make Jerkface his bitch and give him a taste of his own medicine,' Brendan seethed.

'One can only hope,' Liam agreed. Alannah's jaw hit the floor. Liam was usually more concerned with justice than vengeance. 'Commendable job in there, by the way.' He directed his comment to Brendan.

Brendan's eyebrows launched up. 'Um, thanks.'

'I'd best hit the road. See you both later.' Liam shook Brendan's hand before jogging down the steps and up the sidewalk.

Alannah was gobsmacked. 'What the? Did he compliment you and shake your hand?'

'Yup. I wonder if someone has kidnapped my real brother and sent an illusionist in his stead.'

She shrugged. 'Suits me. I could get used to this reasonable imposter.'

'Not too used to him I hope.' His tone was light and jovial, but Alannah could see the anxiety in his aura.

'Please don't worry about me and Liam. That relationship is well and truly over.'

'Are you sure?' He scrutinised every inch of her face.

'Yes, I promise you I'm done with Liam.'

Brendan released the breath he held and leaned in to kiss her.

He got as far a peck on the lips when Nick's hand clamped him on the shoulder. 'Come on guys, we're going to the pub to celebrate.'

Brendan smacked Nick upside on the head. 'You and Cara are seriously cramping my style, you damn cockblockers.'

Laughing, Nick nudged him in the arm and took off down the street.

Turning back to Alannah, Brendan smiled with pursed lips. 'They're being persistent. Are you okay to go to the pub for a bit?'

Alannah nodded. 'Yeah. It'll be a nice way to unwind.'

Returning to the familiarity of her old watering hole, Alannah felt as though she was seeking comfort by a friend's roaring fire in the middle of a storm. Cara bought them a round of drinks and squeezed into the booth to flank Alannah, with Brendan on her other side. The fiery redhead held up her beer. 'Let's toast to Alannah's crushing victory over those self-entitled wankers who tried to put her down and keep her down.'

There was a resounding chorus of 'Cheers!'

Beaming, she clinked her bottle with each of her friends. Even Bianca was there and not the least bit bothered by the way things had developed between Alannah and Brendan.

Cara gripped Alannah's arm. 'So, chickadee, how does it feel to be free again?'

Alannah grinned. 'Fantastic.'

'Just in time for Beltane tomorrow, too.' Jacob waggled his brows.

'Oh my Gods yes!' Cara clapped her hands. 'You should come to the festival with us, now you've cut old Stiffneck loose.'

Alannah tensed. She had not had a chance to talk to Brendan about her plans yet.

Brendan groaned. 'You're the worst, Hughes. First you stop me from taking Lana straight home, and now you're inviting her to an orgy? Have you considered the poor girl might want a bit of peace and quiet after her ordeal?'

Caleb sniggered.

Brendan glanced at Caleb. 'Something funny, Thornsy?'

'We all know why you want time alone with Alannah. Don't sugar coat it, man.'

'What's your problem, bro?' Brendan gritted his teeth.

'Oh, you think boning my sister gives you the right to call me your bro?'

Brendan paled. 'Where did you hear that?'

'Bridey told me.' Caleb narrowed his eyes at Alannah. 'I'd watch my sister if I were you. She's a real prickly one.' Rising, he left the group as a shiver ran down Alannah's spine.

Cara's eyes popped out of her skull. 'When did you sleep with Bridey?'

Brendan sighed. 'First night she arrived in town.'

'You're a moron, Winters. I can't blame Caleb for being pissed.' Cara's complexion turned a shade of red matching the roots of her dye job.

He winced. 'Can we please drop this now? It's killing the buzz for Alannah.'

Truth! Alannah had not realised how difficult it would be to deal with Brendan's past. *Will I keep looking at the women in town wondering if they were one of his many conquests? If they still have designs to get in his pants?*

Brendan's hand grasped her leg as he spoke in her ear. 'Hey, just remember they meant nothing. You're everything to me, gorgeous.' His words and calming touch did a lot to settle her thoughts, but not to remove the seed of doubt taking root deep inside.

Conversation shifted to lighter topics and the general mood improved.

When most of their group had scattered around the bar, Brendan squeezed her thigh again. 'Hey, what did you want to do for Beltane? I could set up something special at home if you like.'

She smiled at him. 'I appreciate the gesture, but I had something else in mind.'

His brows rose. 'Oh? Is it kinky, 'cause you know I'm down, right?'

Alannah bit her lip. 'Please don't hate me for this, but I'd like to try the full Beltane maiden experience at the official festival. I never got to do it when I was with Liam and if things become serious with us, I don't know if I'll get another chance.'

'Oh hell! Are you sure that's smart? The mage community haven't exactly warmed up to you again yet. What if you're partnered with an arsehole?'

'I trust the Gods will do right by me.'

He shook his head. 'You're putting a lot of faith in the Gods, Lana.'

'I have legit reason to do so.'

His left brow arched. 'What reason?'

'It's a long and difficult story I'll explain later.'

Realisation dawned on Brendan's face. 'Damnit! If you do this, you know you can't have sex for five days either side of Beltane. I wanted to ravish you tonight.'

Alannah snorted. 'Sorry to burst your bubble, babe, but I'm looking forward to a long bath followed by an early night. I have a lot of sleep to catch up on.'

After heaving a huge sigh, Brendan nodded. 'Of course. I'm sorry.'

'I want to do the Beltane thing, but I'll only go if you do it too.'

Brendan gaped at her. 'Earlier you were freaking out about the notches on my bed post and now you want to send me into a situation where I could end up screwing any number of random women?'

'This is different. Beltane is a sacred festival. Besides, there's a chance we get paired.'

'You know, a great way to increase those odds is to stay home and have our own private celebration.'

'You're missing the point, Brendan. I see this as an exciting opportunity.'

He studied her eyes for a tense moment. 'Are you sure this is what you want?'

Alannah nodded. 'Yes.'

'Then I'll do it.'

Having parked his Jag, Brendan turned to her. 'Are you still sure about this, Lana? It's not too late to go home.' He gave her an impish grin. 'We could still have our own private Beltane celebration.'

As tempting as it sounded, with the butterflies multiplying in her gut and spreading through her bloodstream, she needed to do this. 'I'm sure.'

Exhaling sharply, Brendan got out, rounding the car to open her door. As soon as she stepped out, he hugged her tight. 'Just know I'm gonna be praying something fierce to get paired with you.'

She grinned. 'Thank you.'

He squinted. 'For what?'

'Praying for me.' Alannah kissed his lips chastely before pulling out of his arms. 'Good luck in there.' She winked at him, turned, and walked through the estate gates. Parting ways with Brendan pinched at her heart. But Alannah felt the need to embrace what may be her only night as a single woman for a long time—or hopefully ever, if things went well with Brendan.

When she queued at the registration desk there were a few locals peering down their noses at her. Ignoring them, she turned her attention to the nearby display of old farm equipment. Rusted chunks of metal had never fascinated her so much. Her body began to thrum as the iron in her blood resonated with the ancient machinery's, opening her matter attunement for a second before the crowd pushed her forward.

An unfamiliar middle-aged blonde woman greeted her from behind the trestle table. 'Good evening miss. Blessed be.'

'Blessed be.' She submitted her finger to the pinprick test to prove the purity of her blood.

The woman dropped Alannah's blood in a potion vial and watched it turn the green substance clear. 'Thank you miss. Have you abstained from sexual intercourse in the last five days?'

Alannah giggled. 'It's been weeks actually.' She glimpsed the woman's gaping mouth. 'Sorry, you didn't need to know that.'

'You are cleared for entry, miss. Are you here alone?'

Alannah took a deep breath. 'Yes.'

'Maiden or mother?'

'Maiden.'

'You seem nervous. First time?'

Alannah nodded. 'First time alone, yes.'

The woman offered a sympathetic smile. 'You'll be fine, doll. I remember my first time. It was delightful. The maidens are gathering to the far East.' She pointed in the direction Alannah needed to go.

'Thank you.' As she moved through the warded barrier, she caught sight of a familiar face stopping her dead in her tracks. Liam lined up alone at the registration desk and he stared straight at her. *Crap!* She did not anticipate seeing him there. *Did he know I was coming? It will be beyond awkward if we get paired.* Blinking, she turned away from his penetrating gaze and continued to her destination.

After passing through a thicket of scrub populated by red gums, grass trees, and wattles, Alannah reached a large, fenced-off clearing. Her own boots joined the hoof prints spotting the paddock, reminding her of the first time she attended Beltane with Liam. She had made an off-hand remark: 'I hope the cows don't interrupt us. Might kill the mood, somewhat.'

Liam had grinned. 'Don't worry, Kieran has all the cattle shifted to other pastures to enjoy their own form of Beltane.'

With a sigh, she dismissed the memory and made her way to the Easternmost bonfire, joining a group of women for the disrobing ritual. This stage of the courtship and fertility rites of Beltane was new to her. She had spent previous Beltane festivals with Liam at the central fire where other committed couples worshipped the Gods without undressing. They had then found their own private spot to make love. Not that all couples spent Beltane this way—only those who were uncomfortable sharing their partners.

An acolyte priestess—one of the devout crones of the mage community—cast a large circle. Alannah watched with wide, attentive eyes as the powerful woman called upon each of the fertility Gods and Goddesses.

The priestess invited Alannah forward. 'How do you enter the circle?'

'With love and peace.' Alannah removed her white velvet robes and handed them to the crone.

'Blessed be.' The priestess turned and threw the robes in the sacred fire.

Alannah had researched the Beltane rites, so she expected this part of the ritual sewing special robes for the event.

Once everyone was in the circle, the priestess prayed, 'These maidens surrender themselves to you, oh Great Ones. Watch over them and bless them with the gifts of love, happiness, and fertility. And bless their children with the gifts of your magic.'

Alannah stepped up to the earthenware urn painted with gold Celtic knots that would decide her fate. She dipped her hand inside and retrieved a small slip of paper with the number three written on it. This told her which of the small campfires she needed to make her way to. The Gods would choose her partner. But she still stopped to pick up one of the staghorn crowns as insurance. This was her way of giving consent. Even though mages put their faith in the Gods to choose a suitable match, they could make the final call on who to mate with.

Approaching the site sign-posted with a large number three, Alannah marvelled at the vast estate with at least two-hundred other small fires dotted about the place. She gave thanks for the warmer weather because being naked on a crisper night would have been uncomfortable, despite the warmth of the fires.

Sitting on the wooden bench in front of the fire, she put the crown aside and examined the contents of the cauldron bubbling away. The fragrance of the mulled wine washed over her, easing her jitters, so she returned to her seat and waited. A few minutes later, she heard footsteps behind her. She remained frozen in place. Something touched her head and she realised it was a wreath of flowers. The man had not even seen her face before declaring his intentions.

A second later, a pair of warm hands rested on her shoulders and a familiar voice spoke, 'Remind me to send the Gods a thank you note.'

Brendan could not believe his luck when he found Alannah at his campfire. He stood in front of her and grinned, taking in the glorious view. She wore nothing but the floral crown upon her head. The vision sent signals straight to his dick. *By the Gods, he'd never seen such a perfect body*! Her skin was flawless, and her breasts were firm and perky. A twinkling of light drew his attention to her navel: the diamond adorning her midriff—beautiful and sexy. It was a superb match for the dainty stud piercing her nose. 'Nice body piercing.'

'I could say the same for you.' Her eyes darted south a moment before returning to lock with his.

It did not take his mind-reading skills to know she referred to his Prince Albert rather than the silver sleeper in his left nipple. 'Can I get you a drink?'

She rewarded him with the most precious smile known to man- or mage-kind. 'Please.'

Brendan ladled the warm, spiced wine into a pair of ceramic goblets, and handed her one. After casting an eager glance at the golden stag horns remaining on the edge of the bench next to Alannah, he took his seat beside her.

Alannah drank a few mouthfuls of the wine before turning to Brendan. 'Do you remember when we used to play those pretend games as kids and Liam was always the hero who rescued me from you?'

The memories made him smile. 'I'll never forget those days. Even when I complained about being the rogue, I loved every minute of it. Chasing you around the garden was exciting.' He winked at her.

She gave him an impish grin. 'Something about those times occurred to me recently. There was a reason I preferred having you play the villain.'

'Oh?' His heart raced as his mind considered the possibilities.

'Because of the thrill I got from having you catch me and press kisses on my lips.'

Brendan gasped. 'Lana?' he whispered.

'Shh.' Alannah placed a finger on his lips. A second later, she put the staghorn crown upon his head.

He was already hard, but even more blood surged south. The rest of him rose and pulled Alannah up with him. Their arms clung to each other as Brendan's mouth claimed hers. When he hoisted her feet off the ground, her legs wrapped around his waist. *Gods!* Her strong thigh muscles felt like vice clamps. *She is divine!*

Like most of her skin, Alannah's lips were soft and smooth, yet she writhed and moaned, kissing him with an unbridled passion telling him she was anything but fragile. Brendan carried Alannah to a patch of grass near the brazier and laid her down, breathing in the scent of her hair as he did so. Strawberries mingled with the smell of smoke from the woodfire. *Gods! How is it possible to get more aroused?* He brushed his lips across her ear.

'Is it okay if I use my powers tonight? To enhance the experience?'

'If you promise me one thing.' Her voice was deep and breathy.

Brendan gazed deep into her eyes, running his fingers through her long black locks. 'What's that?'

Alannah's gaze darkened. 'Promise me a mind-altering experience.'

He grinned. 'I promise[1].'

---

[1] For more juicy details, check out this bonus scene: *The Heat of the Beltane Fires.*

Chapter Eighteen

Watching Alannah sleep in his arms after the night they shared was surreal. Brendan did not even care if it made him a creeper. She was the sexiest, most beautiful woman he had ever seen, and she was finally his. Her peaceful expression, the way her luscious lips parted, and the frame created by her long black hair all added to the picture of perfection he could not get enough of.

He felt wrecked because they had gone until dawn before returning home, yet he was still too hyped to get any sleep. His dick did not want rest either. If Alannah had not insisted on honouring the sacred customs, he would have given into temptation, waking her up for another round. But the sun had risen to herald the end of Beltane, marking day one of five. He understood the reasoning was to ensure any child conceived in this period was the result of the Beltane rites.

Brendan placed his hand on Alannah's abdomen, wondering if he had put a baby in there.

The thought would have terrified him if she were anyone else, but the idea of starting a family with the woman he loved thrilled him. And it amazed him because he had never considered himself dad material, but as he lay there holding Alannah, he thought anything was possible.

The doorbell startled him out of his reverie. Glancing at the clock on his bedside, Brendan saw it was almost two in the afternoon. *Wowsers!* He had spent the last six hours watching Alannah sleep. Being careful not to disturb the angel in his bed, he crawled out from under the quilt and slipped into his trackpants. As the door swung open, he froze mid yawn.

'Hello, handsome. Looks like you had quite the Beltane.' Bridey drawled in a deep voice.

'What the hell do you want?'

She narrowed her gaze. 'Are you going to let me in, or do you want the neighbours to hear us discussing business?'

Grumbling, Brendan opened the door for her, and led her down the hall to the living area. He leaned against the breakfast bar with his arms crossed. 'Well?'

Bridey stepped close to him and trailed a fingernail along his bicep. 'Your latest shipment is late.'

He gulped. 'Don't you normally send your goons for jobs like this?'

A wicked grin formed on her face. 'Normally, yes. But we have a special arrangement in place.' Her hand moved from his arm to grope his junk.

Brendan flinched as he glared at her. 'Not gonna happen.'

'Shame. I guess I'll send the Collectors to Jacob.'

He grimaced at the thought of his friend suffering.

Her eyes flashed with delight. 'Hmm. I thought that might make you reconsider.'

Grinding his teeth, Brendan thought about Alannah sleeping soundly only a few metres away. *Sorry Jacob, but there is no real choice here.* 'Still not happening.'

Bridey's brow arched. 'Wow, and here I thought you cared for the scamp. You must be turning dark, after all.'

'Brendan? I hope you're making coffee,' Alannah's voice approached, sending his heart into palpations.

Lady Violet cocked her head. 'Or could it be the infamous Brendan Winters has actually fallen in love. Oh, this is priceless.' She began to bring her arms up around him, but Brendan pushed her back across the room.

Alannah entered the room wearing only a silk dressing gown and he could feel her heart beating fast as she looked from Brendan to their visitor. Bridey turned to Alannah, taking in her dishevelled appearance, one side of her mouth curling up. 'Seems like you also had a delightful Beltane. Tell me hun, did Brendan keep you up all night too? His endurance is exceptional, isn't it?'

Alannah blinked her bleary eyes and glowered at Bridey. 'Who the hell are you?'

'Lana, this is Lady Violet, and she was just leaving.'

'Lady …' Alannah's jaw hit the floor.

Bridey clicked her fingers. 'Of course, that's where I recognised you from. You're the cousin who barged in on my four-way with Brendan. I've heard so much about you, *Lady Ebony*.'

Alannah eyes widened. 'You're Caleb's sister?'

'Yes dear, why? Has he mentioned me? Caleb is such a sweet boy.'

Her eyes pierced Brendan. 'Why didn't you tell me Bridey is your Syndicate contact?'

'Because she isn't. Jacob is my contact. Lady Violet is *his* boss, not mine.'

Alannah crossed her arms, her face turning red. 'A minor technicality, I'm sure. You should have told me.'

'Lana, can we please deal with Lady Violet first? We can discuss all the things I should and shouldn't have done once she leaves.'

She huffed. 'Fine. Lady Violet, is it?'

Bridey nodded.

'What do you want from Brendan?'

'Lana,' Brendan warned.

Bridey's face lit up with a mischievous glint in her eyes. 'Would you like the comprehensive list?'

'Just the business particulars, thank you,' Alannah clipped.

'Brendan is late on his shipment of mother tincture. I came to collect, with interest.' She added the last detail with a lewd smirk in his direction.

Alannah turned to Brendan. 'Do you have the potions?'

'No. I've been a bit preoccupied lately. Kind of hard to prepare essence of joy when the woman I love is locked in prison at the mercy of sadist pricks.'

Her expression softened. 'I'm sorry.'

'This is touching and all, but I have a business to run. Handsome here should be able to channel other people's emotions if he can't evoke the feelings in himself, although now you're here, Lady Ebony, I'm sure he'll have all the inspiration he needs. You have until tomorrow to pay up. Including the interest.'

Taking one step closer to Brendan, Alannah unfolded her arms. 'What's the interest?'

He gritted his teeth. 'You don't want to know.' Brendan turned toward Bridey. 'I want out of the business, Violet. I'm done making your damn potion.'

'Sorry, handsome, but you're under contractual obligation for a full year.'

Brendan gasped, feeling the air grow too heavy. 'What? Since when?'

'Since you put your signature to this piece of paper.' She pulled a copy of their contract from her purse and handed it to him.

He snatched it from her. Sure enough, it was the deal he had signed. This time he read the full terms and conditions more thoroughly, feeling the blood drain from his face. Violet had even spelled out the nature of interest payments for late shipments: *Sexual favours of Lady Violet's choosing to be provided by the aforementioned primary producer.* His jaw dropped. '*Oh hell!*'

'Did you fail to read the fine print before signing, Mr. Winters?' Bridey grinned. 'Tsk, tsk.'

Alannah grabbed the contract and tensed as she read it. 'Oh Gods, I think I'm gonna be sick.'

'As you can see, the only way *you* can break the contract is by dying. Payment tomorrow, Mr. Winters. And I will have my interest, with or without your consent.' Bridey kissed him on the cheek and walked out of the house.

Alannah flew to Brendan as he collapsed to the floor. He drew his knees close to his chest and looked at her from beneath his heavy brow. Her heart ached for him.

'I'm sorry, Lana. I messed up big time. It was stupid of me to sign that thing. I should have read it properly. I didn't know…'

Kneeling before him, she wrapped her arms around his and kissed his lips. 'Shh. It's okay, we'll sort this out. Perhaps we could use your recent crash course in legal studies to search for loopholes in the contract. And I could try calling in a favour with Scarlett.'

'No! Don't take any more risks with her. I don't want you getting wrapped up in my mess. You've been through too much lately.'

She pulled his hands into hers, placing one over her heart as she did the same on his chest. 'Feel that? Our hearts are beating as one now. We are in this together, no matter what. This is what it means to be in love.'

He sucked in a breath. 'Gods!' Dropping his legs, he pulled Alannah into his lap to kiss her deeply. When he broke the lip contact, he smiled. 'How do I deserve you, Lana?'

'By being awesome.'

He cocked his left brow. 'More awesome than Liam?'

'Way better than Liam.' Alannah bit her lip a moment, wondering if she should tell him.

Brendan gave her a sidelong glance. 'Tell me what, Lana?'

Her cheeks flushed. 'Let's just say after last night, there are several more items for that list.'

His entire face broke out in a victorious grin, and he squeezed her tight. 'Tell me all of them.'

Alannah laughed. 'Seriously? Isn't it enough to know you're better overall?'

'Nah, uh. I'm not letting you go until you tell me all.'

She flashed him a devilish grin. 'What if I don't want you to let go?'

Brendan groaned. Rising to his feet, he pulled her with him. She wrapped her arms and legs around him, hanging on tight as he walked her down the hall, eyeing her with ravenous need.

Alannah squealed as her dressing gown fell to the floor. 'What are you doing, Brendan? You know we can't have sex yet, right?'

His lustful eyes narrowed on her. 'Doesn't exclude all forms of pleasure, gorgeous. I've been hungry for another taste of you since last night.'

She felt a rush of desire and tingles all over her bare skin. 'But we still need to sort out your contract dilemma.'

'Hmm. Dilemma you say. Should I eat you now, or after hours of studying contract law? That is a dilemma.'

Alannah laughed as he laid her down on the bed. 'How about before *and* after?'

Brendan licked his lips. 'Brilliant suggestion, my love.'

…

When they cuddled together after, Brendan's eyes twinkled as he played with a strand of her hair. 'You're incredible, Lana. Best I've ever had.'

She beamed. 'Awesome. I'm glad I compare well to all those other girls.'

Brendan straddled her, pinning her arms to the bed as his mouth moved to her ear. 'You are infinitely better than those other girls. Please stop worrying about my past, gorgeous.' His lips trailed kisses along her jawline until he reached her mouth and claimed it passionately. But he jerked back when his dick grew hard again. 'I'm gonna take a cold shower before I do something sacrilegious.'

She snorted as he disappeared into the bathroom. Getting up, she threw some clothes on before returning to the living room. After brewing some coffee and fixing herself a quick afternoon brunch, she sat down to study the copy of the contract Bridey had left. There had to be a way for Brendan to get out of the interest payments in the very least. *I will not let that endarkened bitch touch my man!*

'So, I'm your man now, huh?' Brendan clamped his hands down on her shoulders.

Alannah jumped out of her skin. 'Jesus, fuck! You scared me.'

Brendan moved around to the chair beside her and sat down, smelling of fresh shower gel, hair still damp and dripping. 'Sorry, gorgeous.' He gave her an impish grin. 'For the record, I've always been yours. You just took all this time to stake your claim.'

Breathing in deeply, she leaped into his lap, and kissed him fervently. 'Gods, I can't get enough of your lips.'

'Mm. I know exactly how you feel. I can't get enough of you in general, but especially these.' He brushed his thumb over her lips and groped between her legs. 'And these lips.'

When Alannah felt the bulge in his pants grow, she rolled her eyes and moved back to her chair. 'You are insatiable.'

'Yup.' He grinned. Sighing, he grabbed the contract and studied it. After reading over it several times, Brendan grabbed a textbook on contract law and got comfortable on the couch.

Alannah took the agreement and sat next to Brendan as she kept reading over the clauses.

After about an hour, Brendan threw the book across the room. 'This is useless. There's no point turning to the law on this when dealing with criminal activity. The contract is illegal anyway, so it's not like Violet will use legitimate channels to enforce it.'

She sighed. 'True. That's why we need to focus on the wording of these terms and conditions. I can't believe she put a sexual favours clause in here. The woman is repulsive. I can see why Caleb doesn't like her.'

'You don't know the half of it,' Brendan replied.

Bile churned in her gut. 'What do you mean?'

'Let's just say not even her brother was safe from her coercive charms.'

'Ick!' Shivering, she returned to reading. '*Of course!* It's right here. Reference is made to you as the primary producer, a term Violet defined as "the mage who produces the mother tincture for the potion known as Rhapsody". What if you aren't the only primary producer?'

Brendan beamed. 'Lana, you're a genius!'

'I hope you're right about this.' Jacob paced across their warehouse. 'What if Violet still insists on the last shipment with interest?'

Brendan offered Alannah a reassuring smile. He had asked Jacob to arrange for the meeting to occur at their place of business to save Alannah from seeing Bridey again. But she had insisted on coming with him, promising to floor the bitch if she tried anything. 'That's why I'm making it a condition of the deal,' Brendan explained. 'She'd be stupid to refuse my offer and Violet is a lot of things, but she's not stupid.'

'No, but she is a sick, twisted bitch and she's not touching my man,' Alannah added.

Jacob laughed. 'Gods, I still can't get my head around you two being a couple now.'

The buzzer sounded at the front door. Brendan glimpsed Bridey with two of her goons on the security monitor.

'Here goes.' Jacob got up and answered, creating an awful grating sound as he pulled the metal beast of a door open, then closed again.

'Thank you, Associate.'

'Madam.' He bowed his head.

Bridey cast an inquisitive eye at Alannah before focussing on Brendan. 'Do you have my potions Mr. Winters?' She drew close to him—too close.

Brendan gulped. 'I have something better.'

Her brows furrowed. 'You'd better not be—'

'Shoosh.' He put a finger up to silence her, flinching when he accidently touched her lips in the process. 'It is apparent demand for Rhapsody is high, yes?'

Still gobsmacked by his brazen move, she nodded.

'So, it makes savvy business sense to have more than one primary producer, right? I'm willing to sell you the full recipe for the mother tincture, complete with explicit instructions for essence making, along with this warehouse, on the condition you find me a replacement and allow me to exit our contract unharmed and unmolested.'

'How do I know you won't set up a competitive operation elsewhere?'

'I'm willing to sign a non-compete and non-disclosure agreement.'

'Hmm.' She went silent for a few tense minutes. 'What about Jacob?'

'He remains in the Syndicate. This is his world, not mine.'

Sighing, she circled around him, trailing a finger along his shoulders. 'Pity. You had such potential as a dark mage, and we could have had so much fun. Lady Scarlett clearly misplaced her faith in you and Lady Ebony.'

Brendan could feel his traitorous dick responding to Bridey's mild attempts at coercion. Alannah advanced on them, but he shot her a warning glance as he spoke in her mind. *'Wait, Lana. She's only toying with me.'*

'I will expect a discount considering you have not fulfilled your last shipment,' Bridey continued.

'Of course. Jacob will negotiate the particulars. Do we have a deal?'

She grinned. 'Yes, Mr. Winters. We have a deal.'

He let all the air gush out his lungs.

Bridey clasped the erection through his pants and leered at him. 'If you ever need a real woman to take care of your darkest desires, you know where to find me.'

Alannah sucked in a sharp breath between clenched teeth.

'I already have a real woman,' Brendan hissed, pushing her away.

'See you later, Mr. Winters.' Bridey winked at him and left.

'Thank the Gods!' He collapsed onto the couch and watched as Jacob pulled the heavy sliding door closed, filling the air with the screeching sound of metal parts grinding together.

Jacob grabbed them each a beer from the small bar fridge. 'Congrats, bro. You're a free man.'

Brendan clinked his bottle with Jacob's, followed by Alannah's, before pulling her into his lap. 'Cheers to that. If I never see Violet again, it will be too soon.'

Chapter Nineteen

The front door slammed, startling Alannah and making her botch the stitches in her latest sewing project. She cursed under her breath, pushing her work to one side of Brendan's dining table. Odd how she still did not think of the place as hers. They had not yet talked about her moving in officially. She still had a lot of her stuff at Liam's and moving would mean an awkward confrontation she was not ready for.

As soon as Brendan appeared, holding a black leather collar with attached lead, she knew she was in trouble. He gave her a wicked grin. 'The wait is over, gorgeous. Beltane was six days ago.'

Yep, sweet, sweet trouble. She bit her lip and simpered. But she felt the stygian channel stir through her blood and instinctively knew her eyes appeared more demonic than angelic.

He stalked toward her, holding up the collar. 'Do you know what this is, Lana?'

'It's a bondage collar.' She knew enough lifestyle kinksters to recognise it.

Brendan smiled. 'Do you know what it means to wear one of these?'

'The collared person submits to their dominant partner.'

When he reached her, Brendan circled his arms around her waist, letting the collar hang from his elbow. 'I see you've been talking to Cara and Amy about this stuff.' His fingers trailed along her arm, bringing goosebumps to the surface and she wondered how far he wanted to take things. 'Don't worry, gorgeous. I'm not interested in the full lifestyle. Let's focus on exploring those dark fantasies of yours, plus a few of my own. Sound good to you?'

Heart pounding, Alannah bounced on her heels. 'Uh, huh.' Her voice dropped low, becoming breathy.

He followed up his lascivious grin with a passionate kiss. 'First, we'll need a safe word. Something not associated with sex and the more repugnant the better.'

'How about Richard?'

'Love it. Richard it is.' Brendan twirled a strand of her hair in his hand. 'I know you've had some traumatic experiences with restraints lately, so we can forget the bondage if you prefer.'

Gods, I love this man! 'No, I trust you, Brendan. And bondage is an important part of my fantasy. Just don't use handcuffs or anything cold iron and we'll be fine.'

'Are you sure, Lana?'

'Yes, I'm sure.'

Brendan inhaled deeply. 'Any other limits?'

'No. I meant it all those years ago when I told Emma there's nothing I wouldn't let you do to me. That's still true.'

Brendan's breathing became heavy. 'Even after what that creep did to you? I will understand if any form of anal is off the cards.'

She brought her hand up to cup his cheek. 'Everything you do to me is going to feel spectacular. I'd like to have more pleasurable associations with all of it, and I know you can give me those. So, try anything and if it gets too much, I'll use the safe word.'

'Ah heck!' He kissed her again. Straightening, he ogled her. 'Are you ready for me to collar you?'

'Yes.'

He smirked. 'You don't look ready.'

Without further ado, Alannah stripped herself naked and knelt beside Brendan. Instinctively falling into her role, she bowed her head.

'Gods, Lana! I'm already hard and we just started.' The moment the collar attached to her neck, the air between them became superheated.

Crawling on all fours, she followed his lead towards the bedroom.

Brendan positioned Alannah face down, tying her to his bed in record time. After placing a red satin blindfold over her eyes, he straddled her back and rasped in her ear. 'I'd like to try something magical tonight. And I mean in every sense of the word, Lana. I reckon with what we're about to do, we can establish a two-way empathic link. Would you like that?'

'Yes, sir.'

'Mm, you are such a good girl. Although I do hope you will give me some reason to punish you tonight.'

She grinned. 'You don't need a reason, sir.'

'True. So, getting back to this idea of mine. I'd like for you to try and channel my emotions and my senses simultaneously. Can you manage that?'

'Yes, sir.'

'I'm going to have my empathic link active, which means I will feel everything you do. This will have an amplifying effect when you channel my touch, enhancing all the pleasure and pain I subject you to. Will you be able to handle it?'

Desire coiled around every nerve ending, like elastic bands winding up. 'Mm, yes sir.'

'Excellent. I'm going to start by massaging you. Once you have the channels open, let me know and I'll start to ramp things up, okay?'

'Okay, sir.' As Brendan's hands rubbed her back, Alannah focussed on his emotions first, being the more familiar power source. She felt a jolt of tingling pleasure the moment she connected, followed by a strong rush of arousal flowing through her. Senses mana was a new one, though, and she needed a visualisation. Given what they were doing, sex with Brendan was the obvious option. So, she cast her thoughts back to Beltane, bringing to mind the sight of his naked body, the sound of his husky voice, the smell of his musky cologne, the taste of his salty lips mixed with the mulled wine, and the feel of his big, strong hands all over her body. Recalling the full sensory experience, she became hyperaware of his hands on her skin. 'I'm ready, sir.'

'What's the safe word, Lana?'

'Richard.'

'Good girl.'

The impact play came next, and Brendan worked his way up through spanking, flogging, whipping, and caning. She had never experienced anything so exhilarating. The hot wax followed. For this, he drove himself inside her first, making love to her as the droplets of heat seared into her skin. It was a true test of her pain threshold, and without the added pleasure, it might have been too much. But instead, it took her over the edge, releasing the wound tension in those elastic bands around her nerves. The moment Alannah surrendered herself to Brendan, they came together.

'Gods! That was extraordinary.' Brendan removed her bonds and collar before collapsing beside her. He drew the quilt up to cover them both and hugged her. 'How are you doing there, gorgeous?'

Alannah turned to face him and smiled. 'Overwhelmed, in a rapturous way.' She brushed her lips against his and closed her eyes.

He held her for a few minutes before moving. 'I'm gonna run us a bath; be right back.'

When Brendan left the room, Alannah felt a strange sense of loss, like part of her soul was missing. A moment later, her hand felt wet. 'What the hell?' she muttered to herself. But then it dawned on her. 'Brendan?'

He returned to the bed. 'Yes, gorgeous?'

She reached forward and pinched his arm.

'Ow, what was that for?'

Alannah grinned. 'It worked. I can feel everything you do.'

Beaming, Brendan moved in to embrace her. 'You have no idea how happy that makes me, Lana.'

'Actually, now I do.'

The moment Alannah opened her eyes the next morning, she found Brendan staring at her. 'Hey.'

'Morning, gorgeous.'

'How long have you been watching me?' Her voice was still gruff from the dryness in her mouth. Sitting up, she grabbed the water bottle beside the bed and gulped down two large mouthfuls before snuggling into Brendan's arms.

'Only a few minutes this time. I slept like a rock after last night.'

Memories of their night flooded Alannah's mind: after a bath and take-away dinner, they had spent several more hours going at it, although they eased up on the more painful stuff. She felt warm and tingly from the recollection. 'Mm. Beltane was special, but last night was easily the best sex of my life.'

Brendan rolled her onto her back and straddled her as he peered into her eyes. 'Do you mean that?'

'Yeah. It was even better than kinky vampire sex.'

'I love you so much, Lana.' Before giving her a chance to reply, he crashed his lips to hers and kissed her ardently. Within minutes, Brendan plunged deep inside her.

'Wait, Brendan. I'm still not covered by birth control after Beltane.'

He pressed himself deep inside her and gazed lovingly into her eyes. 'Does it matter? Whether I impregnated you at Beltane, or if it happens now, I'll still be with you to raise our child.'

Her eyes bugged out. 'You've thought about this?'

'Yes, Lana. I promised you once, I'll never leave you, and I mean it. You're stuck with me now.' He thrust into her and before long they were writhing together.

An hour later, they collapsed alongside each other, still panting. Regaining control of her breathing, Alannah glanced at the clock: 9AM. 'Oops! You're late for work.'

'I called in a sickie. I want to spend the whole day with you.'

She arched a brow. 'Are you sure that's wise after all the time you took off recently?'

Brendan shrugged. 'Those kids are a lost cause anyway.'

Playfully shrieking, Alannah slapped his arm. 'How could you say that!'

'Because it's true. I'm better off becoming a lawyer to defend their delinquent arses in court.'

'Are you honestly considering such a career change?'

'Yup. What do you think?'

Alannah contemplated the idea. 'You'd be a great lawyer. And if you defend dark mages, you'd be like the Devil's Advocate.'

His eyes widened, grabbing and pinning her to the bed. 'Are you comparing me to Keanu Reeves?'

She giggled. 'No. I meant the Neiderman book character. Aside from the black hair, you don't look anything like Keanu.'

'No?'

Alannah shook her head. 'Nuh, uh. You're way hotter. More like Ian Somerhalder.'

'Oh? Still have a thing for vampires, do you?' He dived for her neck and nibbled the skin.

It tickled at first, but before long the intensity of his bites increased. She arched her back as moans escaped her and their foreplay escalated into another hour-long lovemaking session.

When they finished, Alannah heard something growl. 'Is that my stomach or yours?'

Brendan smiled. 'Both. Come on, let's eat.'

As he moved away, Alannah felt the same aching feeling of loss, so she rushed after him. Sticking close to his side, she helped Brendan cook up a full Irish breakfast. They were halfway through the meal before she broached the topic. 'Thank you for staying with me today. I don't know how I'd deal with the pain of separation so soon.'

Brendan peered up over the slice of toast he'd bitten into with raised brows. 'What do you mean?'

'You know, with the empathic link? When you walk away from me, it hurts. I guess I need to work on switching it off.'

'Oh wow. I'd forgotten about the pain after acclimating to it long ago. I can still feel the distance between us when the link is active, but it doesn't hurt per se. It's more like a homing signal drawing me to you.'

She huffed. 'Great! I'm the one who gets stuck with the separation anxiety and you get the stalker power.'

'Hey, you might still be able to track me. We haven't tried yet. I have an idea. Why don't we spend some time in town testing it out?'

Alannah frowned. 'Didn't you hear me say it hurts?'

He gave her a wicked grin. 'Incentive to find me sooner.'

She punched his arm. 'You are such a sadist!'

A lopsided grin formed on his face. 'Well duh. But I didn't see you complaining last night.' Rubbing the red mark on his bicep, he gazed at her lustfully. 'Don't forget I'm also a masochist.'

After gaping at him a moment, she made the connection. 'That's why you were able to keep the link open when you were caning my arse last night.'

'Bingo, babe. Are you going to finish eating those?' He pointed his fork at her plate.

Huddling around her food, she glared at him. 'Don't touch my hash browns buddy.' She made a show of scoffing them down as quick as possible and licking her lips.

Brendan's eyes darkened. 'Damn that was hot.'

Alannah used to think he was teasing her when he said such things, but this time she could feel the extent of truth in his words. She rolled her eyes. 'Is there anything I do that doesn't turn you on?'

He paused for thought. 'Hmm. Only one thing comes to mind, and you better not do it anymore.'

'What?'

'Boning my brother. He's the one man I would never consider sharing you with, so you can forget *those* threesome fantasies.'

She should not have taken her final sip of coffee because she sprayed it all over Brendan. Words failed her.

He wiped the coffee from his face. 'On that note, it's time for a shower.'

'So, what's the plan?' Alannah glanced at Brendan as he drove north along the Esplanade.

'How far do you feel like walking?'

'What do you mean?'

'I'll drop you off somewhere, then I'll go hide. You will need to walk to find me, so how far are you willing to travel?'

The thought of parting ways with Brendan, even for a short time, was like pilers pinching at her heart. *Weird*. She hated the idea of dependence on any man, even if he was the love of her life. 'I dunno. Maybe three k's.'

He sniggered. 'You *do* have it bad for me.'

She glared at him. 'Do you want me to hit you again?' As the grin formed, she added, 'Wait! Don't answer that.'

'I'm sorry, Lana, but I love teasing you. Always have, always will.'

Always will. Two simple words became music to her ears. Alannah's expression softened and she knew in her heart Brendan was hers forever.

'Right, here we are.' They had stopped outside the boatshed, north of the bridge leading across to the small island housing the Sailing and Lifesaving clubs. 'I'll text you when I reach my destination. If you can't pinpoint my direction within thirty minutes, call me and I'll come get you, okay?'

'Okay.' She leaned across the car to peck his lips and hopped out.

The Jag sped through the middle of town a moment later.

Alannah doubled over from the pain once he disappeared. 'Crapola!'

Footsteps came running toward her, and strong arms caught her before she hit the ground. 'Gods! Are you okay, Alannah?'

She smiled at Connor's concern. 'Yeah, I'm okay. Just a strong muscle cramp.'

'Do you want me to look at it?'

'No, I'll be fine. But thank you.' She noticed his hair was wet. 'Have you been diving today?'

'Yeah, just finished collecting and processing some aquatic plant samples. I'm heading into town for an early lunch. What are you up to?'

'I'm looking for Brendan.'

'Ah, well I saw him—'

'No! Don't tell me. I'm trying to use magic to locate him. It's a training exercise.'

Connor eyed her askance. 'O-kay.'

Alannah sighed because Connor was not stupid. Magical tracking was rare and usually involved a clairvoyant using scrying crystals on a map. 'We have created an empathic link. Well, my side of the link is new; Brendan's felt me for years.' She grimaced. 'That sounded dirty. Anyway, I'm testing whether or not I can use the link to find him, like he can with me.'

Connor cracked up laughing. 'You guys are adorable. I'm glad you finally hooked up. Would you like some company on your hunt? In case you have another muscle cramp?'

Figuring some conversation could distract her from the pain, she nodded. 'Yeah, sure. Give me a minute.' Alannah checked the message she received from Brendan.

{Brendan} **Ready and waiting for you, gorgeous.**

Closing her eyes, she focused on the part of her soul linked to Brendan's. *He feels excited*. She sensed it, the strong pull. Opening her eyes, she headed for the centre of town. 'This way.'

Gobsmacked, Connor followed her. 'So, if you have this link, does that mean you are attuned to emotions and senses as well?'

'Yeah, I suppose it does.'

'So, how many attunements do you have now?'

She counted them in her head. 'Seven.'

'Woah! That's more than the High Magus.'

Alannah smirked. 'Good point.' They walked in silence for a few minutes, giving her a chance to confirm the direction they headed. 'Connor, can I ask you a personal question?'

He cocked a brow. 'You can ask, but I can't promise I'll answer.'

'Do you and Amy ever swap roles, or is she always the Dom?'

'No. We aren't switches like Jacob and Cara. I like being Amy's sub. Why do you ask?'

'Just curious.'

Connor's eyes narrowed. 'Does Brendan know you're interested in kink?'

Alannah laughed. 'You should know there's no hiding this stuff from Brendan. Of course he knows. We even dabbled last night.'

'Is that so? Did you establish roles, because I'm having a hard time placing who would be the Dom in your relationship?'

'I subbed to Brendan.'

'Wow. I can't imagine you subbing to anyone.'

Alannah sighed. 'I guess the bedroom is the one place where I feel I can let go. It's nice to give up all sense of control sometimes, you know?'

'Yeah, I know exactly what you mean. So, are we gonna start seeing you and Brendo at the dungeon?'

'No. At least not anytime soon. We aren't planning to take things beyond the bedroom.'

Connor shrugged. 'Shame though. It'd be fun to have you guys visit on occasion.'

'Does the club allow visitors?'

'There are nights when we can invite friends.'

Curiosity got the better of her. 'Has Brendan ever gone on these nights?'

He bit his lip. 'Maybe you should ask *him*.'

'He totally has!' She sniggered. 'No wonder he knew what he was doing last night.' Alannah felt Brendan's presence close by. She tuned in to the sensation and glanced in the direction she expected to see him. When her gaze fell upon the VETERINARY SURGEON sign, her heart almost ruptured from all the love she felt. She had been thinking about how much she missed Nora that morning. Ross had cancelled the last family dinner due to Beltane, and Alannah had been in prison the fortnight prior. When she thought about it, the last proper chat she had with Nora was seven weeks ago. She turned to Connor. 'Well, thanks for the talk. This is my stop.'

'No worries, Alannah. See you round.'

As soon as she stepped into the waiting room, Brendan jumped up and ran to her, pulling her into his arms. 'I guess it worked.'

Smiling, Alannah pushed up on tippy toes and kissed him. 'Yeah, it worked.'

Brendan tightened his hold and deepened the kiss.

'Naw, you guys are such a cute couple.' Ben's voice drew Alannah's attention. She noticed he was wearing scrubs, with his long hair tied back.

'Aren't they just?' Nora agreed. 'I haven't seen the two of them this happy since… well, ever. Hi, honey.' She opened her arms and Alannah flew into them.

'Hi Nora.' After their hug, Alannah turned to the man in scrubs. 'Hi Ben. I didn't know you work here.'

Ben smiled. 'Yeah. I started a couple of months ago after finishing my studies.'

'Ben is my assistant. He has exceptional rapport with the patients here,' Nora explained.

'The discount medical bills are a bonus too.' Ben gave them a toothy grin.

'I just have to keep him away from these little ones.' Nora walked over to a large cage holding a few playful kittens, all with plastic cones around their necks.

Alannah heard Ben's inner dingo growl as she approached the cats. 'Aww, they're adorable.' Brendan moved in close to her side as she put her finger through the bars. She addressed them with a cutesy voice, 'Why are you here to see Dr. Winters, hmm?'

'The local animal shelter brought them in for de-sexing and shots as part of their adoption program,' explained Nora.

Brendan gasped. 'You mean to tell me these poor critters will never know the joys of sex? I'm horrified, mother.'

Alannah laughed and elbowed him in the ribs.

Ben snarled. 'We don't need more of those filthy things breeding.'

A pure white kitten pounced at Alannah's finger, reminding her of another white cat she had once met. 'Oh Gods, my heart just melted. This one is too cute.'

'Would you like to hold her?' Nora stepped up beside her.

Alannah's eyes widened. 'Could I, please?'

'Of course.' She opened the cage and retrieved the white fluffball. 'Here. Be careful of these stiches.'

As Alannah cuddled the kitten, it stared at her with wide blue eyes.

Brendan's arm circled Alannah's waist as his other hand joined hers in patting the kitten. 'You wanna adopt a fur baby together?'

She shot him a look. 'Can we? I mean the place is a rental.'

'Won't be a problem.'

'Then yes, I'd love to take this precious girl home. How much does the adoption cost?'

'Don't worry about it, hun. I've got it covered.' Her aunt smiled.

'Really?'

Nora nodded.

'Thank you, so, so much.'

'What do you want to name her?' Brendan asked.

'I have the perfect name. I want to call her Luna.'

Chapter Twenty

Later that afternoon, Alannah curled up on Brendan's couch to read from her book of shadows with a kitten snuggled in the crook of her neck. It was the sweetest, most heart-warming sight he had ever beheld. He moved behind her to pet the sleeping fluffball. 'I'm going to die from cuteness overload here, Lana. You know, I still can't believe you called her Luna.'

'What's wrong with Luna?'

'Don't you think it sounds a lot like Lana?'

She shrugged her free shoulder. 'I suppose it does. I named her after another white cat I'd met in foster care after Dad died.'

Brendan sat beside her. 'That's all well and good, gorgeous, but don't get mad at me if I mix up your names.'

She snorted. 'So long as you don't call out for the cat during sex, I'll deal.'

Laughing, he glanced at the book in her lap. 'How are you going? Find anything yet?'

Alannah was searching for a spell or ritual to help her control the empathic link so Brendan could do stuff like run to the shops and go to work without subjecting her to excruciating pain. 'Nothing helpful yet. From what I've gathered, these empathic links generally require a strong spiritual connection.'

'I always thought we were soulmates.' He gave her a big dumb grin.

She arched her brow. 'Corny much?'

'Yup. But I know you love it.'

'Not as much as I love you.' She leaned in and planted a sloppy kiss on his lips.

The movement disturbed Luna, who scurried off Alannah's shoulder and skidded across the room where she hid under the entertainment unit. They both laughed at the kitten's antics before returning their attention to the book.

Alannah flicked through a few pages when a few Gaelic words stood out to Brendan. 'Wait. What about this one? "Ceangal Anamacha" means the connecting or binding of souls. Didn't you say the pain feels like having part of your soul torn away?'

'Hmm. Valid point.' She pulled out a translator and continued reading.

Brendan would have read along with her, but Luna decided to attack his leg, so he scooped her up and cuddled her. He had never thought of himself as much of a cat person before, but this kitten stole his heart, much like Alannah had. Perhaps it was the experience of caring for another being together. As Luna curled up and drifted off to sleep on his lap, he became distracted by thoughts of raising a child with Alannah.

'Oh my Gods! This is it!' Alannah's outburst sent the kitten running again.

He focussed on the book. 'Fantastic. Let's get started. What do we need?'

She pursed her lips. 'Oh. Sorry, this isn't about the empathic link. But it is the secret of the lich. It has to be. Look here.' Alannah pointed to a passage of the ritual. 'It talks about preventing true death by binding the soul to a crystal.'

Brendan's eyes widened as he read the passage. 'You're right! What sort of crystal?' He scanned the rest of the page, finding it and tapping the word. 'Clear quartz.'

'For real? The stuff is like way too common for such powerful magic.'

'Rarity has nothing to do with it. The magic powers of crystals come from their chemical composition and origins. Clear quartz has strong psychic and spiritual properties. Mages also know quartz for its stability and longevity, with some crystals being billions of years old—so it makes sense.'

She gaped at him. 'How do you know all this stuff?'

'I've been studying magic theory since I could read, Lana. Crystals always fascinated me.'

'Hmm. Fair enough.' She returned her attention to the book. 'Apparently the crystal glows once the mage binds their soul to it.' Her mouth gaped open. 'I remember seeing a crystal like it in Mum's mystic chest. I kept it with the others in your parents' training room until…' Alannah jumped from the sofa.

Brendan sprung to his feet. 'What is it? What's wrong, Lana?'

'I took the crystal to my sanctuary with a bunch of others because Scarlett—I mean Tara—suggested they would be useful for my training.' She ran to the door and put her shoes on.

He rushed after her. 'What are you doing, Lana?'

'I need to go and check if the crystal is still there. What if she took it? Or, better still, what if she didn't? We could have the means to destroy her once and for all.'

A light switched on in Brendan's mind. 'Do you think destroying the crystal would bring about her true death?'

'That's exactly what I'm thinking. It makes perfect sense. Maybe this is why she trained me all along. She wanted me to bring the crystal to her.'

He sighed. 'If so, I doubt she left it there.'

'Only one way to find out. Come on, let's go.'

Brendan insisted on driving, knowing how many thoughts distracted Alannah's mind.

The moment they arrived, she bolted into the glamoured shed and rummaged through her stash of crystals. 'Damnit! It's gone.' Alannah dropped to the floor.

He sat next to her and pulled her into his arms. 'On the plus side, we can be even more certain the crystal is the key to Tara's true death. She is less likely to leave something so important lying around in the hands of the enemy. Maybe we need to find her current hideout.'

Alannah sighed. 'You're right. I guess it's time to see if I can meet her again.'

Tara examined Alannah and Brendan when first entering the sanctuary an hour later. 'This is a curious development. I suppose congratulations are in order.' She directed her gaze at Alannah. 'You have made an excellent soulmate choice, dear child. Brendan is a more suitable match for you than Liam. That boy is too much of a Council pet, like his father.'

Alannah could feel Brendan's chest swelling. She turned and smiled at him, before returning her attention to Tara. 'What are you talking about, Madam?'

'Please tell me your soul link connection is an intentional choice.'

'You mean the empathic link we have? It was Brendan's idea, but I was delighted to make it a two-way link. But how did you know about it?'

Tara laughed haughtily. 'Have you seen your auras lately?'

Alannah's attention shot to Brendan. 'Have you?'

'No. I don't need to see your aura when I can feel your emotions strongly now. Give me a sec.' He took a few steps back to study her.

She read his aura too. Knowing what to expect from his outer colours, she focused on the main aura. 'Wowsers… that's different.' The right side was still his usual yellow, although murky from the dark magic he had been mixed up in. But the left side of his aura was orange.

Tara drew up close behind Alannah. 'I assume you are both aware your auras are a visual representation of your soul. Brendan is now seeing a mirror image of what you can see, dear child. Soul linking is the ultimate commitment mages can make to each other. No one has performed it in these parts for decades. Couples often accompanied the private ritual with a public declaration involving a handfasting ceremony. They chose ribbons based on the colours of the joining souls. Am I going out on a limb here to assume your ignorance on these matters means you did not know what you were getting yourselves into?'

'Not entirely,' Alannah agreed. 'Did you know, Brendan?'

He shook his head.

Alannah tilted her head. 'But why did Brendan already feel the link before we, uh, joined.'

'You do not need to act coy on my account, dear child. I am aware of what soul linking entails. Besides, I have indulged in acts of debauchery that would make your head spin.'

Ew, too much information Grandmother!

Ignoring Alannah's thoughts, Tara went on, 'If Brendan felt the connection before, it meant he already devoted himself to you. So much so his soul instinctively chose yours.'

Brendan grinned at her, conveying a telepathic message, *'Told you.'*

'So, it had nothing to do with Brendan's attunements?'

'Actually, being an enchanter has a lot to do with Brendan's inclination towards the link. The traditional joining ritual requires both partners to channel emotions and senses during the act of intimacy. It took some mages years to master the arts necessary, making the commitment even more meaningful.'

Brendan chuckled. 'So, what you're saying is Alannah and I had the magical equivalent of a Vegas wedding?'

Tara smiled warmly. *Such an odd sight*. 'That is one way of putting it.'

Alannah decided to leap on the opportunity. 'Why does it hurt me every time Brendan leaves my side?'

'You are suffering a symptom of the honeymoon phase. It should wear off after a month.'

'Honeymoon phase?' Alannah and Brendan chimed in unison.

'Newly linked soulmates are supposed to spend their first month focussed on each other as way of kickstarting their family.'

'How do I switch my side of the link off and on like Brendan can?'

'With practice, you should be able to push thoughts and feelings for Brendan from your mind using mindfulness, bringing them back in much the same way. This will help modify the physical aspects of the soul connection.' Looking at Brendan, she pursed her lips. 'I guess years of unrequited love gave you plenty of opportunities to hone this skill?'

He nodded, eliciting a sharp pain in Alannah's gut. Squeezing her hand, he spoke in her mind. *'Don't worry about it, gorgeous. All water under the bridge now.'*

She gazed into his eyes, feeling lost in them a moment.

Tara cleared her throat. 'Was there another reason you called me here, or have we finished?'

Blinking, Alannah sighed. 'Yes, actually. I noticed one of my crystals have gone missing, a white quartz. You took it, didn't you?'

'Hmm. I see you have discovered the secret of the lich. Yes, I took my soul crystal back, and I have hidden it safely. I know you still don't trust me, and it would be foolish to leave the instrument of my undoing in your hands.'

Alannah gasped at Tara's candid response. 'If you are aware of my intentions, why are you meeting with me?'

'Because I am not your enemy, Alannah. I had hoped our training sessions and everything I have done for both of you would have proven this.'

Brendan snorted. 'What have you done for me other than send me a potion book that landed me in a world of trouble, then given me a mind shield to protect me from the legal consequences?'

Tara huffed. 'Show some respect, boy. What you did with my book was your own choice, Brendan. When I saw you had aligned yourself with the Syndicate, I stepped in to mediate matters for you. Without me, you would be at Lady Violet's mercy. And why do you think you were able to absorb so much knowledge during your crash-course in legal studies? I have been looking out for the two of you in more ways than you realise.'

They were both gobsmacked. Brendan dropped to his knees in front of her, adopting a playful tone, 'Please Lady Scarlett, I beg you to share your magic wisdom with me. Like the trick of yours for quick learning.'

Tara laughed as Alannah rolled her eyes. 'Brendan, please stop grovelling; you look ridiculous.'

Casting his gaze her way, he poked his tongue out at Alannah, before pulling himself up to his feet. 'Seriously though, I'm keen to learn.'

'I would be happy to teach you both everything I know.' Tara moved across the room and sat at the table.

Alannah watched with a frown as Brendan followed Tara like a faithful puppy. Before joining them, she needed the truth. 'Lady Scarlett?'

'Yes, dear child?'

'Has your goal been to turn me and Brendan dark?'

Tara's brows rose. 'Did you not meet your father?'

Brendan's head snapped in Alannah's direction; his brow creased.

'Yeah, I did. But how did you know?'

Her grandmother smiled again. 'Because I arranged the meeting. What did he tell you, Alannah?'

'Wait a minute,' Brendan interrupted. 'When did you meet your old man and why am I only hearing about it now?'

Alannah sat down next to him. 'Because it is difficult to talk about that time. I met him in the Celestial realm when I was… defiled.'

'Oh, hell!' Brendan gasped, jumping to his feet. *'You died? That bastard killed you?'*

She shook her head. 'No! Please calm down, Brendan. It was more like… astral projection.' When he returned to his seat, she continued, 'When I met my father, he told me he was proud of me and I was on the right path; he guaranteed my place in the realm if I stay on this path.'

Tara nodded. 'What does that tell you about the nature of my influence?'

Alannah scratched her head. 'But you are cursed and tried to curse me. You tried to damn my soul!'

Tara sighed. 'You have much to learn, dear child. It was never my intention to hurt you. Cursing was a means to an end. I needed your allegiance and as Queen at the time, I saw an opportunity to bring you in line when you became close to Austin. It was a short-sighted approach and I am sorry for what transpired.'

'Why didn't you ask me directly?'

'To protect you from the Council. They cannot see you working willingly with me. Surely you gathered as much from your time on trial?'

'I still don't understand.'

'Because you still have much to learn and revealing too much too soon will put you in extreme danger.'

'Danger from whom?' Brendan demanded.

'It is best you do not know yet. Knowledge can be a dangerous asset to possess in a world full of mind readers. Richard may be gone, but they will appoint another Inquisitor soon enough.' She placed another mind shield on the table and pushed it toward Alannah. 'This should help in the meantime, but both of you need to study the art of deception and perfect your skills before I tell you much more.'

Alannah hated the idea of becoming a deceiver, but she had suffered enough at the hands of the Council to appreciate the need. 'Okay then, guru. Teach us how to become liars.'

Catching her breath, Alannah moaned pleasurably. 'I'm loving this honeymoon phase concept.' It was late afternoon and they had spent the day making love. In fact, it was day seven and counting of their staycation and she was more than thankful Brendan had chosen to spend the full month by her side, to prevent the pain of separation. At least she had learnt to switch off the link when she needed to focus on other tasks.

Brendan's fingers trailed along her bare stomach. 'Mm, yes. Best idea ever. Pity it only lasts a month, 'cause I could spend all day, every day like this with you, Lana.'

As if sensing another break in carnal activities, Luna jumped onto the bed and rubbed up along Alannah's side, purring profusely as she did.

Alannah giggled from the sensation. 'Hey kitty, that tickles.' The cat pounced. 'Ow, Fuck! Luna, you bad kitty!'

Brendan jack-knifed, wearing a huge grin, and clutching his nipple. 'Did she bite your boob?' When she replied by biting her lip and blushing, he rolled onto his side and roared with laughter. 'Too. Damn. Funny.'

With their empathic link still open, she could feel his mirth and let it infect her as she joined the hysterics.

The sound of Timberlake singing 'Sexy Back' through Brendan's phone ended their fit of amusement. Naturally, he had to answer with a well-timed, 'Yeah… Hang on Cara, slow down. I'm gonna put you on loudspeaker so Alannah can hear you, okay?'

With the phone held in front of her, Alannah leaned in. 'Hi hun, what's going on?'

'Hi Alannah. I'm freaking out because I can't get hold of Jacob. When was the last time either of you saw or spoke to him?'

'At the pub, three nights ago.' Brendan exchanged a glance with Alannah.

'I haven't been able to contact him since flying out Sunday night. It's not like him to miss my calls and not return them. I'm worried. Can you please check in on him at home?'

'Okay. Do you want us to stay on the line while we head over there?' Brendan asked.

'Yes, please.'

'Just give us a minute to get ready, okay?' Alannah added.

'Okay.'

When they got there, they found Jacob and Cara's door locked, so Brendan thumped it with his fist. No response. He hammered against it.

Alannah held the phone. 'The door's locked and he's not answering, Cara.'

'Can you use your matter attunement to pick the lock?'

'Alright. Hang on a minute.' She handed the phone back to Brendan and placed her hands over the door and the lock while she connected with the material mana source. When the familiar power source flowed through her, she visualised the locking mechanism and liquified the pins. 'Done. Sorry, hun, but you'll need a new lock.'

'Least of my worries right now,' Cara replied.

Brendan and Alannah both withdrew combat knives from their belts and made a stealthy entrance. It did not take them long to scout the place and confirm all was in order, except for the complete lack of Jacob.

Brendan retrieved the phone from his pocket. 'There's no sign of him, Cara. Place is locked up tight, no sign of a struggle or anything out of the ordinary.'

'Shit! Where the hell is he?' Cara's voice increased in pitch and volume.

'I can think of one likely avenue to explore, but I'll need to sign off and call you back later tonight,' Brendan explained.

'Okay, please don't be too long.'

'I'll do my best. I promise.'

'Thanks, Brendan.'

He signed off and looked at Alannah. 'You know I wouldn't do this if I didn't absolutely have to, right?'

Her heart sank because she realised what Brendan had in mind. 'I know. This is for Cara and Jacob's sake. At least let me come with you.'

Brendan smiled. 'I wouldn't expect otherwise, gorgeous. Come on. We better hurry.'

An hour later, they were walking into the underground lair of Bridey Hawthorn, aka Lady Violet. It was everything Alannah would have expected of the endarkened enchantress: opium den meets brothel, with Victorian boudoir furnishings of purple velvet and black leather.

Her leather-clad guard, Aiden, stopped them in the hallway beyond the main chamber to announce their arrival.

'Let them in,' Violet's voice called out in response from beyond the velvet curtain.

When Aiden pulled the curtain aside, Alannah stared aghast at Bridey sprawled out on a chaise longue, wearing nothing but a corset and smoking something herbal with a cigarette holder, while a guy with long black hair continued to eat her out. Several other men in various states of undress surrounded her. *This woman has no shame.*

Alannah also sensed Brendan's discomfort as he dragged his feet forward.

Bridey tapped her current lover on the head. 'Oh look sweety, your friends are here.'

When the endarked man turned his head to face them, Alannah's stomach churned from the recognition. But Caleb maintained a passive expression as he leaned back against his sister's naked thigh.

'The hell?' Brendan thundered. 'Violet, let him go—right now!'

'Why, handsome? Did you want to take his place?'

Caleb snarled at Brendan.

'Hell no. Enthralling your brother is twisted and wrong.'

Bridey tittered. 'You seem to be of the mistaken impression Caleb doesn't want to be here. Tell them, sweety.'

'It's true. I love my sister and want nothing more than to please her.'

Brendan shook his head. 'Unbelievable.'

Alannah glared at her. 'Would you mind covering up?'

'Aw, what's wrong petal? Are you afraid your new soulmate won't be able to resist my feminine wiles?'

Alannah's eyes widened.

'Oh yes, I can see the link. Brother dearest, did you know we have a pair of newlyweds to congratulate?'

'What?' Caleb squinted.

'Brendan and Alannah made the *ultimate commitment* and linked their souls. Isn't that sweet?

I wonder how long it will last before one of them *begs* me to sever the connection.' Bridey sat up and closed her legs, forcing Caleb to rise and join the rest of her (reverse) harem. 'You know, severing soul links is one of the many services I offer in this fine establishment. Is this what brings you here tonight?'

'No. We are content with our link, thank you,' Brendan hissed. 'We are here because Jacob is missing, and I want to know what you have done with him.'

Bridey burst into laughter. 'Oh, you are precious, Brendan. You ought to know better than most how the sneakthief can get himself in plenty of trouble without my help. Why would you assume I have anything to do with his disappearance?'

'Because you're his boss, for one. And I have firsthand experience with the underhanded ways of the Syndicate.'

'Well I have no idea what happened to him. But do let me know when the scamp shows up. He owes me an interest payment.' Bridey winked at Brendan.

It took all of Alannah's self-restraint to hold back from clawing the bitch's eyes out.

'If you want my advice, I'd start by checking all the warlock holding cells around the state. There was a big potion bust on the weekend. Failing that, try the local drug dens. Now, unless you want to join the merriment, Aiden will show you out.'

They both spun on their heels and strode out of the cesspit of sin.

Chapter Twenty-One

Silence prevailed on the drive to Cailleach Estate. Breaking the news of their soul link to the family would be awkward, but it did not weigh as heavily on their minds as their missing friend. They had spent the last twenty-four hours searching for Jacob to no avail and Cara was beside herself. Alannah wanted to be with her, but Cara had insisted on bringing Liam into the search, which meant resolution time.

As the Jag came to a stop, she turned to Brendan. 'Are you okay?' It was a stupid question. Alannah could feel his mood was not pretty.

'I should be out there searching for him, not enjoying a family meal.'

Alannah sighed. 'I know, but we promised Cara we would try this her way.'

'Well, let's get this over and done with.' Brendan made his exit from the car and Alannah followed close behind.

Nora squealed with delight when they entered the kitchen. 'There's the happy couple.' She pulled up short of hugging them when she noticed the clouds hanging over them both. 'What's wrong?'

'Jacob's missing,' Brendan replied.

'Oh sweety, I'm sorry. I know you are close to him. I'm gonna have to insist on that hug now.' She pulled Brendan into her arms and opened the embrace to Alannah.

'What's with the group hug?' Ross crossed the room.

Nora stepped back and smiled at him. 'They have good and bad news to share tonight.'

'Best get the bad news out the way so we can have the good news over dinner,' Ross advised.

'What bad news?' Liam entered the cramped room.

'Alright, everyone out of my kitchen. Take it into the dining room while I finish up in here.' Nora pushed them all out the door.

Once they sat, Brendan turned to Liam. 'Jacob Bennett is missing. I know you're not a big fan of his, but I'm hoping for your help in tracking him down. We could use police and Council resources on this.'

'You're right, I'm not a fan. He's an unseelie, Brendan. The Council won't spare him a second thought and I don't owe him anything.'

'No, but the police ought to. He is still a citizen,' Alannah added. 'And we are asking you to do this for us and for Cara. I know you still care about her, despite your complicated past.'

Liam sighed. 'Fine. What do I need to know?'

Alannah smiled at him. 'Thank you, Liam.'

Brendan filled him in on the details, avoiding any mention of the potion business.

'If he is as dodgy as he sounds, I can't promise I won't be locking him up when I find him.'

Anticipating Brendan's hostile response, Alannah intervened. 'At least we know the Council will keep him safe, right Brendan?' She placed a reassuring hand on his thigh.

'Right.'

Nora's timing with dinner was perfect for a change in conversation. And topics were much lighter while they ate.

Alannah breathed easier knowing she had succeeded in winning Liam over for the help they needed.

When dessert came out, Nora also brought out a bottle of expensive champagne and winked at

Alannah. *Oh Gods!* It was the moment she had been dreading. This time, Brendan gave her the reassuring hand squeeze.

Liam's eyes narrowed on the glass flute Nora poured sparkling wine into. 'What's with the bubbles, Mum?'

Brendan smirked. 'This is the good news bit—although you might want a stronger drink, Brother.'

Liam's eyes flicked from Brendan to Alannah, and he paled.

'Dad, you can stop trying to set me up with pure mages, because I have the perfect woman right here.'

'I figured something was going on between the two of you. So, are you an official couple now? Is that what we are celebrating?' Ross asked.

Liam locked Alannah in a stare as Brendan's words spilled out.

'Yup. Alannah and I have made the ultimate commitment.'

'*What?*' Liam's attention snapped toward Brendan.

'Have you heard of soul linking, Liam?'

Liam's face turned red. 'Is this some kind of joke?'

Dropping his guard briefly, Brendan let his colours show. 'No joke. Just ask Mum. She can see our mirror image auras *right now*.'

Liam turned to Nora, who nodded while squirming in her seat. 'Shit!' Liam leaped out of his chair and stormed out the back door.

'I'm sorry.' Nora hunched over her place at the table. 'I didn't think he'd take the news so disagreeably. I thought he knew the two of you were together and he'd had time to deal with it.'

'I'll go talk to him. We still have a lot of unresolved issues.' When Alannah stood up, Brendan made to follow her. 'No. I have to do this alone. I'll be able to deal with the short distance.'

'Okay.' He pecked her on the lips and sat down.

Alannah found Liam on the swinging loveseat hanging from the Moreton Bay Fig and sat beside him. 'Talk to me, Liam. What's going on?'

'Not much. My life has been pretty uneventful since you left it; oh, except for the bit where you ripped my heart out.'

'That's hardly fair, Liam. You left me, remember? You even pushed me into Brendan's arms, so don't tell me you're surprised by how things turned out.'

'Biggest regret of my life. I thought if you got him out of your system, you'd eventually find your way back to me when he messed up and did the dirty on you like he does with every other girl. And when I saw you alone at Beltane, I allowed myself to hope. I didn't expect things to escalate this fast… so honestly, I am extremely surprised.'

She stared aghast at him. 'That's stupid logic, Liam. And what you did by dumping me in prison was wretched.'

Tears fell from his eyes. 'I know and I am so damn sorry, Lana. I still can't forgive myself when you won't even forgive me.'

Seeing how much he was suffering melted her heart. Without thinking, she moved a hand to his face to wipe away his tears. 'I forgive you, okay.'

Liam grabbed her hand and pulled her into his lap to kiss her savagely.

His attack on her senses blindsided Alannah and it took her several seconds to realise what was happening. She pushed back out of his arms. 'Liam! What the hell?'

Kicking off from the swing, he rose. 'I'm sorry, Lana. I've had a harrowing time living without you.'

'Well, you're gonna have to get over me because I'm with Brendan now. And what I have with him isn't a passing phase. He and I are forever.' A moment later, Alannah collapsed to the ground as the familiar agony winded her.

'What's wrong, Lana?' Liam rushed to her and scooped her up from the dirt.

The pain she felt could only mean one thing. 'Brendan crossed the threshold. He must have left already.' When he squinted, she summarised the honeymoon phase symptom.

'Why would he run off?' Liam's brow furrowed.

'I don't know. Maybe he got word of Jacob? Let's go find out.' Thanks to the crippling pain, she hobbled back to the house with Liam's help. When they got back, Alannah directed her question to Nora: 'What happened to Brendan?'

'He was on the phone, then rushed back inside to tell me something urgent came up before he drove off.'

'Sounds Jacob-related to me,' Liam agreed.

Alannah tried ringing him, but the phone went straight to voicemail. 'Hey. Just wondering what's going on. Call me as soon as you can. Love you.' She looked at Liam. 'Can you please give me a lift home?'

'Yeah, okay.'

The air was thick with tension even after Liam and Alannah had left the room. Brendan averted his gaze from his father's cold glare. 'I'm gonna check in with Cara.' Pulling his phone out of his pocket, he stepped out onto the back porch.

'Hi Brendan. Please tell me you have good news.'

'Sort of. Liam has agreed to help.'

'What a relief. Thank you so much.'

He sighed. 'Don't thank me. Lana talked him around.'

'I knew she would. Please pass on my gratitude.'

'Will do. I'll keep you posted.'

'Okay, bye Brendan.'

He had not even realised he had been walking into the garden until he hung up, but it made sense. Alannah's pull on him had been much stronger since completing the soul link. As soon as they came into view, he stopped himself from advancing. Brendan did not want to eavesdrop on their conversation, contented to gaze upon the beautiful woman he loved. The woman who was finally his—mind, body, and soul.

Her hand touched Liam's face, and Brendan froze. When she leaped into Liam's lap and kissed him, something deep inside Brendan broke, along with all the promises they had ever made each other. Unable to watch anymore, he turned and fled.

Rushing back through the house, he cried out, 'Something urgent came up.' Jumping into his Jag, he gunned it out of there. 'Fuuuuuuck! Fuck! Fuck! Fuck!' He banged his hand against the steering wheel. *How could I have been so stupid? Of course she would still have feelings for Liam*. Brendan never even gave them a chance to resolve their issues before besieging her with his own love.

Tears streamed down his face as he reached the expressway. In addition to the grief, he felt the tearing of his soul—something he had not experienced for years.

Brendan only knew one way to deal with what he felt. When he got there, he barged in and dropped to his knees before her. 'Please make the pain go away.'

'Well, that didn't take long now, did it handsome?' Bridey smirked.

'Please. You said you could sever the link. I want it gone. *Now*.'

'It'll cost you.'

'Name your price.'

'Mm. You are precious. I want a year of your sexual servitude.'

'Done. Now make it stop.'

When Alannah got home, curling up in bed was all she could manage. The pain became unbearable. 'Please, Brendan, come home to me soon,' she whispered to the empty room.

Luna jumped onto the bed and batted at her nose. 'Meow.'

'Hey kitty. Are you hungry? Let's get you some dinner.' Hauling herself out of bed, she clung to the walls as she walked down the hall. She struggled with the ring pull on the cat food tin. 'Fucker!' The bastard snapped. She flung the can across the room and poured some biscuits in Luna's bowl instead. Sinking to the floor, she watched the cat eat. At least it took her mind off the pain.

A few minutes later, she began to nod off as the pain eased. *Are you on your way home now, my love?* Alannah crawled down the hall to the bedroom, remembering with fondness the first time she had done so; only Brendan had been by her side then. She stripped herself bare in anticipation of his return and climbed back under the quilt. Try as she might, she could not hold sleep off any longer. *Brendan will have to wake me when he gets back.*

Alannah woke with a start. The room was dark, and Brendan's side of the bed was empty. She moved her hand into the vacant space. 'Still cold.' Her separation pain had subsided. *Odd*. She got up. 'Brendan?' Searching every room of the apartment to no avail only served to intensify her heartbeat. Grabbing her phone, Alannah checked for messages. Nothing. She rang him again.

'Hi this is the voicemail of Brendan Winters. I'm currently bringing sexy back, so you'll need to leave a message after the tone…'

She sighed as the beep sounded. 'Hey baby, I'm getting worried now. Please call me; or better still, bring your sexy arse back to bed. I love you.' She typed out the same message in a text and sent it to his phone and every one of his social media accounts.

After a few deep breaths, Alannah tried to focus on their spiritual connection to see if she could track him. But she felt nothing. 'Crap, that's scary.' Normally she could at least gauge his mood and feel what his hands were doing. When she failed to get a read on Brendan, the jitters set in.

Finding Cara in her contacts, she hit CALL.

'Hey hun, please tell me you have good news.'

'Have you heard from Brendan tonight?'

'Not since he rang to tell me you got Liam on board. Thanks, by the way.'

'You're welcome. But listen Cars, Brendan's still not home and I'm freaking out.'

'What do you mean he's not home?'

The tears chose that moment to start. 'I think he went to follow up on a lead regarding Jacob and I can't get hold of him.'

'Hang on, can't you track him with your soul link?'

'I tried,' Alannah sobbed. 'But I can't get a read on him. I can't feel him at all, Cara. Oh Gods, what if he's unconscious in a ditch somewhere. Or worse?'

'Hang on hun, I'm coming over.' The line went dead, followed a few minutes later with knocking on the door.

Still naked, Alannah threw on one of Brendan's rock band t-shirts that was long enough to be a nightie. Cara assaulted her with a massive bear hug.

'Come on, let's start the ring around.' Cara attempted to smile but grimaced instead.

Alannah pulled up her friends contact list. Most of them were clueless on Brendan's whereabouts and a couple of the guys did not pick up, which was fair enough considering the early hour.

Cara pursed her lips when they exhausted the friends. 'It's time to bring in the big guns.'

She nodded through her tears and rang Liam. It took a couple of tries to reach him.

'Hey Lana, it's 3AM. Is something wrong?'

'I can't find Brendan,' she cried into the phone.

'Can't you use your link?' He spoke with a hint of acrimony in his tone.

Alannah choked back a sob. 'I can't feel him at all, Liam. I'm terrified something awful has happened.'

'Okay, I'll alert the Council and petition a search party. Have you called my parents?'

'No. I don't know if I should yet.'

'You should. Ask them to come over. Mum can calm you down and Dad might give you a potion to help you sleep.'

She lost all control of her emotions and screamed at him, *'I don't want to sleep, damn it. The love of my life is missing and possibly dead! I can't lie back and do nothing.'*

The line went silent.

Alannah realised what she had said. 'Oh, crap! Liam, I'm sorry.'

He sucked in a sharp breath. 'Just call them, okay. You won't be able to help much in your hysterical state. Get some rest and let the Council handle things for a bit. You can join us when you have calmed down.' He hung up.

When Alannah put the phone down, Cara gazed at her with raised brows. 'Well?'

'He will get the Council on the case. Hmph, at least this way they will have to look for Jacob as well, presuming Brendan went after him.'

'I'm sorry, hun.' Cara embraced her.

Pulling free a few minutes later, Alannah picked up her phone again. 'I need to call Nora and Ross.'

Telling them their son was missing and possibly dead was one of the most difficult things Alannah had ever done and calling on their aid made it much worse. But she was thankful they both came to her, doing exactly what Liam had suggested they would.

Cara provided some comfort, snuggling with Alannah in bed as Brendan's scent surrounded her. It was not much, but it allowed the sleeping potion to take effect and Alannah drifted off with dreams of Brendan holding her.

The irritating sounds of Europe singing 'The Final Countdown' startled Liam. He searched the room, wondering where the hell the awful music was coming from. Spotting the illumination on his phone, he groaned at the name on the screen, but picked up the call with haste. 'Where the hell have you been?'

'Chill, bro. What's got your knickers in a twist?' Brendan shouted over the thumping bass line of the music in the background.

Liam growled. 'Are you serious right now? You disappeared for over a week without telling anyone. I half expected to find you dead in a ditch somewhere. Now I'm thinking I'll be the one to put your corpse in said ditch.'

The background music stopped. 'Woah bro, that's pretty harsh, especially coming from you right now.' There was a hint of malice in his brother's voice.

'I warned you to keep your hands off her.'

'Relax, man. It was just a fun tumble in the hay. I doubt it meant much to her considering she has you again now.' Liam attempted to cut him off, but the stubborn twerp paid him no heed. 'And you can tell our princess it meant about as much to me too. Oh, and if she doesn't believe you, let her know I severed the link and I'm now whiling away the hours in the arms of a real woman—one who takes care of all my darkest desires.'

The sickening laugh of a woman's deep voice sounded through Brendan's phone, confirming part of the bollocks he spewed forth.

'If you're content in your newfound *happiness*, why call me? What the hell do you want?' He spat the words into the phone.

'I wanted to say goodbye now I've settled into my new home beyond the state borders. Plus, I had those messages for you to deliver to Lana.'

Liam shook his head. Brendan's behaviour was off the charts, even for the rogue he knew his brother to be. 'I'm glad you left town, Brendan, because you've saved me a homicide charge.' His tone went grave. 'And I mean it when I say, if I see you again, I will kill you for what you did to Lana. Good riddance, *Brother*!'

Brendan laughed as he hung up the phone.

'What are you doing here?' Alannah opened the door for Liam. 'Don't you have a Council meeting?'

He beelined for the lounge area. 'Sit down, Lana.'

'What? Why?' It had been eight days since Brendan's disappearance and, along with Cara, Alannah had begun to accept the possibility that her man was not coming back. They had even turned into a pair of old widows together; at least that was their ongoing dark joke on those few occasions when humour became possible.

'I have news of Brendan.' He frowned, a disconcerting sign.

She sagged to the floor, but Liam caught her and helped her to the couch. 'Is he dead?' Her voice squeaked.

'No. This is much worse.'

'What could be worse than death?' Alannah imagined all sorts of horrid things.

Liam paced. 'See, this is why I warned him not to touch you. I knew he would pull this shit.' He muttered to himself more than telling her.

'Liam, stop wearing a hole in the damn rug and tell me!'

He halted in front of Alannah and faced her with a grimace. 'He's gone, Lana. I'm sorry.'

'What do you mean, *gone*?'

Liam clenched his jaw. 'He left you.'

'*No!* He promised he wouldn't ever leave me. Brendan loves me and he told me I was his everything. His forever.'

'You wouldn't be the first girl he promised to world to, Lana. He told me to tell you the sex was meaningless, just a bit of fun,' Liam spat.

Shaking her head, she screamed at him, '*Did he want to impregnate those other girls too?*'

'What?' Liam was gobsmacked.

'If the sex was meaningless, why did he tell me he wanted to raise a family with me?'

All the blood drained from Liam's face. 'Did you stop using all forms of contraception?'

She nodded.

'I'm gonna murder that perverted bastard!' He clenched his fists.

'Liam, please. I'm freaking out here. What's going on?'

He sighed and collapsed on the sofa beside her. 'Brendan must have figured you wouldn't believe me, hence the message.'

Alannah's eyes widened. 'You spoke to him? Is he okay?'

'More than okay, by the sounds of it. I don't want to tell you this, but he has a message for you.'

Her heart beat double time. 'Go on.'

'He said that he severed the link and that he's now wiling away the hours with a real woman. One who takes care of his darkest desires.'

A sliver of hope returned. 'Bridey! She must have enthralled him.' Alannah plucked up her phone, thinking for a moment.

'Who's Bridey?' Liam asked.

'Caleb's sister. Can I borrow your phone? Caleb won't recognise your number.'

He nodded and handed it to her.

'Hello?' Caleb spoke with caution.

'Caleb, it's Alannah.'

'Son of a mother!' He mumbled. 'I'm not getting involved.'

'Wait! Tell me one thing: Did she enchant him?'

He sniggered. 'No. Brendan came willingly. And I can't say I'm surprised.'

Alannah's heart stopped. For one split second, it forgot to beat. 'You don't have to be such a jerk about it.'

'Hey, I just call things as I see 'em. Shall I send Brendan your regards?'

'Whatever.' Alannah ended the call as she doubled over from the excruciating pain of her soul shattering into tiny shards.

Liam pulled her into his arms as she howled the house down. When her throat was too hoarse to vocalise her pain, she continued with sobs until her eyes dried out.

'Come on, Lana. You shouldn't be alone tonight. Let me take you home.'

She nodded numbly.

Liam helped Alannah to her feet as Luna rubbed up against his legs. 'Hey you. Do you want to come too?'

The kitten meowed, triggering a new stream of Alannah's tears. She reached down and picked up Luna, leaning into Liam as he carried her outside.

When they got to Liam's place, he went to put her in the spare room, but it still smelled like Brendan. 'This won't do. The place reeks of him even after all these months.' Instead, Liam tucked her into his bed and stood back. 'I'll be on the couch if you need me.'

'No, wait! Please hold me.'

Liam hesitated a moment before sitting on the edge of the bed to slip out of his shoes and stripped down to his boxer shorts. He climbed under the quilt and eased himself up to her side, where he gingerly pulled her into his embrace. 'I'm sorry, Lana.'

Sniffling, she gazed into Liam's big blues and remembered the caring man she fell in love with years ago. Alannah did something she thought she would never do again. She leaned in and kissed Liam's lips. Tentative at first, but when he returned the kiss, she climbed into his lap and deepened it.

Awareness of Liam's arousal knocked the air from her lungs, and she jerked back. 'Shit! Too soon. I'm not ready...'

Liam closed his eyes and drew a deep breath. He forced a smile and tucked a strand of hair behind her ear. 'It's okay Lana, I shouldn't have taken advantage of your vulnerability. I'm the one who should be sorry. If you decide you want me back, I swear I'll never leave you again.'

'I wish you guys would stop making empty promises,' she choked out between sobs.

Liam pulled her into a bear hug. 'I mean it this time. You will have to kick me out if you want me gone, because I am not making the mistake of letting you slip from my arms again.'

She let him tuck her into bed where he spooned her. As Liam drifted off to sleep with his arms around her, Alannah accepted the harsh reality that Brendan had left, and he was not coming back.

Chapter Twenty-Two

The harsh reality of another day dawned, and Alannah groaned.

Liam snuggled into her side. 'What is it, Lana?'

'I hardly slept a wink.'

'I'm sorry, gorgeous. I wish I could make the heartache go away.' He kissed her forehead. 'You should stay here and rest as long as you need.' His lips caressed her left cheek, then her right before hovering above her lips.

Alannah felt numb as she returned the gentle kiss Liam pressed to her lips. Uncertainty plagued her mind, so she inched back from him. 'Shouldn't you be getting ready for work?'

'Yeah,' he sighed. 'I wish I could spend the day with you though. Will you be okay on your own today?'

'I'll be fine.'

Liam jumped out of bed and headed for the bathroom. He returned ten minutes later wearing a towel around his waist. 'Shower's all yours.' Not even the sight of water trickling down his naked chest did much for her anymore.

Taking her time getting ready, she did not hear the commotion at the front door until she opened the bedroom door.

'What do you want?' Liam fumed.

'Tell me where Alannah and your brother are, and I'll leave you alone.' The horribly familiar voice of the ex-Inquisitor acidified her blood and gripped her spine with ice. She ducked back behind the bedroom door.

'I'm not telling you anything. By rights, I should be blasting you and sweeping up your remains with a broom.'

'Do that and you'll be taking an innocent life right along with me,' Richard smirked. 'Not that he's exactly innocent. The boggart and I had an interesting chat, didn't we Jacob? You should hear the mischief he's been making.'

Jacob? Alannah had to know he was okay. Peeking around the corner, she noticed there were three silhouettes at the end of the hall, but she could not make out Jacob's features thanks to the glare of the morning sun through the window. She tip-toed a few steps closer, freezing when one of the floorboards creaked beneath her feet. *Crap! That's a new one.* Alannah used to know all the panels to avoid when sneaking through the house at night.

Liam's head jerked towards her. 'No! Get out of here, Lana!'

Too late. Richard glared at her with malicious intent. 'Hello, Alannah. I must admit, I'm surprised to see you here. I thought you were living with Brendan. Is he with you, or are the brothers sharing you now?'

A low growl crept out of Liam's throat.

She registered Richard's words, but Alannah focussed on the sorry sight of Jacob's battered face. Bound in cold iron cuffs, his shoulders hunched, and he stared at Alannah with wide eyes while Richard used him as a shield. The last Jacob knew, she was celebrating her honeymoon with Brendan. But the duct tape on Jacob's mouth prevented him from voicing his thoughts. 'I guess you didn't hear.' Alannah kept her attention on Jacob. 'Brendan left me for Bridey.'

Jacob's eyes bugged out.

Richard sniggered. 'An interesting turn of events. I guess he went darker than I thought he would. Never mind, I'll catch up with him later. The four of us are going for a drive now.'

'I'll pass, but thanks for the invite,' Alannah deadpanned.

Sparks lit up Richard's hand. 'You seem to be under the misconception that you have a choice in the matter, Miss Winters. If you value this boggart's life, you will come with me. *Now*. Both of you.' He opened the door for them and pointed to the black SUV with darkly tinted windows in the driveway.

Alannah stepped beside Liam. 'Your dispute is with me. Leave Liam out of it.'

Shaking his head, Liam grabbed her arm. 'I'm not letting you go without me, Lana.'

'How touching,' Richard grinned. 'Liam will join us whether you like it or not. I need to be certain he won't go to the Council. Now get moving.'

Jacob shook his head furiously, but Alannah refused to leave him at Richard's mercy. She could not live with herself if she let him die and Cara would never forgive her. Alannah strode out to the car, with Liam following close behind.

Once they settled in the back, handcuffs appeared out of nowhere and fastened themselves around their wrists. Alannah studied Richard, who took the front passenger seat, and saw him close his eyes as he mouthed a spell. He pulled their phones from their pockets and took possession of them. A glance of the demonic driver was all Alannah needed to confirm her suspicions without the need to read Richard's aura. 'Looks like you've turned dark too.'

Once the SUV had turned onto Main Street, Richard turned toward them. 'I do what I must to survive as an outlaw. Oh, and speaking of dark mages, Liam—did Alannah tell you about Brendan's extracurricular activities?'

She paled as Liam eyed her.

'What is he talking about, Lana?'

Alannah opened her mouth, but no words came out.

'Oh, now you go quiet.' Richard laughed. 'Jacob was much more open to sharing Brendan's secrets than you, Alannah. Does that mean he was more susceptible to torture, or just less loyal to Brendan than you were?'

'Lana, please tell me. I promise not to freak out on you.' Liam's eyes drilled into her.

She sighed. 'Brendan was the source of Rhapsody.'

'*What?*' He was gobsmacked.

'And Jacob was his business partner for dealing on the Unseelie Market,' Richard added.

Liam appeared furious as he turned toward Jacob. 'You bastard! I knew there was something fishy about you.'

Alannah was glad she sat between them; else Liam may have used his elbows to add to Jacob's injuries.

After a few deep breaths, Liam regained his composure. 'I can understand your need to protect Brendan, Lana. You don't need to explain. But I can't pretend I'm not disappointed you kept this knowledge to yourself, especially after what he did to you.'

'It wasn't relevant anymore. By the time I found out, he was in the process of pulling out of the business and last I knew, he *was* out.'

Liam frowned. 'At least that's what he led you to believe. Gods know what actually transpired, given his current choice of lover.'

Tears trickled down Alannah's face.

'I'm sorry, Lana.' Liam lifted his bound hands and attempted to caress her face and wipe her tears away. 'Just knowing what he did to you… and now this potion business; it all makes me angry and disgusted with him.'

Jacob mumbled something from behind his gag, so Richard telekinetically tore the tape away. 'Ow, bloody heck!' Jacob rubbed the raw patch of skin around his mouth gingerly. 'I don't know what the hell Brendan was thinking when he left you Alannah, but I know he loved you and he definitely left the potion business when he sold the mother tincture recipe to Lady Violet. Maybe she enchanted him to pull him back into it?'

Liam squinted. 'What am I missing here? Who's Lady Violet?'

'Lady Violet is Bridey's pseudonym, and she is an underboss in the Dark Syndicate,' Alannah replied. 'And I already thought of that, Jacob, so I rang Caleb. He confirmed Brendan went to her willingly.'

'Let me get this straight,' Liam interrupted. 'Brendan made Rhapsody with Jacob and sold it to Caleb's sister, who is actually a crime boss for the unseelie Dark Syndicate? And now he is shacking up with this same whore?'

'Yes. That about sums it up,' replied Alannah. 'Except the Dark Syndicate isn't just an unseelie organisation. It includes dark mages and Lady Scarlett runs it—aka Tara Winters.'

'Oh hell!' Liam stared at her wide-eyed.

'An interesting titbit you left out, Jacob,' admonished Richard.

Jacob scowled at him. 'Must have slipped my mind.'

Alannah peered past Liam and out the window. 'Where are we going?'

'The middle of nowhere, about nine hours northeast of here. I'm hardly going to seek my revenge on the notorious Alannah Winters in the middle of her own territory, am I?'

She exchanged furrowed brow looks with Liam, who twisted in his seat to accommodate her in his lap. Curling up against him, Alannah tried to make the most of what could be her last hours with Liam—*or any man for that matter*.

'Hey, are you awake Lana?' Liam's hushed voice spoke in her ear.

Alannah's eyes fluttered open, and she sat up to stretch her stiff neck. After yawning, she chanced a glance at the passing scenery: mostly open plains with a sparse scattering of trees. 'Where are we?'

'We crossed the New South Wales border. We'll be passing through Broken Hill soon,' he whispered.

She had never travelled so far north, and the countryside became barren. 'Hmph. Pity my first time in this state isn't under more favourable circumstances.'

'Tell me about it,' Liam agreed.

She looked deep into his blue eyes. 'If we survive this, Liam, I want to give *us* another chance.'

He grinned. 'Something to look forward to.'

They huddled together in silence as the car journeyed on, and every so often, Liam would kiss the crown of her head. After passing through the township of Broken Hill—where they took a quick rest stop—the driver headed due north. A large reserve to their right signposted as THE LIVING DESERT intrigued Alannah.

The rocking motion of the vehicle eventually lulled her back to sleep when they hit a dirt track. But a sudden stop startled her awake. An old stone farmhouse sat amid a desolate field. Richard had not been kidding about the middle of nowhere.

Their captor opened the back door for them. 'Right. Everyone out.'

Liam stumbled as he tried to exit the car with his hands still bound.

'Jacob, you can lead the way to the cellar.'

Filing in after him, with Richard on their rear flank, they entered what would have once been a wine cellar, or possibly even food storage. The place was easily two hundred years old, if not more. Alannah froze the moment her eyes fell upon a wooden structure fitted with leather restraints. Thanks to her recent foray into BDSM, she knew exactly what it was and trembled at the thought of Richard's intentions.

A pair of strong, rough hands gripped her shoulders. 'How do you like my St. Andrew's Cross, Alannah? I see you recognise what it is, but after what you and Brendan got up to, I'm not surprised.' Pushing her forward into the dungeon, he closed the door. He tied Liam and Jacob to wooden chairs cemented to the floor and gagged them both.

Dread found its home in the depths of her soul as Alannah drew some nasty conclusions.

With the guys fixed firmly in place, Richard grabbed her and pulled her over to the cross. 'I wonder Alannah, does Liam know you let Brendan tie you up and beat you?'

She could see his eyes bulging out of their sockets as she shook her head.

'Or how you enjoyed every minute of the punishment? It's no wonder I didn't get far with my torture. You enjoy pain a bit too much. But I was going easy on you back then. I won't make that mistake this time.' Producing a pair of scissors, he cut away her clothes, leaving her exposed to all three sets of eyes in the room.

Alannah's stomach twisted, shooting acid up her throat.

Richard released her cold iron cuffs and threw them aside. In the split second she had,

Alannah tried to summon a weapon to hand. But Richard laughed when she felt an oppressive weight blocking her mind. 'I figured you might try a conjuring spell. Are you forgetting my attunement to the nether? I can easily block any of your attempts to use magic against me.'

She narrowed her eyes on him. 'But not my attempts to escape.'

'Oh, I know you won't escape, because if you do, I'll kill your friends over there.' He directed her attention to Liam and Jacob, who both sat wide eyed.

'You weren't wrong to refer to me as a sadist, Alannah,' Richard continued as he pressed her front to the cross and strapped her in. 'Perhaps more than you realise. What I'm about to do to you will bring me pleasure, not only for the pain I deal you, but because the sight of your suffering is going to torture one if not both of our onlookers.'

'You're not only a sadist, Richard—you're a psycho!'

'Perhaps.' Once he finished tying her in place, he pressed his body into her back. 'I thought we could start with a full re-enactment of the first time you indulged your fantasies with Brendan. Let's show Liam what a deviant whore you are.'

Alannah's mouth fell open. 'How would you know?'

'I got the whole thing on video thanks to the cameras I hid about the place when the Council released you on bail. Kieran must have forgotten I had surveillance on you when he booted me out of the state. I connected those nifty devices to my phone, and they proved quite the source of entertainment.'

'Fuck!'

'Indeed, Alannah. Now, let's skip the massage and get straight to the spanking, shall we?' The intensity of his blows started stronger than Brendan ever had, and he did not bother to rub her arse in between each one. Nor did the assault bring her any of the pleasure she had felt with Brendan.

But she managed to keep quiet, not wanting to give him the satisfaction. Her strategy worked right up until he brought the cane down across her thighs, at which point she let out a gut-wrenching scream. Alannah hated how Richard was poisoning the memory of her most intimate and erotic time with the man she loved; not even Brendan's betrayal had done so.

The smell of burning wax filled her nose with smoke and her throat with bile as she heard the zipper of his fly. Alannah gulped, unable to bear the thought of another man raping her, especially in front of Liam. She remembered what her father had told her: '*Some magic is more powerful than anything earthly.*' Nether was not exactly earthly, but it was still inferior to Aether. *Worth a try*. Alannah prayed for divine strength.

A second later she felt the power flowing through her as she burst out of her bonds. Richard was halfway through undressing when she spun around and sent a shockwave from her body into his.

He fell on his backside and stared at her with his mouth agape. 'What the hell?'

'More like heaven.' Alannah stood over Richard and kicked him in the head with as much force as she could muster. It was not much, but it did knock him unconscious. She tried to focus on conjuring a sword, but something continued blocking her connection. 'Crap! I still can't channel matter near him. His nullification spell must still be active even while he's unconscious.' She crossed the room to free Liam of his bonds, starting with the ball gag.

'What are you doing, Lana? Get out of here while you still can.'

'Are you kidding me? There's no way I'm leaving either of you here. I could never live with myself if I let you guys die. Besides, I've already lost Brendan—I can't lose you too.' As soon as he rose free of the bindings, she helped Jacob.

Liam ran across to Richard and attempted his own magic to no avail. 'I guess I'll have to rely on brute force to deal with him.'

Releasing the last of Jacob's tethers, Alannah noticed Liam grab Richard in a choke hold. Everything sank into slow motion as the arsehole opened his eyes and sent Liam flying with a kinetic blast.

She watched in horror as Richard's fingers sparked. 'Liam! Watch out.'

He ducked in time to avoid the lightning bolt. *'Get out of here, Lana!'*

'I'm not leaving you, Liam!'

Dodge-rolling got Liam out of the path of another attack, then another. 'I'll hold him off while you go get help.'

Tears sprung forth. 'I can't.'

Liam managed to get close enough to punch Richard in the jaw, staggering him for a moment. *'Lana, please get help!'*

Seeing Liam hold his own, Alannah conceded. 'Promise you won't die on me, Liam.'

'I promise. Now go!'

Sensing a ley line beneath them, Alannah grabbed Jacob and magiported the hell out of there.

Liam was royally screwed and the rictus grin on Richard's face confirmed his opponent knew it too. His best bet was to remain on the defensive and try and tire the man out, both physically and magically, hoping his own stamina was beyond Richard's. With the adrenaline pumping through his blood, Liam felt like he could go for days, although he knew the rush would only be short-lived.

Ducking and weaving Richard's attacks put Liam in mind of training sessions with Brendan. Thanks to his brother, Liam had spent years learning to hide his true intentions and mask them with bluff tactics to fool even the most skilled mind reader. This was one of those rare occasions when he was grateful for something the twerp had done.

As a fireball grew in his opponent's hands, Liam let Richard think he would dodge to the right, when in fact he went left. *Perfect! That damned wooden cross is ablaze.* He still could not believe how close he had come to witnessing Alannah's defilement *again*. Only this would have been right in front of him, and he would have been helpless to save her. Nothing had made him feel so impotent and useless before.

'I see you have developed some effective deflection skills. Am I right in guessing your dark mage brother helped you with those?'

Liam growled at him. 'You don't know jack about my brother.'

'On the contrary, I believe I know more than you. Did you enjoy my re-enactment? There was much more I could have shown you. Based on what I saw him do to you precious Alannah, I suspect he might be even more sadistic than me.'

Damnit! Liam had not banked on this strategy. Richard knew exactly how to poke the grizzly bear inside Liam that begged to come out and play.

Another fireball came hurtling towards him, so he dropped and rolled out the way, kicking out as he did so, which brought Richard to the floor. Liam grabbed the opportunity to jump on the guy and deal another blow to his face, this time clocking him in the left eye.

Richard sniggered. 'Tell me Liam, what was it like spending all those nights alone knowing Brendan was banging the woman you love.'

'Screw you, arsehole!' He landed a blow on Richard's right eye.

'No thanks. I'll wait for Alannah to get back. Clayton was right, she is a fine piece of arse.'

When Liam brought his hand down again, Richard grabbed it and sent a powerful bolt of electricity through his body, throwing Liam back and giving his opponent the advantage.

Richard's tall, muscular frame towered over Liam's prone body and fire flicked between his fingers. 'This time, when Alannah returns to me, she won't have you or your delinquent brother to save her.'

In her weakened state, Alannah was not exactly fit for travelling by ley line, so the moment they reached the first junction, she stumbled and collapsed into the dirt. But something—or rather someone—soft broke her fall.

'It's okay, Alannah, I gotcha,' Jacob's soft voice reassured her.

Resting her head against his chest for a moment, Alannah allowed herself a few seconds to catch her breath. But she felt something hard pressing against her stomach. Her skin prickled and she scowled at Jacob. 'What the hell, dude? How can you get aroused at a time like this?'

'Ah, hello? Extremely attractive naked woman? I am the hot-blooded man you have your bare breasts pressed against, among other parts. But you can call me Jacob, or whatever you want, since you're on top right now.'

Crap! She had forgotten about her nudity. Glancing up, Alannah thanked the Gods for landing in a deserted field, or whatever the large patch of dirt was. Standing, she took stock of their surroundings. Nothing in sight for miles except for the stunning sight of the setting sun.

Jacob drew up close beside her. 'Not that I'm complaining about the view, but you might want to conjure up some clothes before heading into town.'

She glared at him a moment before doing what he suggested. 'We should try to get back to Broken Hill and call on help from the local mage community.'

He shook his head. 'Correction: we go back, and you call on help. I doubt the local mages will help you if I'm in tow.'

Alannah sighed because he was right. 'Fine. But you should ask the local fae to get you back home ASAP, then send us some reinforcements. Oh, and can you please feed my cat when you get home?'

Jacob nodded. 'Sure thing. Come on, let's go.'

She grabbed his wrist, but he pulled her in closer with an arm around her waist as he winked at her. Rolling her eyes, she tuned into the ley lines and focussed on getting them to their destination. A few minutes later, they were standing on the outskirts of town.

'I'd better lickety-split. But first…' Jacob held his arms open.

Knowing this could be the last time she saw the cheeky boggart she had come to adore, Alannah obliged and squeezed him. 'Tell Cara I love her like the sister I never had.'

'Gods, woman! You're making this sound like a final goodbye.'

'It might be.' A rogue tear and its friend escaped her eyes.

'Nuh, uh. You and Liam are going to kick arse as usual, and you'll come home heroes once again.'

'Thanks for having faith in us, Jacob. I do hope you're right.' They parted ways before one of the town's warlocks greeted Alannah.

The tall man pierced her with eyes to match the blue of his police uniform. 'Miriam was right about someone magiporting into town. Who might you be, and what brings you to this neck of the woods, miss?'

'Hi there. I'm Alannah Winters of the Adelaide district. I seek aid because the exiled Inquisitor kidnapped me and my… boyfriend.' She gulped as the word tumbled out, but there was no time to explain the complexity of her relationship with Liam. ' I only just got out with my life, but Liam's still stuck back there trying to fend Richard off *without* the use of his magic. Please, I don't know what else to do. He took our phones, so I can't even call home.'

'Hold up there, miss. Did you say Winters? As in *the* Winters clan?'

'Yeah, that's right.'

'Ah, hell. And you said this man of yours is Liam? As in Liam Winters?'

She nodded.

'Well, we best be getting my buddies out there to help. I'm Jaxon Hayes, by the way.'

'Thanks, Jaxon.' She offered half a smile.

He pulled out his phone and made a quick call to someone named Shane. Turning back to her, he smiled when the call ended. 'From what I hear, Liam is a great Councillor and warlock to boot. But did you say he doesn't have use of his magic?'

Alannah sighed. 'Yeah. Richard is channelling nether and using a nullification spell. We are going to need weapons and fighting skills to take him down.'

'Hmm. We don't have much of an arsenal out here. I can phone in for some backup from Sydney and Adelaide, though.'

'Backup's prudent. I can conjure up some weapons from home if I know what training you and your men have.'

'Nice. Follow me and I'll introduce you to the lads.'

Chapter Twenty-Three

Liam rolled to the left, narrowly avoiding a fiery death. He pushed himself back to his feet and scowled at Richard. 'Is that the best you've got? No wonder you needed us warlocks to do your dirty work as Inquisitor.'

'Oh, I'm just warming up.'

'Well, come on.' Liam was not sure if it was wise to taunt him, but he was tired of Richard's ramblings.

A long rope flew across the room and wound around Liam's legs. A moment later, Richard dropped Liam to the floor and dragged him closer. 'Try dodging my attacks now.' Liam channelled enough energy mana to break free of the ropes as another lightning bolt struck the floor millimetres away from his head. *His power is waning.*

Rolling on to his front, Liam got up on his knees in time to see the next fireball coming straight for him. 'Shit!' he muttered as he jumped to the right too late to avoid getting his left hand singed.

'*Mothercranker!*' Burns were nothing new to him, having trained with elemental fire magic for much of his life, but they still hurt like a bitch.

Richard grinned. 'Is the great Liam Winters dragging his feet?'

'Why don't you turn off your pussy arse nullification spell and fight like a real man?' Liam spat.

'Now why would I do something so stupid? I know you wouldn't hesitate to kill me, as per your orders. You are the Council's golden boy, after all. Tell me, have you enjoyed living up my brother's arse all these years?'

'I don't have any qualms with Kieran. He's a respectable man and it would seem we have more in common than I thought.'

'Oh?' Flames danced on Richard's fingertips. 'Let me guess, you've taken up stamp collecting.'

What the…? 'Uh, no-o. I was referring to the fact we both have piece-of-filth brothers.' Those flames flared and flickered toward him. But Liam slammed into Richard before the bastard even saw it coming. Next thing, they were wrestling on the floor. Liam pinned him, one hand securing Richard's wrists, while the other pressed down firmly on his throat.

A kinetic blast threw Liam back against the stone wall with enough force to wind him. Liam slumped to the floor, trying to catch his breath as he waited for his diaphragm to settle.

Stalking across the room with a sneer, Richard did not give Liam any time to recover as he shot sparks. The shock carried more charge this time, burning Liam's shoulder at the point of entry.

Liam hissed as blistering agony charred his flesh. He tried to get to his feet again, but Richard grabbed his hair and shoved him back against the wall. Kneeling in front, Richard pressed a heated finger into the fresh wound, causing Liam to howl. Cornered and weakened, Liam failed to resist the pull of Richard's brutal hands as they tore at his scalp, or the cold iron cuffs clamping around his wrists and ankles, fixing him against the wall. He barely even had the puff to vocalise his distress from the constant onslaught of electric shocks. All he managed was praying for unconsciousness or even death to take him.

His prayers were on the verge of being answered when an explosion blew the door in. Something red flashed through the room, throwing Richard away from Liam.

'What the hell?' Richard yelled, as the woman ambushing him pressed a heeled boot into his chest.

The woman grinned down at him. 'We meet at last, Mr. Lane.'

Richard's eyes widened. 'Tara Winters?'

'In the flesh.' She emphasised her double meaning by driving her stiletto into his sternum, forcing out a distorted yelp. 'I have been looking forward to paying you back for all the pain you have inflicted upon my grandchildren.'

Liam blinked in disbelief, possibly more astonished than Richard.

'Oh Gods, Liam!' Alannah shrieked as she ran through the cellar opening a second later. Her warm body pressed against him as her arms tried to embrace him.

Taking in the sweet smell of her strawberry-scented hair, Liam felt his aches and pains soothed by her loving presence. He brought his mouth close to her ear. 'Why is Tara helping us?'

Her gaze focussed on him. 'I told you, she doesn't want to hurt me.'

'By rights I should kill her.'

Tears formed in Alannah's eyes. 'I know, which is why I can't let you out of these cuffs yet.

We need her help. Please promise you won't reveal her identity to the others.'

'Others?'

The trio of armed warlocks who entered the room a moment later answered his question. 'Thank the Gods.' Liam had never been so happy to see sword-wielding mages before. 'Lana, please get me out of these restraints.'

She shook her head. 'Not yet. Besides, you're not fit to fight right now.' Alannah pecked him on the lips, drew a sword from her belt and spun around to join the fray.

The battle appeared tense when Alannah turned back to face Richard. Kinetic blasts foiled most of the guys attempts to approach him, sending them flying and falling unconscious when their heads hit the ground. Only Tara had any luck drawing close, appearing immune to his attacks.

Tara must be using her own nullification spell. She made a mental note of asking her grandmother to teach her the spell the next time they met for training, along with asking her how the hell she had known Alannah was out there and in need of help.

Seeing her chance while Tara distracted Richard, Alannah switched her sword for a dagger and snuck up behind him. She was a hair's breadth from stabbing Richard in the back when he spun around and grabbed the blade, flinging it into Tara's heart a second later.

Crumpling to the floor, Tara sniggered as she bled out. 'You are a fool, Mr. Lane. I am no ordinary cursed being. Not even a blessed blade will bring about my true death.'

Richard grinned. 'No, but what if I destroy this?' He retrieved a glowing quartz crystal from his pocket, leaving Alannah gobsmacked as he approached the prone lich.

Tara's humour vanished as her mouth gaped open. 'Where did you get that?' She garbled the words as blood pooled in her mouth and dripped from her lips.

'Oh, Tara dear, didn't you know demons can have more than one master? They are not the most honest and loyal of servants.' He sent the crystal spinning across the room with enough force to smash on impact against the wall.

'*No!*' Alannah cried.

A white wispy cloud broke free from the crystal and merged with Tara's body, making it jolt and convulse.

Alannah ran to Tara. 'Don't you dare die on me, Grandma.'

The woman smiled warmly. 'This is the first time you called me that.' She spoke in a low, hoarse voice between shallow breaths.

Pressing her hands firmly around the knife, Alannah tried to staunch the bleeding.

'*Lana! Watch out!*' Liam bellowed.

The moment she looked up; Alannah saw Richard launch a fireball in her direction.

Using her body as a shield to protect Tara, Alannah's instincts kicked in as she screamed, '*Damn you to hell, Richard Lane!*' A protective bubble formed around her as the flaming projectile hit it, causing it to rebound with equal force and swallow Richard in the blast.

He ran screaming from the room as fire engulfed his clothes.

Alannah returned her attention to Tara, whose life continued to slip away. 'Gods, I wish I knew healing magic right now.'

An old, frail hand reached for Alannah as Tara's face wrinkled and her eyes drooped. The crone's voice sounded in Alannah's mind. '*It is too late for me, dear child. The blade has pierced my heart. Just know I was never the real enemy. One day you will discover the truth and succeed where I have failed.*'

Alannah ran to her. *What do you mean? What truth?*

'You will find it if you keep striving for greatness. It is your destiny.' Tara's arm fell limp beside her and the last of her glamour faded, revealing the lich who had hidden behind the Scarlett persona.

One of the other guys groaned and stirred as Alannah pulled the knife from her grandmother's chest. It was Jaxon. 'Hole-ee heck! Did you take out Tara Winters?' Before Alannah could correct him, his eyes widened. 'Where's Richard?'

'Lana set him on fire, and he ran away crying like a baby. You might want to stop him escaping,' Liam replied for her.

Jaxon glanced at each of them with wide eyes, grabbing his sword, he bolted after Richard.

'I'm sorry, Lana. I didn't realise how close you'd become to her.'

'Thank you, Liam.' Looking at him, Alannah noticed cuffs still restrained his limbs. She dashed over to him, keeping her eyes averted from his as she used her primordial attunement to channel the kinetic forces needed to break the iron free from the wall. When he fell forward, it took all of Alannah's strength to remain upright as she helped him to one of the chairs. 'Bloody hell! You've taken a nasty beating, Liam. We need to get you home so Ross can patch you up.'

'Don't worry about me right now. Just get out there and make sure the arsehole is dead.' When she hesitated, he added, 'I'll be fine. I promise.'

After a quick peck on the lips, she took off after Jaxon.

When she found him in the front yard, Jaxon stood alone scratching his head. 'I'm sorry Alannah, we lost him. I searched all through the house and there's no sign of him.'

'Damnit! Why won't the bastard die?' She scanned the grounds as best she could in the darkness. *It must be around three or four in the morning by now.*

Jaxon pulled out his phone. 'Do you want me to call HQ and see if we can track him?'

'Yeah, okay. I guess it's worth a try, although his nullification spell will probably block scrying magic.'

'Sure, but it won't stop us tracing his phone's GPS signal.'

'Hmph. With how much magic rules my life, I forgot satellite tracking was even a thing we could do.'

Jaxon smiled. 'My old man had a saying: "Save your magic for when human technology can't do the job. One day you might find that same technology will work where magic doesn't." Wise words from a wise man. Just give me a sec.' He stepped away to make the call.

Alannah went back inside to check on Liam. He was talking to the other two who had woken up from their blunt-force trauma-induced sleep. Shane and Tyler gazed up at her, along with Liam. 'Hey, Lana, what's going on?'

She sighed. 'Richard got away. Jaxon's trying to get a trace on him.' She looked at the other two warlocks. 'Are you guys okay? You both took some pretty nasty blows to the head.'

Shane rubbed the back of his skull. 'Yeah, just a slight bump. I'll be fine.'

'Me too,' added Tyler as he sat up and gazed lasciviously in her direction.

She returned the grin instinctively, either despite or because of Tyler's uncanny resemblance to the jerk who had ghosted her. 'There's no point sticking around here anymore. I assume you have a healer back in town?'

'Yeah, we got a couple.' Tyler's attention remained fixed on her.

'Great.' She broke the eye contact and helped Liam up from the chair. 'Let's get you fixed up before you jump back into the action, soldier.'

He laughed. 'Yes, ma'am.' But before she could take him much further, he pulled her in for a deep, possessive kiss. This time she yielded without hesitation.

Liam could see Alannah fidgeting as she watched Tanya, the town's best abjurer, perform her healing spells.

Once Tanya finished, she turned to Alannah. 'Liam will be fine after a full day and night of rest.'

'What if we don't have a full day and night?' Liam asked. 'We should get back out there as soon as they find Richard. It's better to strike before he fully heals and restores his energy levels.'

'They have to find him first,' Alannah reminded him. 'But if they do find him before the night is through, I will go without you.'

'What? No!'

'Liam, you took a metric fuck tonne of electric shocks and burns. Your body needs time to heal.'

'I can't sit back here while you are out there fighting the biggest jerk known to mage-kind. I need to be in there, helping you.' Liam clenched his fists.

Alannah sighed. 'I appreciate you wanting to help, but knowing you are at greater risk because of your existing injuries will distract me from the fight. You will compromise my safety as well as your own.'

Tanya cleared her throat. 'Your girl is smart, Liam, you should listen to her.'

Laughing, Alannah put her hand on the healer's shoulder. 'I like you, Tanya. Let's stay in touch after this.'

'Sure thing, hun.'

Liam groaned. 'Uh, Tanya? Mind if I have some time alone with Alannah?'

'So long as you don't get up to anything too strenuous.' She winked at them and left the room.

Alannah snuggled up to Liam's side. 'How are you feeling?'

'Okay, I guess. A bit tired, but more frustrated than anything.' The burns still ached like hell, but he did not want to cause her undue concern with everything else going on.

'I don't want to fight over this, Liam.'

With a sigh, he conceded. 'Don't worry. I get it, Lana. If our predicaments reversed, there's no way I'd want you out there in my state.' With his arm, he reached across her waist and pulled her in closer for a kiss. He peered into her eyes and sighed. 'I've been thinking about Tara's death. You should roll with Jaxon's misread of the situation. It would help you regain favour in the Council.'

Her eyes bugged out at his suggestion. 'I can't do that. It would dishonour Tara's memory.'

'I don't think it would. She must have had reasons for making us believe she was the enemy, right?'

Alannah's jaw dropped. 'How did you know?'

'Call it a hunch. I'm not gonna pry into the secrets she shared with you. It's best if I don't know. Much safer to maintain the pretence and I'm sure that's what she would want.'

'You're right. I guess I'm not the only smart one here.'

Liam poked his tongue out and Alannah nipped it between her teeth before drawing it into her mouth and consuming him with a kiss reminiscent of their prior love and passion. Perhaps there was hope for them again after all.

The two of them drifted off to sleep in each other's arms, only to wake a couple of hours later when Jaxon stirred her. 'Sorry, Alannah, but we found Richard and we should launch an assault now while he is still licking his wounds.'

Alannah sighed, looking at Liam. 'I'm sorry babe, but I need to go.'

'It's okay. I'll follow the doc's orders and rest up on one condition.'

'What's that?'

'You kick Richard's arse extra hard for me.'

Smiling, she leant in and planted a sloppy kiss on his lips. 'I love you.'

He sucked in a sharp breath. It felt wonderful to hear her say those words again. 'I love you too. So. Damn. Much. Now go show him who's boss.'

Alannah stepped out of Liam's room. 'Where is the prick hiding?'

Jaxon bit his lip, exchanging a look with Shane, who waited in the corridor.

She narrowed her eyes on Jaxon. 'What?'

Jaxon shuffled on his feet. 'He has presented us with quite the challenge.'

'How so? Is it a hard-to-reach location, or something?'

'No, but we are going to have to be extremely careful about how we approach him,' Shane explained.

'Why?' Alannah did not like how cagey they were acting.

'Because he is in a large population centre,' replied Tyler as he walked out of Tanya's living room.

'Crap! That's unfortunate. Where are we talking?'

This time Jaxon pulled up his big boy panties. 'Right in the heart of Sydney's Kings Cross. He knew we'd be after him, knowing we can't stage an all-out war in such a public place, full of so many non-magicals.'

'Oh hell.'

'Yep, it's like everything's gone to crap and we're all out of bog roll,' Tyler remarked with a smirk.

Alannah grunted as she tried to stifle her laugh. *Just when I thought the toilet paper jokes had gone out of fashion*. 'How are we going to get to him in one of the most commercial and busiest districts of the nation?' She considered their predicament for a few minutes as the guys fell silent. 'We can't use magic anyway, right? So, maybe we need to treat him like a regular criminal—a fucking dangerous one at that. I say we tag him as a terrorist and use our contacts in the feds to help bring him down. We can all get uniforms and cordon off the area. This will get the non-magical community out of our way so we won't expose them to any magic.'

Tyler grinned. 'Hell, I think I'm falling in love with you, Alannah. You can talk strategy to me all night, baby.'

Jaxon laughed. 'Stop mistaking love for lust, bro.' He turned his attention to Alannah. 'The plan is pretty solid, but what do we do about the non-magical cops?'

'Keep them posted around the perimeter where they can't see Richard and make sure they don't have any loaded guns in case we can't contain the bastard and he goes full Carrie White on them.'

'Carrie who?' Jaxon asked, earning a snigger from Tyler.

Alannah rolled her eyes. 'Never mind. Let's get moving.'

As soon as they stepped outside, Tyler flung his arm across her shoulder. 'So, you're a horror fan too, huh?'

Jaxon laughed behind them. 'Give it up bro, she's got a boyfriend already—a powerful warlock at that. You don't want to be crossing my man, Liam.'

As they continued along the gravel driveway, she glanced at Tyler. His green eyes showed an impish glint as they scanned her body up and down before connecting with hers. 'I'm flattered Tyler, but Jaxon's right: you don't want to get on Liam's bad side. He gets protective of me.'

He leaned in to whisper in her ear, 'Why aren't you pulling out of my arms, beautiful?'

A damn good question. But as soon as she thought about it, the painful realisation struck. 'Because you remind me of someone I should be trying to forget.' Increasing her pace allowed her to slip free of his hold and hide the escaping tear.

'Alannah, wait! I'm sorry.' Tyler jogged up behind her. 'I didn't mean to upset you. I thought we had some kind of… connection. But I was out of line, and I'm sorry.'

Wiping her eyes, she smiled at him. 'It's okay.'

When they reached the end of the path, Alannah tuned into the ley lines and mapped a route to Sydney in her mind. She held hands with Jaxon and an over-eager Tyler, leaving Shane to take Jaxon's other hand, and the four of them magiported across the state.

Half an hour later, they had reached a riverside suburb known as Parramatta on the northwest side of the city. Jaxon took in their surrounds. 'We should contact the feds before we get much closer.'

Alannah nodded. 'Okay. You know this city better than I do, so I'll follow your lead on this.'

When he stepped aside to make some calls, Alannah noticed Shane appearing pale and clammy. 'Are you okay?'

Shane waved dismissively. 'Just motion sickness.'

'He always gets like this from magiporting,' Tyler explained.

They both watched on as Shane ran into the bushes lining the road. 'Welp. There he goes. You okay there, buddy?' Tyler followed his friend.

Jaxon returned a moment later. 'Right, we're all set. We just have to rendezvous with the feds and our backup support.' When he observed Shane returning from his upchucking, he sighed. 'I guess we find a car and drive from here.'

Alannah's plan was falling into place. They surrounded Richard's Kings Cross apartment block, and a few non-magical police had gone in to stealthily evacuate the innocent civilians. She hid in the early morning shadows along with her three new friends, hoping to avoid detection. They had figured it would be better to keep all mages back until the humans were safe; less chance of crossing any detection wards and alerting the bastard.

Richard's voice sounded in her mind, and judging by how the other guys jumped, she was not the only one to receive the communication. '*Hello again, Alannah. Apparently, you can't get enough of me. Have you come for another spanking? You can't deny how much it turned you on.*'

The other guys looked at her with wide eyes, although Tyler also tilted his head and arched his left brow.

'It's not what you think. I never enjoyed any of *his* torture,' she explained in a hushed voice.

'*Perhaps I should film us this time and send it to Brendan as way of returning the favour. I know where he is hiding out, by the way.*'

Her face burned hotter than the volcanic pits as she instinctively moved toward him.

But Jaxon held her back and whispered, 'Don't let him taunt you. We gotta stick together for this to work.'

Alannah stopped in her tracks and nodded.

A voice came through Jaxon's radio. 'We're all clear.'

Jaxon gestured to their backup team huddled on the other side of the entrance, letting them know it was time. He led Alannah and the other two guys into the building.

The stairwell was dank and reeked of excrement. It was certainly not the luxury accommodation she had imagined Richard living in. *Perhaps that is why he chose the place as his hideout.*

As soon as they reached the second-floor landing, a rope snaked across the floor, entwining itself around Alannah's shins and pulling her down. She reacted with a sword strike across the tether.

Tyler's outstretched hand helped her to her feet, and the four of them charged into Richard's open apartment as one cohesive unit. Their backup soon followed, filing in behind them. Before long, they had Richard flanked with about twenty armed men.

Alannah glared at him. 'Any last words, Richard?'

'Do you honestly think you have enough force to take me down?'

Her lips curled into a vicious grin. 'Oh, I know we have enough.'

Richard's hand moved forward, directing a kinetic shockwave toward them, but Alannah brought up her Aether shield to block and rebound it. The blow sent him flying into the troops behind him. He struggled free of the man's hold, grabbing his sword and charging at Alannah.

She was ready for him, meeting his attack with a parry. It was satisfying to be able to fight him on equal footing at last.

They exchanged blows for what felt like an eternity, while one of the others would try to cut in every so often, but each time they did, Richard would send them flying. After about the tenth intervention attempt, Richard was sweating, and his footwork slackened. This was the opportunity Alannah needed. Having let him think her moves were predictable and her mind readable thus far, she used one of the mental bluff tactics Tara had recently taught her and went in for the kill. As Richard swung to his right, Alannah aimed for his left side.

A split second before she hit him, Richard dropped to his knees and released his own bubble, sending Alannah flying back into Tyler's arms. 'Are you okay, beautiful?'

She stood up straight. 'Yeah. I'm fine. But what is he doing?'

Richard hunched over on the floor, chanting to himself. Rather than a white radiance of Aether, his shield glowed red.

They heard screams from outside and Jaxon's radio sprang to life:

'Requesting back… *Ahh!*'

'What the hell is that?'

'Oh God, somebody help us.'

'They're coming out of nowhere!'

Alannah exchanged a frown with Jaxon. 'Damnit! He's summoning demons. Jaxon, we need to save those guys out there.'

He nodded his agreement. 'If I take a few of these guys, can you manage in here?'

'I hope so. Either way, we can't leave those men at the mercy of a demon incursion.'

As Jaxon ran from the room, Richard rose to his feet with fiery tendrils flicking out of his shield like a crimson corona.

Tyler's eyes bugged out. 'Gods! Is he summoning hellfire?'

'Afraid so.' Alannah closed her eyes and drew on the strength of her Aether connection and on the conviction of her faith. She did not know of any offensive spells that channelled the Celestial element, so she improvised, drawing on the power of the Gods to smite the fiend who defiled her own realm simply by living in it. If the stygian element could nullify earthly magic, she reasoned Aether could nullify nether.

'Um, Alannah? That's some impressive afterglow you got going there.' Tyler's mouth gaped open.

As Alannah's power intensified, she laughed. 'Just stand back, honey. I feel my climax coming on.' She winked and turned to face Richard.

'Hot damn,' Tyler muttered.

Advancing on Richard cautiously, Alannah maintained eye contact to the best of her ability. His eyes had turned mostly red by this point and looking into them felt like staring at the sun for too long. When one of the flares flicked out at her, it withered away the moment it touched her forcefield.

But another tendril lashed out to her right and she heard Tyler scream.

She spun around to see him bound by a burning tentacle squeezing his waist. He thrashed about, trying to cut it off with his sword to no avail.

'*Tyler!*' Alannah cried out as she ran to him. Extending her own sword within her Aether field, she released him, drawing him close, and wrapping her arms around his waist, she instinctively healed his burnt flesh.

Tyler remained gobsmacked and speechless as she pulled away and returned her attention to Richard.

More tentacles reached out to grab the unconscious guys who had fallen to his kinetic blasts.

'Enough!' Alannah bellowed across the room.

He turned and snarled at her with a noise sounding more monstrous than human.

She rushed at him, cutting through his barrier, and driving her holy blade straight into his heart.

Richard dropped to the floor and tried to speak but coughed instead.

Alannah stood over his limp body and watched as his eyes glazed over. 'Enjoy an eternity rotting in the Underworld, you piece of scum.'

A moment later, a black wisp emerged from his body and sank into the earth.

Relief washed over her like summer rain before she collapsed into a set of waiting arms.

Chapter Twenty-Four

Waking up, Alannah found herself in what appeared to be a hotel room. When she glanced at the clock, she realised she must have slept most of the day because the sun would be setting soon. She got up and peeked through the bedroom door, finding the other guys chatting in a lounge area. After getting dressed, she slipped out of her room to join them.

Tyler grinned at her. 'Hey beautiful, how'd you sleep?'

'Great actually. Where are we?'

'Sydney still. When you collapsed after the fight, we decided it was best to check in to a nearby hotel to rest. Don't worry, the Council paid for it.'

'And Liam?'

Some of Tyler's smile faded. 'He's still recovering in Broken Hill. We can head back there as soon as you're ready.'

Alannah was in Australia's most lively city on a Saturday night and while it would be nice to return to Liam's arms, she knew he needed more recovery time. *Besides, he is in safe hands*. She directed her grin toward Tyler. 'How about we hit the town for a victory celebration before heading home?'

He jumped up from the couch. 'Heck yeah! I'm so down for it. What about you guys?'

Jaxon laughed. 'I think we deserve a drink or ten.'

'I'm in,' replied Shane.

Tyler's arm rested on her shoulders as he guided her back to her room. 'How's about you conjure up something sexy to wear, and I'll show you the best magic club in Sydney.'

'Sounds super.' Alannah broke free of his hold and retreated to the privacy of her room where she got ready. When she stepped back out in her black lace skater dress and fishnet stockings, all three jaws hit the floor.

'Gods, woman! Are you trying to get me killed? How am I supposed to keep my hands off you now?' Tyler rose and stalked across the room toward her.

'You said to wear something sexy. Now where's this club of yours?'

The night club hosted a mix of magical races mingling around the numerous bars and dancing intimately close on the dancefloor while a Satyr DJ pumped out Egyptian tribal beats.

Tyler found them a booth, pulling Alannah in close to him. No sooner had they sat down, than a half-elf waitress took their drink orders.

Alannah cast wide eyes over her surrounds. 'Wow. This place is incredible.'

'I'm glad you think so,' Tyler beamed.

As she took in the sights, a shiver gripped her spine and all the hairs on her body stood to attention. *Is someone watching me?* Scanning the room failed to reveal any such observer. When their drinks arrived, the group eased into some light-hearted discussion, but Alannah could not shake the prickly sensation from her skin.

Several drinks later, the awareness remained, although the buzz of the alcohol helped to dull her worries. Glancing at Tyler, he rewarded her with the warmest smile, so she grabbed his hand and dragged him out of the booth. 'Come on, let's dance.'

As soon as they reached the dancefloor, Tyler's hands beelined for her hips. Alannah encircled his neck with her arms and pressed her body close to his, letting him grind against her.

His lips pressed against her ear. 'Gods! This is like the sweetest form of torture.'

'Uh huh.'

'I've been hard for you ever since seeing the way you handled yourself in combat. Harder still when you plunged a blade deep into Richard's heart.'

Alannah sighed. 'Sounds like something he would have said.'

'So, this other guy I remind you of, is he like your ex or something?'

Inhaling deeply, she caught a whiff of Tyler's spicy cologne. Along with the spiky fringe and lack of piercings, it was one of the few differences to remind her he was not Brendan. 'Yeah. An ex who didn't just break my heart but shattered it into millions of tiny pieces.'

'I'm sorry to hear that. What about me reminds you of him?'

'You're overtly flirting even though my heart belongs to someone else. But also, you could easily pass as his twin.'

'Is he attractive?'

She rolled her eyes as she looked up into his gleaming gaze. 'Extremely.'

His hand moved to her arse. 'Then I'll take it as a compliment, Alannah.'

'Please, call me Lana.' She pressed her head into his solid, muscular chest.

'Did *he* call you Lana?'

'Yeah.'

He sucked in a sharp breath. 'I'm not him, Lana, but if you need to believe I am for one night, I'd be more than happy to oblige.'

Alannah peered up into green orbs peeking out from beneath long, thick lashes. Before she could let logic and decency get in the way, she crashed her lips into his. When she came up for air, the uncanny sensation she felt before had gone, replaced with a feverish rush of desire coursing through her blood. 'Let's get out of here.'

Tyler did not hesitate to escort her from the club and back to their hotel suite. They sank onto her bed in a series of fiery kisses, hastily removing each other's clothes in the process. When there were no more layers between them, he sat back and pulled on a condom. Leaning over her, he stroked her cheek. 'Who do you want me to be, Lana?'

She took a deep breath. 'Brendan.'

He climbed astride her. 'And what do you want me to do?'

'I want you to fuck me rough and hard.'

'Then I will.' He drove himself deep inside her and for a few glorious hours Alannah forgot all the heartache and focussed on the pleasure Brendan brought her.

Rested and healed, Liam stepped outside Tanya's house at first light and magiported his way to Sydney, following the instructions Jaxon had given him over the phone. His insides were buzzing from the news of Richard's defeat. He could not wait to scoop Alannah up into his arms and kiss his praise all over her soft body.

The directions were reliable, and he found the place without any hassles. Jaxon had advised him Alannah was still sleeping after a big night, so he tapped softly on the door.

'Hey man,' Jaxon whispered and shook his hand before letting him into the large four-bedroom suite. 'How was the trip?'

'Fine.' He cast an eye around the place and noticed the other guys were not up yet. 'Which room is Lana's?'

Biting his lip, Jaxon hesitated a moment. 'Uh, that one.' He pointed to the first door on the left.

'Thanks.' Liam headed for the door.

But Jaxon jumped in front of him and gripped his shoulder. 'You probably shouldn't go in there.'

'It's okay, Jaxon. Lana won't mind. We've been together for years.'

Jaxon cursed under his breath. 'You should still wait for her.'

What the hell is Jaxon's problem? Is he trying to protect me? Something heavy took root in the pit of his stomach. They had not told him what condition she would be in.

Barging past the warlock blockade, he burst into Alannah's room. Liam did not expect the sight that greeted him, but it still broke his heart. Her naked limbs entwined around the man who wore Brendan's face.

Liam's initial instinct was to kick the shit out of Tyler, with storming out of the room a close second. But glancing at Alannah's peaceful face, he remembered the promise he had made her and the hell Brendan had put her through. Fighting against all his violent and bitter urges, he slumped down next to her, kicked off his shoes, and climbed under the covers to hold her.

Alannah stirred from her sleep, moaning as her eyes fluttered open. When she registered Liam's presence, she sat bolt upright. '*Crap!*' Her forehead wrinkled as she studied him.

Her sudden movement woke Tyler who gasped at Liam, rolled out of the bed and ducked beside it.

'I… I'm sorry, Liam. I—' Alannah tried to explain.

But he cut her off by pulling her into his arms. 'It's okay, baby. I know you're still hurting, and I understand. Please rest assured I'm serious about my promise. As long as you still love me, I will never leave you again. Not unless you want me to.'

She gaped at him. 'But I cheated on you.'

'I'm not sure you did. I won't pretend I'm pleased with how things turned out, but it's not like we properly defined our new relationship. I'm willing to move past this if you are. Do you still love me, Lana?'

Tears welled in her eyes. 'Yes.'

'Do you still want to be with me?'

She nodded. 'Yes.'

'I love you too, princess.' He claimed her lips with his own, letting his forgiveness show in the fervour of their kiss. Liam was vaguely aware of Tyler sneaking out of the room and closing the door. They were alone in bed and Alannah was still naked. It was the perfect opportunity to show her how much he still loved her.

Waking up for the second time that day was surreal for Alannah. She could not believe how rational and understanding Liam had been.

He smiled at her when her gaze fell upon his. 'Morning, sunshine.'

'Hey. Is it still morning?'

'Barely. Have you rested enough?'

'Yeah. I guess we should get moving. I need a shower first, though.'

Liam rose and followed her to the ensuite bathroom. He did not even bother asking if he could join her. They had reached that level of comfort in their relationship years ago. *Why should we start over again with the formalities?*

When they both finished getting ready, they stepped out into the loungeroom to say goodbye.

'We should be getting home,' Alannah announced. 'I want to thank all of you for your help. I couldn't have defeated Richard without you.'

Jaxon smiled. 'You're most welcome, both of you. I mean in every way possible. Please don't hesitate to call on me in Broken Hill whenever you want or need.'

'Likewise, man.' Liam shook his hand.

Alannah pulled him into an embrace before giving Shane a farewell hug. Tyler hunched his shoulders, hiding his hands in his pockets and carefully avoiding eye contact with Liam. But as she pulled him into her arms, there was no air of discomfort between them. She whispered a soft 'thank you' to which he replied 'no, thank you, beautiful' before pulling back.

She returned to Liam, who grabbed her hand and led her out of the suite, out of the hotel, and out of Sydney.

Alannah's mouth watered at the Summer Solstice feast laid out before her. 'Wow, Aunt Nora, you've outdone yourself this time. But there's too much food for the four of us.'

Nora beamed. 'There won't only be four of us. We have several guests arriving shortly.'

When Alannah glanced at Liam, she noticed the mischievous glint in his eye. 'Wait! You know who's joining us, don't you?'

'Maybe.'

She narrowed her gaze on him. 'Who is it?'

'Telling you would ruin the surprise.' He grinned.

'Hmph. Keep your secrets.' As Alannah crossed her arms, the doorbell rang.

'Would you get that please, hun?' Nora directed her question to Alannah.

After casting a suspicious eye Liam's way, she rose to greet their guests. As soon as the door swung open, she squealed with delight at the five friendly faces. 'Oh my Gods, what are you guys doing here?'

Jaxon grinned. 'It was Liam's idea and apparently your aunt and uncle loved it.'

Liam drew close behind her. 'I figured it was the least we could do to repay our debt of gratitude.'

Jaxon, Shane, Tanya, Tyler, and his friend Samantha were all there. It had been almost three weeks since they had helped her defeat Richard and she had only seen them once since then, although she had also kept in contact via social media and text. The civility of Liam and Tyler's friendship amazed Alannah. Then again, Liam did not know about her more recent escapades with Brendan's doppelganger.

Once all the handshakes and hugs were out of the way, Alannah showed their guests into the dining room.

Alannah watched as everyone finished plating up their meals. 'So, what's the latest in Sydney?'

'Actually, I have an announcement to make,' Jaxon replied.

'Oh?' Alannah sat upright.

He grabbed Tanya's hand. 'This wonderful woman has agreed to marry me.'

Alannah cupped her hands to her mouth for a moment before jumping up to hug them both. 'That's tremendous news.'

A round of congratulations and cheers followed.

But as soon as Alannah took a sip of her champagne, the contents of her stomach decided to come back up, leaving her precious little time to rush to the toilet.

Liam dashed after her. 'Are you okay, babe?' Kneeling, he held her hair back.

When the worst of it was over, she collapsed against the wall. 'Actually no. I feel dreadful.'

He took her hand in his to offer a reassuring squeeze.

Nora appeared in the doorway. 'What's wrong, honey?'

Tyler's concerned face appeared behind her.

'I threw up. I must have some kind of stomach bug. Surely it wouldn't be your food, Nora.'

Nora shook her head. 'You're a pure mage. We don't get infections.' She smiled. 'Alannah, sweety, I think you might be pregnant.'

But when Alannah's forehead puckered, Nora's smile dropped.

'*Oh Gods!*' Tyler quaked.

'Chill, man. It's not likely to be yours.' Liam's grip on her hand tightened like a vice. 'Mum, get Dad in here, *now*.'

Nora nodded and disappeared.

'How do you know it's not mine?' Tyler's voice trembled.

Liam glared at him. 'You used protection, right?'

'Yeah, but—'

'Morning sickness usually takes at least four weeks to manifest,' Liam cut in.

'How do you know that?' Alannah was ignorant of such facts herself.

'I did some research after you told me about… you know.'

She realised why Liam was edgy. Tyler was not the only unlikely candidate. Alannah felt the walls closing in on her, more bile rose, and she leaned over the toilet a second later.

When she finished, Liam helped her up so Ross could examine her in the adjacent guestroom, where she laid down on the bed.

After touching her abdomen for a few minutes, Ross looked into Alannah's eyes with his best attempt at a neutral expression. 'You are definitely pregnant.'

Liam paced the room. 'Is it his? Did my arsehole brother do this to her?'

Tyler sat on the edge of her bed with wide eyes. 'Brendan's his brother?'

She gave him a nod as tears threatened to break free.

Ross sighed. 'If you give me some peace and quiet, I can determine the gestational age.'

'Come on Tyler, honey. Let's give them some privacy,' Nora suggested.

He nodded and followed her out.

Liam lowered himself into an armchair beside the bed.

Ross resumed pressing his hands to Alannah's abdomen and closed his eyes as he did so. She wondered what sort of spell enabled him to learn so much about the baby growing inside her. *Wow*. She had not fully grasped the fact yet. *There is actually another person growing within me.*

Several minutes later, Ross opened his eyes and smiled at her, a reassuring sign. 'Alannah, you have a special child on the way—a Beltane baby.'

Liam's eyes lit up and he pounced on the bed, pulling her into his arms. 'That is such a relief. Congratulations, my love.' Of course Liam would be delighted. He did not know whom she had spent Beltane with, nor would he ask.

But it felt like another piece of her soul crumbled away as Alannah hid her face in Liam's shoulder.

When he drew back to study her face, she forced a smile. He stood and helped her up. 'Come on. Let's go tell the others.'

No time like the present to put Grandma's training into practice. When they reached the dining room, Alannah looked at the faces staring back at her. 'So, um, I've kind of got some big news of my own. I'm pregnant with a Beltane baby.'

Worry lines softened and beaming smiles filled their faces.

Nora squealed and hugged her. 'I'm thrilled for you, honey.'

Tanya grabbed her next. 'Congrats, dude. That's awesome news.'

Tyler pushed his way through the crowd of well-wishers to squeeze her tight. 'That's a big relief, hey beautiful?' He chuckled. 'Seriously, though, congrats.'

Jaxon and Shane demanded their hugs before the party could return to some semblance of order; after which, Alannah relaxed thanks to the exquisite food and affable company. But as the evening wore on, she fell quiet.

Liam leaned in close, placing a hand on her arm. 'Hey, are you okay?'

'Yeah, just getting tired.'

'I guess I better get the two of you home.' He grinned.

'Are you honestly okay with me carrying another man's baby?'

'Lana, this isn't just some random guy's child. You have a blessed baby. I am more than okay with it. But even if you hadn't conceived him or her at Beltane, I would be happy to raise the kid as my own.'

This time her smile was genuine. 'Really?'

He nodded.

'Even if it was his?'

Liam frowned. 'Especially if it was his. Although, happy might not be the best word to describe my emotions in that case. I'm angry at him for what he did to you, but I wouldn't abandon you or the child.'

Alannah pursed her lips, fighting back more tears. 'Thanks.' *But there is still no way in hell I'm telling you or the child who the real daddy is.*

The small island housing the Gaeilge Shores Sailing Club was a feast for the senses on New Year's Eve. Twinkling lights adorned every single structure, including the gazebo hosting a live jazz band. Food carts scattered about the place, producing mouth-watering aromas making Alannah's stomach somersault. Most of the town's population showed up for the biggest party around for miles.

'Here you go. Curly fries and a dagwood dog as requested.' Liam smiled as he handed her the food.

'Thanks.' She pecked him on the lips, before gorging on her second dinner for the evening.

He watched her with amusement. 'I hope all this eating isn't an avoidance tactic.'

She pointed to her belly with a concertina of fried potato goodness. 'I'm feeding two people, remember.'

Liam arched his brows. 'You know that's not a real thing, right? You'll just end up getting fat.'

Alannah gasped. 'Take that back, Liam Winters, before I kick your arse.'

He laughed. 'I'd love to see you try, babe.'

After dropping her food on a nearby bench, she advanced on Liam with a ferocious glare. Laughing, he made a run for it, so naturally she gave chase, ending up in the one place she had been evading: the club rooms. Liam tackled Alannah, pulling her into his side in time to catch some unwanted attention.

Kieran approached them. 'Ah, there you are. I've been hoping to catch up with you, Alannah.'

The humour vanished from Alannah's features. 'Uh, hello, Your Honour.'

'I wanted to commend you on a job well done with Tara and my… uh, Richard. There is still a vacant seat on the Council if you would like to return to it.'

Alannah's mouth gaped open. 'Really?'

'Yes. I feel it is the least I can do after everything Richard put you through.'

Monique sidled up next to Kieran and smiled. 'The girls would love to have you back too.'

She frowned at Monique. 'What happened to making me pay for exposing your uncle?'

Casting her eyes to the floor, Monique shifted her weight awkwardly. 'I uh—I think I misdirected my anger. I'm sorry, Alannah. What he did to you was wrong.' Lifting her gaze, Monique's eyes pleaded with her. 'Please reconsider the lobby group. We could use your help.'

'I won't spare it a second thought.'

Monique pouted.

'What I mean to say is, I'm in. The women's group and the Council. I want my positions back. Although I will need to take maternity leave in about thirty-three weeks.'

Father and daughter Lane both stared with slack jaws.

Liam took his cue. 'Alannah and I are expecting a blessed baby.'

'Well, I believe congratulations are in order.' Kieran shook Liam's hand.

'Excuse me, but did I hear right?' Jessica interrupted. 'Did you say Alannah's pregnant?'

Alannah nodded. 'With a Beltane baby.'

Jessica squealed and hugged Alannah before dashing up to the stage to grab the microphone. 'Excuse me ladies and gentlemen. Alannah and Liam Winters have an important announcement to make. Get up here, you two.' Her arms summoned them with more enthusiasm than a cheerleader.

After rolling her eyes, Alannah let Liam drag her up there. Jessica handed her the microphone, so she took a deep breath and let the news spill out. 'This is awkward, but you will hear it on the rumour mill anyway. I am pregnant.' She caught a few wide-eyed glances amongst the assembly, namely those of her friends who did not yet know.

Cara, the only other person she had told since the Solstice, gave her an encouraging thumbs up.

A dark figure up the back of the room stepped forward. 'So, which cousin is the baby daddy?' Caleb gibed.

Liam winced, grabbing the microphone from Alannah. 'Tradition forbids us from asking who the biological father is because Alannah is carrying a baby conceived at Beltane.' Ignoring the murmurs and hoots from their audience, he turned to face her and smiled. 'Lana, I promise to love and cherish both you and the child the Gods blessed you with. I will help you raise the kid as though he or she is my own. Not because of any sense of duty or honour, but because you are the light of my life, and I cannot imagine a world without you.' He dropped to one knee in front of her, pulling a ring from his pocket. Alannah's gasp echoed through the crowd. 'I adore you, Alannah Winters, and if you would do me the honour of becoming my wife, I promise to devote the rest of my life to keeping you safe and happy.'

Tears trickled down her face as she stared at Liam in stunned silence.

He gulped. 'Lana, baby, will you marry me?'

She nodded fervently until she found her voice. 'Yes. Very yes.'

Liam slid the white gold ring onto her left hand, and she noted the Celtic love knot surrounding a large garnet. He rose and pulled her in for a passionate kiss, earning them all manner of cheers and whistles. As soon as they came up for air, their friends accosted them.

When the onslaught of well-wishers eased, Alannah ducked outside for some fresh air.

Liam drew close behind her. 'Come on. I want to show you something.' He grabbed her hand and led her down to a private spot on the beach. 'I was actually planning to propose to you here, but it felt like the right moment back there. I'm sorry if I embarrassed you.'

'It's okay. You ought to know I'm not self-conscious. I just feel overwhelmed by everything. Can we sit down for a bit?'

'Of course. There's still something I want to share with you here.'

'Oh?'

Laying back on the sand, Liam pulled her atop him. 'I've always wanted to make love to you here.'

She squinted at him. 'This is a public place, Liam.'

He smirked. 'I thought you said you weren't self-conscious.'

'It's not that. I'm surprised *you* want sex on the beach.'

'Why not? The ocean is my home away from home. So, will you…'

Alannah decided they had wasted enough time talking about it and stifled his words with a kiss as her fingers pulled at his fly. A few minutes later she rode him hard and surfed the waves of her orgasms.

There must have been some magic in the air because as they both reached their climax, the sky lit up with the midnight fireworks.

To be continued…

What's Next?

Thank you for reading *Winter's Maiden 2*. I would be most grateful if you could show your support by leaving a rating or even a review.

If you are game to read Brendan's adventures during his time with Bridey, check out *Winter's Thrall*. Due for release in May 2022.

****Trigger Warning**** *Winter's Thrall* is a dark paranormal romance with strong sexual content that blurs the lines of consent. It also includes graphic m/m, BDSM, and incest scenes. Feel free to skip ahead to *Winter's Mother 1,* the next main entry in the series, if such matters are likely to offend or be a psychological trigger.

Alannah's story will continue in *Winter's Mother 1,* coming November 2022.

Keep reading for samples of both books…

Bonus Content

Winter's Maiden 2: The Heat of the Beltane Fires

I appreciate that not all my readers like much explicit content. For those of you who do want a little more, you can read the rest of the Beltane chapter in all its graphic glory…

If you are keen to read this bonus content, you can access it on the 'Freebies' page of my website: www.starlaarts.com.

Acknowledgements

This book took me on an epic journey through a minefield of emotions. I literally cried while tearing a rift in Alannah and Brendan's relationship. Fear not, dear readers, this is not the end for them.

I am so thankful for my hubby who helped me recover from all the writing hangovers I suffered while punishing my beloved characters.

Cheers to my editor Felix for your tireless efforts. You are a champ!

A special thanks to my beta readers for providing such helpful feedback on this book: Ariel Mareroa, Amanda Mashburn, Elli Morgan, Hayley McKenna, and Joshua Wake.

And a huge shout out to all my launch team and ARC readers for your reviews and for sharing this book with the world.

Winter's Thrall

There are dark places in the world where the lines between lesser evils become too murky to distinguish.

Brendan Winters, enchanter mage, playboy, and consummate maker of poor life choices, has outdone himself once again.

In a moment of weakness, Brendan struck a deal that turned his life upside down. The filth he first witnessed in Bridey's den of sin was just the tip of the iceberg. As her new favourite, Brendan is thrust into a world of debauchery where he learns there is no limit to his mistress' depravity. So, when the opportunity to undermine her authority presents itself, he jumps in headfirst.

Sent to investigate a Cult of dark mages with their roots in Ancient Egypt, Brendan embarks on a collision course with organised crime, a God, and his own magical doppelganger. Yet, none of this cloak and daggers business blindsides him more than the companion he finds in the very house of his captor.

What lengths will Brendan go to for a chance to reclaim his freedom?

****Trigger Warning**** *Winter's Thrall* is a dark paranormal romance with strong sexual content that blurs the lines of consent. It also includes graphic m/m and incest scenes. Feel free to skip ahead to *Winter's Mother 1,* the next main entry in the series if such matters are likely to offend or be a psychological trigger.

AVAILABLE MAY 2022

Keep Reading for a sample…

Chapter One

'Oh Shit!' Brendan had several regrets in life, most of which involved Tinder. But looking upon the sleeping form of the naked fae enchantress beside him hit him with a compunction which trumped the lot. In a moment of weakness, he had given up on the single most important person in his life. He had divorced his soulmate and sold himself into the service of a woman he despised. Bridey was an endarkened woman: the wicked fairy, or fae, offspring of an elf and a dark mage.

Feeling the call of nature, he rose from the bed and froze when he discovered metal cuffs around his ankles, tethered to long chains. He bent over to inspect his bonds. 'Cold iron. Damnit!' The material blocked magic and the locked restraints held tight. Even if he could channel a useful mana source or tune into any ley lines, there would be no escaping his shackles. At least the chains had enough length for him to reach the bathroom.

When he returned to the bedroom, Bridey—or Lady Violet in business circles—sat up and gawked at him hungrily. 'Morning, handsome. How do you feel? Has the pain gone away?'

He glared at her. 'The physical pain has.'

'Excellent. I have fulfilled my end of the bargain, now let's discuss yours.' She held out a contract. 'I honestly thought you would've learned your lesson last time you signed one of these without reading the fine print.'

Snatching the page, Brendan stared in horror at his signature, a bloody autograph beneath seven clauses:

1. The subject, Brendan Winters, has agreed to enter a period of sexual servitude in service of Lady Violet.
2. The agreed period for this contract is one full calendar year from the date of signing.
3. Sexual servitude requires complete submission to Lady Violet, who invokes the right to insist upon any sexual act she desires.

4. Failure to submit may lead to the use of compulsion or result in punishment within Lady Violet's dungeon.
5. The subject will dress and act according to Lady Violet's every whim and show due respect to all other members of her household.
6. The subject may not leave Lady Violet's residence during the period of servitude except under her express orders.
7. Attempts to escape will result in punishment within Lady Violet's dungeon and may risk the wellbeing of other members of the Winters Clan.

The chains rattled as he slumped down beside her and tugged at them. 'Are these necessary?'

'I could hardly have my latest acquisition running off in the middle of the night, could I? When you earn my trust, I will permit you to move freely through my home. They are a precaution until such time.'

Brendan groaned. 'How am I supposed to earn your trust?'

'By doing everything I ask and not making any escape attempts when I loosen your tethers.'

'Can I at least go home first and put my affairs in order?'

Lady Violet laughed maniacally. 'Do you think I am stupid, Brendan? I will send Caleb to deal with your apartment when the time is right. For the next twelve months, this is your home, sweetcakes. And when you do step outside, you will remain by my side. Is that clear?'

His last sliver of hope disintegrated as he looked at her with frosty, dead eyes. 'Perfectly.'

'Good. Now get yourself cleaned up. I expect to see you at breakfast in twenty minutes. Levi will collect you at the appointed time.' She strode across the room and left, not bothering to dress before stepping out.

After letting out the mother of all sighs, he pulled himself up and dragged his feet along the floor. Showering challenged him, with his chains tangling several times. He usually preferred to take his time bathing, allowing himself to relax, but it was an impossible ask in his current state. So, he sprayed himself with scalding water and wrapped a towel around his torso.

Stepping out of the steam cloud, he found a shirtless guy waiting for him. By all appearances, he was a half-mage; tall and slim, although well-toned, with tanned skin and a small goatee. Aside from the spiked leather collar around his neck, he wore only a pair of faded, ripped jeans.

Brendan jumped. 'The fuck, man? You startled me.'

'Sorry. Brendan, is it?'

He nodded.

'I'm Levi. Lady Violet told me you were expecting me. Here are some clothes.' He dropped the pile of clean laundry on the bed. 'I hope they're an adequate fit. I have filled your drawers with much of the same. There are also some suits and special outfits hanging in the wardrobe, but you can only wear those upon Lady Violet's request.'

Glancing over the options, Brendan observed an assortment of jeans and leather pants. 'There are no underpants or tops here.'

'She only grants such luxuries when we escort her outside.'

Brendan gaped at him. 'For real?'

'Yes. Lady Violet likes to see as much of our bodies on display as possible and she wants us ready to service her at a moment's notice. We only get pants because of her more… conservative clientele.'

He noticed the bruises on Levi's torso. 'So, you're one of her sex slaves too?'

Levi winced. 'I prefer the term *submissive*, but yes, I am essentially a slave.'

Brendan began rubbing himself dry. 'How many of us are there?'

'She likes to keep our number at seven.'

He snorted. 'What? One for each night of the week?'

Levi laughed. 'If only. No, Lady Violet has a thing about the number seven being auspicious or some shit. But I think she also likes to have a variety of men to cater to each of her different tastes. You should expect her to call upon you several times a week… possibly more, given you're her new favourite.'

Throwing the towel aside, Brendan picked up a pair of black leather pants.

As he stood upright, Levi cast an appreciative eye over Brendan's naked body, lingering a while at the sight of his Prince Albert piercing. 'I can see why Lady Violet likes you.'

Brendan was no slouch when it came to his physique, and he knew his other assets were desirable. 'No offence man, but I'm not into dudes.'

'None taken, but you should know your sexual preference means nothing to Lady Violet. If she wants you to sleep with a man, you will do it if you know what's good for you.'

His eyes bugged out. 'What happens if I refuse?'

'One of two things: either she will compel you to do it, or she will beat you within an inch of your life.'

Brendan gulped. 'Is that what happened to you?'

Levi smiled. 'No. I actually enjoy the way she marks my flesh.'

With a cocked brow, he shot Levi a dubious look. 'Really?'

'It may come as a surprise to you at this stage, but most of us have grown quite fond of Lady Violet. So, don't get any funny ideas about running off.' With a wave of his hand, Levi released the cuffs from Brendan's ankles. 'You will only need to wear these in your room.'

Brendan slid into the tight pants that clung to every ridge and valley of his sculpted legs, emphasising the bulge between them. *May as well look the part.*

'Excellent choice,' Levi nodded his approval. 'Those pants are sure to please Lady Violet. She also insists you wear this.' He stepped forward and attached a collar resembling his own to Brendan's neck.

He brought a hand up to test the feel of the thing. The spikes were sharp, made of cold iron. Not enough to stop him channelling mana, but they would prevent him from magiporting.

'Come on, let's get some breakfast. We must not keep Lady Violet waiting.'

The moment Maurus Hawthorn walked into the dining room that morning, Caleb stiffened. He wasn't in the mood for one of his father's lectures. But when Dad planted his larger-than-life presence directly next to him, Caleb knew that's exactly what he was in for.

Maurus scowled at him. 'Put a shirt on, Son. You look like one of your sister's slaves.'

He snorted. 'I may as well be, with all the demands she makes of me.'

His dad's fist clenched on the table. 'You ought to show her more respect. Bridey adores you.'

'She has a sick and extremely twisted way of showing it.'

As if on cue, the devil herself walked into the room and smiled the moment she spotted Maurus. 'Hi Daddy!' She ran into his arms, falling into his lap as they kissed.

Ick! Caleb still couldn't deal with the level of intimacy they shared. His whole family was all sorts of messed up.

Dressed in one of her many purple corsets and black miniskirts, Bridey moved across to Caleb and straddled him. 'Morning, sweetheart.' As her skirt hitched up, his sister's slick arousal soaked into his jeans and her mouth claimed his with the hunger of a starved lioness.

Caleb detested how remarkable her lips felt pressed against his, how sweet she tasted, and most of all, how much his cock responded to her. 'I didn't realise I was on the breakfast menu.'

Bridey dabbed his nose with one of her manicured fingertips. 'Caleb, dear, you are always on my menu.' She moved to her own chair to his left and watched as servants spread the actual food on the table.

'Have you started training yet?' Dad's gruff voice pulled Caleb's attention away from Bridey's huge breasts.

'No.'

Maurus growled. 'I've been patient with you, Son, because of what your mother did, but I'm done waiting. You could be a great necromancer, Caleb. It's about time you lived up to your potential.'

'Not gonna happen. I don't wanna go dark.'

His dad chuckled. 'I've got news for you, my boy: your soul is already damned. You may as well embrace it.' Then all signs of humour fled. 'It's time to man up and start pulling your weight in this family. You have two options: either join my business or join Bridey's.'

Caleb hated the idea of working for his father. From what he'd gathered, it was more of a cult than a company: one practising some of the darkest magic known to mage kind. It made Bridey's life of crime look like a teddy bear's picnic. 'Fine. I'll join the Dark Syndicate.'

Bridey gasped and clapped her hands together. 'Oh, Caleb, do you honestly mean it?'

He looked at her and nodded.

She pulled him into a firm embrace. 'I love you so much! I can't wait to work together.'

A young woman in a skimpy French maid costume announced, 'Breakfast is ready.'

Bridey pulled out of Caleb's arms. 'Thank you, Isabelle. The seven may enter.'

The maid bowed, turned, and opened the door for Bridey's harem.

Caleb had been dreading this moment since the previous night.

As soon as Brendan entered—head lowered, as expected of a slave—Caleb observed how Bridey's eyes lit up. Her reaction didn't surprise him either. He had never seen a man pull off tight leather pants so well. The bastard even rocked the slave collar better than anyone. Ironically, the whole outfit on Brendan's imposing frame made him look more Dominant than submissive.

Maurus erupted from his seat. 'Are you insane, Bridey?'

Having thought as much for ages, Caleb couldn't help the snigger.

Her jaw dropped open. 'What's wrong, Daddy?'

Dad thrust a hand toward Brendan. 'This. Him! Surely you realise your latest catch is a pure mage. Don't you think the Council will notice he's missing?'

Bridey moved across the room and encircled the shoulders of her latest prize with her arm. 'Don't be silly. Brendan here came to me willingly. Didn't you handsome?'

Brendan's gaze lifted and immediately fell upon Caleb. 'Yes, Madame.'

Pure delight registered in her expression.

Maurus shook his head. 'He must be a spy. You cannot trust him, sweetheart.'

'He is not just any pure mage. We have history. Brendan, honey, this is my dad, Maurus. Please explain the situation to him.'

Stepping forward, Brendan offered his hand to their unimpressed father, who shook it reluctantly. 'It's a pleasure to meet you, Sir. Your daughter refers to my involvement with the Dark Syndicate. I was the original source of Rhapsody.'

Caleb almost choked on his coffee. This was news to him. He hadn't realised all those previous visits had been business calls. After Bridey told him about the time she'd fucked Brendan, Caleb had assumed a more sexual relationship existed between them.

Maurus narrowed his eyes on Brendan. 'Let me see your aura.' A moment later he grinned. 'Well I'll be damned a second time. A bloodline mage with balls enough to dabble in the dark arts.' He glared at Caleb. 'Yet my own son, born with a tainted soul, won't even practise a modicum of necromancy.'

Christ! Even my old man prefers Brendan.

Dad turned his attention back to Brendan. 'What clan are you from, son?'

'The Winters clan, Sir.'

'No shit? You're *the* Brendan Winters?'

Caleb rolled his eyes. *Trust a fellow womaniser with a track record more infamous than Dad's own to impress him.*

Maurus clapped a firm hand on Brendan's back which didn't even make him flinch. 'So, it took a minx like my baby girl to reel you in, huh?'

'Ha! You are precious, Daddy. I wasn't the woman who stole his heart, but I do get the honours of mending it after the bitch went and broke it.' Bridey took Brendan's hand and kissed it.

'Is this true?' Maurus asked Brendan.

'Yes, Sir. Alannah, my soul mate, betrayed me. Lady Violet severed the link for me.'

Caleb had seen and heard as much when Brendan's miserable arse came crawling back to Bridey. He couldn't believe Alannah would do such a thing, but Brendan had seen it with his own eyes.

The old man offered him a nod. 'Women can be vicious creatures. I've had my fair share of heartache too, son. But stick with my girl here and she'll treat ya right.'

Bile rose in Caleb's throat because Dad knew shit about women. Mum leaving was his fault. Dad had corrupted Caleb's sweet sister and turned her into the monster who, in turn, took Caleb's innocence. Mum was only trying to protect him.

'Yes, Sir,' Brendan replied.

Caleb missed the flippant Brendan he once knew. *Is this all an act of compliance to protect himself from Bridey's wrath, or has Alannah majorly damaged him?*

Everything about Maurus Hawthorn sickened Brendan. Knowing this man's history did not help, but even if it had been a true first impression, there would be nothing to recommend Maurus. The long black hair—moustache and beard—along with the biker tattoo sleeves all added to the sicko sleaze vibe. But his aura spoke extensively for him: a pure black soul covered in a thick layer of lust pulsing brightly every time he looked at his daughter. It went some way in explaining Bridey turning out the way she had.

Brendan could clearly see Caleb's hatred for his father, but the jealousy oozing from him was a mystery. *Did Bridey stick her claws into Caleb that deep?*

'Come on, handsome, I'd like to sit with you for breakfast.' Bridey tugged on his hand, pulling him onto a chair. Of course, her idea of 'sit with' meant making a seat of Brendan's lap.

His famished stomach groaned at the sight of the feast laid out on the table and he wondered how he would actually eat with a fae enchantress perched atop him. Fear prickled across his skin as he glanced at the other slaves who took positions on the floor around her feet. They were all skinny men, with pale complexions and hair that varied in length from medium to long. Brendan could see how he fitted the aesthetic, although his muscular build stood out like a tall poppy. *Does she starve these guys? Will I wither away too?*

With a heeled boot pressed into Levi's back, Bridey leaned over the table and filled her plate with an assortment of fruits and pastries. Once she had served herself, Caleb and Maurus followed suit.

After throwing a few scraps to the floor for the other guys to fight over, Bridey turned to straddle Brendan. 'Don't worry, handsome. You will all get a chance to eat the leftovers once I have finished. She handed him her plate. 'Feed me.'

His eyes widened with shock, but he smacked the metaphorical mask back on his face, remembering what Levi had told him. 'Yes, Madame.' Brendan took the dish and broke the food into smaller chunks. He brought a piece of croissant to her lips.

She grazed his fingers with her teeth as she took the pastry into her mouth. The gesture was too damn hot, and he felt himself slipping. As soon as she had swallowed her mouthful, Bridey sucked on his fingers with a lascivious gaze piercing the last of his composure.

'Fuck!' He exhaled the muttered curse.

Bridey beamed as she ground against his hardening cock. 'Later, handsome.' She opened her mouth for another bite. Brendan continued to oblige, and as he lifted a grape, she flashed him a wicked grin. 'I want to take those from your teeth.'

Oh hell! It amazed him how this woman could turn something as simple as breakfast into an act of foreplay. Gripping the fruit between his teeth, he braced himself for the contact. But nothing could have prepared him for the heat of her lips as they pressed against his. Memories of their first night together flooded his mind. Her kisses were still among the most erotic he had ever experienced. Logically, he knew she achieved this through her magical attunement to his senses and emotions, pulling the same tricks he often used to enhance the experience; but his body still responded favourably to her touch.

'Mm, delicious.' She licked her lips and eyed the plate to indicate she wanted more.

This time, she bit into the grape with her lips pressed against his, letting the juices explode into his mouth. It was the sweetest torture to have his stomach grumble while the rest of his body cried out for more of what Bridey could offer. Yet his mind and soul wanted none of it. He could not have been more conflicted if he was Parliament.

A sudden commotion broke the spell between them, and the maid appeared at their side. 'Sorry to interrupt, Madame, but Lady Scarlett is here to see you.'

Bridey tensed and swivelled around to face the girl. 'Thank you, Isabelle. Let her in.'

'Yes, Madame.'

When Isabelle stepped aside, Tara bust into the room like a storm cloud. As soon as she spotted Brendan her eyes flashed with lightning, and she unleashed her fury on Bridey. '*You stupid girl!* I warned you to keep your hands off him. Do you have any idea what you have done?'

Bridey scoffed. 'I'm sorry, Madame, but I'm not the one who broke his heart. Your precious Alannah did that without my help. No offence, but I still don't get what you see in the girl.' She leaned into him and rubbed his bare chest. 'Brendan, on the other hand… I can definitely see his potential.'

Eyeing him, Tara spoke to Brendan telepathically, '*Does she speak the truth about Alannah?*'

He opened his mind to his grandmother, letting her see for herself as he replayed the memory of Alannah leaping into Liam's lap and kissing him. The recollection emotionally traumatised him, but at least the physical pain he had felt as their souls severed had dissipated. Bridey's ritual had successfully severed their link.

Tara's wide eyes betrayed her surprise. 'Is there some way you misread the situation?' she asked aloud. 'Alannah has the entire Council looking for you, Brendan. She worried about you. When I sensed you here, I assumed my misguided *employee* was holding you against your will.'

Shit! Doubts plagued his mind. *Why does Alannah care about me? What am I missing?*

'Shit!' Maurus cut in. 'See, sweetheart, this is why I warned you to stay away from the bloodline mages.'

'Relax, Daddy. Brendan wants to remain hidden, don't you, my dear?' Bridey's nails dug into his thigh as she smiled at him sweetly.

Shielding his thoughts from Bridey's mind reading, he shook his head. 'No, Madame.' Addressing Tara telepathically, he admitted to selling his freedom. *'I'm one of her slaves now, please get me the hell outta here.'*

Tara gave Bridey a sidelong glance. 'If Brendan is not your prisoner, why is he wearing a slave collar?' Her own thoughts entered Brendan's mind. *'You are not ready, darling prince.'*

'A mere formality,' Bridey continued. 'We have a mutually beneficial arrangement, which I assure you he enjoys as much as I do.' She squeezed his hard nipples to emphasise her point, drawing a pleasurable moan from his throat. 'See? What I'd like to know, Lady Scarlett, is how you were able to sense him here when I have wards up strong enough to conceal this place from the Council's detection magic.'

'Not ready for what?' Brendan demanded.

'Not ready to leave here, to return to Alannah.'

'Please, Grandmother, I'm begging you here. Don't leave me to rot in this place.'

Tara's arctic eyes pierced him with shards of ice. *'Enough! My word is final. Accept your fate and wait for the right time.'* She returned her attention to Bridey. 'Some magic is more powerful than anything of Earthly origin.'

Bridey sighed. 'Always so cryptic. I may not channel Aether or nether, but I know they can't be used in scrying spells. You are not soulmates, so the only other possibility is blood magic, which would require…' Her voice trailed off as her eyes flicked back and forth from Brendan to Tara.

Tara laughed drily. 'Has it taken you this long to figure it out, Violet?'

Caleb furrowed his brow. 'Wait, what's going on?'

Brendan bit his tongue.

Bridey ignored him as her eyes narrowed on Tara. 'You died.'

'A minor inconvenience for a lich, I assure you.'

'The fuck?' Caleb glared at Brendan. 'Did you know?'

He nodded. 'Kinda hard to fail in recognising one's own grandmother.'

'Was this why the Council were cagey about letting us in to watch Alannah's trial? Because they discovered the truth and wanted to cover it up?' Caleb asked.

'Alannah's relationship with me was the premise of the trial.' Tara admitted. 'They charged her with treason and the practice of illegal magic… magic I taught her.'

With eyes bulging, Caleb's whistled a single note. '*D-amn*. How'd she get outta that mess?'

Tara directed her gaze toward Brendan and smiled. 'She had an excellent lawyer.'

Caleb shot him a look. 'You represented Alannah?'

Brendan nodded.

'Gods, dude. Is there anything you don't excel at?' Although light-hearted, Caleb laced his tone with envious undertones.

He could think of plenty of his own flaws and failures, but he did not want to go there. Especially not in present company.

'I still do not trust you, Violet,' insisted Tara. 'As a show of good faith, you will accept Brendan's help on your next job.'

'Wait, don't I get a say in this?' Brendan demanded.

Tara grinned at him. 'Trust me, darling prince, you *will* want in on this job.'

Winter's Mother 1

Most mistakes have consequences. This one has a legacy.

Alannah

Following the birth of her daughter, Alannah slipped into a deep depression. Many blamed it on the hormones, but they did not know the truth: this precious baby girl was the spitting image of her father, a man who broke Alannah's heart and shattered her soul.

After years of escaping her grief, either at the bottom of a whiskey bottle or in the arms of Brendan's doppelganger, Alannah is finally sober and on the road to recovery when the devil himself walks back into her life. Will his return spell her ultimate destruction, or will they find a way to reconciliation and a second chance at love?

Brendan

Having escaped sexual slavery, Brendan has become the master of his own universe and Boss of the unseelie underground. Everything is good until work takes him back to Gaeilge Shores where he discovers the daughter he never knew existed.

Old wounds reopen and priorities change when he throws himself back into Alannah's life. And all this family drama takes place amidst an apocalyptic threat. Can Brendan help the Council save the world, and reunite with his soulmate?

Warning: This book contains coarse language, adultery in a crumbling marriage, and explicit scenes, including steamy m/f/f romance, that may upset or offend some readers. It also ends on a cliff-hanger, with the sequel launching in May 2023.

AVAILABLE NOVEMBER 2022
Keep reading for a sample…

Spoiler alert! The following sample will spoil some aspects of *Winter's Thrall.*

Chapter One

Sixteen years following the events of Winter's Maiden 2

Glancing at her reflection in the bedroom mirror, Alannah cringed. She studied her cotton unicorn pyjamas and felt the beginnings of a mid-life crisis set in. *When did I trade in the black satin slips for these pyjamas? How am I only noticing how frumpy I look these days?* With a bamboo brush and some concerted effort, she managed to tame her wild bed hair. It had been another restless night.

The house was quiet when she made her way to the kitchen. The silence was unusual, but not alarming. Being a summer Saturday meant Liam was likely at the beach already, making the most of the surf. She turned on the coffee machine and looked across the open plan living space. Her daughter sat at the dining table, watching something on her laptop.

Neve was using headphones which explained the lack of noise. But the sound of grinding coffee beans got her attention. 'Morning, Mum.'

'Morning, hun. I didn't expect to see you up before me on a Saturday.'

'You do realise it's nearly midday, right?'

'Oh shit! Really?' Alannah looked at the old grandfather clock. She had recently acquired the timepiece from an antique auction for a bargain price. 'Damn. I guess I overslept. Did you get yourself some breakfast?'

Returning her attention to whatever YouTube had to offer, Neve shook her head.

Alannah took her fresh brew to the table and sat next to Neve. 'You know, if you want your father and I to show more lenience, you are gonna have to start behaving responsibly. That means looking after yourself more.'

'Spare me the lectures, Mum. I get enough of those from Dad. Besides, I remembered to feed the cat.' Neve gestured at the ball of white fluff sleeping on the couch.

Sighing, Alannah returned to the kitchen. She threw together some avocado and cheese toasted sandwiches. 'Here, eat this.' She put one of the plates beside Neve's laptop, then sat in front of her own computer.

Sipping her coffee, she scrolled through her social feed. Not much engaged her foggy brain beyond some cat memes. She clicked like on a few and went to close her laptop when a news bulletin caught her attention.

'Mum, can—'

'Wait a sec, hun. Come look at this.' She opened the live video feed and gasped at the aerial footage.

'The Victorian Government has declared a state of emergency. Melbourne residents flock from their homes amidst the City's collapse.'

'Oh wow! Is that a volcano erupting?' Neve asked. 'It looks awesome!'

'The dormant volcanoes erupting form part of the Newer Volcanic Province. This disaster follows a series of earth tremors. Experts claim the odds—'

Alannah muted the sound. 'It's devastating is what it is. Don't forget I spent nine years of my life living in that city. I have friends there.'

Remorse filled Neve's bright green eyes. 'Shit! Sorry, Mum. Can you call to check if they're okay?'

'Now's not a good time to be clogging up the phone towers over there. I hope they've marked themselves as safe.' Alannah's hands trembled as she clicked over to Melissa's profile. Nothing. She looked at Emma's and Cole's next. *Damnit!* None of them had checked in.

'Mum?'

'Mm?' Alannah was too distracted to give Neve her full attention.

'Is it okay if Cat and Fi come over for a bit?'

'Yeah.'

Neve disappeared down the hall. Alannah switched between face-stalking her friends and watching updates on the disaster. The more she watched, the more uneasy she felt about the whole thing. The reports coming from the scientists only fed her suspicions. *Why is a dormant volcano with such low odds of current activity erupting in such a prominent place? Could this be the work of dark mages?*

The issue warranted some investigation, so she sent a quick email to Kieran Lane, the High Magus of her state. She included a link to the newsflash with the question: *Could this be dark magic?*

When Kieran did not reply within an hour, she grew impatient and rang him.

'Yes, Councillor Winters?' His curt tone was typical even after years of working with her.

'Did you get my email, Your Honour?'

'I did.'

'And?'

A loud sigh crackled through the line. 'Why are you asking me about the goings on in another state? You know I don't have any jurisdiction over there.'

'Are you not the least bit concerned for them?'

'I sympathise, sure, but it's not like I can do anything. If High Magus Hanigan has need of us, I'm sure he'll be in touch. Now if you don't mind, I am in the middle of something.'

'Of course. Sorry to bother you.' Alannah hung up and flung her phone at the couch out of frustration. *Sixteen years on and I still haven't earned enough respect from the man.* Then it struck her. *If this volcano business is a dark magic conspiracy, they could hit South Australia. What if I can uncover such a plot and prevent devastation at our doorstep?* Surely *doing so would raise Kieran's esteem.*

With newfound enthusiasm, Alannah dialled her friend Monique.

'Hey girl, what's up? I hope Caitlin isn't causing you any grief.'

'What?' Alannah remembered the girls were over and hanging out in Neve's room. 'Oh right. No, she's fine. Have you seen the news?'

'No. Why? What happened?' Monique's cheerful tone plummeted.

'A volcano in Melbourne. It's all-over social media, so you should check it out. But listen, I was hoping you could hack into your dad's work files. I need some contact details for the magic community in rural Victoria.'

'You thinking foul play?' Monique was always more astute than her father, the High Magus.

'Yeah. Your dad's too stubborn to look into it, so I need to use some back channels to check it out.'

'I'll see what I can do.'

'Thanks.' After signing off, Alannah returned to checking on her friends. A little relief washed over her when she found Emma's update declaring she was fine and out of the danger zone. She continued to wait for news from the other two.

'Well, there's go my plan to fly under the radar.' Brendan huffed as he stuffed his phone back in his pocket. Zipping his small carry-on case closed, he became thankful for the decision to pack light.

'What do you mean?' asked Caleb.

'My flight got cancelled, something about a volcano in Melbourne spewing too much ash into the air. Now I need to magiport there, which sucks 'cause I'm not keen for High Magus Kieran to know I'm in town.'

Caleb's big, dark, soulful eyes looked so pretty when they grew wide with surprise. 'A volcano in Melbourne? Are you for real?'

'Yup.'

Grabbing his own phone, Caleb became engrossed in footage of the volcano erupting. 'I didn't even know we had active volcanos in Australia, let alone under cities.'

'Hmph. We should have paid more attention in school.'

Sardonic eyes peered over the small screen in Caleb's hands. 'You were the one playing hooky all the time. I kept my head down and got the work done.'

'That's right.' Brendan cast wistful thoughts back to their youth. Stalking around the bed, he backed Caleb up against the wall. 'I'd almost forgotten you were a nerd back then. Hm, I wonder... Would I have noticed your beauty sooner if your hadn't buried your head head in books so often.' He brought a hand up to Caleb's face, tucking a strand of long, black hair behind one of his pointy ears. The proximity aroused them both, their dicks tenting against each other.

The pitch of Caleb's voice lowered. 'Perhaps, but then I would have been nothing more than a distraction. A passing fad like all the girls you used back then.'

'Touché. Instead, your timing was perfect. You were like my life raft in a sea of despair.' Brendan drew Caleb's lips into a deep, passionate kiss. When the calendar alarm on his phone sounded, he groaned as he pulled back. After silencing the damn thing, his gaze returned to Caleb's mouth. Subconsciously, Brendan grazed the pad of his thumb along the bottom lip. 'Gods I'm gonna miss these sweet lips.'

Caleb's mouth curled into a mischievous smile. 'Jacob has pretty soft lips.'

'You sly fox.' Brendan laughed. 'You never told me the pair of you hooked up.'

'Sure I did. I told you about all the times I partied with him whenever I paid our hometown a visit.'

'You told me about the gang bangs, but you never related the details of being intimate with *him*.'

'My bad,' Caleb replied with a wry smile. 'I figured you'd assume we fucked.'

Brendan drilled into Caleb's soul with a stern expression. 'You know I don't like it when you leave me guessing. When I ask for details, I want *everything*. The who, the where, and most definitely the how. I am going to have to punish you for such insubordination.'

A slight moan escaped Caleb's lips as his eyes darkened with lust.

With a wicked grin, Brendan stepped back, breaking all body contact. 'I can see how much you want me right now, Thornsy. But you see, punishment is never about what *you* want.'

Caleb's eyes lowered. 'Of course. I'm sorry for offending you, Sir. What is my punishment?'

Seeing his submissive stance sent signals southward and tested Brendan's willpower. It would have been too easy to dish out a few lashings and take him then and there. But what he had in mind would be more fun in the long run, and it would give Caleb time to reflect upon his actions. 'No intentional sexual release until I return home. You will not touch yourself and you will not initiate intimate contact with anyone else while I am away. I'll let Bridey know the deal too, so she won't let you get off.'

Caleb gasped.

'What's wrong, Thornsy? Are you afraid of a little celibacy?'

'Not afraid, more… frustrated. I can't remember the last time I went so long.'

Closing the distance, Brendan reached inside Caleb's pants and gripped his erection. Then he leaned in to press his lips to Caleb's ear. 'If you think this is frustration, how do you think you will feel in two weeks?'

'Ah Gods!' Caleb gritted his teeth against the torture of Brendan's teasing touch.

'Will you be good for me Caleb?'

'Y-yes Sir,' he replied with a shaky voice.

'Good man. Now I want my goodbye kiss.' Embracing Caleb, Brendan kissed him with ardent fervour. Their passion rivalled anything Hollywood ever put on the big screen. He walked out sporting a massive smile and the boner to match. At least he could use magic to control the latter. Although he didn't have time to hide it before finding Bridey in the parlour.

She glanced at his situation and grinned. 'Oh dear. Has my brother left you unsatisfied?'

'Quite the reverse, I assure you.' He dropped his case beside the chaise longue and straddled her lap. 'At least I can do something about mine, unlike Caleb. I forbid him from seeking relief for the next two weeks. Can I rely on you to police him for me?'

'Certainly, Sir.'

'Thank you, Bry.' The farewell kiss he shared with Bridey was much more savage, like a pride lion with his lioness. By the time he left, Brendan considered the merit of Caleb's suggestion. Seeking out Jacob might prove necessary. The pickings in Gaeilge Shores were slimmer after the Council had exiled him. He was not even sure if Bianca would welcome him back in her bed.

EDM blared from Neve's speakers as she sat on her bed with the girls. Clicking next on the photo slideshow, she gasped at the fine specimen on her laptop.

Fiona squealed with delight, 'Oh. My. God. Dorian Pearce is so hot!'

'I know right! And you know what they say about vampire bites.' Neve licked her lips.

'Your parents would have a fit if they heard the two of you lusting after a vampire,' Caitlin scoffed. 'Especially your mum, Neve.'

Neve shot Caitlin a suspicious look. 'Why do you say that? I know my dad can be an arrogant arse, but Mum is more tolerant than most bloodline mages.'

'Didn't she ever tell you about her vampire ex?'

After scooping her jaw up off the floor, Neve questioned her blonde friend, 'My mum dated a vampire? I can't imagine her doing something so sordid.' A giggle slipped out as she thought of her mother letting a vampire bite her.

'She did. He was Dorian's late uncle, in fact. Austin was working for your great-grandmother who was a Lich. Under her orders, he tried to talk your mum into becoming cursed, which freaked her out, so she dumped his arse. But he went crazy and tried to force the curse on her. A big battle ensued where your mum killed the lich, and your dad killed the vampire.'

'Wow! How did you know all this and how have I never heard anything?' Neve asked.

'My mum told me. She was there. I guess the memory is too traumatic for your mum to retell.'

'Hm, I guess.' Neve continued looking at the photos she had downloaded from her phone. She paused when one of the Rowan family filled the screen.

'Mm, Jasper!' Neve and Fiona chimed in perfect unison.

'At least our folks can't complain about his bloodline status,' added Fiona.

'No, but he is a massive slut. I heard he's already slept with half the girls at Gaeilge High,' explained Caitlin. 'And he is a senior! Good luck pinning him down for more than one night.'

Neve laughed. 'I'd gladly pin him down for a night.'

As if on cue, her phone buzzed with a message from Jasper: **End of summer holidays party at my house tonight. Open invitation.**

Screaming, she threw the phone at her friends. Then using the breathing exercises Mum had taught her, Neve tried to calm her excitement. *Jasper messaged me! The hottest boy in town sent me personal invitation!*

Fiona gave her a wicked grin. 'Looks like you might get your wish.'

'Will you give up your V-card to the rat? Don't you want your first time to be special?' Caitlin asked.

Neve frowned at Caitlin for throwing a wet blanket over the elation she felt. 'With Jasper, it will be special.'

Caitlin sighed. 'To you sure, but not to him.'

'So?'

'So, you should hold out for someone who will treat you with respect. Someone who appreciates you.'

'Ugh, why are you being such a drag, Caitlin?'

'Because I care about you, and I don't want to see you get hurt. What about Lorcán Ó Máille or Kane Sheridan? They are both hotties and they're nicer boys.' Caitlin grabbed one of the carrot sticks from the snack plate on the bedside table.

'They are in our year level, so they're way too young. Boys mature slower than we do, so you need to pick one at least one year older, two years is even better. Besides, I doubt they even look at girls that way yet.'

A loud crunch filled the air, then Caitlin grinned. 'Trust me, hun, they've noticed us. Don't forget mages grow up quicker than humans.'

Neve gasped. 'You like one of them, don't you? Alright, spit it out, who are you crushing on?'

Caitlin blushed, but kept her mouth shut.

'Oh, come on, Cat. You know we won't tell anyone. Your secrets are safe with us, right Fi?'

'Of course,' replied Fiona with an eager tone to equal Neve's.

'Okay. It's Lorcán. He is so… dreamy.'

Fiona cupped her mouth in her hands to hide the big smile on her face. But the joyous expression was still there when she pulled them away. 'Are you in love?'

Caitlin bit her lip. 'Hardly,' she scoffed. 'I don't even know how he feels about me. The attraction is purely physical at this stage.'

Fiona shrugged. 'Let's go to this party. Then you can both find out what the guys think of you. Plus, it would be a great ice breaker before we start senior high school on Tuesday.'

'True,' agreed Neve. 'So, the big question is, what should I wear?'

Liam hung up his surfboard beside the outdoor shower affixed to the back of his house. Peeling off his wetsuit, he slipped under the warm water. He closed his eyes and basked in the feel of the stream cascading over his skin and seeping into his tight muscles. It was his favourite form of meditation. Then a scream, followed by fits of giggles coming from an upper floor window broke his reverie.

'Curse that girl,' he muttered as he stepped out and grabbed a towel.

Wrapping the Egyptian cotton bath sheet around his waist, Liam stepped inside. He spotted Alannah curled up on the sofa with Luna the cat purring beside her.

She was texting someone, tension swirling around her like storm clouds.

Is she oblivious to my presence, or choosing to ignore me? 'Who are you messaging?'

'Hm, what?' Alannah's attention remained on her phone.

Meanwhile his own attention shifted to the sight of her curvaceous body in a skimpy summer dress. He had not seen her wear anything so revealing for years, and the design looked new. 'Who you are chatting to and why do they have you so worried?'

'Oh. It's Emma from Melbourne.' Alannah finally glanced at him, but she took little heed of his partial nudity, or his growing arousal. 'Have you seen or heard the news at all?'

'No. I've been out at sea all day. What happened?' He sat next to her, adjusting himself in a none too subtle way, although she did notice.

Alannah showed him the footage of the volcano erupting in Melbourne.

'Christ! That's horrible. I'm so sorry, babe.' Leaning in, Liam kissed the crown of her head. At least she did not flinch when he did so. 'Are your friends okay?'

'Emma is. But we can't get hold of Mel or Cole.'

When his hand moved to her back, she stiffened. But he refused to pull away from his wife when she needed comforting.

'Neve's friends are here, by the way, so you should put some clothes on.'

So she did notice. Liam dismissed the thought as soon as it occurred. *Doesn't mean she cares.* 'Explains the squeals coming from upstairs.' He rose and headed into his room, closing the door with a little too much force. The last thing he wanted was for Alannah to feel pressured, especially at a time like this. *But what was she thinking when she put that damn dress on?*

Slumping onto the bed, he eased the towel free. He used it to contain the mess he made when thoughts of his last time with Alannah brought him over the edge. Then he threw it in the laundry hamper and fetched some clean clothes. Dressed in black cargo shorts and a tight, white surf brand t-shirt, he returned to the living room.

'Can I get you something to eat?' he asked as he fixed himself a snack in the kitchen.

'Just a coffee, thanks.'

Concern furrowed his brow. 'Have you eaten much today?'

Alannah glared at him. 'I'm not hungry, okay? What do you expect me to do? I can't exactly conjure up an appetite.'

'Jesus, Lana. I'm worried about you. I can tell you're not sleeping properly, and you've been losing weight again. Why won't you let me help you?'

'Because you can't. Let me work through my own shit, okay?'

'You could see your therapist again,' he suggested, trying to be supportive.

She snorted. 'You have no idea what my therapy entails, do you?'

'Not exactly, no. I know you said he uses unconventional methods. You tend to feel better but after a weekend of therapy, and it's those results I care about.'

Neve chose the moment to interrupt. 'Mum, can I go to Naomi's house tonight?'

'Yeah I—'

'Wait,' Liam cut Alannah off. 'Will her parents be there?'

Neve shrugged. 'I dunno. Probably.'

'Unless you can get me confirmation from her parents the answer is no.'

'But Dad—'

'I won't hear it, Neve. I don't trust Jasper anywhere near you. Rowan boys don't exactly have the best reputation for respecting girls.'

Noticing Alannah's shiver, Liam kicked himself for reminding her of Clayton.

'You're so unfair, Dad! All my other friends will be there.'

'So not only are Naomi's parents unlikely to be there, but it sounds like a party. You are most definitely *not* going.'

She gaped at him. 'I hate you, Dad!' Storming off to her room, she slammed the door behind her.

'Fucking brat,' he cursed under his breath.

'Do you have to be so hard on her?' Alannah asked.

'Do you have to be so soft on her?' he retorted. 'She's only fifteen, Lana. Far too young to be going to parties and hooking up with boys.'

'She turns sixteen in July. Have you forgotten what we were like at her age?'

Recalling Alannah's reckless past, Liam paled. He dreaded the thought of Neve following in her mother's footsteps. 'I remember. That's the problem. Especially if she's anything like you.'

Thunder rumbled from inside Alannah as those storm clouds burst around her. 'How. Dare. You.'

Startled, Luna sprang from the couch and skidded along the floor in her attempt to flee the room.

Shit! 'Lana, I didn't mean it like that. I'm concerned about her is all.'

'Right. Like you're worried about me. But there's nothing wrong with *you*, is there?'

Liam froze. 'What do you mean?'

Alannah sighed. 'Never mind.'

'No. I want to know what's on your mind. If I've done something wrong. If I've upset you somehow, I need you to tell me.'

'Do you really want to know what's wrong?'

'Yes. I do.'

A tense moment passed as Alannah studied him. 'You're a lousy lay, Liam. Sex with you is boring. It's why I stopped putting out for you. You don't do it for me.' Her words floored him.

Anger simmered away inside his nerves. 'So what, no sex is better than any sex with me? Is that it?'

A malicious grin formed on her perfect face. 'Who said I wasn't getting any?'

Liam's heartbeat kicked up a notch.

'Would have been so quick to suggest therapy sessions if you knew what they involved?'

Shaking his head, he denied what he was hearing, 'No.'

'Oh, yes, Liam. My therapist fucks me the way I like it because you can't.'

With his blood boiling, Liam took off in a mad dash for the gym where he pummelled the punching bag with his fists. 'Fuuuuck!'

Also By L. Starla

The Phoebe Braddock Books

(Taboo Romance & Forbidden Love)

I Heart Mr. Collins
From Prying Eyes
Crystal's Crucible
Undeniably Wrong

Winter's Magic Series

(Magical Realism / Paranormal Romance)

Winter's Maiden 1
Winter's Maiden 2
Winter's Thrall
Winter's Mother 1
Winter's Mother 2
Winter's Bride (TBA)
Winter's Crone 1 (TBA)
Winter's Crone 2 (TBA)

About the Author

Laelia Starla is an Australian author who often raided her mother's shelves for any form of fiction she could get her hands on. Her first love was the horror genre, but she owes her love affair with the romance novel to her high-school English teacher, who started her on the classics. Given her earlier reading, magical realism and paranormal romance were a natural progression. Along with steamy romance, these are the genres she writes.

Laelia also loves spending her spare time playing tabletop and video games, paper crafting, singing, dancing, and watching anime.

Access Exclusive Content

Join my newsletter to access free stuff like short stories, deleted scenes, fan art, and invitations to future launch events.

Newsletter: www.starlaarts.com>freebies

Follow me Online:
Website & Blog: www.starlaarts.com
Goodreads: 19660804.L_Starla
BookBub: www.bookbub.com/profile/l-starla
Amazon Author Profile: author/l.starla
Instagram: lstarlaauthor
Facebook: StarlaArts

www.ingramcontent.com/pod-product-compliance
Lightning Source LLC
Chambersburg PA
CBHW070149120726
47909CB00001B/37